MURDER ON GALVESTON BAY

WILLIAM WARREN

ISBN-13: 978-1-945532-89-4
Library of Congress Control Number: 2018958113

Printed in the United States of America

Published, Edited, and Cover Design by:

Opportune Independent Publishing Co.
113 N. Live Oak Street
Houston, TX 77003
(832) 263-1700
www.opportunepublishing.com

For more information about this book and the author, please
visit www.williamwarrenbooks.com.

TABLE OF CONTENTS

Discovering a Body of Mischief.................9

The High Sheriff Rodriguez..................23

Apple has a Lunch Date.................27

The Briefcase.................37

Good Ole Boys.................45

Bettis Tom gets Noticed.................55

Colorado Billy and Beer Can Billy.............59

Money Talks.............71

Sheriff Ben Listed.................73

Apple Eyes the Jag.................77

Beer Can and Colorado Watch.................89

Apple Visits the Coast Guard.................95

One More Water Mishap.................105

Looking for "Chump Change".................115

Colorado Billy Goes South.................119

Barton and Cronkite and Clinton.................129

Doubling Down.................139

Galveston or Veracruz?.................149

Big Henry's Bait, Tackle, and Beer.............155

Reporter and Sheriff Collaborate.................165

Fred and Little Joe Make Mischief............177

App is Surprised with New Wheels...........187

Apple Suffers more than Bruised Ego........199

Removing a Catheter is Highly Underrated..209

Colorado Billy Starts Planning.................219

A New Dr. Duke...............................223

Colorado Billy and Little Joe Meet...........231

Things Even Out..............................239

Maggie is on the Case.........................249

Back to Work 257

Dearcorn is Nervous..........................261

BT Visits Mr. Barton Maggie Calls on Little Joe..267

Apple Squeezes Dearcorn.....................281

Hello, and Goodbye, Little Joe................291

Little Joe, You Done Good....................295

Apple and Mr. Barton Go into Business.....301

Houston to NY to San Francisco.............309

Excelsior Publishing Gets Interested..........315

Colorado Billy Develops a Plan..............321

A Heavy Hitter Comes Onboard.............329

The Good Avenger Meets Roy Jacobs........339

Apple is on the Scene........................349

Maggie Gets Close...........................355

Chasing Colorado Billy..............................359
Reminiscing, and Old Movies....................369
Collecting "Chump Change".....................379
The New Editor......................................387
Bettis Tom's Surprise...............................391
The Good Avenger has a Conscious............403

Chapter 1

DISCOVERING A BODY OF MISCHIEF

The two men stopped the Ford four-wheel drive
pickup truck, and the company's security guard opened the
gate in the large wire fence. They drove across the large
expanse of black gumbo dirt, made muddy by the regular
nightly thundershower. The big man wore a badge on the
outside of his stiff starched white shirt. The other man was
wearing an expensive blue business suit. Apple felt he was
a bit overdressed, now he knew it. He ordinarily wore blue
jeans.

Jim Overriver's small 36-foot shrimp boat was
straining against the current, and the heavy pull of the
large shrimp nets trailing from the out-riggers. Jim smiled
as he thought about the large Gulf shrimp filling the black
stringed woven fishing nets. He was sure the demise of the
chemical production plant that had dominated the shore
line for the last 50 years was now bringing the premium
shrimp back to the cloudy, green waters of Galveston
Bay. It always amazed Jim to find beautiful large white
shrimp in the shadow of NASA, and only a few miles from
downtown Houston. He was working his boat today about
a mile from the high bridge at Kemah. Most of the time, it
was tougher to dodge the abundant pleasure boats enjoying
these calm waters, than to find the shrimp. The sailboats far
outnumbered all the other boats and were much more of a

pain in Jim's backside, because of their slow movement. They always seemed to be in his way. Because of the wind, the sailboats were not eager to give up good air so a nasty-looking bay shrimp boat could chug along.

Just a few short years ago, he had to make the long trip near Mexico to find shrimp like these. He never liked that very much. There were Mexican patrol boats even 50 miles from their coast, clearly in international waters, but the Mexicans were very particular about who came close. Jim always suspected they were clearing the way for the drug runners, not just protecting their fishing grounds. Yes, the good old days had returned all up and down the coast. He was very happy. A few more minutes and he would be emptying his nets of what would surely be an exceptional catch.

"What a haul we are making Jim, old buddy," said Rufus. Rufus was Jim's only deck hand on the small trawler. They had worked together for what Rufus referred to as forever, but really was 15 years. Indeed, Jim hired Rufus by the day but used him every day that he worked his boat. They were great friends and enjoyed working together and drinking beer together.

"Yeah, maybe we will make some money for a change," responded Jim.

Jim pulled his nets for shrimp and fished these waters all his life and barely scratched out a living for himself. A good thing he had not married because he never made enough money to support such a thing. But now things were changing.

"Bend over the edge there Rufus and help me grab this end of the net!" Rufus turned from his work of sorting the "trash fish" from the good shrimp after the last net haul, bent low and grabbed his side of the net being raised from the bottom of the bay. The two fishermen were excited with the prospect of sorting shrimp and fish from the catch. And so what if there was a hearty sampling of blue crabs trapped in with the shrimp?

As Rufus and Jim were dumping the haul onto the old boat's paint-worn deck, Jim stood up straight with a start and squinted into the morning sunshine. The sun was bouncing off the green blue water, making it difficult to see.

"What in the world is that?" asked Rufus. It was not too unusual to pull things out of the water besides shrimp.

"Well shoot, it looks like a leather bag, you know a briefcase like one of them fancy lawyers might carry," said a startled Jim.

"How did that thing get here?"

"Must have fallen overboard from some merchant ship."

Both men were breathing hard from the excitement and exertion and did not have time to recover from the surprise of the briefcase when out of the net protruded a soggy black leather shoe with a person's foot inside.

"My goodness!" exclaimed Rufus in a near state of panic. He was so excited he could only stammer after a great deal of effort.

"I am afraid to look further. I don't know where that shoe fits," said Jim. But he knew they would have to stretch the net out to empty the contents. The two fishermen knew they had just pulled a body off the muddy bottom of Galveston Bay from directly beneath where they were standing, on the working stern of the boat. Neither of them had ever experienced anything like this. They had one time pulled a rusty rifle up in their net, but this was something new and unexpected. Both had a strange dread of a serious misdeed.

And Jim, although he did not say, was a little perplexed, wondering what would become of his catch of shrimp and fish. This haul was worth several hundred dollars that Jim and Rufus really needed. This day could be a total loss. Could he still keep his hard-earned catch? Even if the shrimp had been brought up with a body dressed in a business suit?

They dumped the heavy net, and out spilled a man still dressed for his day of business in a corporate office somewhere. The body was not a pretty sight because of several days at the bottom of the ocean. "Rufus, don't do a thing! I've got to call the Coast Guard!"

The two men eased the pickup truck out toward the middle of a huge expanse of black mud and Gulf Coast salt grass. The Sheriff angled toward the open water and brought the vehicle to a stop.

Benjamin Rodriguez was Sheriff of Galveston County. He lived in Kemah, Texas and had lived there for the last 16 years. He was accompanied by Appleton Smith. Smith was a special investigative reporter for the Houston Announcer, the south's largest, and most respected daily newspaper. Appleton had reported on some of the biggest stories in the last dozen or more years, including the NASA shuttle disaster. He had earned respect around the country, especially in the newspaper community for his bulldog attitude in reporting the huge oil spill off the coastal community of Freeport. His exposure of top engineers' cost cutting violations had earned him national acclaim and nearly a Pulitzer Prize for reporting this past year.

The Houston Announcer had just assigned him to work on the most important continuing story of the last 50 years in the south. Many believed it to be the most wide reaching story for the entire country. This story was the total dismantling of BAR Chemicals. BAR Chem was responsible for some of the country's most important Department of Defense alloys as well as chemical compounds used in medicine.

LBJ once said BAR Chem was the most important single industrial complex in the world. A lot of people agreed.

BAR Chem had shut down one of the world's largest chemical plant complexes. Over the next five years they moved the operation to Mexico, and to add insult, had set up operations in Matamoros. With the chemical plant right across the border from Brownsville, they had remained as close to Texas as they could while being out of the country.

All of the people living in this area were convinced their country had sold them out with international treaties allowing companies to relocate. This agreement was good for Mexico, but was devastating for the people of the Galveston Bay area.

Apple Smith said, "Sheriff, are you telling me that where we are standing was once the heart of BAR Chemicals?" The Sheriff answered "Five years ago, this four square miles was home to 25,000 workers, but now it is all gone."

"How in the world did they move all the pipes and equipment and everything else?" asked Apple. Even though it had been written about over and over, the enormity of the project was just now hitting the reporter. "Why that was a bigger job than the Panama Canal!" Of course, his point was that it was a huge effort.

On May 3, 2010, BAR Chemicals experienced a massive explosion in the southern sector of the plant between the highly traveled road and the bay. The horrific explosion and resulting fire killed 345 workers in the plant and ten more outside the plant traveling on Sea Shore Drive between the towns of Texas City and Seabrook, Texas. The company was effectively shut down. Many believed that the explosion was set off by the company itself as an excuse to shut down Texas operations and dismantle the remainder of the plant. BAR Chemicals blamed the explosion on disgruntled employees. Five years later, and feelings were still running high.

This once-thriving coastal area from Galveston to Houston was now experiencing high unemployment. The local people who had spent lifetimes here were now hurting, and people were plenty angry. Their once-steady jobs were now down in Mexico. Fathers, sons, uncles and aunts had worked for BAR Chem and, nothing now, as the locals saw it.

Sheriff Ben's telephone was buzzing an annoying sound. Smith asked, "Sheriff, you going to answer that or let it ring?" The phone had rung three times since the two men had stopped the pickup in the edge of the grass and mud.

"Naw," reported the Sheriff. "If I let it ring long enough, maybe it will stop."

Smith was still fascinated by the first-hand lesson on the plant closing and asked, "So, tell me more Sheriff Rodriguez, how did they move the company and level the landscape?" Sheriff Ben responded, "They worked 24 hours a day for four years. What they could move to Mexico and use, they took. What they couldn't, they sold for scrap."

"What about the employees?" asked the newspaper man. Sheriff Rodriguez shifted the wad of Beech Nut from one side of his jaw to the other and answered, "The company had a massive lay off. BAR Chem just simply told everyone to go home. They kept only the construction workers. And this is the strange part that just infuriated everyone. They paid them daily just like migrant field workers."

Appleton Smith was working on his story. "Didn't they keep some sort of offices here locally?"

"Yes, but they staffed it with just a few company officials from outside this area. The company still runs the Mexico operation basically from the Galveston office building."

App asked, "How do they manage that?" The Sheriff answered,"Engineering, payroll, the works. Everything is decided here and completed with computers. But, they only employ about a hundred people."

"How many down in Mexico?" asked the reporter. "Oh, don't really know, but it must be thousands. It's a big operation, I understand."

Sheriff Ben was speaking from experience because he had been on the BAR Chem Company payroll himself. He was sent a gratuity every month as a security consultant. He was still paid to watch the perimeter, and to keep folks off the property. A job mostly honorary. The company thought it was good business to have the local sheriff on the payroll. Especially one so well liked and re-elected by the voters of Galveston County. Sheriff Ben was a local hero of sorts, a Gulf War veteran with several military decorations. He had graduated from Ball High School and spent his entire life in the county. He liked to tell people that he was "one of them."

"There goes my phone again; maybe I should answer it this time."

"Or at least see who is calling," suggested Smith.

"It appears we are going to have to cut our interview and tour of the plant short. It's the Coast Guard calling this time," as Sheriff Ben checked the digital number viewer on his phone.

"Sheriff here, how can I help the Coast Guard today?" Ben knew the boys over at the Coast Guard substation on the shore at Kemah.

Kemah is small seaside village on the edge of Galveston Bay, popular for good seafood and various yacht marinas. He shared coffee in the crew's mess two or three times a week. He was familiar with coasties stationed there, and called most by their first names. The Coast Guard liked and accepted his company with mutual respect.

Sheriff Rodriguez had enjoyed the brief visit with the newspaper reporter and asked, "How would you like to go for a boat ride?"

"Sure," responded Smith with enthusiasm.

"It seems the Coast Guard had just received a call from a couple of shrimpers. Their boat is about two miles off the Texas City jetty. They have just pulled a body from the water in his shrimp nets. Might be a story in it for you."

The Sheriff was not always this benevolent to outsiders, especially considering all that had happened over the last five years, but he somehow liked this fellow. Smith had done some first class reporting over the years. Apple Smith was always even-handed, whether you were in a position of power or were powerless as a common working family.

"You got yourself a rider, and thanks sir."

"You ever see a body that's been down at the bottom of the sea for a few days?"

The two men met the Coast Guard boat at the Kemah shrimp boat supply pier. The dock was just along the coast from the new sport fishing marina on the south side of the Kemah Boardwalk. Not much of a drive for the Sheriff and Apple Smith.

The boat was right on time, which pleased Sheriff Ben. He was very anxious to get to the bottom of this grizzly accident. He was not considering it anything other than a tragic mishap. The Sheriff was confident he would quickly get to the bottom of this nasty episode.

The seasoned policeman had an ulterior motive for inviting the newspaper man. Sheriff Ben prided himself on being open to his constituents. This would be another opportunity for the public to see what its Sheriff's department was doing, how Sheriff Ben handled serious matters other than domestic squabbles and traffic mishaps. A story from the south's largest daily newspaper written by the renown Appleton Smith would be good publicity, even this accidental drowning. Particularly since this was by all accounts more than a swimming accident. This event was surely going to be written about in the Houston Announcer, and probably make the evening news shows.

A drowning is not usually much news, except locally. Wading fishermen occasionally misjudged the currents and stepped into a deep hole in the otherwise shallow bay waters, but this was intriguing. A man in a business suit? Come on, how could this have happened, thought Sheriff Rodriguez. Probably a rich man with too much to drink tumbled off his boat. More than likely one of those sailboats, which the area was famous for. There were a lot of accidents since the new marina had opened for so many fine yachts.

The pier was slippery from the rain, and a stiff wind was blowing sea water in the air, creating a fine mist. Afternoon showers were common this time of the year, and expected.

"Hey Sheriff, come on aboard," rang a familiar baritone voice. Chief Petty Officer Deckford appeared to be in charge this day. With the Coast Guard you never knew. One day a lower-ranked petty officer might be running things. Chief Deckford was not in this category. He was a veteran of 22 years and knew his way around, widely respected by the crew and officers. Another time, Commander Johnny Johnson would be on duty.

"Hey Chief, yourself," returned the county Sheriff to the Chief Petty Officer.

"Commander Johnson sends his regrets. He is waiting on a call from his boss in Washington. Probably wants to talk to him about water safety," said the slightly grinning Chief. Deaths from drowning was no smiling matter, but the Chief had a funny sense of humor.

The reporter and the cop stepped down a few steps to the deck of the twenty-eight-footer to be greeted by the Commander of the Coast Guard Station himself.

'You know you are beginning to sound just like Chief Decks. I thought it was him making the noise," said Sheriff Ben.

"It was him," responded the Commander. "He is standing by on the helm. You boys come in the wheelhouse and out of this wet. Let's make sure the Chief can get us out of the boardwalk channel without cussing or hitting one of these fishermen."

"What are you doing out in this rain?" asked the Sheriff. "I thought you paper pushers didn't like getting out of your ivory towers," joked the big policeman.

"I thought I would come along," said the Commander, "and see what this business about a body dressed in a suit is doing in a shrimp net. Besides, the brass over in Florida might be interested," he joked.

"I have a bad feeling about this. Something just is not right," continued Commander Johnson. "What in the world do you suppose is behind this?"

"Aw, your imagination is going too fast. Nothing but a fellow with a little too much to drink fell overboard," answered the Sheriff. However, Ben was having private thoughts about this "accident."

The county Sheriff noticed his new friend, Mr. Smith from the newspaper, standing out like a sore thumb.

"Let me introduce you to Appleton Smith from the Houston Announcer. I asked him along for the trip. I hope you don't mind."

"The more the merrier. I just hope you are not disturbed by what we may find. It may be nasty," said the Commander. "Say, haven't I heard of you?" continued Commander Johnson.

"In my business I have seen a lot of unpleasant things," said Apple.

"I suppose you have," said Johnson.

"Maybe too many," replied Apple.

"What brings you down to the coast, Mr. Smith?"

"Please call me Apple or App."

App Smith explained to the Coast Guard Commander about the tour and interview the Sheriff was giving concerning BAR Chemical's relocation to Mexico.

"Gotta see for yourself don't you?" asked the Commander.

Apple replied, "That was the biggest movement since Eisenhower built the highways." Many do not realize President Eisenhower had started the interstate highway system. "I kept hearing news and reading stories about the plant. Finally, I had to see for myself."

"Don't let him kid you," said Sheriff Ben. "I know he is up to more than curiosity. I expect he is doing some investigating on how all this happened. Right, Smith?"

Until now Apple thought he had been too low key and clever for Sheriff Ben to suspect that in reality he was going to do an in-depth report on all the curious and unexplained loose ends about the plant explosion. He secretly planned to blow the lid off this story once and for all. And, if he won a few awards for investigative reporting along the way, well so much the better. He knew there was much more to find out, and this was only the beginning. But for now he was along for the news of tomorrow concerning the drowning accident.

The Commander interrupted, "Have you two forgotten why we are here now? Remember, we have a corpse to check out." Apple Smith said, "I just might just get two stories for one!"

A few miles of rough riding and the Coast Guard began to close in on Jim Overriver's thirty-six-foot trawler. As they brought the guard boat alongside, Jim began to shout, "What took you guys so long? We could have made breakwater by now for ourselves."

Jim had composed himself now, with a little time. He had thought the situation through. At least from his stand point. Jim was complaining about the time it took for the Coast Guard to arrive, but he was secretly happy about that. Jim and Rufus had made themselves busy by emptying their catch into the boat's fish holding tank. Jim did not intend to lose his catch because some city dude somehow managed to fall overboard from his fancy boat.

Two seamen made the boat secure to Jim's shrimp boat. The Commander, Sheriff Ben, and Chief Petty Officer Deckford stepped onboard the fishing boat. Apple was simply watching everything from a good vantage point on the Coast Guard boat.

"What's going on Jim?" asked Sheriff Ben. He knew most of the oystermen and shrimpers that worked around here. He had known Jim Overriver most of his life.

"Well, better days have occurred," said Jim.

Commander Johnson excitedly shouted, "Look at this Ben!" The Commander pointed to a large, round hole in the back of the head of the man wearing the charcoal business suit with the expensive, black shoes.

"Absolutely been shot in the head from close range!" slowly responded Sheriff Benjamin Rodriguez. "This is now a murder case!"

WILLIAM WARREN

Chapter 2
THE HIGH SHERIFF RODRIGUEZ

Morris Barton was meeting in his office at the Houston Announcer newspaper building in downtown Houston with Apple Smith. Morris Barton was the managing editor for the newspaper. It was the first meeting of the day for either man and they were both drinking hot coffee. Barton was obviously enjoying his and Smith was drinking his out of duty and necessity. He did not even like the stuff, but it gave him a sociable moment with his boss, a man he admired.

Barton was a kind and reasonable man. Because of this he was often underestimated by people who did not know him well. And that was a mistake. He was approaching 65 years, but still held an extraordinary flair for reporting breaking news. His position was to make even a car wreck sound in print like a pile up at the Indy Speedway. Barton particularly liked Apple because he could get to the bottom of a story like no one else on Barton's staff at the newspaper.

"OK, so let's hear what went down at Kemah. How is the Sheriff?"

"You know Sheriff Rodriguez?"

"Yeah, a lot of folks know him. He's got quite a reputation."

"Morris, you know I went there to get info to do a piece on the unrest caused by BAR Chem moving to

Mexico."

"Yes, I know, I'm the one that sent you. So what has all this got to do with a body being pulled out of Galveston Bay?"

"Literally fished out of the ocean," said Apple.

"OK, OK, leave the graphics for print," said Morris Barton with a grin.

"Well, you see, Mr. Barton, I think this unfortunate fellow is somehow connected with BAR Chem."

"And how do you know this extraordinary claim?" Apple was expecting this question, and was ready.

'This is what I am excited about. You see, this guy was carrying a briefcase with BAR Chemicals Company embossed on the side of the case! And here is the good part. The briefcase was attached to the man's wrist with a band of some sort!" excitedly explained Apple.

"Am I hearing this right? The man in the suit had a briefcase attached to his wrist with some sort of chain and cuff. And the case had BAR's emblem on the side?"

"Exactly," said Smith. And here is something else, may or not mean anything, but it is nevertheless interesting." Apple was speaking very slowly now. He was trying to entice Mr. Barton in a way to bring the older man's curiosity out. Apple really wanted an assignment to investigate the man's death and his obvious connection to BAR Chem.

"Go on, what is it?" Mr. Barton was indeed interested. His old reporter's instinct smelled something to this story.

"When the Galveston County Sheriff noticed me taking this all in, he deliberately got between me and the body. Then he did a curious thing, he covered the briefcase with a fish net. He didn't cover the body, he covered the

24

briefcase. Now don't you think that strange?"

"What do you make of that?" asked Mr. Barton.

"I think it is pretty obvious Sheriff Benjamin Rodriguez didn't want me to see the BAR Chem briefcase."

"And why not?" asked Morris Barton.

"I am sure he thought it was just an accidental drowning when he invited me along. But, you know, sir, this is anything but a routine accidental drowning."

"Think the Sheriff had any reason for hiding the briefcase?" asked Mr. Barton,

"Yes, and no, who knows. I think he is an honorable man doing his job as best he can. But there are some unusual happenings in Galveston and Kemah since BAR Chemicals moved to Mexico. And, I think this dead man has an interesting story to tell," said Apple. "For instance, did you know Sheriff Ben is on the payroll of the company?"

"Find out the details, Apple," ordered Morris Barton. "And they had better be interesting, remember we got a lot of newspapers to sell." This was exactly what the reporter was hoping.

WILLIAM WARREN

Chapter 3
APPLE HAS A LUNCH DATE

Early the next day Apple packed a few casual shirts and pants, jumped into his pickup and headed south to Kemah. He only lived about twenty miles away, but he was excited about being very close to where the action was. He intended to stay a few days and poke around, maybe eat some seafood and ask a few questions. For example, how much did Sheriff Ben make from BAR Chem? What was the poor guy's name who drowned? What was in the briefcase? Maybe a real big one, like who shot him in the back of the head, and why? He knew all of this was connected directly to the company, and their move to Mexico. The details he presently knew told him this was very sinister, very sinister indeed.

This assignment was great for Apple because he docked his 36 foot sailboat at the Boardwalk marina just under the bridge at Kemah on Galveston Bay. He would be sleeping on his boat for the next couple of days. What a lucky man I am, he thought. Getting paid by the newspaper to spend time on my boat. He was an avid sailor. Apple grew up in Seabrook and spent a lot of time on the bay as a kid. He was a perfect fit to investigate and write this story, having lived his entire life near the area. He understood the people of this waterfront community and what made them tick.

At breakfast the same morning, Sheriff Ben's wife Ronnie asked him, "Why the frown?"

Ben was so deep in his own thoughts that he barely heard his wife speak.

"What's that?"

"I asked you the same, what's going around in your head? That shrimp boat thing bothering you?"

Ben responded to his wife, "Yeah, sure is, there are some strange things going on there."

"Well I know you'll find out the details, you always do."

"Sure, most of the time, but this is no teenage burglary. I have a fearful feeling where this is headed." At that, Ben Rodriguez left for his office.

As he made the drive to police headquarters located near the old lighthouse, he rethought the events of yesterday. There were some important questions to ask someone soon. He thought of his own involvement with BAR Chem and knew that some questions might arise about the monthly "gratuity" he had been receiving. Ben was uneasy about questions that tested his impartiality and his equal enforcement of the law. He always knew this day was coming, and he feared it. A sheriff's county paycheck was just not enough to make ends meet. This investigation was making his stomach feel tight, and he knew it was only the beginning.

As Sheriff Ben drove into the city hall parking lot, he noticed a car with the Coast Guard emblem on the door. He knew Commander Johnson was inside waiting for him. Just what he was expecting. He also took note of an old Ford pickup; he couldn't remember ever seeing that vehicle before.

He opened the door and there sat the Commander

and the Houston newspaper reporter. They were both drinking steaming hot coffee, even though the morning was warming up quickly.

"Hello there, I expected you," as he nodded to the Coast Guardsman. "You driving the pickup?" Sheriff Ben asked Apple. "But, what are you doing here?"

"Thought I would hang around a few days and do a story on the fellow you dragged out of the water yesterday."

"I'm not so sure about that," said Sheriff Ben. "One investigation going on at a time is plenty. When I get something we'll let the press know."

His attitude was entirely different from just yesterday when he was actually quite amiable with the reporter from Houston.

"Listen Sheriff, I plan to do a story with or without your help. Anyway, I know an FBI friend in Houston that might be of use to you. Maybe I could trade him for a little inside info about what's going on around here."

"I don't need any FBI help, and good day to you," harshly returned Sheriff Ben.

"Sheriff, I am only trying to help. Why, for heaven's sake, you don't even know the guy's name yet!"

Apple Smith eased out of the Sheriff's office, pulling the door softly behind. He was thinking to himself, haven't these guys heard of fingerprints? He was a little surprised, but not overwhelmed, or intimidated. It had been his experience that many police get a little nervous when a newspaperman begins poking around. He would just stay low for a while and try not to cross paths too soon with the sheriff. But there was a story here for him and he had no intentions of letting it go. Besides, he had resources of his own and he might just come up with something before the officials.

Inside the Sheriff's office, Commander Johnson and Ben Rodriguez looked at each other and grinned. Neither disliked Apple but both were a little careful around reporters. The Sheriff and the Commander had talked it over last evening well into the night. They were perplexed about what jurisdiction was involved in the investigation of the murder. They had discovered the body in the bay waters but they had definitely returned to the Galveston County line. And the problem was more of a shore incident and not of the sea. The solution to this would be found right here, not at sea. So they agreed to fully cooperate as far as they could. The Commander agreed that the Sheriff had full control over the matter, but he still had some responsibility to get the details right.

Earlier that day, Commander Johnson was sitting in his office at the Coast Guard station on the little peninsula. Being stationed in Galveston was a dream job for a Coast Guardsman. He was commander of 30 enlisted and four other officers. His responsibilities included the star attraction, a 125 foot cutter and six other smaller patrol boats. After all these years, he still enjoyed the smell of the ocean air. The sound and feel of the swirling wind were a part of his soul. Damn, but he enjoyed his life as Commander of this Coast Guard station. This was his domain, and although he shared it with the other coasties, this was his show.

As much as he enjoyed his coast guard life and his friendship with Sheriff Ben, he was troubled by the nervous and peculiar way Ben had reacted last night. Why had the Sheriff insisted on locking the briefcase in his office until today? Why not open it immediately and see what was inside? There could be discoveries waiting that would solve this case quickly. For example, perhaps his name is on the inside. Johnson thought to himself that the Sheriff better not wait too long because that reporter Apple Smith would discover at least his name soon. Perhaps all one had to do was call BAR Chem and ask. However, he had known Sheriff Ben long enough to have faith in his methods, so he dismissed the thoughts from his mind, for the time being.

Ben called the front desk, "Maggie, has that reporter gone?" After verifying that he had left the police station, both men agreed that it was time to open the briefcase.

Apple drove out of the station parking lot in his Ford, traveled about six blocks and pulled over into the lot of a popular seafood restaurant. He got out a notepad and jotted down a few notes. Why did the Sheriff not know what the poor guy's name is by now? It seemed to Apple that was a simple thing. Why was it that the Sheriff was helpful yesterday with the story about the departure of the company, but today practically kicked him out of his office? Why hide the briefcase from him? That made no sense. Why wait an entire night to open the briefcase? Again that made no sense. Hell, how difficult could it be to find out the victim's name? He decided right then to do it himself and tried to get a few sentences prepared for this afternoon's edition of the Announcer.

He picked up his phone and called his office and asked for Ms. Hannigan. She came on the phone and said, "What you want, App? I'm pretty busy here. Remember we have a paper to put out today." Bernadette Hannigan was the Associate Editor, fact checker, proof reader, and all around go to person on the news floor; she was the real editor even though she did not have the title. Apple told her that he wanted her to call BAR Chem and simply ask what the guy's name is and what was he doing on a boat last

31

night. App thought it just might work. Ms. Hannigan said, "Not so fast." Apple had to explain some of the details to get her to do his favor. She was pretty intrigued and agreed to make the call. App would do it himself but he had other details to see to.

The Sheriff flipped the latch and the lock on the case immediately sprang open. Commander Johnson thought it strange how easy the lock had opened, and wasn't the latch locked last night?

Apple's phone rang. It was Bernadette Hannigan from the office. "Hey kid, got something for me?" asked App. "Sure thing, in-the-field reporter." App disliked the term; that is why Bernadette used it frequently. "Yeah, I got news, but the old man is not too pleased with me. He seems to think you are on some kind of secret mission or something. What are you up to anyway?"

"Tell you later, right now I am in a bit of a rush. So, did you get me a name?" asked Apple.

"His name is John Bishop."

App asked, "What does he do?"

"He is an attorney for BAR Chem, but after that, info is shady. BAR Chem will not talk about employees. I got this from an old friend who was a paper pusher, before the explosion. Of the many employees, I just happened to remember this one, and she worked in the legal office. Pure luck. And, the name might not be right, so keep that in mind."

App said, "You're the best, I owe you."

"You owe me big time, maybe dinner sometime. Knowing how much you like to dress up, I'll wear my best jeans"

As App sat in his vehicle near the newly completed City Yacht and Marina Club, at the heart of Kemah, he sat waiting and thinking about how he was to overcome the lack of cooperation from the Sheriff's department. He wondered if Commander Johnson, when alone, would help sort through this, without Sheriff Ben looking over his shoulder. Perhaps so. And, now he had a name to go with the murder victim. He was not sure, but he was sure that one or both would have to help. Or, he would have a difficult time reporting on a murder in the city and on the bay waters. What he needed as he thought to himself was an inside source.

Smith decided to concentrate on the murder. He was sure the murder was tied to the demise of BAR Chemicals. He felt himself lucky to have been in the right place at the right time. What are the chances I would have stumbled onto this murder while writing about the huge transformation of BAR Chem? He mumbled, "I wonder, have there been other strange deaths before this one?" Apple decided to find out.

Apple made it a point to speak to all the secretaries and office people he came in contact with, and the Sheriff's secretary was no exception. He plied his craft expertly when he noticed the pretty woman attending to the Sheriff's correspondence. He was not sure if his immediate attraction was to the pretty lady or his need to know someone close to the Sheriff. At any rate she was a looker, and he did need information.

As App waited, he pondered whether or not to try to make the afternoon newspaper deadline for at least a short paragraph on the victim of the murder. His information was scanty, and the real story on the incident wouldn't be for a few more days. Maybe tomorrow. "What the hell, give Morris Barton something." Apple rang up the paper. and this is what he wrote for tonight's late edition:

33

*Drowning victim on Galveston Bay off Kemah
appears to be a murder victim. The name of the
middle aged man is John Bishop. Bishop is a
current employee of the well know chemicals
firm BAR Chemicals Manufacturing. It appears
he works in the local area with the remaining
employees at their Galveston office. As noted,
BAR Chem relocated to Matamoros, Mexico
about five years ago after the horrendous fire
and explosion decimated a portion of the
manufacturing plant. Tensions still run raw
after the decision to move the plant. It is not
known if this apparent murder is connected to
that move or not.*

Maggie drove up to the Marina Club in her little
vehicle that looked like a BMW, but was really a little
Japanese imitation. She was to meet the curly haired big
city newspaper reporter for lunch.

Apple and Maggie made their way to a table near
the windows fronting the marina. They sat, and Apple
began some small talk about how great the view was from
the Marina Club. Apple remarked, "What a beauty." The
Sheriff's secretary knew immediately the reporter was
talking about the 46 foot Hunter sailboat tied to the pier
immediately below their seats. Indeed, many cruised to the
Marina Club, tied up, and enjoyed dinner or drinks in the
club restaurant and bar.

"This place has turned into a see and be seen for the
entire Houston area, a kind of gathering place this area has
needed for so long."

"Well, I can see why," returned Apple. "This place
has a great view of the boats and the water. Everybody

likes the water."

They ordered lunch. Maggie had a seafood salad, liberally sprinkled with fresh crab meat, and Apple had the blackened red fish. This place was special because it only served fresh seafood from these local waters. They ordered iced tea. Apple wanted a beer but thought the better of it. He really wanted to cultivate a friendship with this attractive lady. He knew she could provide him with inside pieces of information he could get nowhere else. After all, she had access to all the Sheriff's official records. Mayor Butterfield's office and conference room were just down the hall, and this lady covered most of those meetings.

"Aw hell," thought Apple. "Waiter, bring me a Saint Arnold ale." Saint Arnold was a local Houston craft beer brewery that Apple particularly enjoyed.

"I'll have something cold. Please bring me a Budweiser," said Maggie. "I was thinking what is all this iced tea stuff? We're having seafood," continued Maggie. Surprised, Apple turned a slight sideways glance out the corner of his eye to his luncheon companion.

WILLIAM WARREN

Chapter 4
THE BRIEFCASE

"What the, that thing is full of money!" excitedly
exclaimed the Coast Guard Commander as Sheriff
Rodriguez opened the briefcase and spread the soggy
contents on his desk.

"Sure is, and letters, and looks like graphs and some
sort of reports," brought back the Sheriff. Stacks of cash
secured with rubber bands shocked Commander Johnson
and he forgot his earlier idea about something being
"fishy."

He was sure the case had been locked the night
before. He thought it strange the briefcase had opened
so easily after being down in the ocean for at least a day,
maybe more. But all that was forgotten now.

They counted the damp money, and after some few
minutes agreed that laying before them was $200,000.00
dollars, mostly in twenties. The Sheriff put the money in
four plain brown paper shopping bags and returned it to
his office safe. Then he shut the briefcase intending to do
the same with it, when Johnson said, "Hold it! What are
you doing? Let's look at the other papers in that thing."
Secretly he felt as if Ben was intentionally avoiding the
letters and other papers.

"Oh yeah, I guess we need to examine those."

"What you mean? You better believe we need

to look at those. This is still Coast Guard business too! Remember, a man died yesterday."

"I just forgot. I was thinking of something else," said the Sheriff

"You okay? You seem a little out of it since we left here last night." asked Commander Johnson. He thought it very strange that he could be thinking of anything but the curious briefcase.

Maggie and Apple made small talk.

"You been with the Sheriff very long?" asked App.

"Seems like forever. He's been Sheriff for about 15 years, and I have been here for 13. Would you believe it, in the beginning there was no budget for the Sheriff to have a secretary. This city has gone through some hard economic times, and times are as tough as they have ever been. What with the closing of BAR Chem. Can you believe they did that?" Maggie said to herself as much as to the reporter from Houston. The local people were suffering, but the tourists were still coming to the bay and the beaches in Galveston. The boats and harbors were all doing well, just the same, while many who had worked at the chemical plant were missing paychecks."

"If you ever need a reference or perhaps would like to move to the city, call me up. The Houston Announcer can always use good help." Apple was using this offer to his hoped for good advantage, but inside he was sincere. Another pretty face around the office couldn't hurt.

"I appreciate that, but like many here, I could never leave this place. Besides things are picking up with the opening of this new marina."

"Looks like business is good," said Apple. "Hire mostly locals?" he asked.

"Yes, mostly, but a lot of the work is seasonable,

and the pay is not like running a big chemical plant. And, not only do I like this place, I like working for Ben."

"He's sort of a living legend around here, isn't he?"

"Sure is. You know he has arrested and solved some pretty big crimes around the bay," added Maggie.

Apple asked, "Didn't he solve a case about the kidnapped twin boys, some years ago?"

"Yeah, how did you remember that?"

"I had a professional interest in the case. I reported that story for the Announcer."

"You know, the entire state was interested in finding those two kids, and the Sheriff found them safe and sound. Some around here think those two weirdos who took those boys were intimidated by Sheriff Rodriguez into not harming them. He did take a personal interest in the case."

"Didn't he even arrest some cattle thieves once?"

"Yes, he did. That guy is something. You know the fellow who was stealing all those cattle was once a county commissioner of Harris County. He was here before Ben took office. He even stole a bulldozer and some trucks. But, he made the mistake of bringing his stolen stuff to Galveston County where Sheriff Ben busted him."

Apple said, "It seems folks around here think highly of their Sheriff." App continued, "What does he think about the poor guy we fished out of the water yesterday?"

"You know, he is pretty tight lipped about that deal. He usually confides in me about almost everything, but not so much on this case. Of course it was only yesterday, and he has been very busy concentrating on the details. I think he wants to shield me from that awful story. Sheriff Ben seems pretty shook up about this murder, as he calls it now."

Apple knew he had made a friend. And, more

importantly his inside source sat across the table from him. He knew he was good at this.

"What do you mean?" queried App.

"Last night I was driving home late from the movies over at the Clear Lake Cinema on the Gulf Freeway. I always go there in the middle of the week. I love movies, and it is not crowded during the week. And, I am sure I saw the Sheriff's car at the office. He seldom goes there after closing the office for the day. He says that is the secret of his long tenure. He separates home and work. And very seldom overlaps them. His wife has only been to the office a couple of times during his entire time there. Yes, I am sure that was his pickup."

'Why didn't you turn in?" asked Apple.

Maggie continued as if she did not want to answer that question. "You know what is strange?" asked Maggie as she forked at her seafood salad. One day last week I am sure that the guy who drowned was in the Mayor's office meeting with him." The county and the city shared a substation office complex in Kemah.

"What! Why do you think that?" asked App,

"All I know is what I saw, and what the Mayor's secretary told me. I put two and two together and that is what I came up with. I am not one hundred percent sure. But pretty darn sure."

"What did you see?" asked Apple.

"I saw a man in an expensive looking brown suit walking down the hallway to the Mayor's office. Someone that I had never seen before."

"Doesn't the mayor meet with a lot of well-dressed people, who?" Maggie interrupted, with her voice rising just a bit, "I saw the man carrying that brown satchel, you know the one with BAR Chemical Company insignia embossed in gold. It was very expensive looking; you don't see those every day."

Apple was trying his best to conceal his excitement with this news. He purposely slowed his speech when he asked "You're pretty sure of this, aren't you?"

Maggie was offended. "Hell yes!" She never swore. Apple said, "You must be shocked." Maggie asked, "Well, don't you wonder what that guy was doing in the Mayor's office?"

Apple silently exclaimed, "Oh yeah, I wonder!" And, he thought to himself, I intend to find out pretty soon. Wow! What a piece of info. This lunch had been worth $42.50.

Apple changed his mind. This pretty woman was not pretty, she was beautiful.

Commander Johnson picked up a stack of loose papers held together with a large paper clip. He removed the fastener and spread the papers across the desk.

"Will you look at this!" he exclaimed. "It looks like lists of names and dates." Sheriff Ben held a sheet close to his eyes. "The water damage makes it hard to read," said Ben Rodriguez.

"Yes, but I can read this! You better see for yourself." Commander Johnson handed what looked to be a routine memo from someone's office to the Sheriff.

Apple hated to do it, but he needed to call Morris Barton at the newspaper. He did not want to because he was fearful that Morris would want to go to press with the information he had uncovered so far. Especially after the teaser he had written a few days ago. The Houston Announcer was paying his paycheck. He knew they still had to sell papers to keep doing that. What he had uncovered was great news and even greater intrigue. The info he had discovered so far was the type of reporting that sold newspapers. There was an important story here that needed to be explored for the public good. App also knew that if Mr. Barton went too far and printed what he had uncovered so far, then his days of courting Maggie for information was over. And, Ben Rodriguez would never allow him in his office again, or invite him on boat rides. Smith faced a dilemma, to tell all to Morris, or to give him enough to keep him interested. He decided to lay all on the table and plead with Mr. Barton to hold off with the story until he knew more. But, he could wait until tomorrow, because it was late. App thought it would be better to sleep on it.

Before hitting the rack on his boat where he was planning to stay a few days while working on this story, he checked his phone messages and heard, "App, this is Bernadette. Did you know BAR Chem owns a very large yacht? They keep it at the Galveston Yacht Club Marina. Call me." It was very late, App decided to wait until morning to see what the message was about. He thought it would keep through the night. App went to bed, and after tossing and turning because of the message, he decided to call Bernadette Hanningan and find out more about her earlier message. There was something urgent about her voice on the phone. It was near 2 a.m. and he was apprehensive, but went ahead and made the call. A good thing all the key people in the newsroom had their numbers available.

Bernadette answered almost immediately, "What took you so long, in-the-field reporter?"

App asked, "What about this news that BAR Chem owns a yacht? Lots of big companies have yachts."

"Yes, but were they all out for a cruise the night before you found John Bishop in the bay?"

"How did you find this out?" replied Apple.

"Hard work, buster, doing my work and yours. And, there is more. Some shady guy that is associated with BAR uses the boat often. He took a small party out that night. It seems this guy is licensed to skipper and was in charge that night."

Apple asked, "Who is this guy?" "Don't know but the talk is he is some kind of bad dude. Reputation as some kind of operative from here to Washington to eastern Europe."

"I think I will take a little trip to Galveston tomorrow and poke around at the marina a little bit. Besides, I haven't had the boat out in a while. Wanna go?"

Bernadette said, "Maybe, short notice. Don't know if the boss will go for it."

"Tell him you are my assistant." Bernadette laughed, "Hell, you will be mine, I need a curly haired boy assistant anyway. If I can make it I will, depends on what the boss has me lined up for tomorrow. Don't wait for me if I don't show."

Apple knew she would be there. Her reporter instincts were still running high. Bernadette had at one time been a very good reporter, but now she was more important in management at the newspaper. But she still loved the in-the-field work. The 20 mile trip on his boat down the hundred year old Houston ship channel, that had been cut through Galveston Bay, would be a welcome diversion.

WILLIAM WARREN

Chapter 5
GOOD OLE BOYS

The big conference room was dimly lit, but you could still see the lavish decor. The walls were of the old traditional dark paneling. Everyone knew they were in fact walnut of the most expensive kind. This room was famous in the area, and in the old days, before the move, the company even included it on tours to the public when it was not in use. It was a little strange that the company with its operations in Mexico was still run from the same offices on the bay just outside of Galveston.

Five men sat huddled at one end of the table. The blinds were closed and the curtains drawn in tight. This group evidently had not gotten the news about tobacco. The nostril-stinging acrid by-product of cigar and cigarette, smoke hung heavy in the air, and clouded the dark furniture all the more.

Maggie would recognize the man in the brown suit, if she had been present. He was the same fellow that had caught her attention in the mayor's office some years earlier. However, he was not the main force today. He was a listener.

Jeffrey Chung Dearcorn was the man in charge. Dearcorn was the Chairman of the Board of BAR Company Chemicals. He was in control and he knew it. Rarely did he ask for advice, nor take it. He was ruthless in his quest for power. BAR Chem provided him with the means to exercise immense power. He was widely known in Washington on the hill. Congressmen knew him to be a person not easily ignored. He was so wealthy in his own right that he could often get his way in the back rooms where policy was written and decisions made. And with the might of BAR Chem behind him, he usually got his desires. It was widely believed that he even had the ear of the current administration. In fact, Barrett Stockman, the longtime head of the CIA was his regular dinner host whenever Jeffrey Chung Dearcorn was in town.

Bettis Tom Stovall was dressed in blue jeans, with a loose fitting, yellow Hawaiian style shirt hanging on his rather average build. Bettis Tom was 49 years old, but he looked much younger, probably because of his daily workout regimen. Running and lifting kept him in top physical shape. He had an ordinary face with one exception. His dark eyebrows constantly crunched low on his steely blue eyes. This gave him a perpetual frown, even when he was smiling. Which he rarely did. His work did not lead to smiles very often.

Bettis Tom was the enforcer, the muscle, the eyes and ears in these tense times of the company. This was not spoken about, but was well known to a select few who ran BAR Chem. And, in fact everyone with the exception of Dearcorn was fearful of him. They hid it well with their expensive suits and air of superiority, but they knew and had heard tales of Bettis Tom. They showed him a certain amount of tolerance. Probably because of the .357 tucked in his pants at the back. Oh, you couldn't see it, but they all knew it was there.

"Alright let's get down to the serious matter we've come to discuss," said Dearcorn.

Besides Dearcorn and Bettis Tom, there was Roy Jacobs, M. Ellis Winston, and Everett McIvoy. All were heavy hitters in the company, and were only a few notches below Dearcorn himself. They were powerful men in the world of finance and big business, as well as the higher halls of Washington. They were all ruthless. They would stop at very little or stoop to any level to get their desires. They all desired money, the way to power. That was what had elevated each to their lofty positions in perhaps the world's most powerful company, BAR Chemicals.

Elton Fulbright, late of the Attorney General's office, was one who came to mind. He had pursued BAR Chemicals on their bad record of polluting the bay and rivers near them for the better part of two presidential terms, until he was caught by Bettis Tom in a compromising situation with one of his young female staff. That ended Mr. Fulbright's quest of BAR Chem. Indeed, he now was an advocate for the company wherever he had the power and chance. Overnight he had been persuaded to only do what was beneficial for the interests of BAR Chem. That was only one of the methods this group of five, led by Dearcorn, dealt with people in their way.

The room was secure. Bettis Tom had personally made sure to debug the entire floor. He had secured his best electronic operatives to oversee the task.

"So men, let's begin to see how we can make BAR Chem strong for the next one hundred years," said Dearcorn.

Roy Jacobs said "Get down to it Jeff. What is all this secrecy about?"

"I thought things were going pretty good," said Ellis, "Except for all that damn union trouble here in Galveston."

The workers' union that represented the dispatched workers, the Association of Chemical Manufacturing Workers, continued to speak out against BAR Chem, even though the company had moved out of the country five years ago. The union knew they had no chance of bringing back the jobs or the company, but their goal now was to be a watchdog over the entire industry with special attention paid to BAR Chem.

"Hell, let me take care of that," said Bettis Tom. "I know how to deal with the union trouble."

"When you gonna do that?" asked Ellis. "Seems all you do is talk about things since you got Fulbright to come over." Ellis was the one in the group that would say his mind. He had an argumentative, straight forward manner that sometimes went down the wrong way with people.

Ellis had graduated near the top of his class at the University of Texas Law School, and had made millions in private practice before sitting on the board of BAR Chem. He was the only one that was considered able to handle Bettis Tom, besides Jeff Dearcorn. The M. in his name stood for Maythorpe, which explained some of the brittleness in his voice. He had to constantly live down the name. Later in life, after graduating from law school, he decided to go with the initial. He felt that would make it easier, besides it looked good on the door. Some of the people he had schooled with knew his real name and used it to advantage in many of his court appearances. They would say "Your honor, Maythorpe," and his concentration would evaporate. Maythorpe Ellis Winston had developed an abrasive attitude after dispensing with the Maythorpe and just went with M. Ellis Winston. Ellis was not impressed with Bettis Tom, as were the others. He felt Bettis Tom was quicker to bristle and more prone to bluff than to take action.

"I said I'd handle it, and I will!" fired back Bettis Tom in reply to Ellis.

"All right, hold it down, we're all on the same team here," said Dearcorn, "Besides, we have much bigger items on the agenda today."

"I suggest we get to it," said Roy. "I got a plane to catch." In fact Roy Jacobs' important flight was actually a trip in a long black car driven by a company chauffeur to meet his so-called secretary. Jacobs thought he was a real ladies' man. In fact he was a big balding man with an overbearing attitude and a world class comb over. He really thought that someday he might get into politics and run for president. That was his fantasy. In fact many of his associates called him "Mr. President" when he was not in earshot. Some of the more brazen sometimes called him that to his face. Mainly Bettis Tom. Roy's wealth and power enabled him to be seen in the company of very attractive ladies. His wife knew and loathed him for it, but put up with it to keep all the luxuries she had become accustomed to. If it meant putting up with his roving ways, then so be it.

Dearcorn started by going down a long list of red ink the company was suffering at the present time. High insurance rates, cost of raw materials, bribes to almost every politician with any influence, and the biggest of all, the constant rebuilding of the plants were piling up. This had been evident for perhaps the last five years. He privately thought that the move to Mexico had been a mistake. Even though profits were still coming in, the company was suffering severe downturns. The uncertainty of the stock market, with huge weekly swings, was a big concern. Dearcorn could not accept this.

"Steel," shouted Roy. "The prices we are paying are out of this world. We are being systematically raped by those damned foreign steel companies." And so they were. But it had been Roy Jacobs himself who, some 10 years earlier had been an outspoken advocate for the company to take their business overseas for the steel necessary to keep a big chemical plant operating.

BAR Chem was approached by US of America Steel Company for a sort of merger. This business arrangement would have saved US of America from declaring bankruptcy. It probably would have been a good business deal for BAR Chem in the future.

Roy was interested in the present and not the future. In fact he had cast a "no" vote on the merger. In the long run it had cost the company millions. They were now buying their steel from Sweden and Italy. The inferior steel was priced exceedingly high worldwide, costing millions each quarter. The problem was so serious the five had even asked Bettis Tom what kind of worldwide pressure could be put on the Ministers of Commerce in both countries. Bettis Tom said anything could be done, but it would be a maximum risk. They decided to table the question for the time being, only asking Bettis Tom to think about it.

Now came the crux of today's meeting. "Gentlemen," began Jeffrey Chung Dearcorn, "We, that is the company, can no longer continue operating as we are. The plastics, medicines and all the other raw materials we produce are being made by others in foreign countries. Between our meddling congress, the stupid decisions made in Austin, and hell, even our own workforce, we are being driven out of the markets." Indeed even moving the company south for cheap labor was not working. Between unqualified workers and the Mexican government, it was more costly than the production had originally been in Kemah.

"We all know that Jeff, what can we do about it? Bribe or get rid of a few senators?" sneered Everett McIvoy. He spoke, as he always did, with a turned up little grin on his lips that came off as petulant and spiteful. He never offered useful insight to problems, only his usual sarcasm. "I suggest we send Bettis Tom out on some useful errands." The only reason McIvoy was kept around was his brilliance with numbers.

"That is exactly what I have in mind," spoke Jeffrey Chung Dearcorn.

"I am not so sure I agree with what you are suggesting," said Roy Jacobs. "We still have that congressional subcommittee on business oversight and practices or whatever they call themselves, hanging over our shoulders. Is this the time to send Bettis Tom out for more shenanigans?"

"I intend to do just that," answered Dearcorn. "Only this time I am suggesting Ellis, our legal mind, help Bettis out. You know, just to keep him from going overboard as he did last time. We certainly don't want anyone getting hurt again, just a little lesson in minding their own business."

"Help him out with what?" returned Roy Jacobs. "Dumping the bodies?"

Everyone just dropped their chin on their chest and looked down, as if to signify they had nothing to do with Bettis Tom. No one ever spoke out against Bettis Tom's methods, mainly because they worked, and they were good for the company.

Everyone drifted out of the big room. Ellis hung around a bit until everyone was gone and out of earshot when he approached Dearcorn. "Jeff, I have some deep concerns about Bettis Tom and what was suggested concerning Bettis Tom. I think we are headed down a dead-end path for all of us."

"Don't be so pessimistic Ellis, everything will work out ok, just like it always does."

"Look, I don't like Bettis Tom, or his methods. Someday all this will backfire in our faces," said Ellis. I do not want to work with him. Keeping him out of trouble is impossible. The more power you give him the more out of control he is. He's going to end up killing someone and I don't want to be anywhere around that crazy man. Hell, he's still carrying that gun. He thinks he is Jesse James or Capone or someone like that. He scares me!"

"Bettis Tom is better than you are giving him credit for. Remember, he has been with us a long time. Has he ever gotten you in trouble?"

"You are giving him too much latitude."

"He has my complete support. You know the company is in trouble, right? The big moves we have made in the last few years are yet to yield as we thought they would."

Ellis said, "How much do you know about the John Bishop affair? You know the Sheriff is now investigating, and a Houston newspaper man is poking around into our business. Too much daylight and we could be on thin ice. John Bishop was found in the bay with a bag of money or something. Did Bettis Tom have anything to do with it?"

Jeffrey Chung Dearcorn said, "That was just an unfortunate accident, I'm sure Bettis T. had nothing to do with it."

"You do know Bettis Tom was out on the yacht that week? Seems any investigation would show that. No coincidence. I don't want to get in the way of BT."

"Is that what has you worried? Bettis Tom knows where his fortunes lie. And, that is with us. You and me, and this company."

"I'm going to watch him closely, and I expect you to back me up."

Jeff said, "Rest easy my friend, this company has not seen her best days. We are going to personally make millions more."

Ellis uneasily said, "I wish I had your confidence about this."

As both men gathered their things and turned to exit the big conference room, Jeff said "Remember, Sheriff Ben Rodriguez is on our payroll."

WILLIAM WARREN

Chapter 6

BETTIS TOM GETS NOTICED

Apple Smith could not get the man with the briefcase chained to his wrist, wearing a charcoal business suit out of his mind. Oh yeah, there was the other small matter of a bullet hole in the back of his head. App had not actually seen the bullet hole, but he remembered Sheriff Rodriguez saying "Absolutely been shot in the head." Apple did not think that would escape his mind any time soon. And he wondered aloud "Was the Sheriff acting peculiar?" He thought it was almost as if the Sheriff recognized the businessman. Well, surely that was unlikely, wouldn't he just say, "Hey, I know this guy?"

Apple was thinking about how much he would like to get a close look at that briefcase, especially inside. Apple said to himself, "Now you're thinking, why not? Why does everything have to be difficult?" Hell, just ask him. He might even do it. App thought about calling Maggie and suggesting to her what he had on his mind, and see if she thought the Sheriff would see him. Instead he decided to just drive over to the Sheriff's office and go right in. His reporter sense was kicking in. That's when he is at his best.

Apple started the 20 mile trip from his downtown office at the Announcer. He had been in the office all morning doing a bit of research on the BAR Chemicals Company explosion and move to Mexico. He did not particularly like working from his desk in the newsroom because of the constant interruptions from friendly folks, but he could use some additional research help. On his computer he was able to come up with some new information he had not known before. Such as a string of interesting characters coming and going from BAR Chem. It was interesting; they seemed to have access to important people at a moment's notice.

The most interesting was a fellow named Stovall. He stood out because he did not seem like a businessman, a scientist, a bean counter, or anything similar. What exactly would you call Bettis Tom Stovall? Apple discovered that Stovall's main employment up until the time he appeared on BAR Chem's payroll was as a soldier of fortune. He had contracted to at least three companies doing private security work around the globe. Several senators and congressmen had his name appearing in the shadows of legislation, scandals, and little known back door politics.

Apple Smith noticed that Bettis Tom (he liked being known by this double name), had been on the job a short time when an important Italian government official close to the Minister of Commerce was assassinated. He had been overseas two months when this occurred. A curious thought came to Apple. Didn't he remember reading something about the official being shot in the back of the head with a large caliber bullet slug? Probably from an American manufacturer? He decided to store that thought in his memory and check on it later.

Soon after Bettis Tom returned home he made a short visit to BAR Chem. Only one more month passed and Italy had signed an important trade agreement with BAR Chem. The company was treated as if they were an independent country being granted most favored trade nation. Steel prices eased significantly for the company. Apple wondered if these kinds of deals were at the root of their move to Mexico. Out of the country the company could move with almost total authority without regard to trade agreements or regulations from congress, or meddling states. App decided right there to keep this thought as he was investigating his story.

The same scene seemed to repeat itself with the Eastern European nation Hungary. Not with steel but with a specific research compound discovered in a Budapest University research laboratory. The discovery is used to treat severe migraine headaches and has since been used to treat many other nerve disorders. Many have called it a miracle breakthrough.

BAR Chem had bought the formula for what would have been considered low rent payments, and turned the new medicine into billions of dollars in profit. BAR Chem's competition was surprised they had secured the exclusive rights to manufacture and distribute the new medicine. At the same time, Bettis Tom's personal bank account soared.

WILLIAM WARREN

Chapter 7
COLORADO BILLY AND BEER CAN BILLY

I now have several questions that need answering, thought App. The questions seemed to be running together, but how? First of all, who murdered John Bishop, the man in the charcoal suit? And, why is the Sheriff holding the briefcase attached to the man's hand so close to his vest? He asked himself why this character named Bettis Tom Stovall was turning up at such strategic times in the life of BAR Chem. Perhaps the most important of all, was BAR moving out of the country under cover of a massive explosion? Was it set intentionally and by whom? I know the Sheriff knows more about the body in the bay than he is saying. Why?

Two days had passed and Apple still had a lot of questions and no answers, except for the victim's name. He and Bernadette Hannigan were approaching the Boliver Roads in Galveston Bay. This is an area where the Houston ship channel crosses the Intracoastal Waterway. It is a beautiful place, the channel crossing the bay heading to open water through the Galveston jetty. The water is blue, with dolphins playing across the bow wake of every ship, including all the pleasure craft crisscrossing the bay. Apple's boat was no exception. Bernadette was particularly enjoying the trip. She knew this was a business trip, but enjoying the boat and the water was great. They could easily have taken the car. Galveston is very accessible by way of the causeway bridge stretching almost two miles. Altogether a beautiful drive, but very exciting on a boat.

"App, How long have we been friends?"

"I came to work at the newspaper ten years ago, right out of college."

"I had been there doing mostly reporting for ten years when you got there. Remember?"

Apple replied, "Yep, I remember. I remember you scolding me like a child. I remember you correcting my stories like a teacher. I especially remember how you scrutinized my expense reports."

"Then you must remember all of those times I saved your butt from the old man. Mr. Barton wanted to bust your chops more than once, and I spoke up for you."

Apple said, "You know he really liked me, but he just had to appear rough. I remember that."

Bernadette said, "Do you remember the stories you did on the wasted money spent on the Astrodome? Did you know how close the Mayor's family was to Morris? You almost got fired for that one."

"Yeah, but in the end I was right, and he gave me a raise. Remember that?"

They were referring to the scandal regarding one of Houston's landmarks, the Houston Astrodome. Several county commissioners got in trouble about the spending to upgrade the building and lost subsequent elections over it. That was a big mess. Apple Smith, as a young reporter, exposed all of the mishandling of funds and was rewarded with several awards from the city and press for his investigative reporting.

Bernadette and App were good friends. She had indeed saved him from Morris Barton on more than one occasion. They had even gone to dinner a few times. But no romance issued from that. Bernadette was more than ten years older than Apple and imminently more mature. She recognized what a mistake that would have been early on, and deflected his advances. Now they were very good friends who helped each other from time to time at the newspaper.

Bernadette continued, "Then if you remember all that, then I want you to listen to me real good. I think you are onto a story more explosive than you know with this BAR Chem stuff. Do you realize the implications of the man found in the bay waters? I just have a feeling of dread where this is heading. Why, for heaven's sake, the man was a well-placed executive with the company and showed up murdered, dressed for business. Who do you think is responsible?"

"I don't know, but I intend to find out. I take that back, I do know who's responsible. Someone in the hierarchy of the company knows." He paused here and took a big breath and continued slowly, "I think Sheriff Benjamin Rodriguez knows a lot more than an outsider should know, even as the Sheriff of Galveston County."

Bernadette said, "That's what I am worried about. Just don't go down with the ship. And, don't take me down with you." Then Bernadette did something she had never done before. She asked Apple why not just walk away? Let it be. What's done is done. BAR Chemicals is not coming back. She was uneasy about the direction the body in the bay was leading. It was leading straight to the top of BAR Chem.

Apple responded easily with, "You know I can't do that. Besides, it is just getting fun."

"Alright, don't say I didn't warn you. Now, what

do you think we are going to learn at the yacht club?" Bernadette had resigned herself to his answer and was prepared to go along for this bumpy ride.

"I hope to find out who is licensed to captain that big boat and who had it out this past week. Maybe we will get lucky and find out who was on board that night."

Apple got on his VHF radio and made the call to the marina for an assignment for a boat slip. His call on channel 16 went unanswered. He assumed no one was in the office. He quickly looked up the phone number on his iPad and called on his cell phone. The phone was answered after one ring. "Hello, Galveston Yacht Basin, how can I help you?"

App asked for a transient boat slip for one night.

"No problem, turn right at the fuel dock then left, go down to the end of the pier and tie up at slip number six near the shower house. After you are secure, walk around to the office and check in." Apple and Bernie found the slip, docked App's boat, the "What's News" and walked around to the office.

Apple gave the information about his boat, then he asked, "Who could possibly help me with some info about BAR Chem's boat?" The lady asked, "The big one or the little one?" Apple did not know the company owned two boats. The lady, whose name was Jessie, asked App, "Why you asking about their boats? Why don't you just ask them? I think the care taker is down there right now."

"Right, thank you Miss."

Apple and Bernadette walked out of the marina office, and Bernadette said, "Hey App, why don't you just ask them? Now do you see why you need my help?"

"Why don't we just ask them?" said App. Sometimes things are so easy you just miss them.

"We forgot to ask which slip, we are some good reporters."

Bernadette said, "I think we can find it since it is the biggest on the entire Texas coast. Why don't we start with that big one over there?" she smiled as she said this rather sarcastically.

As Bernadette and Apple walked down the pier he was thinking "Wow! What a boat, must be worth millions." Bernie was mulling a few thoughts of her own about who can use this expensive ride. And, somebody has to know who was on it the night that John Bishop went overboard. She was sure Mr. Bishop went from this boat to the water, and somebody around here has those answers. Bernie was also thinking this could be a dangerous plan. She was also thinking Apple has no clue about who we are dealing with.

Apple was always interested in characters that lived on their boats in the marina. Since he was a boat owner they came to his attention easily. He always enjoyed talking to them because many had been to interesting places cruising on their boats. They were a different breed than most folks. They seldom worked or held regular jobs, so they were either older people with an income or some younger ones working odd jobs or waiting tables in one of the many eating establishments in Kemah or Galveston. One thing they had in common was their independence; they moved to their own desires and rhythms. But, they always knew what was going on in the marina. Who was friendly, or not, who gave good parties late into the night with plenty of booze, who used their boats frequently, and so on. If they wanted, they could tell you a lot about comings and goings. App had once done a short piece for the paper about some of these characters, a special interest story for the Sunday edition when people were more likely to read such.

As Bernie Hannigan and Apple Smith walked down the pier towards the big yacht docked at the end, he noticed two fellows standing near one of the many sailboats. Interesting guys, thought App. Maybe keep them in mind for later.

As they approached the large yacht, they noticed the name of the boat at the same time, quickly turned to each other and broke into a large grin. Bernadette said, "Just the name of a boat for a bunch of arrogant bastards to come up with." Apple couldn't keep from grinning as he spoke, "I think this shows who we are dealing with." The name of the boat was "Chump Change."

Apple said, "I once knew of a large sailboat named "Petty Cash" which was cool but it was nothing like this. This thing looks like it could belong to a Sultan or the dictator of a middle eastern county."

"I wonder what the stock holders think about this monster?"

Indeed, this had to be the biggest on the coast. Yet one had to admire the stainless steel shinning in the sun. They saw no one moving about so they approached the gangway. Apple was loudly saying, "Is anyone home?" A young fellow appeared from the side dressed in working clothes of white shirt and trousers. He appeared like a dishwasher rather than a nautical caretaker. "Can I help you?" Not too friendly but not unapproachable either.

"Yes, I am from the Houston Announcer doing a story on interesting vessels in the Galveston area. Maybe you could answer a few questions? Like who owns this beautiful boat?"

"She belongs to the BAR Chemical Company. Have you heard of them?"

The man named Robert agreed to answer a few

questions, but informed Apple that a he was not really the one to do so, but would since he was the only one aboard.

"Does the boat move very often?"

"Yes, but only a few people at a time. Seems such a waste since she is so large."

"Do you ever go yourself on trips?"

"No, my job is done in port. I polish and clean everything on deck. Keep her looking good."

Apple was disappointed in the information he was getting out of Robert, but decided to try one more, "Did they have a trip a few days ago?"

Robert said, "Yeah, but it was strange that she was only out one night and returned first thing the next morning. Maybe I shouldn't answer any more questions, I don't really know much. Mr. Stovall is very strict about strangers and questions."

Bernie thought, "Bingo."

For the first time Bernie added to the conversation, "Would that by any chance be Bettis Tom Stovall?"

"You know Mr. Stovall?"

"Only by reputation. I hear he is a pretty nice guy. Does he still work for BAR Chem?"

"Yes, I guess he works for them, he uses their boat a lot. But, just between you and me, he is very stern. Doesn't joke any and has no sense of humor. I am just grateful he does not talk to me much."

"What do you mean?"

"He lets me be, and do my work without bothering me much. Just keep the liquor cabinets full and the towels fresh and everything will be OK."

Apple asked, "Does he have any regular guests?"

"I can't really answer that or anything else. If Mr. Stovall found out I was talking out of turn he would probably fire me. He talks a lot about loyalty to the company. Hell, I'm just a working guy trying to make a living. Please just ask him yourself."

"How could I do that?"

"I don't really know. He just usually shows up."

After thanking Robert for his help, Apple and Bernadette turned to exit the boat ramp. Apple told Bernie he had an idea. Why don't they try to find a few neighbors home near the "Chump Change?"

There they are thought App. He knew the two guys they had passed earlier would still be there. He decided to ask around a little more about Bettis Tom and guests.

"How ya doing?" asked Apple.

"We're doing good, how about y'all?"

After introducing themselves, Apple told them about their trip down the Houston Ship Channel this morning to Galveston. Apple told them it was such a nice day they just wanted to get out of the office for a little while.

They were a couple of real interesting looking characters. The more talkative of the two introduced himself as Billy who hailed from Beaumont. Billy weighed about 220 pounds and was about five foot ten, suntanned face, and a two foot ponytail braided tight, hanging down between his shoulder blades. He volunteered that most called him Beer Can Billy. Obviously from his penchant for, you guessed it, drinking beer. Which he was doing at the time. The other chap was average and thin, and not drinking beer, but reeked of tobacco. He said the reason for the Beer Can Billy was because his name was also Billy. And, that was one way of telling the two apart. He was called "Colorado Billy." Colorado Billy also wore his gray speckled hair shoulder length long.

App said, "Well, hello Beer Can and Colorado.

MURDER ON GALVESTON BAY

What's going on?"

Apple was going to engage in friendly banter, just one boat lover to another, before asking too many questions about who was coming and going on the "Chump Change."

Bernadette added, "I'll bet you see a lot of interesting folks being docked so close to that really big yacht." She knew these two would talk to a pretty girl quicker than to Apple. She was right. Beer Can Billy and Colorado Billy were eager to talk about things at the marina. Apple and Bernie found out that the main captain was Bettis Tom Stovall, although a local captain was occasionally used. On those occasions Stovall was never present. When he used the yacht, he was the skipper. They found out in conversation that the boat was used a couple of days ago, and that Bettis Tom had been on board. Out of the blue, Apple decided to go for broke, "Did you notice how the passengers were dressed?"

Colorado Billy said, "Sure. Most were dressed very casual. Just like anyone going for a cruise on the bay.

"A funny thing last week though," said Beer Can Billy, "There were a couple of fellows that really stood out."

"How so, Beer Can?"

"Well, one was carrying a briefcase, very fancy it was. Not a casual bag with a change of clothes, but a fancy schmancy leather case, like a lawyer might carry into a court room."

"Sure was," said Colorado Billy. "Me and Beer Can Billy were laughing about how silly that looked. We said must be full of loot or his stash of weed."

Both fellows got a good laugh out of that, so Apple and Bernie laughed along with them. These two were full of information that Apple could not have wished for.

Beer Can volunteered, "Stood out like a sore thumb. He was wearing a sharp-looking business suit."

Apple was trying to contain his excitement as he was thinking that this surely is John Bishop. And, he had two sources, namely these two characters, Colorado Billy and Beer Can Billy alias Beaumont Bill. Wow! he thought. You can't make up stuff like this.

Bernie was smiling. She was reading Apple's mind. She was wishing she could write this story, but this was Apple's swing all the way. Of course she would do everything to help him. Growing inside her was the fear she had experienced earlier. She and Apple had stumbled upon a really big story. Stack this on top of the already existing BAR Chem story, and this was becoming explosive.

Apple was thinking he did not want to overstay his welcome. But he would be back for more, you could count on it. Perhaps he would even catch Bettis Tom around here himself another time, soon.

They turned to go when Bernadette stopped, turned around and asked, "You said there were two that stood out. How about the other guy? What stood out about him?"

Beer Can said, "Surely did stand out. He was wearing khakis, starched white shirt, wearing a cowboy hat, a badge, and a gun. Some kind of lawman for sure."

Bernie exclaimed out loud, "Bingo!"

"What'd you say? Miss?" asked Beer Can.

When Apple and Bernie were barely out of sight, Beer Can and Colorado looked at each other with the same thought in their minds.

"Sure was a lot of questions. What do you think they are up to?"

Back on Apple's boat, he and Bernadette discussed what they had just found out. Could that be John Bishop they were describing? Probably more important, were they talking about Sheriff Ben Rodriguez?

"What we need is a description of the mayor. Something tells me he is a player here. Did I tell you Maggie thinks John Bishop visited the mayor a few times before he turned up in the bay?"

"Maggie?"

"She is the Sheriff's assistant."

"Apple, you sure get around fast." She was a little jealous, but she did not know why. She had absolutely no interest in Apple Smith, but she did enjoy their friendly banter.

Colorado Billy and Beer Can Billy talked about the other interesting things about the big yacht. They were always remarking to each other about how often parties were going on there. Both guys were convinced a big poker game was held there about once a month. They did not care, they were just curious. They decided that they would keep a little extra watch since the reporter from the Announcer seemed to be interested. This was fun. Maybe stay up a little later at night and see who came and went. Hell, maybe they would be in the newspaper.

WILLIAM WARREN

Chapter 8
MONEY TALKS

The Association of Chemical Workers continued to meet and discuss their problems. In fact they had grown stronger through the support of unions throughout the country, after the demise of BAR Chem. They were stronger now than they were before the explosion and move of the company to Mexico.

The union was considered a phenomenon by business leaders and workers alike because unions from all the states had stepped forward with financial support to keep the Houston ACW going. No one could remember garment workers, auto workers, hotel workers, and all the others actually doing anything to actively support another union so far removed from their own.

The effect of this was the ACW had turned into the spokesman for all the unions. Not in an official way, but in an informal advisory agreement. They pressured congress, state houses, and corporations. The ACW worked by finding out everything possible about their adversaries. The long list of opponents included senators, judges, heads of corporations, even foreign heads of state when necessary. They vowed to never allow another large company to "slither" away to a foreign country, and take those valuable jobs, without a fight.

In a strange twist of fate, their original enemy, BAR

Chemicals Company conducted much of its influence and business in about the same way. Both would exert pressure on a precise individual until they began to see the ACW or BAR Chem's view. The ACW continued to be the company's bitter foe.

The ACW, soon after the closure of the chemical plant, desperately wanted to hire Bettis Tom Stovall as a consultant. Bettis Tom always did what was right for himself, so he figured he was better off doing what he does for BAR. Besides, the ACW had no yacht for him to play around with. Bettis Tom had grown over the last five years to hate the ACW. None of his tricks and operations so far had any effect on the union. They played just as rough as he did. BT had tried one of his favorite ploys on two of the top union leaders. Bribery with cash.

The two union representatives were paid to tone down the pickets and the rhetoric. They took the money but kept right on doing the same things. Bettis Tom was personally embarrassed in addition to being held to some ridicule by the boys in the board room. Jeffrey Chung Dearcorn was particularly upset. He had always protected and endorsed Bettis Tom.

Chapter 9
SHERIFF BEN LISTED

Commander Johnson looked sternly at Sheriff Ben. "You better take a look at this Ben. It appears to be a list with names and dollar signs next to the names. And your name is on the list."

"Let me take a look at that." Ben took the water-stained list and examined it for some time. "Where?"

"Right here! It is dim but it sure as hell looks like SBEN to me."

"How do you get Benjamin Rodriguez out of that?"

"Sheriff Ben."

"You know I get a payment every month for providing security to their property. That is no secret, even you know that. The mayor and the council all know and are fine with it. I drive around the property on my own time. Never any trouble. I chase kids off hunting rabbits and riding three wheelers, not much, and they pay me for it. No big deal."

"I know you get paid for that. Can you get me in on it since it is $20,000?" The Commander was trying to make the tense situation a little light hearted. Ben was his friend. He knew there was an explanation for this. But to him the note did say SBEN. Sheriff Ben, that was obvious to him.

"What? It is $1,500 a month, not $20,000."

"Then how do you explain it? There must be a

reason," emphatically declared the Commander.

"I don't frankly know, maybe I got a raise."

"All right, let's stop kidding around. You know Ben, this is serious. Remember this stuff comes from a water-logged briefcase carried by a dead man. How did your name get on a list in his possession?"

After examining the note, they found the mayor, several councilmen, a local state representative, and most shocking was the name of a prominent district court judge. Not to mention the head of the local EPA office. Also the most intriguing of all was Maggie, the Sheriff's administrative assistant.

"Man, on the surface it looks like they have everyone with any influence on their payroll." said Commander Johnson.

"But why is my name on there? I have no influence over matters that affect BAR Chem. Listen Johnny, this looks very odd, but believe me, I have no idea about that list. I have never received more than the $1,500 a month. And, why in hell is Maggie's name mentioned?"

"Here is an idea, just between you and me. Maybe they are about to ask your cooperation on some problem they are having or about to have."

"I don't know how I could help a big company like that, especially 20 grand worth."

"Have you forgotten we are investigating a murder of one of their employees?"

"OK, perhaps they want me to go lightly on the investigation. I don't know, but I am going to find out shortly. I never liked those bastards anyway. You are my witness that the money is all still here. I never took any of it. This list with amounts backs me up."

"That never crossed my mind." Commander

Johnson was lying, it did in fact cross his mind. Maybe the Sheriff was into the company more than he imagined. "Naw, that couldn't be," he thought to himself.

WILLIAM WARREN

Chapter 10
APPLE EYES THE JAG

Bettis Tom Stovall and M. Ellis Winston were to meet at a local ice house off Hwy 146 in San Leon.

Ellis was driving the short five miles from his upscale condo on Clear Lake to the meeting. He was wondering what the hell Bettis Tom wanted with him? Jeffrey Dearcorn had assigned Ellis to work with Bettis Tom a few days ago. Ellis thought that was beneath him, but someone had to keep an eye on Stovall. He was an unpredictable fellow, and prone to violence.

Ellis did not know this for sure, but he suspected heavily that BT was involved in more than a few disappearances. Bettis Tom was nearly indicted in Italy a couple of years ago over the shooting of the Italian Commerce Commissioner. That had cost the company a lot of money to local attorneys and judges to get him home without an indictment. We should have left his ass over there, thought Ellis. Of course they could not do that. What if Bettis Tom started talking? The company would have a lot of difficult questions to answer. No one wanted that, so they bailed him out. Bettis Tom Stovall would probably be wise to never return to Rome. And, I would be wise to put some distance between myself and BT.

Ellis was a brilliant attorney. That was the reason he had been assigned to keep an eye on BT. Give him some good advice, etc. There were two problems. First Jeffrey Chung Dearcorn told him to help BT out. The second was he was scared to death of Bettis Tom. Actually three reasons. He was almost as fearful of Dearcorn as BT.

Dearcorn was vicious, and would think nothing of professionally destroying Ellis, so he resigned himself to his duty at hand. Try to keep Bettis Tom on a chain. Keep him from stirring up more than the company could handle.

Ellis parked his new Jaguar alongside the ice house. Wondering as he made sure the shiny black Jag was locked secure, why was it called an ice house? They sold beer and hamburgers, not ice.

The Jag was very conspicuous lined up along the pickups and battered sedans. "How in hell do these guys afford these new stretch cab pickups? Where do they work?" Houston is a big city. Ellis never thought there were places to work other than BAR Chem.

Besides the Jaguar, there were no other vehicles that he could guess if Bettis Tom was here yet. That would be an insult to Ellis, having to wait on BT in this place. The ice house, Jerry's Ice and Beer, looked as if it were constructed from salvaged lumber and driftwood. In fact it was a well-known local eatery and drinking place, having been here more than 50 years. Actually some of the planking was salvaged from Hurricane Carla back in the sixties.

Although Ellis lived within five miles, he had never been on this end of San Leon, and of course never been to this place. Why they could not meet at the Houston Club or the Petroleum Club in downtown Houston, where Ellis held VIP memberships, made no sense. Bettis Tom is already calling the shots, thought Ellis.

Ellis entered the ice house and was surprised when he walked through the door. The place opened up to a veranda facing Galveston Bay. Even Ellis had to admit, one of the more pleasant views he had seen along Texas' Gulf Coast.

Ellis chose a place in the shade, but as near the edge of the veranda as he could get. He preferred a good view with no one between him and the water. No worry, the place only had a few patrons at this time of the day. He sat, and was surprised at the very pretty waitress that appeared quickly. She was near 50 but very attractive. Ellis thought, "Maybe this won't be so bad after all."

"What'll it be, hon?"

"I'll have a martini, as quick as possible." Ellis would like to have one down before Bettis Tom showed.

"We don't have martinis."

"Just tell the bartender, he'll know how to make it."

"I am the bartender."

"You wait tables and bartender at the same time?"

"As you can tell it's pretty slow this time of the day."

"You know, my dear, there are only two ingredients, vermouth and gin. Just like Sinatra liked them."

"Please mister, just choose something else."

"How about Jack Daniels and Coke? You got that?"

"Jack and Coke it'll be."

It will have to do thought Ellis. He was beginning to understand this was an ice house where most of the patrons drank beer, cold beer.

Where was Bettis Tom? As Ellis finished his drink, he ordered a second and was half way through it when BT came striding across the floor to M. Ellis Winston's table, with his pale blue shirt adorned with faded red painted flowers hanging loosely down over the top of his Levis. Ellis thought, "Who the hell does this guy think he is, a 20 year old surfer on the north shore? I hope he does not have that stupid pistol stuck in the back of his pants." Ellis was a good attorney, so he knew how much trouble they could be in if someone noticed. Even in Texas you can't just stroll into an establishment, selling alcohol, with a gun tucked under your shirt, in your belt. "The dumb bastard. What does he want?"

Bettis Tom slouched into his chair and as close as he could muster, smiled. "How you doing. Maythorpe?"

"Don't call me that." returned Ellis. "And what do you want? Why do you want to see me?"

"We'll get to that, relax."

"Next time we meet, and maybe we won't, let me choose the place."

"Look Ellis, at one of those places you go to downtown everyone there knows you. So just relax, you might get to like this place. You are pretty conspicuous driving that Jag, and wearing that suit. If we wait another hour, the plant workers will begin to arrive, then you will really be noticed."

"What'll it be, hon? Oh, hello BT. I should have noticed it was you with that shirt."

"Don't order a martini. They don't have martinis."

The pretty waitress stared at Ellis for a full ten seconds, then turned to Bettis Tom. "I know you, cold beer in a long neck."

The two men were taking the measure of each other and did not notice the pretty woman sitting across the room, enjoying her drink and looking at the water. Her curly haired lunch companion strolled in a few minutes later, spotted her and walked to her table unnoticed.

"Hello Maggie."

"Right on time Apple. You know that is a unusual

name. I never even heard of anyone else called that."

"You ever hear of Appleton. I much prefer Apple or App." They were enjoying each other's company, unlike the tense meeting going on across the room. "By the way Maggie is pretty rare too."

"Are you kidding me? Maybe it was popular in the 40s, not now."

"OK, but I think Maggie Smith and Maggie Hatcher, and Maggie Monroe. Well, maybe not that last one, were pretty famous. Ever hear of a famous person named Apple? Hey, what are you driving these days? Last time we met you were driving a little import."

"Exciting, I just bought a new car, a Cadillac CTS. Can you believe that? My mother told me I would never get anywhere working for Sheriff Ben. I guess I showed her. Yes, I love it."

"I am happy for you. Guess what? My mom told me the same thing. In fact she told me that just last week. I would never get anywhere reporting for the Announcer. She wants me to write, maybe a novel, or for the Times or the Journal. Mama, it is the largest newspaper west of the Mississippi and east of the Rio Grande. I guess she is right so far."

Apple and Maggie ordered drinks. The attractive waitress promptly brought them cold beer in long neck bottles.

Maggie said, "Did you notice the black Jag parked alongside the building? Giving my new car a run for the money."

Apple looked around the large patio and said, "I bet you I can guess who is driving it."

"How you gonna do that?" asked Maggie.

"It is sort of a gift, a second sense I have. And, I

will bet you I can guess what he does for a living. See that guy over there? The one wearing the pin stripped Brooks Brothers suit. That would be him."

"That was easy, how about the guy in the Hawaiian shirt?"

"He would be more difficult. I can tell you this: he is not what he seems to be. Maybe a land developer or some kind of tricky encyclopedia salesman, you can be sure he is some sort of a tin man hawking aluminum siding. Maybe burglar alarms."

"You're kidding aren't you?"

"Not altogether. The suit guy just might be the tricky one and Mr. Hawaiian shirt might be the lawyer. But the guy in the suit is definitely driving the Jag."

"Want to hear a funny thing? I think I have seen the suit guy somewhere," said Maggie.

"Hey, now you are not a land speculator are you?" All this time, Apple kidded around. "I thought you were the Sheriff's assistant."

"Guessing was easy. How we going to prove you are right?"

"I know. I will ask them." With that Apple quickly got up and walked across the patio to where the two were sitting. Apple was never intimidated by strangers or awkward in asking people questions. After all, he was a newspaper reporter.

As he approached, Bettis Tom and Ellis suddenly stopped talking and looked straight at Apple. Not too friendly, but probably the type of look anyone approaching a stranger in an ice house might get. Apple put on his most engaging smile and said, "Sorry to disturb you, but my girlfriend and I were having a little guessing game, and I am hoping y'all can help us out. I told her I could guess who is driving that handsome Jaguar parked out in the lot." He turned to M. Ellis Winston, "My guess is that would be you. Am I right?"

Ellis was flattered, which was the effect Apple was hoping for.

"You were right, my friend, that is my car. I have been driving Jags for a while now. A real performer."

Apple said, "And a real eye catcher. Does the opposite sex like it? I will bet that they do." App was really flattering Ellis and it was working.

"Just open the door and they get in," said Ellis.

"I also bet my girlfriend that you were an attorney. How close would that be?"

"You are right again, my friend," and with that he casually handed Apple a business card. Apple pocketed the card and turned to Bettis Tom. "I also told her that you would be much harder to guess. My guess was land developer, or something along that line. Am I in the ballpark?" he asked BT.

Bettis Tom looked him up and down and simply said, "Beat it, buddy. Guessing game's over," then turned back to Ellis.

Apple said, "My apology for interrupting you." As he turned to leave, he handed Ellis a business card with the Houston Announcer in bold print and Apple Smith lightly printed across the bottom with his office and cell number.

Apple returned to his table where Maggie was wearing a big smile. She could tell that App had been summarily dismissed. "So how did it go? Was he a lawyer and was he driving the Jag?"

"Right on both guesses." As Apple glanced at the business card for the first time. A look of surprise instantly came over his face, "Well I'll be. And dear, that is why I am a good journalist. I am incredibly lucky!

"I've heard you are a good reporter."

"Yeah, from who?"

"None other than Sheriff Ben himself."

"Really? I was under the impression he did not like me very much. But no matter, look at this!" Apple handed her the business card with M. Ellis Winston's name on it. And the card said, legal office, BAR Chemical Company. Apple's quick mind was racing with thoughts. He excused himself from Maggie with, "Gotta go to my car for a minute. Be right back." He returned rather quickly with his iPad and began striking keys. "Do you know who we just stumbled onto? That guy is so high up in the company he advises Jeffrey Dearcorn himself. He is on the board at BAR Chem. Boy! Would I like a few minutes with him."

At that Apple got up and walked over to Ellis's and Bettis Tom's table and said," I had no idea who you were when I very frivolously interrupted your conversation a while ago. Allow me to introduce myself." Ellis just glanced down at Apple's card and said, "I think I know who you are now."

"Mr. Winston, I am doing a piece on the company's movement to Mexico and, I would very much like to have an interview with you. I would be very grateful."

"Have you talked to my secretary about a time?"

Apple answered that he had and that he had discovered Ellis was a very busy man. Apple pushed his point for a few words now, but Ellis politely declined, stating that he was presently busy and, could he make an appointment with the office.

Bettis Tom again told Apple to move along. Apple said, "Who are you by the way? Do you work for BAR Chem also?"

Bettis Tom dismissed him with a wave of his hand. Apple retreated also with a wave of his hand. Question in his mind, who is the surly one? I'll bet he works for BAR Chem also. Apple was thinking that he couldn't really be that lucky. Could that Hawaiian-shirted fellow be the boat captain, the one with the country boy name, Bettis Tom Stovall? He made a mental note to call Bernie and ask if she had any idea what Bettis Tom looked like. With those thoughts, he turned his iPad just so, and took a picture of the two sitting and discussing something in obvious serious tones. Apple thought, if I could just hear what they are saying, now that would be technology.

When he returned to his own seat Maggie asked if he was the one Apple thought he was. Then she said, "I remember where I have seen him. He has been to visit the Mayor. And I am pretty sure that the Sheriff has spoken privately with him also."

"Do you keep an appointment book for Sheriff Ben?"

"Yes, but this would not have been on the agenda. He just walked in and went straight to the office of the Sheriff. I"m pretty sure the Sheriff was expecting him.

Bettis Tom told Ellis, "See, you attract attention with that fancy suit and the Jag. Let me see that business card." Ellis handed Apple's card over to BT. Bettis Tom took one look at the card and his face changed color from his normal red to white. "You know who this is, right? Which is why I asked for this meeting"

"The only thing I know about him is this business card. I know he has written some important pieces for the Announcer, but other than that, no, I don't know anything about him."

Bettis Tom threw a derisive small laugh in Ellis's

direction, then said, "He and a female companion, I think also works for the paper, visited the yacht in Galveston recently, asking questions about who uses the yacht, when it moved last. You get the picture?"

"I know you use the yacht more than anyone, but why would you be concerned with questions being asked?"

"Do you know anything? You ever hear of John Bishop? Don't you understand everything that happens to the company affects all of us?"

"Your uncalled for heavy handed methods concern you, not me or the company. You need to calm down Bettis Tom."

"My methods are what keeps this company profitable, my friend, and they are about to involve you, directly."

Ellis was having a hard time keeping his mouth shut, but he remembered the private conversation Dearcorn had with him recently where he had been assigned to keep an eye on Bettis Tom. So, he sat and listened. Bettis Tom took everything in a different light. Ellis was working for him, and he intended to use him in a clever way, at least to BT's way of thinking.

"Listen to me, Ellis, that reporter was on board the coast guard boat when the shrimpers discovered the body. He was already doing a story about the plant explosion and the events that followed. And do you know who was showing him around? You guessed it, Sheriff Rodriguez himself. And he has permission from the newspaper to explore more in depth because of John Bishop."

"Yes, well whose idea was it to have Bishop dancing around with a briefcase full of cash? If you don't remember, I believe that idea came from you. I advised Jeff against it, and now we have a big mess on our hands."

"I'll give you that one. It is a problem, and you are going to get things headed right again."

"How do you propose to do that?"

"You are going to go to Morris Barton at the newspaper and talk him into pulling our Appleton Smith back. Tell him a story is fine, even allow him to criticize us about the movement of the company and the mistreatment of our former workers. Just get him to pull back on the story about John Bishop and the money."

Ellis asked, "How do you propose I do that? Just walk into the editor's office and ask him to stop writing the story? Why would he do that?"

"That is exactly what I propose. Remind him how much money we spend there advertising. Hell, he might even know how many products we have investments in. Just because BAR Chem is not written on the labels doesn't mean we are not the owners of hundreds of products. You remind him of that, Ellis. Also tell him the Senator would like for him to oblige us in this matter. He'll know who you are talking about."

Ellis said, "I am uneasy with this entire plan."

"Now you relax and listen to me. This is what I am good at. We are not in your courtroom now. We are in the real world of business. I know how to get these things done. Use that smooth talking way you have and convince the good Mr. Barton how much we appreciate it. You just might be surprised how much Barton thinks of BAR Chem."

M. Ellis Winston had no way to refuse Bettis Tom's heavy handed idea. Besides, it just might take the heat down a bit. He asked BT, "Alright, so we get the newspaper to pull back. We still have the Sheriff to deal with. You know he is not going to back off. And even if he does, we still have the Coast Guard to deal with."

"The Coast Guard will be no problem. They rescue people, not investigate murders." That was the first time Bettis Tom had mentioned the word murder. It made Ellis very nervous.

"OK Bettis Tom, have it your way. I will give it my best shot, but if this blows up in our face, remember whose idea this was."

Chapter 11
BEER CAN AND COLORADO WATCH

Apple was on his way back to his boat to do some thinking about this whole affair. Who was M. Ellis Winston? Was the other fellow Bettis Tom Stovall? That should be easy enough to find out, Winston would be listed on the board of directors of BAR Chem. Probably a biography would be available on the internet. The other fellow would be a little more difficult. He already knew Bettis Tom was on the payroll at BAR Chem. He surely had more duties other than running the yacht. Apple really did not know if the guy was indeed Bettis Tom Stovall, but he intended to find out soon.

Why not right now? He had a picture and he was only twenty minutes from Galveston. He would simply pay another visit to the two Billys, that being Beer Can Billy and Colorado Billy.

Apple was excited as he drove over the causeway, down Broadway to the Galveston Yacht Basin. As he pulled into the parking lot, he was in luck. He would not have to spend time looking the two fellows up. They were standing near the same place he had left them day before yesterday, predictability drinking beer out of an ice chest setting at their feet on the pier.

Apple approached easily, stuck out his hand and said, "Hi fellows, remember me? I spoke to you a few days ago." Beer Can Billy shook hands and grinning said, "We been advised not to talk to you anymore." Colorado Billy stood by rather passively, and did not join in the conversation.

"Really? Now who would advise you that?"

"Never saw the fellow around here before, but he was definitely connected with the big yacht, Chump Change."

"Well Colorado, Beer Can, if you would rather not, I'll understand. I know some of the fellows that use the big boat have a reputation for playing pretty rough."

Beer Can drew himself up to his full height of five foot ten inches, puffed out his chest and returned, "You underestimate us sir. I have personally sailed single handed around the world twice, right now I am thinking about going back to Indochina to retire, and Colorado here just returned from the Azores where he spent the past year. The ocean does not intimidate us, nor do little people from down the pier. They are chumps from the 'Chump Change'."

Whereas Colorado took over, and taking his guide from Beer Can stood up to his full height of six foot two inches, and spoke, "Have you ever been so hungry you ate a sea gull, never mind the feathers? Now that is tough. We take it as a personal insult when someone down the pier dictates to us who we can talk to and not. No sir, we don't take that kind of rude behavior in a man, never will. Besides we like you much better than those folks. Didn't you sail your Hunter sailboat down from Kemah the other day? We like boat people."

Then they grinned big and Colorado Billy said, "Especially your lady friend who was with you, no offense."

Apple told them he would let her know their sentiments. Then he showed the photo on his iPad to them. "Do you recognize this guy?"
Beer Can and Colorado took a quick glance at the photo and said, "Heck yeah, that's Stovall."

"You're sure!" "We're dead sure." Then Apple asked, "How about this other guy?"

"No, don't think I have seen that fellow," said Colorado, "Me either," said Beer Can. "I will tell you this, many of the fellows that show up to the boat are snazzy dressers like that guy."

Apple took a wild guess and asked, "Have you ever seen a brand new black Jaguar on the pier?" Then he described the car. They both believed that they had seen that car before but not recently.

Apple thought, "I have done a good day's work, definitely Bettis Tom and M. Ellis Winston having drinks together. Iron clad because of these two witnesses."

Apple left a warning to Beer Can and Colorado as he departed, "Be careful boys, I think that "Chump Change" is a mean crowd. Particularly the one named Bettis Tom."

"Don't worry about us, partner. Nobody gets in the way of our fun," said Billy and Billy as they waved goodbye.

Apple was grateful for the information, but left the marina a little concerned about his two new friends. Those two knuckleheads had no clue who they were living down the pier from. Apple had a dread in his heart that he had to look no farther for the murderer of John Bishop. And Bishop was one of theirs; no telling what Bettis Tom and his boys would be capable of doing to a couple of outsiders.

Several things still bothered Apple about his story, as he still called it. Why was Bishop killed, and why were

Bettis Tom and Ellis Winston meeting? He thought he sure would like to get a look in that briefcase. What else was inside? Was it too early to simply ask Sheriff Ben for a peek? The answer was probably no. And the last question, which probably wasn't anything, just curiosity. How did Maggie afford a new expensive car on her salary as an employee of the county? Maybe he would just ask her the next time they got together, and he hoped that would be soon.

It was late in the day, so he would call it a good afternoon's work and head on over to Eagle Point for some oysters. There was a good place located on the point to enjoy the sunset, beer, and great seafood.

He needed to call Bernie at the paper, but it was late in the day and he did not want to call her at home, so he decided to wait until tomorrow morning. He needed to catch her up on what he had found out about Bettis Tom and M. Ellis Winston. He made a mental note to tell her the boys at the marina missed her today. Maybe he would ask her to do some checking on Maggie. Some reporter I am, he thought, I don't even know her last name. Bernadette could find that out easily enough, she had more resources than anyone at the newspaper. She was frequently asked when the TV networks wanted a quick answer on a local issue. A last thought came to his mind, "I wonder if I could find out anything about the briefcase by asking Commander Johnson. He seemed to be a little more approachable than the Sheriff over this matter. With that he pulled up into the parking lot at the oyster house.

After dinner he would drive the five miles to his boat and watch the Astros play the Angels. App was a big baseball fan and his hometown team was in a tight pennant race. For the first time in ten years the Astros were interesting to watch. He was very relaxed as he made the way to his boat for the night. He was a little saddened by the news that the great Yogi Berra had passed away. App smiled as he remembered a small boy going to the Astrodome and seeing the great player coaching his team, the Astros. That would have been about 1988 or 89. He sighed and thought to himself that they don't make them like they used to. He smiled as he remembered a Yogi saying. His wife asked him some time ago where he would like to be buried, Yogi replied, "Surprise me." He thought no, they really don't make them like they used to make them. Watching the game would serve a useful purpose - to clear his mind and sharpen him up for tomorrow.

WILLIAM WARREN

Chapter 12
APPLE VISITS THE COAST GUARD

Apple awoke early after a very restful night. He was a good sleeper because he was a very calm person, even when things were not going so well. He made it a point to never worry about things he could not control. It was too early to call Bernie at the paper, but, he thought, not too early to call Commander Johnson. He did make the call, and the Commander agreed to meet him that morning. He seemed particularly agreeable, even adding, "Bring your coffee mug. We make pretty good coffee around here."

Apple jumped into his 20 year old Ford pickup and headed to the little Coast Guard station on the east end of Galveston. He received grief from fellow workers at the paper about his old pickup. She did need a paint job, but otherwise ran like a top. He felt if newspaper man Leon Hale could drive an old pickup, then he was not too good to do the same. Besides, he lived in Houston where pickups were driven by the rich and famous, the plant worker, and everyone in between. There was even an idea picking up momentum across town to pass an ordinance requiring public parking lots to enlarge their spaces so that stretch cab pickups could park more easily. He smiled as he thought, "Only in Houston."

Apple felt good as he approached the small parking lot at the station. Above all, the question he wanted answered was what was in the briefcase that Mr. Bishop would have the thing securely attached to his arm? Damn, that question kept coming back to his mind. Only one thing made any sense. The case was either full of money or the formula for a gasoline substitute. He knew the last idea was fantasy, so the briefcase had to be full of cash. But if money is the answer, why didn't the killer take the briefcase? A small concern was if Sheriff Ben would arrest him if he went back to the office. He smiled as he thought this. Surely the Sheriff had nothing personal against him. At least he hoped.

This was Apple's first time visiting the Coast Guard station, and he was impressed with what he found. The shiny white coast guard cutter was massive tied to the large pier. He estimated the war ship to be about 225 feet long, and very tidy. Maybe he could get someone to give him a tour, not for anything to do with his investigative reporting but for his own enjoyment. He had passed this place many times over the years, sailing by in the Galveston harbor, but had never had a tour. There were several other smaller patrol boats tied to the pier, including the one he had ridden with the Sheriff the day John Bishop was discovered in the shrimper's net. He grew grim at this thought.

As he walked from his pickup across the parking lot, Chief Decks strode out to meet him. "Good morning sir,"

Apple, recalling the Chief to be an outgoing, informal person, asked him to simply call him Apple, or App and drop the sir.

"Alright, Apple or simply App, how you been doing? I have been reading your paper and watching for a big story on the drowning, or something on BAR Chem, but haven't seen anything."

Apple decided to ignore the drowning comment.

Chief Deckford was there that day on the bay. He certainly knew that Bishop had been murdered. Apple said. "Well Chief, you missed my big story. A couple of days ago we ran about five lines on the body being pulled in by a couple of shrimpers. My boss didn't think I had enough info to warrant any more print. That is why I am here, to see if the Commander knows any more. That and to admire your ship. How about a tour sometime?"

"Anytime Apple. Maybe you could go on a training cruise with us sometime. We often take civilians along as observers." He smiled as he said, "You could tell everyone how good we are."

"I'll keep that in mind, I would like to do that very much."

Chief Petty Officer Decks showed Apple to Commander Johnson's office, where he quickly had a steaming hot cup of coffee in his hand. It was approaching eight a.m., and the station was a hub of activity.

"Welcome to our little part of the world," said the Commander.

"Thanks for seeing me." Apple went straight to the point because he figured the Commander was a busy man. "What do you think my chances are of finding out what was in the briefcase?"

Then Commander Johnson said, "Pretty good. Just ask me. I have been through it very thoroughly."

"What's in it, besides a lot of money?"

"Damn good guess. How did you figure it is money?"

"I used the old Sherlock Holmes method. I threw out everything thing that made no sense. The only thing I could see a fellow having in a briefcase rigged to his arm, was money."

"Before I go any further, you have to understand this investigation is in the very early stages, and anything I tell you has to be very much off the record. If you can agree to that, I will trust you to keep your word and only go to print at your paper after I give you a go ahead. If you agree, then I will tell you what I know."

Apple gave that a quick once over in his head and agreed on his one condition. He had to have one day notice before the rest of the press was notified. After all, he was already working on the mystery himself. He knew there was valuable information in the briefcase besides the money, and the only way he would know was through the Commander. Sheriff Ben was not going to tell him anything. He knew that John Bishop's death was tied to BAR Chem. He was beginning to dislike those bastards if they hired people like Bettis Tom Stovall.

"Why are you trusting me in this way, Commander?"

"I know of some of your work, I did a little investigating of you myself. Your reputation of fairness and honesty is a good one. I also figure that somewhere down the line we may need a little help from you and your resources. So, I am confiding in you."

Then Commander Johnson told him of the money, the names with figures beside their names.

Apple was not surprised to find leading politicians from the area, nor was he surprised to find the name of the Houston-Galveston EPA authority listed. That actually made sense from BAR Chem's perspective.

"Did you know Sheriff Rodriguez has been paid a monthly payment from the beginning of this BAR Chem move to Mexico?" Then Johnson explained the $1,500 monthly fee, and his feelings of perplexity, and his astonishment at seeing the sum of $20,000 next to the

Sheriff's name.

"What do you make of that?" asked Apple.

"I am sure Sheriff Ben is not on the take from the company. I have known him a while and he is the most trustworthy and honorable man I know. That is one reason I am taking you into my confidence. Help me find out the answers to this."

Apple asked if he had any answer to that question himself. "Here is the way I figure it. Some of the names on the list have been taking what could only be described as bribes. The company wants favorable outcomes to some of the problems it faces here, concerning their current and past operations. But in Sheriff Ben's case, I think that was an amount Bishop had been authorized to offer Ben for future favors. However, I can't imagine what Ben could do for the company that would be worth offering him that kind of money. Of course, Ben has no answer for the $20,000. He swears he has never received anything like that and has no idea of why his name appears on the list.

Apple asked the Commander if he thought it would be good to tell the Sheriff of this meeting they had.

"As a matter of fact, I called him this morning and told him that I was going to meet with you."

"And what was his response?"

"The Sheriff said he was fine with it as long as you would stay out of his way and you would not act too hasty in your own inquiries."

"Do you think he would be open to talking to me?"

"Yes, by all means, call him, if for no other reason than to pay your respects."

Apple thought that was a good idea, and said he would very soon.

For some reason Apple did not understand himself,

he did not tell the Commander about Bettis Tom and M. Ellis Winston meeting at the icehouse. Nor did he speak of Beer Can Billy and Colorado Billy. He just wasn't sure of his details yet, so his reporter instincts told him until he knew more for certain, not to talk out of turn. He did appreciate the Commander and was certain that he could work with what he had learned.

As Apple and the Commander were concluding their meeting over their second cup of coffee, the Commander hit Apple between the eyes with his last bit of info. "My friend, I saved this for last because it is so surprising, there were two more names on the list." Smiling, he continued, "One of your new girlfriend. Maggie's name was on the list. But the paper was so wet and soiled the amount was not readable."

Apple said, "What in the world would BAR Chem be doing paying Maggie for anything?"

"My guess is just to keep an eye on the Sheriff."

"You mean inform the company if the Sheriff strays too closely to any details that might be harmful to the company?"

"Yeah, something like that."

Apple thought to himself that might explain the new car. But wait, she hadn't got the money because it was in the Sheriff's possession. What if she had been taking money in the past? He did not tell the Commander about her new car. He knew he was probably getting carried away with his conspiracy ideas.

Then the big one, "The name of your boss, Morris Barton's name was on the list also. We could make out the amount on this one. It was $10,000."

Now Apple really couldn't believe what he was hearing. He said to the Commander, "Just as you believe in the Sheriff's complete honesty, I can tell you Barton is such a man of integrity, even Hitler himself would not be able to make Morris Barton cross that line. Perhaps the money offered was to be used for future favorable reporting? It appears the only people not on the list are you and me, Commander." This is serious stuff, but the Commander grinned as he said, "Shows where we are on the pecking order, right?"

Apple thanked the Commander for his cooperation and vowed that he would keep his word with the new information the Commander had trusted him with. He also intended to use this insider knowledge to the best for himself and for the paper.

Apple realized he was beginning to connect with John Bishop in a strange way. Even though he was evidently just a highly paid bag man for the company, he deserved to have the truth published about his death. He wondered what BAR Chem had on Bishop. Was he caught in a compromising position either with a woman, man, or was he playing with the company's money

He made a mental note to call Bernadette to find out what John Bishop's family situation was. Apple was pretty sure that BAR Chem was bribing the union leaders, the EPA, and at least one local county judge. He also believed that a United States Senator was involved. He was having a hard time getting his head around Sheriff Ben taking a bribe, but if he was taking money, what was it for? Apple knew for sure that Mr. Barton was not taking any money from BAR Chem. He would enjoy being in that meeting when he was being bribed. I am sure BAR Chem would quickly be shown the door.

If they did or if they were going to try to bribe the paper, who from the company would show up at Mr.

Barton's office? There would probably not even be a note as to who came calling. Morris Barton was a newspaper man and saw anyone who showed up at the paper and asked to see him. He knew that sometimes information from these anonymous meetings was truthful and could be gotten no place else. If a person had time to prepare for an interview, how much was true and how much self-serving?

Apple got into his car and immediately called Bernie at the office. She answered the phone and immediately began with, "Hey stranger, I thought you were an employee of the paper. Where you been?" Bernie obviously believed she would have heard something from Apple before, considering they had made the trip to Galveston two days before.

Apple began giving her an update on his meeting with Commander Johnson at the coast guard station at Galveston. App told her of his chance meeting with Bettis Tom and M. Ellis Winston, how he had just walked up to them without having any idea they were connected with BAR Chem. He asked her to see what she could find out about Maggie at the Sheriff's office, what her background would indicate.

Apple told Bernadette, "The Commander revealed some very interesting information about what was in the briefcase, for example, Maggie's name was on the list. I can't figure that one out. What could she know that would bring her to the attention of the company?"

Bernie replied, "It is pretty clear to me App, she is just reporting to the company what the Sheriff is up to. She probably only knows a little bit, nothing important. What would be interesting though, is how long she has been being paid. More to the point, was she receiving money before John Bishop's murder or after? If the answer is after, then

BAR wants to know what the Sheriff is doing towards the investigation."

"I think she knows a great deal about the Sheriff's ideas concerning the Bishop affair, as she is up to date on just about everything the Sheriff does. I don't think she knows much about the contents of the briefcase though."

"Apple, you had better be real careful in dealing with these people. I think everything you know indicates BAR Chem is up to no good, and now you are asking questions that might hit close to home. You know your girlfriend might just be keeping an eye on you too."

"She's not my girlfriend, but I do like her a bit. Hey, maybe I am keeping an eye on the Sheriff's office through her. Ever think of that?" Apple was smiling as he spoke to Bernie.

"It doesn't hurt your investigation that she is a real looker, does it?"

"How do you know what she looks like?"

"You are so simple. I am looking at her profile as we talk. The county personnel office has a record on all the employees."

"Isn't that personal records? How do you get hold of that information, and so fast?"

"Remember who you are talking to, kid. I am good."

They both had a good laugh over that.

Then Apple took a serious tone with Bernadette. "Also, there is one more important bit, Morris's name was on the list of, I am assuming bribed folks, or maybe people targeted to be bribed."

"What?"

"Morris's name." Bernie broke in, "I heard you. How is that possible?"

"Relax, I am sure that nobody has bribed Mr. Morris

Barton, but I think he is targeted for an approach. I believe that someone from the company has already or will try to get him to back off of any investigation of BAR Chem. They want no stories of any kind being printed, neither about the operation of the company and surely nothing about the death of one of their employees in Galveston Bay.

Apple asked Bernie to update Mr. Morris on all the details of his work, and especially that his name appears on a list found in the briefcase. He also asked Bernie to let him know if anyone she didn't recognize had any kind of a meeting with Morris. Apple told her to be extra watchful for anyone looking like Bettis Tom or Ellis Winston.

"I am pretty sure that it will be Ellis who approaches Mr. Barton. He looks so very much like a successful businessman, and he will know how to tread lightly around the issue. Remember he is an attorney."

"I've got both of them pegged. I happen to have a picture of Bettis Tom lying on my desk right now. As soon as we hang up, I will hit Morris with this stuff."

"Thanks, Bernie, you are the best."

"I know."

With that Apple hung up his call with Bernie. Good because one of the noncoms from the Guard was approaching his pickup truck. He was still sitting in the Coast Guard parking lot.

Chapter 13
ONE MORE WATER MISHAP

The young coastie hailed Apple with a serious expression, "The old man, that is, Commander Johnson would like to see you. He said it is urgent."

Apple went striding back into the Commander's office. Before he could speak up, the Commander beat him to it ."There has been an accident with a possible drowning over at the yacht basin."

Apple's instincts went into overdrive. The only people he knew at the marina were Beer Can Billy and Colorado Billy.

"Since we were together on the last incident, perhaps you are supposed to come along on this one. Want to?"

Apple most certainly did want to come along. Two drownings in this area were too much of a coincidence. He wondered if the Sheriff would be there.

"Oh yeah, by the way, Sheriff Ben is on his way to the site."

"Think he will mind if I am there?"

"He invited you last time to come along. Perhaps he will be expecting you."

"Oh, I don't think so."

The Commander jumped into an official Coast Guard vehicle and started in the direction of the marina. Apple insisted on taking his old pickup so that he could leave when necessary. After all, this might not involve him at all. They were followed close behind by Chief Decks and a Seaman. The short drive was less than a mile.

At the marina entrance was a Sheriff's Deputy waiting for the Commander. He directed them to the far side of the Galveston Yacht Basin where Apple and Commander Johnson could see a small crowd of people gathered. Also parked at the foot of the pier was an ambulance with several emergency lights flashing. Marked on the back door was a light print with The University of Texas Medical Branch Emergency stenciled.

Apple could clearly see the makeup of the crowd. There was the Sheriff, two or three of his deputies, a couple of EMTs, and several of what looked like boaters from around the marina. Three things stood out immediately to Apple. Number one, they were standing near the same spot that he and Beer Can Billy and Colorado Billy had their discussion yesterday. Apple had a real sense of dread as he realized that he saw Colorado Billy, but not Beer Can, that was number two. The third thing he noticed, but he considered very important, the BAR Chem Company yacht, "Chump Change," was absent from its pier.

The Commander, Apple and Petty Officer Decks and the Seaman strode down the pier toward the little crowd that seemed to be looking in the water at the edge of the pier. Sheriff Ben greeted them with a handshake to Commander Johnson and The Chief. Then he turned to Apple with a serious, but cordial nod, extended his hand and said, "I think I understand now why you are such a good reporter. You seem to keep turning up at the right time, or maybe the wrong time, whatever your point of view." Then they shook hands.

The Sheriff indicated to them that the body was still

in the water. There was a diver in the water from Sheriff Ben's office coordinating with a small boat also in the water. They were struggling to get the body into the small boat.

Suddenly Apple let out an audible sigh, as he got a good look at the person. It was Beer Can Billy appearing lifeless as a drowning victim would.

The Sheriff said "We don't have a positive ID yet, but we will when we get him on the pier." Apple said," You don't have to wait that long Sheriff. There are two on this pier that can positively identify him."

"Who would that be?"

"That would be me," and he turned a few steps and grabbed Colorado Billy by the arm, "and this gentleman here."

Colorado Billy said to Apple and not the Sheriff, "I don't really know his name, other than Beer Can Billy, but we have been friends for about six months. Ever since he brought his boat in here from his trip to the Virgin Islands where he has been for about two years. I think specifically Road Town in the British Virgin Islands."

Apple was shocked to get to the marina and find out that his new friend was the drowning victim. Somehow he had known on the short trip to the marina that it was going to be one of those two. He felt that some of the responsibility for this tragedy was partly his. What had Beer Can Billy done to warrant this? Beer Can and Colorado were very independent and a little impulsive. Had they asked the wrong person the wrong question? Had they poked around the big yacht at the wrong time?

The Sheriff was summoned closer, now that the body was removed from the water to the pier. "Sheriff, you better have a look at this," the young female EMT said.

The Commander and the Sheriff bent down for a close examination, turned and looked at each other. Beer Can Billy had been hit from behind, on the head with something blunt.

Sheriff Ben looked slightly angry as he said to the Commander, "Perhaps he hit his head on the edge of the pier, and fell into the water."

The Sheriff's department now had a detective on the scene and he said to the Sheriff, "I don't think so Sheriff. Have a look at this." At that he held Beer Can's wrist in his hand and gently twisted it. "It appears that his thumbs on both hands are broken."

Commander Johnson spoke, "That only indicates this entire incident is no accident."

Sheriff Ben agreed that it was highly unlikely Beer Can Billy could have bumped his head so hard he fell into the water and broke both his thumbs at the same time.

"Sheriff, are you saying that this is also a case of homicide?" asked Apple.

The Sheriff looked tired as he simply said, "Yes."

It appeared that the Commander was not going to contest with the Sheriff whose jurisdiction this was. He seemed to want nothing to do with this murder on the dock of the Galveston Yacht Basin. He was still puzzled about John Bishop and his satchel full of money, but he was a ship's captain, not a homicide investigator, so he let it be.

"Ben, you can count on me for any assistance the Coast Guard can provide," Commander Johnson said, effectively taking himself out of responsibility for the investigation into Beer Can Billy's death.

"Mr. Smith," asked Sheriff Ben, "What is it you know about what is going on here?"

Apple answered, "Very perceptive, Sheriff. How

did you know that I wanted to talk to you?"

"Well for one, you seem to know one of the witnesses rather well."

"The truth is, I only made their acquaintance a few days ago. I came to the marina looking for the "Chump Change" and ran into these two guys who only introduced themselves as Beer Can Billy and Colorado Billy. They are both live-a-boards on these two boats. They are in the right place to see who is coming and going on the "Change.""

"And why would you be interested in what is happening on the yacht?"

"As you can see it is not in port at the time, and belonging to BAR Chem, it is of interest to me. Especially since John Bishop was found in the bay a few miles from here. For example, Sheriff, you must know from your own investigations that the "Chump Change" was out all night the night before Mr. Bishop was found in the water by the shrimpers."

"And you find that interesting?"

"Damn right! Don't you?"

Apple was thinking the Sheriff seems to be taking this information personally, not as he intended,. Maybe the Sheriff is still upset with me for digging into this murder investigation.

"I also find it very interesting that the boat seems to take a lot of trips to three places."

"Where are these three places you find so interesting?"

"I find it interesting she seems to go to South America and Veracruz a lot."

"What is so strange about a large company yacht visiting those places?"

"I think they are either bootlegging something or

dealing with some contraband of some kind. I also find it interesting how good an alibi being away from the pier provides for some interesting characters."

"You sure find a lot of things interesting around here," said Sheriff Ben.

"Another thing of interest I have found is the guy who is the captain on these voyages always is one, Bettis Tom Stovall. Ever heard of him, Sheriff?"

The Coast Guard Commander was listening to this conversation, when he added, "Apple, how did you find out all this information? And by the way, who is this Bettis Tom character?"

Apple said, "The most interesting thing I have stumbled across is, Sheriff, you have been a visitor to the "Chump Change" more than once yourself."

"What are you saying, Smith?" The mister had been dropped by the Sheriff. Apple was beginning to touch a raw nerve with his inquiries, and the Sheriff did not like the implication, Sheriff Ben was aware of Commander Johnson's meeting with Apple, and he assumed correctly Apple was told of his name being on the "bribery" list.

"Listen Smith, I know you have a good reputation as a reporter, so I am just going to tell you to let your reporter's sense be overruled by your good common sense. A word to the wise, you're way in over your head. These are murder investigations. You're insinuating everybody from BAR Chem to me is involved, and I am beginning to take your remarks as personal." With that Sheriff Ben dismissed Apple. As he turned to walk away, Apple said, "As to the in over my head, please let me remind you that this case is no cattle rustling crime." He referenced a case in the past that Sheriff Ben had been involved in solving, and had gotten a lot of publicity over. Cattle rustling still happened frequently in Texas and was taken seriously.

"It's just possible I could help in some way. Remember I am the one who knew Beer Can Billy."

"That's no help. What am I supposed to do? Write in my reports the victims' name is Beer Can?"

"Beer Can Billy is more than you know now."

"His real name is William Harry Wilson from Beaumont, Texas. My boys have been by the marina office. I'll tell you what Smith, this is the wrong place to have this conversation. Meet me in my office at eight tomorrow morning and we'll see what happens."

"Thanks, Sheriff, I'll be there."

Apple glanced over at Colorado Billy. Colorado had a tear in his eye. He mouthed the words, "Can I talk to you alone?" Apple nodded his head up and down in the affirmative. Colorado had already talked to the Sheriff and was puzzled at what all this meant. He asked the Sheriff's detective if they were finished with their questions where upon Colorado started to walk down the pier to his own boat. Apple followed in the next half minute.

Apple stepped on board the near 50 foot Island Packet sailboat, and whistled below his breath, he thought wow! What did old Colorado do before becoming a cruising sailboater? Colorado's boat must cost a small fortune. He knew this boat was one of the best boat builders in the world. Island Packets were simple, but expensive, and very tough.

Apple said, "Some boat Colorado, what did you do before sailing? Rob banks?"

"Well, I wasn't always a marina bum. I owned several small businesses back in Colorado Springs. And, actually, I am very well off. My late wife used to say I had money to burn and it was her job to burn it. That was before I had enough of snow and long winters. So, about 15 years ago my wife passed away and I took off for the Virgin Islands where the air is soft and warm. And now this. What the hell has just happened?"

"That is what I am hoping you can help with. What the hell did happen, Colorado?"

"Was Beer Can really murdered?"

"It sure looks that way."

"If he had only fallen into the water, hit his head and drowned, that would be understandable. You know he suffered from dizzy spells that were sudden and severe. He would not be able to walk for a couple of hours, but his thumbs broken? How can that have happened?"

Apple asked him to tell him everything that he and Beer Can did yesterday, in particular anything about the "Chump Change." Colorado related how they had been watching the boat, "But we never went aboard. At least I didn't, Beer Can might have after we turned in last night. You know he was a fun loving guy, and he was really getting into checking things out. We never cared much for the characters that seemed to come and go, so this was sort of an official way of keeping track. And by the way, a very well dressed fellow driving a black Jag did come by and go on board about dark last night."

"So the boat was here when you went to bed last night?"

"Yes, and it was gone when I got up about eight o'clock this morning. Soon after I began looking for Beer Can and found him floating in the water near his own boat."

"What do you think happened, Colorado?"

"Well, I think Beer Can did go aboard and look through the port holes and saw something he was not

112

supposed to see, and he got caught spying."

"But what could he have seen to have caused someone to be so crazy they broke his thumbs and murdered him?"

Apple continued, "I don't know, but I am beginning to get some ideas, and I intend to find out."

Colorado told Apple, "I am more than a little concerned for my own safety. I keep a gun on my boat, but I am a sound sleeper, and I have to get off the boat once in a while."

"What could you possibly know that someone would come after you?"

"Maybe they think I have seen something more than I have. I don't really know even their names, except for Bettis Tom."

"Was Bettis Tom here yesterday?"

"Yes, I saw him around here all day. Checking things as if he were about to pull the boat out."

Apple thanked him for the talk, and told him he would check on him tomorrow. "Take care now."

Colorado answered, "If I'm here tomorrow."

"Why, you going somewhere?"

"Perhaps it would be a good idea for me to sail on down to Barbados for a while. I have friends there, and when it is calmed down here you can let me know."

"I wish you good luck on your cruise. That might be a good idea. Just for a while, I plan to find out who did this to our friend Beer Can."

Apple drove out of the marina very pensive, concerned for Colorado Billy. Many thoughts were coming to him, such as where is the "Chump Change"? Is it just a coincidence that the boat departed in the night? The same night Beer Can Billy was murdered? What could Beer Can have stumbled onto that led to this tragedy? And, could he and the Sheriff work out some agreement of cooperation on this matter? After all, they had the same goal in mind. Would Apple have to promise not to publish anything until the whole story was solved?

Chapter 14
LOOKING FOR "CHUMP CHANGE"

Apple drove his old pickup out of the Galveston Yacht Basin, crossed the Strand district and moved onto Broadway, heading to his office at the newspaper in downtown Houston, about one hour from Galveston, when he suddenly turned around and started back to the Yacht Basin. He caught the Commander in his white Coast Guard sedan at the front gate, signaled him with an arm wave. Commander Johnson slipped into a parking spot, and got out of his car as Apple pulled in the space next to him. The way the Commander quickly got out of his car made Apple think that he actually was glad to see him. Perhaps he has something for me, thought App.

They both walked to the front of their vehicles, nodded and the Commander started talking, "What do you think is going on here?"

"I'm not sure what the motives are in either John Bishop's case or Beer Can Billy's, but I am sure they are both connected with BAR Chem in some way or other. I don't have any good idea about Bishop, since he apparently was a trusted employee of the company. What is so confusing is the briefcase full of money. If the case had been empty that would make more sense. What do you make of it all?"

The Commander responded, "Perhaps the whole Bishop affair was planned? Did anyone know you were meeting with Sheriff Ben the day the body was discovered?"

"Only my editor at the paper. Wait a minute, Maggie in the Sheriff's office knew. She was the one who set up the tour of BAR Chem's abandoned property. I never actually met the Sheriff until that morning."

"Was there anything for the company to gain by your being at the scene of the discovery of Bishop's body? What if the company wanted all of this to become known? The money could have just been the enticer. The real heart of the matter is the list of names."

"What would be the good of knowing who was on their illicit payroll?"

Commander Johnson continued, "I think extortion is the answer. Some of the names are legit, but I still don't think Sheriff Ben is on their side."

"And I know Morris Barton is not. So where does that leave us?"

Commander Johnson said, "Here is a very far out there idea. What if BAR Chem wanted to come back to their old property in the area, and they could use help from some of those people? I would guess the head of Houston's area EPA would have to be hit over the head with a bag of money before the Environmental Agency would grant a permit to occupy any of the company's old properties."

Apple continued with that thought, "That might not be so far-fetched. I have heard that the Company is not doing so well in Mexico. Labor issues, unqualified workers, payoffs, shipments, the list is long."

"I know," added the Commander, "the local ACW would have to be granted a long list of promises before the leadership would back such a plan."

"And that is why the two union leaders Randy Filbin and Mario Santiago are on the list. To convince the union to back such a move. Right?"

This all was beginning to add up to Apple. "But how does Beer Can fit in all of this?"

The Commander could only issue a guess. "I think your friend, completely by bad luck, just stumbled onto something no one wanted to share. For example, he witnessed someone he recognized taking a wad of cash from this character Bettis Tom."

"There is one question I would like to ask. Is there any way the Coast Guard has access to the movements of the Chump Change? I think that boat holds some answers."

"Well, I'll give that to you, it is curious that the yacht seems to turn up as missing at both of these incidents."

"Further than that, I think the reason for the deaths has something to do with where the boat travels, and why it moves to those locations. So if we had a picture of the boat destinations we could have a clue to what she is doing there," said Apple.

Commander Johnson promised to look into the boat's movements, but reminded Apple that it was a private vessel and not for hire and was not required to make sail plans. The Commander's plan was to check with his counterpart at the Naval Station located in Roosevelt Roads, Puerto Rico. They would certainly notice a vessel like the "Chump Change". And perhaps it had made its way to San Juan and they would know of that. The Commander would also ask around with his Mexican friends in Veracruz. The folks in Cancun were not so friendly, but perhaps they would be in a good mood and would cooperate, if indeed the boat had been there recently.

The Commander was more than cooperative with

Apple, and this made App wonder why. Apple's speculation was that Commander Johnson wanted to prove that his friend, Sheriff Ben had nothing suspicious about his relationship to BAR Chem. He promised to get back with Apple if he found out anything of interest. And he added as their conversation broke up, "I am going to station a patrol boat at the mouth of the Galveston jetties and when he turns up I plan to find out where he has been, and why he has been there." The Commander seemed finally involved in this whole matter, much to Apple's delight.

Apple determined that he was going to find out who did this to Beer Can Billy. Commander Johnson might be the spark that solved the entire terrible affair. He knew whoever had murdered, and by the broken thumbs, made Beer Can Billy unnecessarily suffer was also responsible for John Bishop's murder. Apple did not know Bishop and was thus somewhat detached, but he took Beer Can's death personally. After all, he had just finished a convivial conversation with him only two days ago. It was a short visit, but App had immediately liked both of the Billys, especially Beer Can. He determined again to find out who killed Beer Can. BAR Chem became secondary, but he knew somehow they were responsible, if nothing else, by the way they ran their business. He would find out.

Chapter 15
COLORADO BILLY GOES SOUTH

At precisely eight a.m. Apple's cell phone rang. He picked it up instantly, almost as if he was expecting a call. The voice at the other end was Colorado Billy, who spoke in a nervous tone, "Apple, I was awake all night thinking about this whole terrible affair, what with Beer Can's death, and my close friendship, I have decided to leave Galveston and head to somewhere safer," he added, "and somewhere less exciting."

"I understand, but where will you go?"

"I would rather not say exactly. Actually I don't have a strong idea yet. I just know south, far south."

Colorado did not want to tell Apple exactly because he did not want anyone to know for sure where he was. He wasn't certain if a court could call him back to testify, but more importantly he was concerned about his own safety. If someone had broken Beer Can's thumbs before killing him, then they could do the same thing to him. And, he really did not know anything about the motive for his friend's death. Surely all he had observed was a few fellows that looked like they were gathering to play poker, and perhaps a few hookers joining them from time to time. But would someone kill Beer Can over this? He thought not. There was something more serious and sinister going on than gambling. Hell, he thought, I would probably join them if they had asked. No, he had just better put some space between himself and whoever did this to Beer Can Billy.

Apple got the picture and told Colorado he was sorry for the loss of his friend, and that leaving for a while was probably a good idea. He felt he would be safe in Barbados.

They both got the picture. Colorado had mentioned Barbados previously, so Apple knew that was where his new friend was headed. He felt that if he needed Colorado Billy in the future he could find him easily enough. With that he spoke simply, "God speed, my friend."

Apple's phone rang again almost the instant he disconnected with Colorado. It was Maggie from Sheriff Ben's office. "Hello, Maggie from Sheriff Ben, how you doing?" he asked. Apple tried to sound light and unconcerned in spite of what had just happened at the Galveston Yacht Marina. App was trying to use an old reporter's advice given to him by Morris Barton some eight or ten years ago, to never become too personal with your story. Keep a detached attitude, but in this case of Beer Can, he was having a tough time remaining separated from the story. Apple was anxious to know why she was calling. It was an obvious business call, and had to be connected with the murders, but instead, in his usual way of ignoring the obvious and going from another angle, he surprised her with, "How about dinner tonight?"

"I'm free. I'd love to have dinner. But first I need to get to the reason I called. You might not want to have dinner with me when you know why I am calling."

Apple gave in to the urgency in her voice. "OK, so what's cooking?"

"Sheriff Ben regrets to cancel your meeting

scheduled for this morning."

"I am not surprised. Sheriff Ben doesn't care for reporters much, particularly this one."

"That may be true, but that is not the reason."

"Alright, now you have my attention. What is the reason?"

"He did not exactly say, but my guess is something to do with Commander Johnson's call this morning. I think the Commander wants Ben to keep his schedule flexible for the next couple of days. And it has to do with a yacht watch or something like that."

App immediately realized the Commander had a lead on the "Chump Change" and wanted Ben available to be on board when he stopped the yacht just short of Galveston. That had to be it.

Apple knew that his new friendship with Maggie was paying off with this bit of information. He was sure Sheriff Ben wouldn't notify him of finding the yacht, and might not be too happy if he knew Maggie, although unknowingly, had spilled the beans. Apple was sure the "Chump Change" would be boarded today or tomorrow. He wondered if the Commander would invite him to join the boarding party when the time came. Apple did not think so, but would stay loose himself. Just in case. He might not be invited, but he would sure as hell be close by when the yacht came in. He would really like to be there just to see what Bettis Tom's face would reveal when the Coast Guard patrol boat pulled alongside. What a photo, he thought, a simple, small, gray, made for rough business, boat tied to the side of the yacht, made only for pleasure. Also, there would be a curious collection of people aboard, and no telling what a thorough search would reveal!

Apple said, "Alright, now the business is finished.

Where shall we dine this evening? Would you like to get out of Kemah for an evening?"

"Sure, what you got in mind?"

"How about Italian? Ever been to Prego's in the Rice Village?"

"Middle of the week, shouldn't be too crowded. I would love to. Besides, I love to watch that Yuppie crowd strut."

Prego's Italian eatery was a small place in the Rice University Village populated with doctors, college professors, and anyone who could afford a house in the area. And the food was great.

Apple asked Maggie if she would pick him up in her Cadillac. His condo was near, and he was sure she would like to drive her new car. She had seen his pickup truck and was not too impressed. It would also give him a chance to ask her how she afforded the new car. It would be an easy subject to slip in, since they would be riding in it.

Since the day was early, Apple started out for his office downtown. He had intended to go in today anyhow, and since his early meeting with Sheriff Ben was cancelled, he would put this time to good use. He very much needed to talk to Morris about his story and its continuing development.

He drove his pickup out of the marina parking lot. As he made his way over the high bridge on Highway 146 in Seabrook, his main thought was whether or not he should scoot by his apartment near Minute Maid Park for a quick shower and a change of clothes. Working at the paper was a pretty informal place, but he had been wearing the same pair of Levi's for at least two days. He could not really remember, other things were mostly occupying his mind.

He turned onto NASA Road 1. As he passed in front of the big sprawling complex, Apple was amazed as he always was, being this close to such an important place. He glanced over to his right and saw the impressive display of the jumbo 747 with the space shuttle riding piggy back. Apple had a twinge of local pride at this display. He was not old enough to remember Lyndon Johnson from personal experience, but knew what an integral part the ex-president had played in bringing NASA to Houston.

He also had regret that the shuttle was only a trainer and had never actually flown in space. How could the government, in making that decision, have over-looked NASA as a permanent display for a real space mission flying shuttle? He broke into a wry grin as he thought of New York and Los Angeles getting the real thing. What had they to do with the space shuttle? Florida was okay; they had really participated, and deserved their gift, while Houston had to make do with a mock up. A good one, but still not really a space traveler. "Oh well, that's politics." Politics had brought it here, and politics had misplaced the space shuttles. He thought, where was an LBJ when we need him?

Apple continued on the Gulf Freeway toward downtown Houston where his office was located on Texas Avenue. The traffic was heavy. That always surprised him. Why so much this time of the day? It should not have surprised him. This old freeway was outdated many years ago, but was virtually unchanged for most of his life. App was generally a patient person, but today he was very irritated at the slow pace. He was apprehensive about his looming meeting with Morris.

When he had spoken to Morris earlier, he had been chomping at the bit to speak to Apple about the BAR Chem

story. As he neared downtown he was headed north up
I-45, catching a glimpse of Sam Houston Park, watching
carefully for the Texas Avenue exit, he peeled off to his
right on Texas passing near the Alley Theater and crossing
Travis, and turning into the parking garage near his office.
He loved this city.

As Apple entered the building, Bernadette was
waiting at the door for him. He had talked to her on his
drive in. Bernie told him she wanted to talk before he
spoke to Mr. Barton. She caught his eye and greeted him
with a business handshake, then put her left arm around his
shoulder and gave him an old friendship hug, "How you
doing, in-the-field reporter?"

"Good, good, real good."

"That good, huh?"

Apple admired Bernie Hannigan in many ways,
but their close working relationship made it impossible to
connect, other than a wonderful friendship. App thought
"Maybe someday when one or the other is not working at
the Houston Announcer."

She seemed to know what he was thinking, but
quietly ignored his thoughts and asked, "OK, you're doing
good, but what is really up?"

"Do you know about the latest turn in my story?"

"What story? You've only turned in about ten lines
for the second page. I am beginning to think you are out
there just playing around with your new girlfriend, you
remember that Maggie girl?"

"Quit kidding around, I am very serious now."

"OK, go for it kid, what's happening?"

"Do you remember those two fellows we met down
on the Galveston dock?"

"You mean the two with the funny names? Beer Can

Billy and Colorado Billy? Appeared to be two harmless old marina buddies."

"Yesterday Beer Can Billy was pulled from the water near his very own boat. And, he was severely injured from a smack to the back of his head."

Bernie was stunned. She had not heard this horrific news.

"Are you sure? How did you learn about this? Maybe there was some mistake."

"No mistake. I was there. Colorado Billy and I together identified the body on the pier."

"No witnesses? Maybe it was an accident."

"No accident. Both his thumbs were broken. Perhaps like a gangster movie. Even Sheriff Rodriguez said it was a homicide, and his top homicide detective agreed."

"Any ideas about who is behind this?"

"I am sure it is tied to whoever murdered John Bishop, and I am positive someone in the board room at BAR Chem is either directly involved or knows who is."

"Whoa friend, those are strong accusations!"

"I think everything about BAR Chem Company comes from its board of directors."

"Well if you think the board knows all, you are about to learn a lot more about at least one member of the board."

Apple could not imagine what she was talking about. "What gives?"

"M. Ellis Winston, that's what gives. That is why I have spent the last 30 minutes hanging around this door. I wanted to alert you before you meet with the old man. Morris had an interesting visitor that arrived late yesterday. Just arrived at the front desk and asked to speak to Mr. Barton, said he was an attorney with BAR Chem. Of course

Morris ushered him into his office, and ended the meeting in progress with the editorial advisory staff. Interested?"

"I knew it. That sleazy peacock showed up. Got any ideas about what they talked about?"

"No. I was not invited to the meeting, and the old man didn't tell me anything at all about the discussion."

"Nothing at all?"

"I can tell you it was not about an invitation to dinner. Morris did a lot of hand waving and finger pointing. The meeting lasted about ten minutes, then the old man showed Winston the door. Morris had the window blinds open and I could see everything but not hear a sound. It was late in the day and Morris left very soon after Ellis hit the door. I am surprised they were not on the same elevator."

"Wow! I can't wait until my meeting. I hope he brings it up. If he doesn't then I will. And speaking of dinner invitations, have you found anything about Miss Maggie from Sheriff Ben's office?"

"I do all the leg work and you get the credit. Is this how it works?"

"OK, let's switch, you get my pay and I get yours."

"You may not know this, but your girlfriend comes from a pretty prominent family. An old established family tree from Seabrook. The last few years her mother has lived in one of those million dollar homes fronting the bay. Her parents have been divorced for about ten years. The dad lives in New York. He is some kind of surgeon. I think back surgeon, but I'm not sure. He previously was on the staff at MD Anderson Cancer Center, but left for new ground soon after the family split up. Maggie has lived with her mother until recently. I guess you know she has an apartment around Kemah, somewhere. She probably has plenty of money to buy herself a new car, if that is where you were headed."

Bernadette knew all about the list with names and money amounts found In John Bishop's briefcase, including the boss, Morris Barton. She also knew Maggie was now driving a new CTS, and that Apple was trying to tie money to Maggie and the Cadillac.

"Maybe she hasn't accepted money. Her family seems to be doing well enough."

"Yeah, her Mom is one of the top realtors in the bay area. You should be familiar with her billboards. Marilyn Stosselberg."

"Well I'll be," said Apple. "Well it's easy to see where she gets her good looks. Maggie Stosselberg."

"You mean you didn't know her last name?" replied Bernie. "Some news hound you are. Then you didn't know your girlfriend was a Rice University graduate. Surprised? Well, that isn't all, she is also a South Texas School of Law graduate, and a current member of the Texas State Bar Association."

"Then what in the world is she doing answering the phone in Sheriff Ben's office? I can tell she is sharp, but I had no idea." Apple was surprised at this bit of information, but could not tell if it had any bearing on his story at all. But all considered, very interesting. Maggie had previously stated that she enjoyed her work. Apple thought enjoying your work is one thing, but wasn't she a little over qualified?

They hopped on the elevator without any other comments because there were several others riding with them. As they got off on their floor, Apple thanked Bernie profusely for the information, not just about Maggie, but more importantly for the heads up on M. Ellis Winston. Now he had his mind on the subject and was more mentally prepared for his meeting with the old man.

Chapter 16

BARTON AND CRONKITE AND CLINTON

As soon as Apple approached Mr. Barton's office, Morris stuck his head out the door and beckoned him in. He greeted App with a smile and a handshake. "Welcome, my boy! Where the hell you been keeping yourself?" Morris knew he was working on the BAR Chem story; it was just his way of greeting.

Apple was relieved to see Morris in such an amiable mood. The truth is Apple had not been around much the last several days, and had not been reporting much either. He was too busy.

App was not fearful of Mr. Barton. They had an old mentor and a learning reporter relationship. Apple was now an award-winning journalist, but he still respected Morris, and listened to him. He was still the boss, and he would blister everyone from time to time with his fiery dialogue. App wanted none of that today. But instead of that Morris seemed to be most eager to discuss the issues of the BAR Chem story. Apple did not think he even knew of the latest murder connected with the company.

Apple walked into the managing editor's office and as always could not help himself from glancing around with a little bit of awe and curiosity showing on his face. "What you staring at my boy? Act like you've seen a big shot before," said Morris Barton with a little wry smile on his face. He always appreciated Apple's respectful attitude. He also knew that App was one tough interviewer when it came to "his" stories, so his admiration only went so far.

The first thing that always stood out to Apple was the photo of Morris with Walter Cronkite. There they were, big as life from a still shot, arms around each other's shoulders, mugging it up for Mr. Barton's wife armed with her camera. In fact, Morris's late wife had taken most of the photos on the walls. Walter and Morris were both dressed casually, ready for a day on the water aboard Cronkite's big 64 foot, sailing yacht, WYNTJE. Mr. Barton often talked about Walter's love for that boat.

Tucked over in the corner away from attention and framed in dark walnut was a photo of Bill Clinton and Mr. Barton. An unusual shot, because Barton was looking at a newspaper, likely the Houston Announcer, with the President looking over his shoulder. Barton and Clinton both were smiling broadly. Apple always thought to himself that they probably had a copy of Playboy hidden from view by the paper. That always brought a smile to his heart, even if it did not show on his face. Apple had once shared that with Morris, and he quickly said it was a very favorable article written about Bill from one of the staff on the editorial section at the newspaper. Mr. Barton claims that the article was praising the President because of his penchant for jogging through the streets of Washington while keeping a watch for a McDonald's.

Also hanging on the wall was a painting, small but an original work by a local artist, of Master Sargent Roy Benavidez, Medal of Honor award winner. Mr. Barton much admired the Sargent, and was most proud that he was a local boy, from El Campo, just south of Houston. He felt a special kinship with Benavides because Barton himself had served in Vietnam in '68, the same year Roy won the medal. The old man had hated the war because so many boys were killed for nothing. Just LBJ and his ego and pride. Barton hated that President, but he still loved the men he had served with.

Barton's office walls looked like a collection of American culture from the last fifty years. He also had photos of Margaret Thatcher, Elvis, and his latest photo hang was Lady GaGa. The Lady had recently appeared at a local theater with Tony Bennett. Mr. Barton being Mr. Barton had gotten a private audience where the photo was taken. Apple thought that Morris was quite taken with her. What a girl he mused. If you were a famous newsmaker, chances are you are on the wall. Morris Barton liked to say his office walls were a tribute to the Houston Announcer, but he admired his photo collection just because he liked the people hanging there.

"Alright App, now tell me what is going on with the BAR Chem story. Have you talked to anyone from their Board of Directors?"

"No, not officially. But I did meet one in a bar in San Leon."

Mr. Barton wanted details. "It was all luck, or being in the right place at the right time."

"You are lucky that way. What happened?"

Apple related how he was having lunch with Sheriff Ben's assistant when just by luck and intuition he happened upon M. Ellis Winston and a character named Bettis Tom Stovall.

Mr. Barton had a surprised look on his face when he asked, "You met those two together having lunch?"

"Yessir, both together."

"You know Apple, I haven't figured it out yet. Are

you a good reporter, or are you the luckiest guy in the newsroom? To catch those two together is just blind luck."

"Well, sir, I was poking around in the right place."

Mr. Barton asked App if he had any idea who they were.

"I know Ellis is a big shot attorney that sits on the BAR Chem board. I'm not too sure about Bettis Tom, but his name keeps turning up close by anything connected with the two murders on the bay. And since he is connected to BAR Chem in some way, then the company is connected too."

"Did you say two murders? I only know about the Bishop affair."

"Yesterday a fellow named William Harry Wilson was found floating in the water about 200 feet from the yacht owned by BAR Chem. Bettis Tom seems to be the only one using the "Chump Change." He must have free reign to use the boat for his own pleasure whenever he wants."

Mr. Barton asked if it could have been an accident, and App explained the curious broken thumbs. He also added that Sheriff Ben's own homicide inspector said murder.

"But, why would BAR Chem hurt anyone not connected to anything to do with the Company?"

"Well, Morris," App explained with a little reluctance, "They were kinda working for, or helping me." It is not unusual for an investigative reporter to enlist someone close to the story for information or a little help. They usually enjoy helping or adding something to the newspaper story. But, in this case Morris Barton was a little taken back, "How was he working for you? You didn't pay him did you?" That could possibly make the

132

paper responsible in some way, and Morris was concerned. "Did you say they, how many "helpers" did you have?"

Apple explained how Beer Can Billy and Colorado Billy were involved, and that Colorado Billy should be well out of harms way by now. He would be perhaps 150 miles out in the Gulf on his way to the islands, or as Apple thought on his way to Barbados. He just hoped Colorado Billy didn't pass too close to the "Chump Change" which probably will be making its way to Galveston.

"I think Beer Can was caught a little close to the yacht, and watched money or something passed between someone he recognized, and someone could not leave such an eye witness around. They weren't sure how much he saw, so they began twisting his thumbs to find out exactly what he knew, and when they found out, they coldly murdered him. That's the way I have it figured," said Apple.

Mr. Barton agreed. "My boy what have you stumbled into? One of the largest chemical manufacturers in the world involved in things such as this. I don't know?"

Apple then told him, they have to be involved at some level. It is too much coincidence, so close to that yacht, and so close to Bettis Tom. "Perhaps Bettis Tom has a little side business going on and is using the "Chump Change" as his personal vehicle? Without the board knowing what is going on."

Mr. Barton said, "That is a possibility. And, perhaps they don't want to know the details. At the end of the day, they are all culpable, or at least have some questions to answer.

"OK, Apple, so we have two possible murders, and they both seem to run through this Bettis Tom character, and ultimately to BAR Chem. So the question is what is BAR Chem up to? Whatever it is has got to be something outside the normal rules, and there must be a lot of money at stake. Otherwise, why not just bribe all the politicians just the way they usually do?"

Apple said, "There must be a kink in the chain, one person of high standing in the EPA or maybe the statehouse in Austin blocking their way. Or maybe there are a lot of small bureaucrats holding up the works. I have heard that they possibly want to move back to the coast. Perhaps even on their old abandoned land."

"Could be, my boy, otherwise, why so many names on their bribery list that are so far down the line of command, such as your girlfriend in the Sheriff's Office?"

"She is not my girlfriend." Apple returned with, "Just a friend in a good place, know what I mean?" He was smiling broadly as he said that to Mr. Barton.

"Bernadette tells me she is quite a good looking girl, with a lot of money. By the way where is Bernie? She should be in here."

Barton stuck his head out the office door and bellowed, "Bernadette, get in here!"

After a few minutes Bernie walked briskly into the office. "What you two want? You know I don't bring coffee."

"We don't want coffee." How well they knew she didn't bring coffee, in fact she wouldn't allow anyone in the office to serve her. She never cared for special attention. "You seem to know more about what Apple is doing than Apple does. I want you to add anything he leaves out, even if he leaves it out on purpose. You got that?"

"Got it, boss. Have you told him your big news yet? I thought I would tell Apple anything you leave out also, fair enough?"

Apple added, "What big news?" He quickly thought to himself, what could he know that I don't? He is in the office while I have been running back and forth to Galveston every day, and have seen two bodies pulled from the water. What could he know?

Mr. Barton began slowly. He got out of his plush chair and walked around to the front of the desk and sat on the edge, while leaning a little closer to Apple who was sitting right in front of him. Bernie, who had been standing, walked over to the empty chair and sat beside Apple.

She knew what was coming and so did Apple, but Mr. Barton commanded the room, just like he always did. The old man had presence.

Apple was eager to hear what M. Ellis Winston had to say to Mr. Barton. Did he offer the old man a reward of sorts, for what in return? I'll bet he got an ear full.

"M. Ellis Winston, by the way the M. stands for Maythorpe, if that was my name I would use a shorter version too, showed up at my office door yesterday, and in lawyer talk asked to have a minute of my time. We talked for about half an hour until he got to the…"

Apple was impatient, he had been working on this story for over a week, and now he might find out something important and interesting, "What did you discuss for 30 minutes? Had you ever met this man before your meeting?"

"Easy boy, we'll get to that."

"Yessir."

"Now where was I? Oh yeah Mr. M. Ellis Winston's visit."

Even though he might be impertinent, Apple could not hold back, "I just have one question. Are you aware of the list found in the briefcase with your name on it?"

Mr. Barton could not help himself, as he burst into a roll of thunderous laughter. "My boy, you would interrupt the President if he were talking. Just hold your water a few minutes and we will all figure this out together. I think some facts are beginning to come together, and when we arrange them correctly, we will really have a headline."

Apple said, "As of right now, I really don't have that much info on BAR Chem. Every time I get ready to work on that part of the story, someone ends up dead in the bay water."

Bernie added, "I have a feeling you are making someone in the company very nervous. Surely they know you have been asking some questions. Remember, your girlfriend in the Sheriff's office is keeping tabs on everyone coming and going there. I believe she reports to someone at BAR Chem, maybe even your Ellis fellow, or perhaps our friend, Bettis Tom. Remember you have met with the Sheriff, and the Coast Guard Commander, and you talked to Ellis in person at your little beer joint at San Leon."

"She's not my girlfriend. But maybe she will be my informant."

Bernie smiled, and Mr. Barton did also.

"Can we get back on track?" said Morris Barton. "As I said, M. Ellis Winston showed up at my door yesterday, acting like he owned the place. To make 30 minutes short, he wants us to lay off the BAR Chem story. I explained we did not have a story as of yet, but when we did it would be fair and truthful."

"Did Ellis mention that the company has an interest in returning to their old company site?"

"Yes, and I told him how difficult that would probably be, considering how much pollution and contamination they left behind. But, I did say how much the area missed the jobs they abandoned with the move. Then Ellis informed me there were methods to work around the pollution problem. He reminded me that they still owned the land, and were in a free country. At this point his attitude changed from a friendly approach to a smart ass. He began to act like a bully on the block."

"Come on Mr. B., get to the point," said Bernie.

Mr. Barton grunted then said, "He also offered me $10,000 if I would stop your investigation and articles about the company. I then asked him if that included stories about John Bishop in the bay, and the money in the briefcase. I said please tell us how one of your employees ended up with a bullet hole in his head with a bag full of money, and what the hell was my name doing on their lists."

Mr. Barton was now getting worked up. How could his name be on one of their slimy company tricks? He was not happy about that. "Of course our friend Ellis had no answers to that. It was at this point that our meeting ended. I told him to get the hell out of my office, and our building. I advised him about even waking on our sidewalk out on Texas Avenue. Maybe I went too far, but the very idea that they could bribe me. I wonder if he even saw the photo of Cronkite and me."

Apple asked, "So, now what?"

Mr. Barton looked first at Apple then over to Bernie, and said, "You know this newspaper will not back down, withdraw from the story, that is out of the question. What I want you to do, App, is to double down. Write everything you can find out about Bishop, and your late new friend Beer Can Billy. What an unusual nickname, I also want you to see if you can arrange to be onboard the Coast Guard boat when they stop the yacht. Don't make any accusations you can't back up. Keep as close to the murders as you can, for there is the real story. It is all tied up in BAR Chem deep down. This is a big story and up to now it is all exclusively ours. Let's keep it that way. Bernie, try to keep it to a minimum in the office. Perhaps there are others around here they have offered money to influence our thinking."

"Gee, they seemed to offer everybody money except me. I feel left out," said Apple in his light breezy way.

Bernie said, "Watch your step boy reporter. I feel they might have some more important plans for you."

"Bernie is right, you be very careful. Remember the police are investigating this also. Let the cops do their jobs and we will concentrate on ours. App, don't get hurt," Mr. Barton said with some feeling. "And one other thing, until we go to press with this, I want you to report in to Bernie every day. No more two or three day absences from you, every day. I mean it." Mr. Barton closed the conversation in his usual way, "And next time you come in here, try to wear something appropriate, sneakers and blue jeans, too casual."

Chapter 17
DOUBLING DOWN

The next morning Apple was at Sheriff Ben's office precisely at eight o'clock. He was hoping to catch the Galveston County High Sheriff in a good mood. But what were the chances of that? App thought to himself that Sheriff Ben must be under a lot of pressure.

Apple was trying to convince himself that the Sheriff had no relationship with BAR Chem except as a security patrol around their abandoned property. He knew with such an important client as the company, pressure must be coming from their headquarters, perhaps from Bettis Tom, himself, or maybe M. Ellis Winston, especially since Ellis had personally tried to bribe Mr. Barton. He thought, does the Sheriff know Ellis paid a visit to Barton? Just maybe I should bring that up, stir the pot a little, see where the Sheriff sits on that. Apple was good at reading people, just from observing the face and their body mannerisms at precisely the moment they were put under pressure. Maybe Sheriff Ben would just answer straight up with how much he knows about the operations of BAR Chem.

Or maybe he should walk carefully around the Sheriff and not push him too far. After all, he is wearing a big gun on his side, and if he is too close to the company methods, things might not go so good for Apple. He thought, "Naw, that would be following a murder mystery novel a little close."

Apple braced himself as he opened the door to his old Ford pick-up. He looked around at the nice, shiny, cars parked at the city hall offices of the mayor and the county sheriff, and thought maybe I should get rid of my old truck and get some new wheels. But he thought, why? Just to keep up with the others? He thought no, that is not my way. Apple didn't seek attention, but he didn't mind it either. He got more attention from his truck than he would a new BMW. It was so ugly that heads turned when he pulled into the garage at his office or somewhere in the theater district. He liked it, and after a bit the girls he went out with came around to the attraction of an old pickup. Most considered it chic to be hauled around town in the truck. And, it had as much room as a limo. Apple liked being a little different, and he liked his pickup.

As he walked across the parking lot, he remembered what Mr. Barton had said, "Double down," on the story, and that is what he intended to do. He felt he owed that much to Beer Can. After all, it was he that had brought the "Chump Change" to the attention of Beer Can and Colorado Billy.

Now one was murdered, and the other was right now making his way out of harm's way, figuring he would be safe deep in the Caribbean. What a hell of a thing he had fostered. Now Apple felt bad about that. He knew he was somehow responsible for some of this misery.

After the culprits were summoned to the bar, maybe he and Colorado Billy could make another sail together, he on his Hunter and Colorado on his Island Packet. Just sail off to Virgin Gorda or one of the many almost deserted islands in the region. His mind began to wander a little to the matter at hand as he thought that maybe Maggie or even perhaps Bernie would accompany him. Apple knew Colorado would like that; he was somewhat taken by Bernie, from the brief visit to the Galveston marina only a few days ago. It seemed much longer. The tension was growing.

As App strolled across the lobby, he noticed Maggie's absence from her desk positioned across from the Sheriff's office door. She probably was not due at work for almost another hour. He hoped she was OK, because they were to have dinner tonight. He wondered if the Sheriff knew of their recent relationship, or what the Sheriff would think if he knew about their date for this evening.

Apple stuck his head into the open door of the Sheriff's office as he simultaneously gave a polite knock, Sheriff Ben looked up from a pile of papers, got up from his desk and immediately stuck out his hand for a shake. "How you doing, Mr. Smith?"

Apple asked him if he would drop the Mr. and just go with Apple. "Thanks, Sheriff, how about you?" The niceties over, Apple quickly glanced around the office of the man in charge of enforcing the law across Galveston County. He had the standard awards and photos required of officials and politicians on the walls of their offices.

One photo that caught his attention was a very young Sheriff Ben wearing the green beret of a Special Forces member. He also noticed an autographed photo of the Sheriff and former Houston Astros great, Nolan Ryan, hanging in a special place. Ben was obviously very proud of that one.

But, the one that really stood out was a very large photograph of a middle aged man wearing a cowboy hat. Imposed in the background was a 1934 Ford Deluxe riddled with bullet holes. Apple realized the car once belonged to

Bonnie and Clyde, and the stern looking man was Captain Frank Hamer, the man who caught up with the famous bank robbing duo. Sheriff Ben had it in a prominent place on the wall. Hamer was someone he obviously admired. He had put to rest the crime spree of the infamous duo.

Sheriff Ben began by saying, "The other day at the crime scene was not the time or place to go into a question and interview session."

"Sheriff, no disrespect, but you are a hard man to catch up to, and harder to ask questions of."

"Being cautious around a newspaper man is something you learn early on in my job. I know you have questions, and you seem to be more interested in this case than just doing a job."

"It has become a little personal with the death of William Wilson, because he had befriended me, and I liked the fellow. I feel it was because of this friendliness that he was murdered. In a way, I contributed to his death."

Sheriff Ben said, "Nonsense. You had nothing to do with Wilson's death. Just as you had nothing to do with John Bishop."

"Thanks, Sheriff, I appreciate that."

"But, you do have a way of turning up at very tense moments. Did you ever finish your tour of the old property of BAR Chem? At the moment I am too occupied with the crimes of the last week, but I could get one of my deputies to finish the tour we never completed."

"No, thanks, but I saw enough."

The Sheriff then said, "OK then, let's get to what you came for. We're both pretty busy. I will answer any questions you have, but I would like it to be off the record."

Apple responded, "No can do. I will promise to inform you of any pending pieces that will appear in the paper before they go to press, but we are too far down the road to cover over any facts. My intention is, as it was in the beginning, to write a series of articles about the move of BAR Chem to Mexico. John Bishop just turned up at the right time, if that is appropriate to speak of him in those terms. You know, and I know he was murdered, and was an employee of the Company, and to further add mystery, he was carrying a briefcase full of money. And, some of it was earmarked for you. Where is the money, and did you receive any of it?"

The Sheriff bristled at this question and it's implication before he answered.

"Mr. Smith." The Apple had quickly gone away and the more formal Mr. Smith returned. "I am not obligated to answer any questions from you, but I am going to allow you a few, out of professional courtesy, and I expect you to do the same. A little respect will be required.

"If the question is out of line, I will withdraw it. How about where is the money and the briefcase now?"

"Locked in the department safe, here on this location."

"Is anyone aware of the money except you and Commander Johnson?"

"Mr. Smith, you insult me with these kinds of questions. The case and all its contents have been inventoried and turned over to the District Attorney in Galveston."

Apple knew Sheriff Ben was very touchy about the money, which could only come from his name on the list inside the briefcase of John Bishop. Also he had a relationship with BAR Chem, if only as a security agent over the previous site of the company. He knew he should walk carefully around the questions he still needed to ask the Sheriff.

Sheriff Ben said, "Apple, let me now ask you a few questions. I know you have a nose for news. Since you have been checking around yourself, have you found out anything that I don't know, that would be useful in this investigation?"

Apple decided to tell him about Ellis's meeting with Morris Barton. "Are you aware that a member of the board of directors from BAR Chem visited Mr. Barton? Do you know Barton is Chief Managing Editor of the Houston Announcer? M. Ellis Winston paid Barton a visit at Barton's office and asked him pointedly to stop printing articles about BAR Chem."

"Is that against the law? If it is I am not aware of it?"

"Does it violate laws if he offered him $10,000? I would consider that a bribe or extortion. That must be violating some kind of law."

Sheriff Ben did not seem to be surprised at this bit of news. After all he had the list of names locked away in his safe. He was wondering when someone would surface with a story like this, since there were some important names on the list. Would this start a landslide of people coming forward with this bribery idea?

"I did not of course know that, but I am not surprised. What I am surprised about is Ellis Winston being the one delivering the message to Mr. Barton. That is more like something Bettis Tom would be in charge of."

"So you know both Ellis and Bettis Tom?"

"Ellis Winston is well known to lots of folks around here. His name was in the news frequently when BAR Chem was making its move. As for Bettis Tom, I am the Sheriff around here, I know lots of shady characters in this county."

"Sheriff, have you ever been on the Chump Change?"

"Of course. Many times. As part of my duties for the $1,500 I am paid monthly, I am to check on the yacht frequently, and I do. I also have a book that I log into after each visit. Dates of my visits are on record. Mostly to protect myself with the company, if anything happens to the boat, you know, like loose lines, that sort of thing. Sometimes I don't even get out of my vehicle to check on it."

"Sheriff, did you ever meet John Bishop?"

"No, and why would you ask that?"

Apple would have to be very careful now. "My sources tell me that he was seen in this very building on more than one occasion. Why would he do that?"

The Sheriff was not used to being asked questions. He was usually the one asking. Apple was admiring how cool he was. Did he know Bishop? That was a game changer, but Ben remained very cool, and almost casual.

Apple hoped that he did not get Maggie into a jam with the Sheriff, since she was the one that had told him early on she thought she recognized John Bishop visiting the Mayor.

"You have sources inside my office? Are you spying on me, Smith?" The hard tone had returned to the Sheriff's voice. "I think I can guess where your hearsay comes from.

"If John Bishop ever visited here, he was here for some other reason. He did not visit me. Remember, this is a pretty big office building. Taxes, building permits, all types of regulations are conducted here. You even pay traffic tickets here. Perhaps he was called for jury duty. Municipal court is held here also. From my investigations,

John Bishop was an attorney for BAR Chem. He would have had occasions to visit this building many times."

Apple thought the Sheriff was expanding here very strongly. If he didn't know the guy, that is all he would have to say.

The Sheriff continued, "And what if he had visited me, what the hell would that have to do with his death? You think I murdered John Bishop? Is that it, Smith? I should kick your ass out of my office, but I'm not going to do that. I am going to answer all of your questions, then I want you to move on with your investigation, or story, whatever you call it you're doing!"

Apple started with a different tact, "Sheriff Rodriguez, why do you think our friend Beer Can Billy was murdered?"

"He just got too close to some bad fellows."

"Do you think it had anything to do with the BAR Chem yacht "Chump Change," docked right down the pier from Beer Can's boat?"

"I haven't come to that conclusion as of yet. We are still investigating the movements of the yacht."

Apple asked one more question to the Sheriff. "Are you going to be on board the Coast Guard boat if they stop the "Chump Change" before entering Galveston?"

"Yes, and I have an idea, why don't you come along? You seem to turn up every time my department gets an emergency call. I just ask you again to respect my position before you go to print with a story that could jeopardize my investigations."

Apple Smith was stunned from this turn around in attitude from the Sheriff. App quickly agreed, this time to the Sheriff's request. He really wanted to be there when Bettis Tom and his pals were put on the hot spot. Perhaps a little pressure would make him do something irrational. Apple quickly accepted the invitation to again ride along.

WILLIAM WARREN

Chapter 18
GALVESTON OR VERACRUZ?

Apple called the headquarters of the Association of Chemical Manufacturers Workers Union. He asked for an appointment with Randal Filbin, Executive Director of the Association. Apple was expecting to speak to a secretary or a front desk. Instead, a raspy voice said, "Filbin here, what can I do for you?" When Apple identified himself as a reporter from the Houston Announcer, and wanted to get the Union's view about the move of BAR Chem to Mexico, Filbin said, "What does the paper want news about? That's old news." He informed Apple that he was busy preparing for the regular scheduled meeting that would be taking place at seven o'clock. When App asked, "Seven, what date?" the raspy voice asked him where he had been. "Tonight, been scheduled for two months. You would be welcome to attend. Some press might be a good thing for us. How about it?" Apple said he would be there.

Next on App's agenda included a call to Maggie at the Sheriff's office. He would have to cancel their dinner date for tonight. When he called, he was caught off guard when the Sheriff answered, just as Filbin had just done. Sheriff Ben told Apple she had not shown up for work today, and he had no idea where she was. Now App was sure the Sheriff knew who the "spy" was inside his office.

Since dinner had been replaced by the union meeting,

App knew he needed to do some research on Randal Filbin, and Mario Santiago. The two powerful leaders of the ACW. He knew they were outspoken leaders, critical of just about everything concerning BAR Chem. Some of the rhetoric coming from the ACW headquarters bordered on slanderous. They were particularly vicious in their pointed criticism of Jeffery Chung Dearcorn, as the Chair of the Board of BAR Chem. They blamed him personally for the move of the Company, and the invectives never stopped.

Roy Jacobs was high on their list for special attention. Jacobs was an easy target, frequently in the news for the jet setting life style he lived. Filbin and Santiago also remembered Jacobs for his no vote on moving the company to Mexico. They thought he might be useful to the union someday. He was considered easy to manipulate. Simply put, he did not care for BAR Chem with the fervor shown by the other board members, so the thought was he could be used in some way in the future.

Bettis Tom sat back in his comfy captain's chair in the wheelhouse, puffing on a Cuban Cohibas cigar, blowing smoke up from his lips, over his nose, rising to his forehead. His head was covered in a blue haze. Even though tensions were easing with the Cubans, these imports were still, for the time being, illegal at home. BT took some pride in knowing these were the same cigars Fidel had once enjoyed himself.

Everybody gets old, he pondered to himself. Bettis Tom, through his numerous trips to the islands, always had an ample supply, and enjoyed giving them to his friends. One friend enjoyed smoking them so much he tried it on the floor of the Texas House, where he was immediately called to task. Not for smoking a Cuban, but for smoking on the floor.

BT always got a grin when he thought of the episode. The Houston Announcer had run a story on the politician and his penchant for smoking big cigars. There was a funny picture of the fat Texan wearing a Stetson, pants supported by his red suspenders, kicked back, puffing, at his historic 150 year old desk in the Texas House. Everyone got a laugh out of that stereotype. CNN even ran the picture. Yeah, Bettis Tom enjoyed seeing his gift cigar used in such a good scene.

Bettis Tom knew how to relax. He was puffing and holding a tumbler of JD and Coke when he heard the faint chop, chop, of a helicopter approaching. That was not unusual; the Gulf had numerous oil platforms in the region. The problem is the "Chump Change " was about 125 miles out from Galveston. The closest rig in this area was 35 miles away, give or take. There were no rigs in this area, BT was sure of that. What was the chopper doing this far out?

He stepped out of the wheelhouse of the big yacht, onto the deck for a better look at the approaching chopper. BT felt no concern. The thing is, plenty of ships to look at from time to time, not too many low flying helicopters.

The chopper was descending now, and beginning to make a long slow circle. BT asked the deckhand, Arnost, at the helm to see if he could make contact by radio with the chopper. No luck, just silence. BT knew that contacting an aircraft from the boat was a long shot. The chopper was disappearing from view, and BT walked back into the wheelhouse and again settled into his comfortable captain's chair.

He took a long draw from his whiskey glass, and breathed a deep, slow breath, just to relax, when he heard the chopper approaching from dead astern. BT sensed,

"Something just ain't right." Before he could turn around to get a good look at the strange chopper, it passed directly overhead at a low altitude. It was then he noticed the big red stripe on the white background of a Coast Guard chopper, and he silently thought, "Must be looking for a lost vessel."

Roy Jacobs emerged from down below, "What the hell was that? Sounded like a freight train running us down."

Bettis Tom didn't care for Roy very much. Partly because he insisted on coming on a lot of BT's trips to the islands. His presence just complicated everything. These trips were business to BT and strictly pleasure for Roy. BT thought, "The dumb bastard doesn't even have a clue what we are really doing out here. He is just along for the ride."

"If you would come out of your hole once in a while you would know what is going on."

"Yeah, well it is more interesting down below than up here glinting in the sun." Roy enjoyed the company of pretty girls that he always brought along. "You don't need me in the wheelhouse, I'm sure you can guide this thing without me."

"Yes, while you have been up to more interesting things, we have just been buzzed by the Coast Guard!"

"Does that matter? We haven't done anything wrong. They're probably just out for training exercises. They do it all the time."

"Right, we've not been doing anything wrong, but we sure don't want to attract attention of the Coast Guard. The last thing we want is them taking an interest in the "Chump Change.""

Roy said, "Then relax, BT, take a load off." Roy could sense that Bettis Tom was nervous about this fly over, and he did not know why. It was not illegal for the BAR Chem yacht to have a little leisure, and what if we had some beautiful ladies with us? That is our business, not the business of the Coast Guard.

BT sat silent in his chair, deep in thought. Roy had disappeared below decks, and it was quiet in the wheelhouse. "Arnost, something is wrong about that chopper." Arnost was at the helm, even though he had the big yacht pointed by the autopilot.

He had been employed by BT for a little over a year, and had earned Bettis Tom's trust. Not complete, but enough. He was good on the boat and would do what BT told him. No questions asked. It was not good to get between him and BT's orders. BT considered him trustworthy. That is why he gave Arnost orders about Beer Can Billy, then turned and walked away. Arnost knew what was required.

"Arnost, plot us a new course."

"Sure BT, where we going? I guess that chopper has made everyone nervous."

BT said, "Just safe, not nervous. How about we go to Veracruz for a few days? We can refuel and enjoy the night life before going to Galveston. Just stay idle a bit and see what develops."

"Veracruz it is. I like that place. Good food. Coming left."

WILLIAM WARREN

Chapter 19
BIG HENRY'S BAIT, TACKLE, AND BEER

As the chopper landed, Commander Johnson was waiting on the pad. "How'd it go? Spot her?" the Commander asked his Chief Warrant Officer piloting the chopper.

"You betcha Johnny, right where you said she would be." Most of the officers under his command called him by name, not by rank, but the only enlisted man allowed such familiarity was Chief Petty Officer Decks.

"How fast was she traveling?"

"I would estimate about 15 knots, seas were calm, she was skating along pretty good. According to our fix, she was 125 miles south east.'

"Did you see anyone on deck?"

"Yessir, and I was jealous. Maybe I am in the wrong business," grinned the Chief. "That deck lounge had more bikini clad ladies than Stewart Beach in the summer."

"Well, you can't find fault with that. Did you see anyone near the wheelhouse?"

"Yessir, two men looking at us like we were a flying saucer. One of them was dressed just like you said, wearing jeans and a yellow Hawaiian shirt."

"You positive?"

"Absolutely, I was close enough to see that he had a drink in one hand and a cigar in the other. Besides,

Commander, we took a few photos."

"Outstanding! That would be old Bettis Tom Stovall, and now we have dated and timed photos of his whereabouts. Might be important later. We'll see. Good job to you and your crew."

At about the same time, Apple was on his way to the Union Hall near the Galveston Causeway. It would be his first time to see the two union bosses in person.

As App slowed his pickup, looking for the address of the meeting house, he was baffled. The place of the meeting appeared to be Big Henry's Bait, Tackle, and Beer, est. 1951. Underneath the name, in smaller letters read "Friend of the working man."

Before Apple could turn into the parking lot, he had driven by the turn off, and was forced to drive half a mile before making a u-turn under the freeway and circling back. He turned into the parking lot and checked to see if he had the correct address. He did.

Apple had been over this bridge hundreds of times in his life, and had scarcely paid any attention to this old weathered barn-looking building. He could not tell you the name of the place until now. With water on three sides, it blended into the marsh and salt grass landscape. Unless you were a fisherman familiar with the area, you would drive right by it.

He got out of his pickup and ambled toward what appeared to be the front door when he noticed the boat ramp over to the side. Two men were loading a small aluminum fishing boat onto a homemade trailer, pulled by an even older pickup than his own. He smiled at this. He was unable to resist the temptation to ask, "How was the fishing?"

"Fair," one of the men answered, as he held up a

string of speckled trout. Apple was impressed. Salt water speckled trout was just about the best-tasting fish anywhere, and these two had a bunch of them.

Just as App was about to get more closely acquainted with the fishermen, his cell phone rang. "Excuse me fellows, gotta take this."

Commander Johnson was on the line. "Hello, Apple, I offered you an invitation to join our little party intercepting the BAR Chem yacht. If you still would like to go, be at the station in one hour. We have spotted the boat headed this way, and we are making preparations to check them just outside the Galveston ship channel. Still want to go?"

Apple was obviously disappointed to tell the Commander that he had accepted an invitation to attend tonight's union meeting, and since they only met every two months, he had to attend.

The Commander was actually relieved that Apple could not be with them as they stopped the "Chump Change." He had regretted his earlier decision to invite him along. He did not want to seem like he had courted the publicity that would come along with his action. He might even have to answer more questions than he would be comfortable with, if this little action actually appeared in print. But, he had asked him along and now he was keeping his word.

Commander Johnson had no way of knowing that Bettis Tom had smelled something strange about the fly over of the chopper, and had altered his course south west to Veracruz. There would be no boarding party today. Maybe someday, but not today.

Apple stepped back over to the two men now cleaning their catch at the bait house fish cleaning board.

One of the men asked him, "Whatcha up to? You ain't dressed to go fishing."

Apple answered, "Maybe you can help me. I am here to attend a meeting, but perhaps I have the address wrong."

The two fellows smiled at each other, and one of the guys said, "Don't tell me, I'll bet you I can tell you your name and what you do for a living."

"Bet you can't," Apple said, playing along with the friendly banter.

"Alright, buddy, how about this? If I can guess, you buy a round for everybody at the meeting when it is finished. If you win I will buy you a beer. How about it?"

Apple knew he had just been suckered into a bet that he was going to have to pay. How did this fellow know who he was? The only ones that knew he would be attending were Filbin and Santiago. Then it dawned on him. "How about we call it even if I can guess your name and what you do?"

The fellow grinned, stuck out his hand, and Apple said, "Mr. Mario Santiago, Associate Director of the Galveston Association of Chemical Workers, better known as the ACW, let me introduce myself. I am Apple Smith, reporter for the Houston Announcer." They all laughed at this.

Apple had just run into the two bosses of the union in a most unorthodox way. He assumed they would be inside prepping for their meeting. Obviously the meeting was going to be an informal affair. He hoped the rest of their associations would be this amiable, but he doubted it. He had some serious questions for these two. Apple was sure they would have some for him too.

Apple relished this kind of environment, knowing

the chances they would be hostile to his questions, but he was prepared. He had just made up his mind to ask his questions from the floor. Up until now he had been preparing for a private meeting with one or both Filbin and Santiago. Why not put the two bosses on record with their own constituents? The thought of the challenge brought a smile to his lips.

The parking lot quickly filled with cars and pickups, and these people, in no particular hurry, flowed into the meeting area. The meeting began just like any other civic meeting. The only exception was the bar was open. Big Henry's Bait, Tackle, and Beer was smart. Big Henry donated space for the members to meet, free of charge, and in return he kept the bar open. Big Henry figured he was ahead of the game.

The only problem was the meetings always were heated. No fist fights, but plenty of opinions on what should happen to BAR Chem. Filbin and Santiago did a pretty good job of keeping the lid on by strictly enforcing parliamentary procedures, but they allowed everybody to vent. These folks were still angry about the company move to Mexico leaving them high and dry.

The meeting was called to order exactly 22 minutes late, which was about normal. The members noticed Apple sitting a few rows from the front. App wanted to be in such a place that he could not be ignored from the floor. The meeting started easy and friendly enough, more like a meet and greet. There had been so many of these union meetings with no results - they were still unemployed - that members did not expect anything to come from one more meeting. Expectations were low, to say the least.

Santiago started the meeting with old business, a report on the progress being made in Washington and

Austin to enlist either compensation or revenge upon BAR Chem.

Santiago, warming up to his brothers, who were grunting softly and moving their chins up and down, in approval of what he was saying, then finished his summation with, "Even as we speak, our friend Roy Jacobs from the board at the company is enjoying himself on Cleopatra's Barge somewhere in the Caribbean." The reference to Cleopatra was most assuredly speaking of the "Chump Change."

At the mention of Roy Jacobs, the crowd stirred noticeably. They were booing and hissing, and waving their fists like they were at a heavy weight boxing match. The ACW blamed the board of the company for the move that had upset their lives so much. At the front were Jeffrey Chung Dearcorn and the other board members. They rejected the idea that it was just good business. The members took it personally. Roy Jacobs was high on their list for scorn, mainly for his very visible presence.

Then it hit Apple. Did he just get his foot stepped on by a race horse? "How the hell did Santiago know Roy Jacobs was on board the "Chump Change?" He wondered who makes up the pipeline to the bosses. He realized that someone on the stage had direct communication with the company. If that was so, who really was controlling the union?

Besides Filbin and Santiago, there were the treasurer and the business secretary. One of those four was staying in touch with the highest levels at the company. Apple thought, "All of the leadership are playing both sides."

He wished he had access to bank account histories of these guys. He remembered the old adage, "Follow the money." They are selling out their brothers for money he thought, and he had a burning desire to punch someone in the nose. He knew he could not do that, but sure as Nolan Ryan could strike out a batter, he would get to the bottom of this, for Beer Can Billy, and these hardworking fellows who had been thrown under the bus by their leaders.

Suddenly Apple stood up and asked, "Mr. Filbin, have you ever taken money from BAR Chem, outside your official duty as head of this local union?"

If Filbin was shaken by the question, it did not show on his face. He calmly said, "Members, please let me introduce you to Mr. Apple Smith of the Houston Announcer. He, as you probably know, is the award winning investigative reporter of some fame." He continued with, "He is here by special invite from Mario and myself. Please welcome him."

That introduction took some of the wind out of Apple's sails. Apple continued to stand, "Thank you, please, back to the question."

There was an uncommon silence among the members as they awaited Filbin's answer. The answer was a fiery, "Was there an accusation in that question? The answer is of course, no! Have you ever lied in one of your newspaper stories?"

If Apple was taken by surprise it did not show. He expected something of this sort. He was experienced at this kind of forum. Last year he had been at a press conference by Donald Trump. Trump had been questioned by members of the press at a luncheon in Houston hosted by The Greater Houston League for Commerce.

Mr. Trump was in town to discuss a leading edge idea being sold by the GHLC, which included the sale of two of Houston's iconic properties. The historic Hermann Park Golf Course and the west side Memorial Park Golf

Course were offered for sale, on the authority of the Houston City Council, with approval of the voters early next year.

With the money procured with the sale, the city would develop a world class light rail system connecting the entire five county area with all the important business centers of Greater Houston. The issue had a good chance of passing because the city was now gridlocked from east to west and north to south. Workers and business people could not move during the important hours of the day.

Traffic had long frustrated the people, and now was a chance to do something about it, without costing new taxes. Everyone would win was the slogan. A ten year project, but considered worth it. Trump relished the idea of getting his hands on such properties.

Apple had asked him about his number of declarations of Chapter 11 protections involving some of his over the top business ventures. App asked what would happen to the financing of the rail system if this deal failed. Trump answered with, "Trust me," which led to a heated question-and-answer exchange between Apple and Trump.

So Apple knew he could handle an exchange with this union boss. He hoped he could handle the members outside after the meeting.

Apple asked a follow up, with a bit of a twist. "So, has the union ever received money from BAR Chem that you were the controlling administrator over?"

"Mr. Smith, you know very well that the ACW has received money from the company to help members transition from a good paying job to unemployment. I don't understand where you are going with this questioning about money."

Apple rephrased, "Have you or a member of your family ever profited personally from BAR Chem?"

The answer was a tart, "No."

Just as Apple was warming to the challenge, Sheriff Ben walked unnoticed into the meeting, and quietly took a seat at the rear. He was a well-known figure around here, but he was not noticed. It was his practice to wear khakis or jeans and a pressed white shirt. He very seldom wore an official sheriff's uniform, and he was not doing so tonight.

Santiago spoke up, "In response to your question, my answer is, I have taken money from BAR Chem. They loaned me money soon after the company move to Mexico."

"What was the loan for?"

"My house mortgage was in serious arrears, and was about to be repossessed."

Apple knew he was on thin ice here, "Did you repay the loan?"

"No. I did not."

"Why not?"

"I had no money."

The crowd was stirring a little. Apple could not tell if they were surprised by Santiago taking money from BAR Chem, or if they thought he was asking too personal of a question of one of their own.

"Believe me, Mr. Smith, I did not give a damn about paying back money to the group that had just taken my job and welfare south."

"So in effect, BAR Chem bought you a house."

"Phrase it how you will, makes no diff to me," responded Mario Santiago, almost snarling now.

Someone from across voiced, "Who let this guy in here?"

WILLIAM WARREN

Sheriff Ben sat in his place inwardly grinning a little at the spot Apple was quickly getting himself into. At least he thought Apple had guts to stand here before this crowd and question their leaders with tough questions.

Apple stood his ground, "Did either one of you or anyone in this room know a man named John Bishop?"

"I know he is an attorney for BAR Chem, so he is probably a money grubbing creep just like the rest of the BAR Chem crowd."

"Then you did not know the creep was murdered and dumped in the bay last week? Mr. Filbin, do you own a large bore pistol?" Apple wanted to rattle the cage a bit, and that last question did just that.

Filbin shouted, "Sargent at Arms! Remove the gentleman!"

"One more question, Santiago, have you ever been on board the "Chump Change?"

"No, I have not," shouted Santiago.

"Then how did you know Roy Jacobs was on board her at this moment?"

The angry group mulled this over a bit before shouting, "Get him out of here!"

At this time Sheriff Ben arose from his seat and moved forward through the angry group. He approached Apple and spoke to Filbin on the podium. "Easy boys, Mr. Smith is coming with me," as he gently touched App on the elbow and guided him down the aisle and out the door into the parking lot.

Apple was glad to have the Sheriff's company. He knew he wouldn't be buying a round for the house on this night because the easy banter with the two fishermen had been spoiled, at least for the time being.

Chapter 20
REPORTER AND SHERIFF COLLABORATE

As the reporter and the Sheriff stepped out into the damp Gulf Coast air, Apple said to Sheriff Ben, "Thanks, but wasn't that a little bit dramatic?"

"Just campaigning for the next election, my good friend. Besides it looked like you were getting into an uncomfortable position there." The Sheriff was smiling as he said this.

Apple said, "I was in complete control," a little tongue in cheek.

"Oh, yeah? Do you know who those two rather fierce fellows sitting behind you were?" Sheriff Ben continued, "They were the union's muscle. Do you think they were sitting behind you by accident? Your friend Filbin told them before the meeting you would be there."

"How do you know this Sheriff?" asked Apple.

"You're kidding, right? Do you not know I am the Sheriff of this county? Also, I have arrested both of those guys numerous times - two times on union demonstrations in front of BAR Chem for disorderly conduct, and once for roughing up an employee going to work. Both are bad fellows, and intensely loyal to Filbin. I think the union pays both a little money each month. I wouldn't get in their way if I were you."

"Well, thanks Sheriff, I guess. By the way, how did

you know I was there tonight?"

"Just like you Mr. Smith, I have a spy in your office. I called your office today, and a nice lady named Bernadette told me where I could find you. She was good enough to give me your cell, also. But, I wanted to surprise you. You know that is a bunch of rough guys you were doing your best to insult, back there. I thought I would just listen in a bit. Good thing I did."

Apple asked, "But why did you want my number? And, by the way, she is very nice."

Sheriff Ben detected something there, "Don't worry, Apple I am a happily married man."

"I'm glad to hear that, but why were you looking for me?"

"Mr. Smith, when I first met you, I did not care for you very much. I thought you were sticking your nose into affairs where you weren't needed, but Commander Johnson seems to approve of you. Also, you have a knack for turning up on the scene of a murder, once even before me. I figure if I just keep up with you, sooner or later you will lead me to the murderer. Besides, you seem to be making more of an effort to solve my two murder cases than the two detectives working on them. So perhaps we could start over. You can tell me anything you turn up, and I will give you first notice to the press, sort of thing, you know."

Apple thought to himself why this turn around in attitude? He doubted he knew as much as the Sheriff. App could not help but return to the list of names in the briefcase either slated for past bribes or future ones by the company. Sheriff Ben's name was prominent.

But, before he jumped to judgment, he had to remember that Morris Barton was also mentioned. Apple knew there was no way Mr. Barton would take a bribe; for one thing, he enjoyed telling the truth in the newspaper too much. Mr. Barton also took it further and considered it not truthful if the paper held back anything.

"Thanks Sheriff, I appreciate that, but the truth is, I don't know very much."

"One thing you did know was the real name of your friend, what do you call him, Beer Can Billy?"

Apple said, "This may surprise you Sheriff, but I can make more sense out of Beer Can's murder than I can John Bishop's."

"How so? Please tell me what you are thinking, because frankly, I can't make sense out of either one. There seems to be no motive for the violence."

Apple paused, took a deep breath, and looked at the Sheriff. "Well, the way I see it, and remember this is just my opinion, based on my imagination and reporter's intuition. Bettis Tom was commissioned to take John Bishop from Mexico just south of Brownsville on the "Chump Change.""

Sheriff Ben asked, "Why would they take the boat when they could just drive it in about five hours? Or better yet take the prop plane that the execs at the company use all the time?"

"I have given that some thought, and I believe they were taking the cautious approach because of the large amount of money. Remember that much money took the entire briefcase. Because of all the drug trade across that border, they stood a good chance of being searched by Border Patrol at the Rio Grande.

"I understand that the Border Patrol on either side of the river just let vehicles pass if they have a BAR Chem ID hanging from their mirror," said Sheriff Ben.

"Well then, If they aren't smuggling drugs, they

should be," said Apple rather tongue in cheek. I think it was just not worth the risk of getting caught with that much money."

Sheriff Ben said, "Perhaps, and maybe the yacht was already scheduled to return to Galveston."

"At any rate, I believe John Bishop was on board when he was murdered. According to the coroner, he had not been dead long enough to have been murdered in Matamoros. And, he died from a gunshot, not drowning. Leading me to believe he was murdered not far from where the shrimp boat picked up his body. By the way Sheriff, did you ever thank those two guys on the shrimp boat?"

"What do you think? You know Mr. Smith, you really rankle me sometimes. If you and I are going to cooperate, you need to stop asking me disrespectful questions." Apple had clearly approached an area he'd wished he had not. He knew when the Sheriff called him Mr. Smith, things were not going well. He would have to be more thoughtful in the future. He wanted the Sheriff's cooperation.

"My apologies, sir."

"I have known both of those fishermen for a number of years. Rufus has been shrimping the bay most of my life."

"So, I assume John Bishop was on the "Chump Change," and we know the boat was not at her pier the night Bishop went into the water. Both Beer Can Billy and Colorado Billy told me that."

"So, you're telling me that someone on the "Chump Change" murdered John Bishop?"

App forged ahead, "Either that or Jim Overriver and Rufus did, and we both know they did not. Those two are so honest, they didn't even look in the briefcase. What would have happened if they had seen all that cash?"

"The same. Jim wouldn't take a free aspirin if he had a headache."

"Then we are back to someone on the company yacht. You know what I am thinking, Sheriff? You are thinking the same thing. You don't have to look any further than Bettis Tom Stovall."

Sheriff Ben said, "I had ballistics checked on the slug. It was not fired from a .357."

Apple did not know what the Sheriff was talking about. "What about the .357?"

"That's the weapon BT carries in the back of his belt all the time. But it is all legal, he has a license, and he is a registered security officer."

"Apple said, "Don't that beat all? BT is legally carrying a weapon. That means the day I met him, and got a little lippy, he had a gun in his pocket. Now that's scary."

The Sheriff asked, "What?" And Apple explained his encounter at the ice house with BT and M. Ellis Winston.

Sheriff Ben asked, "Your theory is someone on the "Chump Change" murdered John Bishop? Then why didn't they take the money? And why, since they all work for the same man?"

"I think BT wanted the money and John Bishop wouldn't go along. A strange man, Bishop, he doesn't mind bribing and extortion, but he won't give the money over to BT."

The Sheriff added, "He probably felt he was in bad trouble either way, so possibly he struggled."

Apple said, "Exactly. He resisted, and somehow went into the water. I think BT shot him while he swam in the water because he jumped overboard. Then once in the water, lifeless, he got lost in the dark. Remember, the "Chump Change" was seen circling for some time on that night by late fishermen. They were looking for Bishop. I think that will be important later. It puts the company yacht in the area."

"Well done. Here is something you might not know," added Sheriff Ben. "John Bishop was a champion swimmer in college at UT. He was close to making the Olympic team, at least one time, and actually made it the second try. He never competed because he was working and did not have time to train."

App said, "So he did not have any fear of jumping overboard and swimming to shore. It would probably have only been about one mile. He could have swam that easy. That makes more sense now. I did not know he was a college swimmer."

Sheriff Ben said, "Let's step into my car. I have a thermos of hot coffee, and this air is wet." Apple walked around to the passenger side of the Sheriff's car, a Ford Pickup. He was always amazed when he sat in a cop car. Sheriff Ben had everything in there except a microwave. The coffee was good. "Good idea, Sheriff."

"OK, Apple, we have John Bishop solved. How about your friend Beer Can?"

Apple noticed that Sheriff Ben had gone back to calling him Apple. He was pleased.

"You said that you understand his murder more clearly than Bishop's. How so?"

"As you know, those two characters were actually watching the "Chump Change" for me. I feel pretty rough that I might have been the reason they got into trouble."

The Sheriff said, "Wrong. They were working for me. About three months earlier, even before John Bishop's murder, I was watching the yacht because of reports of card games, and other illegal activities. I never knew them by their more colorful names, though. They were to call me when they noticed suspicious things going on."

Apple was surprised to hear this. Maybe he was underestimating Sheriff Ben. "Alright Sheriff, what other kinds of activity? I suspect BT is smuggling lots of illegal items, like cocaine by the tons. He is using that big boat for his own gain. I don't think Jeffrey Chung Dearcorn has a clue what that boy is doing. Unless Bettis Tom is splitting the take with Dearcorn."

The Sheriff said, "Apple, you should be a cop. That is what I have suspected for about a year. I could have busted them for gambling, but I want something bigger. Playing cards is small potatoes compared to what they might be up to. But, back up a bit, why would Dearcorn, who must make ten million a year, risk something like that?"

"Because he may be splitting 100 million with BT."

The Sheriff said, "This whole thing is getting bigger by the moment, talking to you. Remember when you asked me if I needed FBI help? Well, not yet, but that might be worth keeping in mind. Back to Beer Can. What happened to him?"

Apple said, "Sheriff, do you think Filbin or Santiago is taking money from the company while with the other hand waving complaints in their direction? How would they know Roy Jacobs was on board the "Chump Change" this current trip to the Caribbean?"

"Good observation. I have long suspected Filbin of something, I just don't know what. I think he would take money or other benefits without a second thought. Some day he may have to answer to the IRS about that very thing."

Apple raised his eyebrows and thought to himself,

the Sheriff knows a lot more about this than he lets on. "I have an idea, why don't you just ask Roy Jacobs if he was on board the yacht tonight? And, perhaps ask him where he was the night John Bishop was murdered, and the night Beer Can was murdered."

Sheriff Ben paused a moment, then said, "Might be a good idea when the time is right, but not right away. Speaking of the yacht, did you know she never turned up tonight? Commander Johnson called me just before I was to show up at the pier to intercept her. He said she was overdue. He suspects she got suspicious and altered her course. Right now he is calling along the coast to see if she has turned up in perhaps Port Aransas or Freeport.

"It is getting late. Tell me what your thoughts on Beer Can are."

Apple said, "Simple. Beer Can got a little too close to the action the night he was murdered. I think he was perhaps on board and got caught looking through a port. I think he saw someone he recognized taking money from BT. Someone big and important to cause such a violent reaction. Maybe Bettis Tom had his two bouncers do the dirty work for him. I'll bet you that when this is over BT was handing money in large stacks to Filbin and Santiago, and that is what got Beer Can killed. I think the union launders large sums of money for Bettis Tom."

The Sheriff asked, "By the way, do you have any idea where Colorado Billy disappeared to?

"He was scared witless Sheriff. He went deep into the Caribbean, much south of the British Virgin Islands. I know he will be easy to find if you need him, but I promised I would not say where he might be. Please don't force me." The truth was that Apple didn't know exactly where Colorado was, but he had a pretty good idea, and it was true that he knew he could find him if need be.

"He might provide something useful, but I won't ask you to break confidence right now."

"He told me he did not know anything. He swears he was not with Beer Can when it happened, and did not know about Beer Can's terrible fate until he discovered his body the next morning."

Sheriff Ben said, "He must have been plenty frightened if he pulled out the next morning. That's sure short notice to make such a trip alone." The Sheriff continued, "I know what you think, Apple, but let's suppose for argument that Colorado Billy was on the scene when it happened. He could tell us a lot about how to catch the murderer."

"The only flaw with that Sheriff, is I don't think Beer Can's body would have been left in the water over night. Colorado would have immediately called for help if he had seen or been aware."

"So, you don't think it is a possibility that Beer Can spoke to Colorado about what was happening?"

"No, Sheriff, I don't think so. They were loyal friends. Colorado would not have left him in the water."

They ended their conversation and collaboration on that note with Apple promising not to interfere with the Sheriff's investigation.

Sheriff Ben promised nothing in return, but Apple could sense something good in the Sheriff, and he did not want to push too hard.

App did inform Sheriff Ben he was going to write a column first thing tomorrow, but it would not divulge any happenings that would be detrimental to the official investigation. He promised himself that when this thing was over, he would write a very favorable piece on the

Sheriff and his department.

As Apple was backing his old Ford pickup, the Sheriff flipped on his red lights. Apple thought, "What the hell, now?: and pulled over before entering the feeder road to the freeway. Sheriff Ben drove his pickup police car alongside, rolled the window down, and said, "Jump inside, something has just come up."

Apple quickly had a sense of dread because of what had recently happened. His instant reaction was, "Oh no, don't let it be Colorado Billy."

He, very quickly exited his vehicle, walked around to the Sheriff's passenger side and, got in, and said, "What's going on now, Sheriff?"

"Get a grip, Apple, you look like you have seen a ghost. Something very interesting has just happened. A fellow was just stopped for making a turn out of a wrong lane. The Houston Police stopped him."

"Well that is no big deal, even in Houston."

"Here is the big deal though. He claims he works on the "Chump Change", and just left her in Veracruz. And to back this claim up he has a passport that has recently been stamped Trinidad and Tobago, Venezuela, and Mexico."

"Holy smokes! That fellow gets around. He could tell us where the "Chump Change" has been, and maybe a lot more. Maybe you could ask him why they abruptly changed direction, and headed to Mexico instead of Galveston?"

The Sheriff said, "Exactly. It might be interesting to ask him a few questions, but I have to go right now, because Houston is in Harris County and my jurisdiction is only Galveston County. They can only hold him for a short while. Want to ride along?"

Apple was excited, and exclaimed, "You bet.

Thanks Sheriff." Apple knew this would be a long night, he had a deadline for tomorrow's edition of the Houston Announcer, and this could take all night. Especially being the late hour that was.

WILLIAM WARREN

Chapter 21
FRED AND LITTLE JOE MAKE MISCHIEF

Sheriff Ben turned the patrol pickup around in the parking lot and stopped in front of the building, blew his horn, and a fellow appeared from the side. The most enormous man App had seen in a long time. "Good golly, Miss Molly," he muttered under his breath.

Sheriff Ben lowered his window, his words appearing as a fog from the dense cool night air, "Hey, Big Henry, how you doing? Listen Big Henry, this is my friend, Apple Smith from the Houston Announcer."

Big Henry interrupted, "From where? I never heard of no Announcer, where is it?"

"The newspaper, Henry, not a town, this man is a newspaper reporter. Listen, that is his truck parked there. We are going to be gone for a couple of hours. Please watch out for it, will you? We'll be back to pick it up later, Can you do that?"

"Sure Sheriff, don't worry about it. Nice to meet you buddy."

The Sheriff said, "No, he's not much brighter than he appears, but he's a good guy, and after your truck is vandalized tonight, Big Henry will tell us who did it."

"What'd you mean when it is vandalized!"

"Well Apple, it has been known to happen before. Want to know if Filbin and Santiago disliked you?

We'll know when we get back." The Sheriff gave App a sideways glance to see how he would react to his truck being vandalized, but if he expected App to overreact, he was disappointed. App showed no visible sign of agitation.

Apple said, "That is one large man. Couldn't we just ask him to stop the vandalization? I'm pretty sure if he had been at the Alamo, Santa Anna would not have had a chance."

"Big Henry has been in business a long time. He is a good businessman, in his own way. He will play both sides of the coin. He likes the union having its meetings here. But he will also watch the Ford."

Back inside, Randy Filbin and Mario Santiago were talking in hushed tones to Fred Fredrickson and Little Joe Edmonds. Santiago said, "How did y'all like the tone of our friend, Apple Smith from the newspaper?"

Fred and Little Joe were the two characters sitting directly behind Apple during his question session at the meeting.

Little Joe spoke up first. "He's a punk with a big mouth." Little Joe had been employed at the BAR Chem plant before it moved south. He had lost his job, and his house, and his wife because of the unemployment. And, now that he was about 50, employment was hard to come by. He now did odd jobs, anything to make a few bucks. It was pretty well known that Filbin shuffled a few bucks his way; in return, Little Joe did odd jobs for Filbin. He was a small man but mean as a pit bull, carried a large pocket knife and had used it on at least two occasions. Sheriff Ben had arrested him both times. There was no love between the two. Little Joe was one to watch.

Fred Fredrickson had been a pipe fitter at BAR Chem before the company had shut the doors. He had not been a stellar character before, and now was mad at just about everything all the time. His faith had been put in Filbin and Santiago to get his job back. How he thought they were going to do that, he was not concerned. He just felt his chances were better with them than without them. They were both intensely loyal to Randy Filbin and Mario Santiago, and would do whatever they asked. Neither was very bright. Most of the union members did not care for either.

Mario answered Little Joe, "There is an old pickup parked in the lot. It belongs to the reporter, and I know it will be parked there for at least the next two hours. Do you think we should teach him a lesson in respect?"

Little Joe and Fred got the picture. Randy Filbin followed up with, "And I think it would be a good idea to find out where Mr. Smith lives. Perhaps we should pay him a little visit, teach him some manners. No hospital, just get his attention."

The Houston newspaper man and the Galveston County Sheriff drove the police cruiser out of the parking lot and headed north, up the Gulf Freeway toward Houston. It was now pushing 10 p.m.;traffic was thin, so the Sheriff gassed the Ford up to eighty five.

Apple observed, "I wish I could move like this without looking for your black and whites."

Sheriff Ben said, "Being Sheriff has its perks. This is one of them. Anyway, we are on official business. Would you like me to turn on the lights?" He was smiling as he said this.

"I'm pretty sure my old truck won't do 85."

It took no time to cover 20 miles. They pulled up to Dot's Coffee Shop, a Houston landmark, known for its large sandwiches and late night eatery.

Parked in front was a Houston patrol cruiser. "That should be them." said Sheriff Ben. It was unusual for only one police car to be at the diner. Many Houston cops congregated here for coffee time. As usual there was a surprising crowd, especially at this time, and the middle of the week. Dot's was a good, dependable place.

Apple was smiling as he remembered his first time at Dot's. About ten years ago, he had his first attempt at writing published. App had met the publisher here one morning to review the blue lines, as he was told the first copy prior to printing was. He and the publisher had discussed his book and drank coffee for three hours. Yes, he knew this place well.

Sheriff Ben led the way, and quickly spotted his two old friends from the HPD sitting near a window facing the street, in a corner near the back. As the Sheriff and Apple walked through the crowd, the Sheriff was greeted several times by patrons, once stopping to exchange handshakes with a table of four. Apple recognized two of the men. But who wouldn't? The mayor of Houston and a Harris County Commissioner were well known. And Apple being a reporter knew them immediately. Who were the other two fellows?

As App and the Sheriff were retreating to their appointment, a voice spoke up, "Hold it a minute, Sheriff." The Mayor stood up. He had recognized Apple. "Sheriff Ben, you're traveling in risky company. Don't tell this guy any secrets. Hello, Apple Smith, I didn't recognize you at first. How you doing?" Apple and the Mayor knew each other well, App attended many city council meetings and other public press conferences from time to time.

Sheriff Ben said, "Don't worry, Mayor, he has promised not to tell any Galveston secrets. I'm not sure if that applies to Houston," spoken tongue in cheek.

It was a good question from the Mayor because Apple was already running a thought through his mind as to who the other two men were.

As the Sheriff and Apple made their way to the officers waiting, Apple was struck with a thought.

"Sheriff, be right there. Gotta go to the men's room. Apple turned back toward the door and exited into the parking lot. There were about 30 cars or so gathered. App turned and walked to the far side, and there was what he was looking for. He had noticed it as he and Sheriff Ben arrived, but thought nothing of it at the time. The shiny, new black Jaguar! Apple tried to keep calm and think.

He returned to the coffee shop, casually walked by the table where the Mayor and his companions were talking in seemingly friendly tones. Apple got a good look at the four, and sure enough, there sat M. Ellis Winston.

Apple walked by the four and made his way to his own table where Sheriff Ben and the two HPD cops were drinking coffee and chatting. The strange looking, middle 30s, man with them was not saying anything, but was eating a BLT sandwich, and drinking a Coke. Apple was immediately taken by the man's appearance. He guessed that he was only about five feet tall, but muscular, like a circus performer. He didn't appear to be concerned that he was soon to be questioned by the Sheriff and Apple about his knowledge of Bettis Tom Stovall, the "Chump Change" and where she had been this past week.

Sheriff Ben said, "Apple Smith, let me introduce you to friends from HPD's finest, Bob and Stan, old friends from long ago."

Bob said, "Nice to meet you Apple. Sheriff Ben has already briefed us, so let me introduce you to Arnost

Bambenek. Arnost was stopped on a routine traffic stop tonight, nothing serious. He voluntarily told us that he is employed by Bettis Tom Stovall as a deckhand onboard the "Chump Change." Being friends with the Sheriff, we knew he had a slight interest in the BAR Chem yacht, so we called up the Sheriff, and here we all are."

Sheriff Ben began by saying to Arnost, "Sir, you know this is strictly an off the record conversation, and you are here entirely on your own free will. If you prefer to not answer any of our questions that is your privilege to do so."

Arnost replied in an obvious foreign dialect. Apple guessed to be Eastern European, "Your two friends here made that clear, but they also made it clear that it would be in my best interest to come along."

He said this slow and easy with a bit of defiance in his voice. He was most surely not here on his own free will, but preferred this to being detained downtown for most of the night. Apple, from his extensive experience at interviewing, could tell from the start that Arnost would be candid only up to a point. Apple wasn't sure if that would be from his loyalty to Bettis Tom, or from his resentment at being brought to the coffee house for questioning from the Galveston County Sheriff.

The Sheriff caught Apple by surprise when he said. "Apple, you got any questions for Mr. Bambenek?" App just figured that the Sheriff would do most of the talking.

Apple began, "May I call you Arnost? How tall are you?"

"Tall enough. How tall are you?"

If Apple was concerned with Arnost understanding the language enough to respond, that question was quickly put aside. Arnost understood everything, in fact Apple judged him to be above average intelligence. If anything was to be learned, they would have to proceed carefully, and not underestimate Mr. Bambenek.

"Fair enough," said Apple, with a smile. "I only asked because it seems that the "Chump Change" hires a lot of help about your height, and I was wondering why that is so."

That question surprised Sheriff Ben, but he said nothing. He thought, "What the hell is that about?"

"Another of the deck hands on the "Chump Change" is from my old troop. We were a tumbling act for a circus, back in our old country, which by the way if you are interested is Hungary. Bettis Tom hired us because we had both worked on the Mediterranean trading merchant vessel that BAR Chem operates. We made regular trips from Morocco and Algeria up to the Adriatic Sea.

Apple was surprised at this much information. He did not know that BAR Chem was in the merchant shipping business. He thought this might be something to keep in mind for future use.

"What did Bettis Tom have to do with the merchant ship?"

"I don't know, but he was a frequent visitor on the ship a couple of years ago when I worked there."

Apple turned his attention to the Sheriff and nodded his head, and Sheriff Ben asked, "I believe you said that you left the boat in Veracruz. Why?"

"I live in San Leon. I have some personal business here. My landlady phoned and said the city was about to turn my water off if I didn't pay, so since the "Chump Change is only a couple of days from home, Bettis Tom allowed me to come home."

"Arnost, when is the "Chump Change" coming to

Galveston?"

"Don't ask me. Bettis Tom makes all of those decisions. You could probably ask him. I think he will be coming home by plane soon. The second mate will bring the boat home. For all I know, BT is home now."

Apple then asked, "Arnost, do you know of any special cargo that the "Chump Change" carried from either the Caribbean or Venezuela, or maybe even Mexico?"

"I think only cruise food stuffs, you know that is strictly a pleasure craft, right? No special cargo that I know of." Apple asked, "What is your job?"

"I do everything, I cook, clean, drop the anchor, you know, anything a deck hand can do, I do."

"Are there any special storage spaces that you know of? Maybe a special, large locker, or maybe some hidden spaces?"

"What are you asking me, Mr. Smith?"

Apple continued the barrage of questions while Sheriff Ben paid very close attention. The Sheriff thought to himself, where is this going?

"I'm asking if Bettis Tom takes special care of any kind of packages or containers, you might have seen but not allowed to handle."

Arnost answered simply, "Not that I am aware of." But he seemed to pause here a little.

The Sheriff added here, "Arnost, you are not suspected of anything, but if we find out later that you have not been truthful, then you might be in trouble just because you are protecting someone, particularly BT."

Apple said, "Arnost, I believe you are lying, I believe that the "Chump Change" is smuggling drugs into Galveston, and I believe you know about it. There are secret compartments on board her, and you know exactly where those hiding places are. They're small and tight. That's why you were hired, you are small and can maneuver in those places, right?"

The Sheriff broke in here, "Mr. Smith can I talk to you alone a minute?" Sheriff Ben slid out of the booth where he had been sitting next to Arnost, and App pushed his chair away from the end of the table, stood up and turned to walk behind the Sheriff. Sheriff Ben went a few feet away and turned to Apple. "What the hell is going on in there?"

"Sheriff, you asked me to ask questions. I'm asking questions."

"You know, you just accused a man that is here as a courtesy of smuggling drugs and lying about it. What's up with that?"

"Believe me Sheriff, it may have great relevance, and it may just be a shot in the dark. Those are the big questions I have. How about you finish up, but please ask him who was on the "Chump Change. I'll tell you why on the way back to Big Henry's."

The pair returned to the table where Sheriff Ben said, "Arnost, I just have a few general ideas to throw out, like, why did the boat change course? I know it was headed straight for Galveston when you abruptly changed courses and headed for Veracruz. That is where you came from, right? Veracruz?"

Arnost claimed to have been as surprised as the Sheriff. He got off the boat thinking he was in Galveston; instead he was in Mexico.

"Are there any weapons on board the boat?"

"I would say just the usual ones that any boat probably carries. A rifle with a scope, a shot gun, and a few handguns. Nothing significant."

Sheriff Ben had to agree. Most boats cruising like the "Chump Change" carried at least hand guns.

"Was there a fellow on board named Roy Jacobs? Probably did not do any work, works for BAR Chem."

Arnost was taken back a little by that question. "I'm not sure. I may have seen a well-dressed company man, but I'm not sure."

Sheriff Ben was a bit agitated, "Don't lie to me. I can still have you arrested if you don't cooperate. Was Roy Jacobs on the boat?"

Arnost simply said, "Yes."

"One more. Were you on board the night a fellow was murdered on the dock, just down from the "Chump Change?"

"I don't know of any murder or death at the marina, that is news to me."

"Let me make it simple, were you on board the night before the "Chump Change" sailed to the Caribbean?"

"Of course, but so were all the other crew members."

The Sheriff thanked Arnost for his cooperation, and said to the two patrolmen, "Thanks boys, I owe you one."

Chapter 22
APP IS SURPRISED WITH NEW WHEELS

App and Sheriff Ben were making good time heading back to Big Henry's for App's pickup truck. They would be there soon because the Sheriff had his cruiser's needle pointed at 90 miles an hour. Apple was concerned about the speed, but at midnight there was virtually no one on the freeway driving south towards Galveston.

Apple started the conversation with, "Sheriff, did you notice who was having a late coffee with the Mayor?"

"Yeah, a Harris County Commissioner, and Conway, or Connery, I'm not sure of his name, but he is on the Houston City Council. I would say pretty routine. The Mayor meets with lots of folks."

Apple said, "You didn't notice the other fellow? Let me tell you, none other than M. Ellis Winston of the BAR Chem board, and lately the gent that was offering money to Mr. Barton to stop printing articles in the paper about the company. He drives a new, black Jaguar, I noticed it when we pulled into the parking lot."

"Is that when you faked going to the men's room?"

"Yep, I went back to check and make sure. I'm sure."

Added the Sheriff, "I think Ellis probably knows all the politicians, and movers and shakers in Houston since he is leading council for the company. Probably nothing unusual there."

Apple thought there is plenty unusual there, but kept it to himself. He filed it away to think about later.

Sheriff Ben said, "Alright, now what's up with, 'How tall are you Arnost?' That makes no sense to me."

Apple explained his theory that there were hidden storage areas on the "Chump Change" that only a very small person could squeeze into. "That boat just makes too many trips to the Caribbean and Mexico simply for pleasure."

The Sheriff considered that. "She does seem to be continually in transit."

"If it is simply for pleasure, why wouldn't they just keep the boat in St. Thomas, or any number of islands, and just fly down on one of BAR Chem's planes?" said App.

"Well, Mr. newspaper man, that is just a theory, and a pretty amazing one at that."

"Sheriff, you know that stuff about his friend working on the "Chump Change" and being small like Arnost is only half the truth. The truth is, Beer Can Billy and Colorado Billy reported to me that there are at least two more very short people working on the boat. The other two are women. Now why wouldn't Arnost tell me about them, especially since I asked him directly? Why not just tell the truth?"

"You're making a pretty wide jump, partner."

"Listen Sheriff, these guys load the drugs, arms, or whatever, perhaps sensitive electronic parts, maybe even diamonds, could be anything, into tiny little spaces that only a very athletic, small person could get into. I'll bet the spaces are even littered with something nasty like engine oil to discourage a man of say, your size from going into. You would just be told that it is an inspection space for a holding tank or hard to get to, engine space. Morris related a story to me about searching junks during the Viet Nam War."

"Who?"

"Morris Barton, editor of the Houston Announcer, a decorated Viet Nam war veteran. Anyway, he said that the bad guys would store rifles, ammo, in the bottom of a junk, then flood the bilge with water, even raw sewage to discourage anyone searching. And for the most part, it was effective. Hell, who wants to wade nasty water up to your belt to search what is probably just a leaking old boat?"

"And you think this is what may be going on with the "Chump Change"? A pretty far out theory, but maybe that is what smuggling is about."

"The more I think about it," said Apple, "The more I believe it is a real possibility. Safer than bringing the stuff over the border in a pickup truck. And, tons and tons of the stuff."

"What do you think they are smuggling?"

Apple simply said, "Heroin and cocaine, probably not marijuana."

"Why not marijuana?"

"Too bulky, low return compared to coke and heroin."

The Sheriff did not say anything for a long time while this soaked in, then he said, "I had a young nephew that died from an overdose of crystal meth."

Apple added, "Most of the meth comes out of Mexico, some out of South America, and even some out of the Caribbean. How convenient for Bettis Tom, Ellis, Roy, and even Jeffrey Chung Dearcorn. A good deal for them would be how easily that big yacht moves regularly through those areas. Shoot! Sheriff, they take big wigs on

Mexican vacations and load the "Chump Change" with enough heroin, meth, and cocaine to supply New York for a year. No telling how much that would be worth, millions."

Added Sheriff Ben, "And the legitimate guests on board never have a clue. And the nature of the yacht, and who owns it, puts it above suspicion. That would explain Beer Can Billy's murder, but John Bishop is still fuzzy."

Apple said, "No, I think it was purely money. Bettis Tom got greedy and decided to divert the money from its BAR Chem intended purpose, which was simply bribery, and take it for himself."

Sheriff Ben said to Apple, "If I am following you, the "Chump Change" has fake bulkheads full of some kind of contraband, and Arnost and his selected mates are small enough to squeeze into these secret storage areas. And, they make regular runs between Galveston and Mexico and South America."

"That about sums it up. The question is, what are we going to do about it?" said Apple.

"I have dealt with car theft rings, cattle thieves, small time dope dealers, and almost every kind of low life in this county, but this thing is spiraling out of control. If you are right."

Apple declared, "Sheriff, you know I am on to something, even if some of the details are not certain. Scary stuff."

The two turned onto the freeway feeder road and exited at Big Henry's. The parking lot lights were turned off except for one small light in the middle of the lot. They pulled up next to Apple's old Ford pickup before they noticed anything different.

Sheriff Ben quietly whistled under his breath, then said low and somberly, "I hope you have good insurance."

Apple's pickup was a mess. The tires were flat, the front windshield smashed, as were the headlights. Both side mirrors were hanging down, broken off at the base. The driver's door looked as if someone had kicked a boot into the side, and it was standing open. The seat covers were cut with a knife, and the instrument panel was smashed with a hammer or some other heavy instrument.

Apple was stunned, but did not show surprise to the Sheriff. "You said I would find out if Filbin and Santiago liked me. I'm pretty sure they don't think much of me."

"I'm sorry, my friend, I didn't really expect this much damage. I thought that perhaps you would get a key scratch. Saying they don't think much of you is a little mild. I'd say they really have a strong dislike for you," said the Sheriff, who couldn't help but chuckle a little as he spoke.

"You won't think it so funny when I am sleeping on your couch tonight. I think your wife won't either."

"She's grown accustomed to this sort of thing. Sometimes I think she enjoys my work more than I do."

"You better work on keeping her around, most wouldn't think this funny. Why are you laughing, Sheriff?"

"The fun is just about to begin. Let's go wake Big Henry's butt out of bed. I'll bet he can tell us who did this."

The Sheriff rapped on the front door. No one answered. The only sounds were from a dog inside.

"Open up, Big Henry, it's Sheriff Ben. Come on out!"

A light flickered inside, and Sheriff Ben said to Apple, "The old codger, he's probably making us wait on purpose, probably hates to answer the door since he knows there will be hell to pay about your truck." Sheriff Ben seemed to be more upset about the truck than Apple was.

191

"Let's just find out who did it," said Apple.

Finally, from inside, Big Henry's gruff voice loudly said, "Hold your water, I'm coming."

Big Henry opened the door and squinted outside, "Come on inside Sheriff. I guess you want to know about the pickup."

"Damn straight, Big Henry. Who did this? I asked you to watch it so this wouldn't happen."

"Yeah, I saw it happening, but I was scared to stop it."

"Since when have you been scared of anything, Big Henry? Alright, calm down and tell me what happened."

"Who did this?"

"Well, I couldn't rightly say, two kids, maybe. One smallish, one tall and lanky."

"Now Big Henry, who does that description fit? You and I know it wasn't kids, or normal vandals. Tell me who it was, before I take you down to the station, keep you till morning, then ask you again."

"OK, Sheriff, but you know you might be getting me into trouble. You going to protect me?"

"Yes, you know you only have to call."

"I'm looking at that truck, and calling you don't give me any confidence."

"I can't be in two places at once. Now tell me who did this."

Big Henry stared at his shoes and said quietly, "Little Joe and Fred."

"Say it a little louder, I don't want there to be any mistake. I want this here newspaperman to hear you say it."

Big Henry drew himself up to his full height, stuck out his chest defiantly, and said loud enough to hear across

MURDER ON GALVESTON BAY

the parking lot, "You know who I said, Sheriff, Little Joe and Fred."

"And did you see them here earlier in the evening at the meeting?"

"Yes, we all saw them."

The Sheriff politely said, Thanks, Big Henry, I won't forget it. Need anything, call me," and Sheriff Ben handed him a business card with his direct line on it.

Big Henry responded, "Alright, go get out of here, and the next time you come, bring your boat and go fishing."

Apple said simply, "Thank you, Big Henry."

Big Henry mumbled under his breath as he turned to go into his house, "You fish, or just make trouble for folks, with your paper?"

Apple said, "I sometimes fish."

Apple and the Sheriff walked across the parking lot where the Sheriff's police pickup was parked near App's trashed out truck.

"I don't think she can be salvaged," said App.

"Nope, but I tell you what I can do. The thought of getting up in the morning for coffee and finding you on my sofa, doesn't set very well. That's getting work pretty close to the vest, bringing the clients home for an overnight sleep."

"Well Sheriff, you owe me something. After all, it was your idea to leave it parked at Big Henry's."

Sheriff Ben said, "Well we can do two things, I'll let you choose. First, you can sleep on a cot in my jail tonight."

"That's out. What else you got?"

"I can loan you a car for a couple of days."

App replied, "Are you kidding? I'll take the car.

But," Apple asked, "Can you do that?"

"Hey, Mr. Newspaperman, I'm Sheriff of Galveston County. I can do it. Besides, this is official police business. Your pickup was vandalized because of me. The least the department can do is loan you a car for a few days."

The two men got into Sheriff Ben's vehicle and headed towards the police department, only a few miles away. As they pulled into the Sheriff's department parking lot, Apple could see five or six police cruisers, lined up as if ready to go. When they parked and got out of the Sheriff's pickup truck, Sheriff Ben walked directly towards a police cruiser sedan. Apple was surprised. He figured the Sheriff would lead him to an unmarked, ugly dark blue sedan. But no, this was a one year old Chevy Caprice, with lights on top and spotlights on the sides at the mirrors. Apple was thinking, this could be fun.

Sheriff Ben opened the door and could see Apple was surprised, "What were you expecting, a city street sweeper? I am a policeman, this is what we drive. So how you like it? I promise it will do 90."

Apple said, "You're really going to lend me this police cruiser?"

"Yep, this is it. Now let me caution you about a few things. First, this is the switch that turns on the emergency lights. Do not turn them on for any reason. Second, this is the siren. Do not turn it on for any reason. And third, this is the radio. Do not turn it on for any reason. If you do, you might get us both in trouble. So, what do you think?"

Apple was still surprised. Truth is, he couldn't wait to get behind the wheel of this baby. "It'll do. How long can I keep it?"

"Just long enough to get yourself situated."

"One other thing, well two things. Stay out of the

trunk. There may be weapons in there." And with that said he opened the trunk and removed a shot gun and several handguns. "I hope you won't be needing these."

Apple asked, "What's the other thing?"

"You have to buy your own gas."

"You know I live downtown, near Minute Maid Park. Is that ok?"

"OK by me. Oh yeah, if you lock yourself out of the car, it is almost impossible to break into, so be careful. And keep this in mind, if you park it in the street, try to park under a light. You would be surprised how many will take advantage of a vacant police car. They get keyed, or worse, often. Please keep that in mind. Otherwise, treat it like your own, that is for a few days." Sheriff Ben was smiling all the time. He knew Apple was going to enjoy driving this vehicle.

"Alright Sheriff, it is after midnight, and I still have to write a column for tomorrow's paper."

"Good, but don't mention the loan of the car. I don't care if you mention the vandalization of your pickup. But, I would be careful about some of those wild theories concerning short people and trips to the Caribbean if I were the Houston Announcer. Call me tomorrow and let me know how you and the car are getting along. And, by the way, I will call a wrecker and have your truck towed here to the station. This might make you feel better. First thing tomorrow I am going to have Little Joe and Fred Frederickson picked up. Good night, it's been an interesting evening, Apple."

Apple Smith got into the cruiser and drove towards Houston. He needed to get to his apartment soon so he could knock out something for tomorrow's paper. Lately he had been forgetting that he still had a job. His mind was filled with the mysteries surrounding Beer Can Billy's murder, not to mention John Bishop, and the interesting facts concerning the "Chump Change." And he still needed to have a meeting with Mr. Barton. App wanted to learn more about the meeting Morris had with M. Ellis Winston.

But first things first. As soon as he was out of sight of the police station, he switched on the emergency lights. He smiled as he turned them off. He thought I have always wanted to do that. Next was the radio, he only switched it on for an instant, it also worked. App was a little reluctant to flip on the siren, maybe a little more distant from the station. But having the radio on couldn't hurt, as he flipped it on. Almost instantly a familiar voice came on the radio, "Apple, are you listening? I know you are there, answer me."

"Yes, Sheriff, I am here."

"I knew you couldn't resist. Now listen up. My boys went over to pick up Little Joe and Fred, and no one was home at either place. That means they are still out, probably creating mischief, so keep your eyes open."

"But, how would they know I am driving a cop car?"

"They don't, but I'll bet they know where you live."

"You don't really think those two characters would bother me personally, do you? Trashing my truck is one thing, but me, that's pretty extreme just for asking a few questions about the Union's money."

"Listen, to me. Both of those guys have violent arrest histories, so don't fool around. Have you turned on the siren? No, don't answer that. Just drive the car and leave the play toys alone. But go ahead and keep the radio on. Just don't talk on it, unless it is to answer someone specifically calling you. You do know every cop in Galveston County can hear you, right?"

Apple smiled as he said, "Ten-four, over and out." He did not really know what ten-four meant, if anything, but it was fun saying it to the Sheriff.

Apple was sprinting down NASA Road 1 when he spotted a McDonalds still open. He pulled into the drive up window and ordered a burger. He was hungry at the late hour, and he wanted to watch the expressions of the window attendant. He knew he didn't look much like a cop. He was certain a change of careers was not in his future, but he was enjoying this pretending a bit.

As late an hour as 1 a.m., he was enjoying this time. It had been a busy day with the union meeting, his chance encounter with Filbin and Santiago, questioning Arnost, and bumping into the Mayor and M. Ellis Winston at Dot's. Somehow he was not even upset that his old truck had been trashed, probably totaled. All in all a pretty good day. What he could make of it, he did not know. He did know that he and Sheriff Ben were getting a new friendship started. Apple was aware that the Sheriff did not have to loan him a car and was probably breaking some sort of county regulations, but he was going to enjoy his police cruiser for a few days.

WILLIAM WARREN

Chapter 23
APPLE SUFFERS MORE THAN BRUISED EGO

Apple calculated that it would probably take him about one hour to write his piece for the paper before he could call it a day. Apple was tired, but contented.

He drove slowly down Saint Emanuel Street, hoping to find a good spot at the curb as opposed to going into the parking garage, which he disliked. And as luck would have it, he found one near the middle of the block, and not far from his front entry. He remembered what the Sheriff had said about parking in a well-lit spot, but he would have to take what he could find. Not too dark, but not well-lit by any idea. He would take what he could get. Besides, who would really damage a car with Sheriff painted in bold letters down both sides?

Apple briskly opened the door of the cruiser, and was careless in locking the door. He was happy to be at his own apartment near the Astros baseball park.

App had already formulated an outline in his head for the article he had to submit for the next edition paper. He would make the seven o'clock deadline easy.

He would really begin to tell the Galveston Bay murders, and perhaps touch on the seeming connection between the "Chump Change" and BAR Chem itself. App was well aware that he would have to be careful; he had no real evidence, yet. Just two murders in the bay and Ellis's attempted bribery of Mr. Barton. He smiled as he thought, "After this piece, Ellis, Dearcorn or whomever else at BAR Chem would be eager to do an interview with him and the paper." He still had Ellis's rebuff in the icehouse, and his self-important secretary's refusal to give him an appointment to speak to M. Ellis Winston. He thought, "Oh! the power of the pen."

Apple walked through the semi-darkness up the sidewalk when he felt a mind numbing pain across the back of his knees. It felt like someone had hit him with a baseball bat. App immediately fell forward and luckily hit his face on the grass lawn at the edge of the concrete instead of the sidewalk. He was on the verge of passing out as he struggled to his hands and knees, when a second blow from a leather boot struck him full on the right cheekbone below his eye.

Apple could feel the warm flow of blood from the cut immediately. He quickly rose, shaking, to his feet, and threw out his right elbow, striking one of the assailants in the throat, catching him full bore on his Adam's Apple. The bad guy wielding the baseball bat that had been cut off about a foot from the end to make a nasty club, swung the bat again, catching Apple a glancing blow, just below his left eye, opening a cut nearly to his cheekbone.

Apple was bleeding from both wounds on his face. He would remember later that the cut on his left cheek hurt like hell. He was near passing out again from the trauma, and he slowly bent over at the knees and fell to the ground. Now both assailants stepped forward and began kicking him in the back and the ribs.

Apple pulled up into a fetal position as he fought to keep consciousness. One thing he would remember was Little Joe and Fred, swinging fists and kicking him over and over. "The bastards."

As the two walked away, Apple could hear one of them mutter, "Better think it over, smart guy."

Just as suddenly as the ambush had started, it was over. The two assailants quickly disappeared into the night.

Apple laid on the ground fighting the darkness that was closing in on his consciousness. After a few minutes he began to realize what had happened to him. He reached for his cell phone which should have been in his right pants pocket. Not there. App knew he could not walk the 50 feet to the apartment door, and at this hour it was unlikely a passerby would emerge. He was only a few feet from the police cruiser, so he began crawling on his hands and knees to the car door. His only luck was the door being partially open because he had failed to shut it fully. He struggled to the seat of the Chevy police cruiser and began to struggle at the switch that would activate the emergency lights on top of the cruiser. A second attempt and the startling bright lights suddenly flared from the roof. A few seconds later and Apple successfully turned on the siren. That revived Apple momentarily. It certainly woke most of the neighborhood.

The next day Apple would remember how quickly a small crowd gathered around the cop car. One of the bystanders reached into the car, flipped on the radio, and said loudly into the phone, "Officer hurt, 900 block of Saint Emanuel. Come fast. We need an ambulance!"

An ambulance appeared and Apple was quickly attended to, hastily sped off to the emergency room at Hermann Hospital in the Houston Medical Center.

Two hours later and he was wheeled into a room. The doctor advised about two days in the hospital, mostly for observation and to ward off infection. There was a particular worry about an infection moving from his cheeks to either or both of his eyes.

Apple did not wake the next morning until 10 a.m. He struggled to open his badly swollen eyes, and when he did, there was Bernadette watching him from the foot of his bed, along with Mr. Barton. As Apple regained some awareness, he was also aware of the two Houston policemen he had met earlier last night at Dot's. Standing beside the bed was Sheriff Benjamin Rodriguez, starched khaki pants and bright white shirt with the gold badge over his left pocket, looking very serious.

Apple tried to grin and speak, but could only whisper, "What was that train doing on the sidewalk?"

Sheriff Ben said, "You still think cop cars are fun?"

Apple motioned for Mr. Barton to move closer, and spoke softly, "Sorry about the deadline, boss."

Mr. Barton, almost overcome, answered, "No problem, App, Bernie filled in rather nicely. She wrote a short, but nice piece about your mishap."

Bernie said, "Nice going, in the field reporter. You're going to a lot of trouble to get someone else to do your work. How long do I have to keep bailing you out?"

Sheriff Ben moved closer and asked, "Do you know who did this, Apple? I think I know, but I want you to confirm it."

Apple grimaced, "We both know, Sheriff. I got a good look at both of them. Little Joe and Fred Frederickson ambushed me in the dark. I think they sat on the street and waited for me to come home. I never saw them coming."

Sheriff Ben, ever the policeman, said, "Apple, did you see a gun or any other type of weapon?"

"I did see a short baseball bat club. That is what Little Joe hit me first with, and knocked me to the ground."

"Good. Not good that they did this to you, but

good that you saw a weapon. I think assault with a deadly weapon will be easy to take to court. Now if we can find them. Neither one came home last night. But you can bet on it, I will find them soon."

A young-looking emergency medicine doctor came in. "Good that you are finally awake." He asked everyone to soon leave so that his patient could rest quietly.

Mr. Barton was the first to depart, saying, "Take off as much time as you need, App. But, as soon as you are back on your feet, we are going to give that BAR Chem bunch trouble like congress could not. That includes the bunch of union thugs too. I will not tolerate this to one of my employees, you can count on it." He looked over at Bernadette and said, "I know you would like to stay here and tend to your young charge, but I still need you at the paper sometime today."

The big Sheriff said, "Apple, I know you are not in any danger from Little Joe or Fred. They just wanted to get even with you for asking their boss embarrassing questions, but I have an officer on the way here. They will stay here until you are released, or until I feel no danger from them. If we had arrested them this morning, no worry, but they are still out roaming around. So better safe than sorry."

Apple felt so bad, he just nodded his head, thanks.

The Sheriff continued, "Remember Bob from HPD, he met us at Dot's last night? He will hang around for a while, until my officer shows up."

Apple nodded, OK.

The Sheriff turned to leave and said, "Apple, I am going to find out who did this, and I hope soon. In the meantime, I'm taking away your driving privilege. Remember, I told you not to turn on the lights or the siren.

You even used the radio." Sheriff Ben was smiling broadly as he spoke.

Bernie was the only one left in the room. The HPD patrolman was in the lobby just outside the door. She approached the side of the bed. Apple was lying very still with his swollen, blackened eyes shut. He had a row of tightly spaced stitches on each side of his face. Too bad, thought Bernie, this is an incredibly handsome man. Even with his eyes shut and so mistreated, he was still a striking figure. "Maybe when this is over, and he had recovered, I will tell him how much affection I have, but he is so young and reckless. Indeed, Bernie was a few years older than Apple, but not enough to make a difference in a relationship, she mused.

"What're you thinking, office worker?" asked Apple. He caught her unawares, she expected him to return to sleep. She replied, "Not much, my little friend."

"How do I look? I am wary of looking at a mirror. Are my handsome features ruined forever?" said Apple with a small smile twisted at the corners of his mouth. He was kidding, and she knew it. Apple was not vain, didn't much think about how he looked. "Will little children run in freight?"

"Well, probably for a few days. I'm thinking about running myself."

"Not a chance, Bernie Hannigan. You're afraid of nothing, that's why I like you so much. You are a true friend."

As Apple spoke, the door to his hospital room opened slowly, and a female voice said, "Hello, is anybody home?" And in walked someone Apple did not recognize through his mostly shut eyes. He was thrown off, unexpectedly, by the starched khaki pants, and white shirt, with the silver

Sheriff's badge over the left pocket.

Bernie knew it could be only one person. She recognized the figure from her profile in the Galveston County Sheriff's personnel pages.

Apple squinted his sore eyes, then opened them real wide. He was surprised. Standing beside his bed was Maggie. "What are you doing here? And, why are you dressed like that?" asked App.

"You didn't know I was a licensed peace officer with Sheriff Ben's office?" asked Maggie.

"I thought you were a secretary."

"I am, part-time, but I am also a Galveston County Deputy Inspector.

Apple, obviously surprised, said, "Well, I'll be. No, I wasn't aware of your dual status. I thought you worked in the office."

Bernie could see why Apple had cultivated his "source" in Sheriff Ben's office. Maggie was a tall, well built brunette, about 35. Bernie thought, a striking presence, especially with the big side arm holstered on her right hip.

Apple said, "Please excuse my manners, Maggie, Deputy Inspector of Galveston County. Please meet my friend Bernadette, the Associate Editor for the Houston Announcer.

Wow! I am a lucky guy. Two gorgeous ladies tending to my every need. "Ladies, I think I would require some assistance to the men's room, if you please," he said with a big smile. He was proud of his way to make light, even with the throbbing pain in his whole body.

Bernie said, "Don't push your luck, cub reporter."

Maggie thought, "I think I like this lady."

Just as the ice was broken, Dr. Duke pushed open the hospital room door. He was the young doctor who had attended Apple when he was brought into the emergency room a few hours before.

Bernie was the first to speak, "Pardon me Doc, but do you know you bear a striking resemblance to Doctor Red Duke?"

"I should. Red was my uncle."

Maggie said, "Everyone loved Dr. Duke." A simple statement, but very profound, thought Bernie.

Dr. Duke spoke to Apple, "How you feeling, Apple?" Then without waiting for an answer he explained App's wounds. "You got fourteen stitches on your right cheek. They look a lot worse than they are. However on your left side, you've got ten on the inside, and 27 on the outside."

Bernadette spoke up, "What about his eyes, Doc?"

"Hold up, young lady," even though Bernie was probably ten years older than Dr, Duke. "This wound on your left is quite serious. Your cheekbone is broken in about three places. I think it will heal nicely, but in case it doesn't, you may need some surgery later down the line to repair that area."

"How long before I can leave?" asked Apple. "And, how about a timeline for the swelling to go down in my face, especially around my eyes. It hurts to open them."

Dr. Duke went on as if he did not hear the question. "And the gash on the back of your head may give you headaches for a while."

Bernie wanted to ask about the gash, which she had not noticed, but decided to let the doctor finish.

"And the final concern is the beating you took to your torso. You have a bad contusion on your right hip, your kidneys are bruised, and just about every muscle in your back is also bruised. Other than that you are fine.

At least you didn't lose any teeth. As to when you can go home, probably about two days. You need to urinate on your own, and not experience any blood there. Then I will think about it. When you go home, you will probably need some help. Got anybody to stay with you?"

"No, Doc, no one." Apple continued with a grin, "I was just telling my two lady friends that I might require some help in the men's room."

"Can't help ya there, but I appreciate your sense of humor," said the doctor.

Bernadette spoke up, "That won't be a problem. The paper will make sure someone is with him at home. By the way Doc, do you know this is the famous Apple Smith from the Houston Announcer?"

"Famous, how famous are you?"

"Not very, but I almost won an award once. Ever hear of the Pulitzer? Well, I didn't win it."

With that Dr. Duke made his exit. And he did know who his famous uncle was, and that he looked a lot like him, and that he was a damn fine doctor, too.

With the doctor's exit, Bernadette said, "Gotta go, field hand. I'll check on you after the paper goes to print. It looks like you're in good hands. Nice meeting you, Maggie. Don't put up with any of his bathroom nonsense."

Maggie asked, "Is that your girlfriend?"

"No, but she is a very good friend."

"How good?"

"Very good. Hey, are you really here to protect me?"

WILLIAM WARREN

Chapter 24
REMOVING A CATHETER IS HIGHLY UNDERRATED

Apple awoke from an uneasy sleep. He had a morphine pump for pain. He had carefully tried to avoid overusing the crutch because he had on his mind ideas for the column, the one Bernie wrote, that he should have written himself.

Now he determined that he was going to make up for lost time. Instead of the beating frightening him away from his laptop, it accomplished the opposite. He was now going to lay into BAR Chem and their stooges, and Randy Filbin and Mario Santiago at the Association of Chemical Manufacturers Workers, better known as the ACW.

He had vowed before to find out who murdered Beer Can Billy and John Bishop. Apple was still in his first day at the hospital, still feeling pretty rough, and feeling a little silly at having an armed police officer guarding his safety.

Apple rolled over on his right side and immediately felt the sharp pain from the injury to his hip. He quickly changed tactics and rolled to his left, which was difficult since he had an IV in his left arm. He also realized for the first time that he had a catheter attached in a very uncomfortable place. "Hell with it," he thought, "I'm getting up anyway."

In this awkward situation, the door opens and a nurse accompanied by Maggie, approached him. "For the next day, whenever you need to get up, call me," demanded the nurse.

"All right, I'm calling. Please help me to my laptop."

After getting Apple re-settled in his bed, with his laptop perched between his tummy and a pillow, App was ready as he could be for work. And with that began the thought process that went into a well-formed newspaper article.

About five minutes into his work, he could hear Maggie's cell phone ringing from across the room. Really! Way to go, Ben. Where, how?"

Apple could see she was excited about something. "Yeah, the patient is doing well. The nurse came in a few minutes ago, and he was out of bed trying to find his computer. He is writing now. Yes, I will tell him."

Maggie walked over to Apple's bedside and said, "Rest easy, Sheriff Ben just picked up Little Joe and Fred. They were at Jerry's Ice House over on San Leon, sitting back, drinking beer, as if they had no care in the world."

Apple said, "Great! Call Sheriff Ben back and ask him if the tall one has a bruise on his throat or neck. I guess it's not protocol for me to be there when the questioning takes place?"

"No. Two things. First, you are still in the hospital, and I doubt you will walk out of here tomorrow, and second, no, unless you were an attorney representing yourself, Sheriff Ben, for legal reasons wouldn't allow you to be in the room. Believe it, Ben knows what he's doing. And they are probably in there with the two homicide detectives undergoing questioning as we speak.

"Look at his neck? Were you able to fight back? From the beating you took, I thought you were down and never got back up."

"I got about half way up once, just enough to swing my arm and connect with my elbow on the neck of Fred. I knocked that rube back about three feet, but then Little Joe clubbed me to the ground with the bat he was carrying. Then ole Fred gave me this present," he rubbed his right cheek. "He kicked me right in the face when I was down on all fours. I owe both of those guys some payback. Only I will do it with this," as he pointed at his Mac laptop.

"Yep, there goes the old reporter, plying his craft. Maybe when you get back on your feet you and I will start hanging out at Jerry's. That's where they must hangout. Remember Jerry's? That's where we ran into Bettis Tom and your friend M. Ellis Winston. With any luck, in about three years they will be out of jail, and I will wear my Sheriff's badge. Then we can talk to them again."

"Sounds good to me, Deputy Maggie."

"Only then, I will be Sheriff of Galveston County."

"Really?"

"Didn't I tell you? As soon as Sheriff Ben retires, I plan to run for Sheriff, myself. Surprised?"

"A little, but I am beginning to expect the unexpected from you."

"You mean like when you checked into my private life to see how I could afford a new car? Just for your own knowledge, I bought the car on my own. You know, I probably make as much as a local newspaper reporter, and I haven't been beat up yet."

Apple responded, "How did you know that?"

"I am a cop, remember? And I am placed in a position to know what goes on around here. But, we are even. I checked into your personal life, too. But all I found was where you went to college. You're really not too exciting. You know that?"

"Except for when I get beat up. Right?"

Maggie spoke, "So, what is your relationship with Ms. Hannigan? She's the reason you haven't called me, and remember you canceled a dinner date with me."

"Yes, and for that I think I got beat up. If we had gone to dinner I would not have gone to the union meeting and probably would not have gotten my butt ambushed in my front yard. Gee! I wish we would have kept that date."

"I'll take a raincheck. And, I will put my gun in my purse. What'll you think about that? Besides, I would like to know what you asked those people to make them so mad."

"Right now I would like that, but I insist you wear your gun. I'll feel safer," grinning as he spoke. Apple was feeling something new toward Maggie. Along with the growing respect, he admired her cool attitude in dealing with his situation. He knew he looked like a train wreck. Somehow, he felt safe with her around, and not just because of the big sidearm she was carrying, but because of her "I'm in control here" demeanor. And the fact she looked like a movie star, no, better than that, she looked like a model, only filled out with spectacular results.

"Dinner sounds great as soon as I can chew solid food," said a slightly smiling App.

"Great, but for now, I'll be getting back to the Sheriff's Office. I'll check on you tomorrow. Don't get too tied up with your column. Get some rest. I mean it, take it easy."

And with that Maggie took her khakis out the door. Gotta hand it to Sheriff Ben and his guys, they picked up

Little Joe and Fred quickly. Apple was amazed that those two hoodlums had, either out of cockiness or stupidity, gone straight back to their regular haunts. App was sure Sheriff Ben had that place staked out from the beginning.

With pleasant thoughts about Maggie and her badge, he very slowly, with great difficulty, started inching his body into a sitting position so that he could manage his laptop more comfortably.

Then a thought came to his head that he would soon regret. He had not had a look at himself, but to do that he would have to get to his feet and move to the dresser with the big mirror. He could call the nurse but she would probably tell him, "No doing," too early to be moving about.

With that he slowly sat up on the side of the bed. Pain was surprising because it came from places he did not expect, and the areas that he expected were fine. His ribcage and the wound on the side of his right hip were burning with pain. The stitches in his face were causing no more discomfort than when lying down. He was surprised at this.

He grabbed the catheter bag and hooked it on the rolling pole with an IV bag attached. Then he noticed that the IV had been removed from his arm, so he just held the catheter bag in his hand. He slowly wiggled his feet on the floor, grimaced, tried to stand, then sat back down. App was feeling a little woozy. His head began to throb slightly from the wound in the back of his head.

He was struggling to keep from lying back, but he was determined to get a look at himself. He wasn't sure he could do this when the door opened and in walked Bernie. "Whaddya think you're doing, big guy?" She was obviously displeased.

Apple said, "C'mon Bernie, I need a hand."

"Not the bathroom ploy again?"

"No, no kidding this time, I need some help to the dresser. I have got to have a look."

"Alright buddy, if you insist. But you ain't gonna like what you see. Why don't you wait a couple of days?"

"No, now."

Bernie held the bag, Apple held on to the side of the bed and shuffled his feet to the dresser, where he got his first look at the message left behind by Little Joe and Fred.

"I thought I felt bad, but this looks worse than I feel."

"Good, I think that's good." responded Bernie.

"Listen Bernie, I want to look at my back, that's where a lot of pain comes from. But I need some help, and I need you to act like my mother for a few minutes."

"Sounds serious. What do you want me to do?"

"Lift my gown, and don't peek at my butt."

"Can't help myself there."

Apple stood there looking at the contusion on his right hip, and the bruises on his back. He was paying no attention to Bernie holding up his gown, and his rear reflecting in the mirror, when Dr. Duke and Mr. Barton softly knocked and, without waiting, immediately entered the room.

Mr. Barton was amused at the sight, and Dr. Duke smiled, and said, "Some guys will do anything to get a little attention from a pretty girl."

Mr. Barton said, "You must be feeling a little better." And Dr. Duke added, "I think I will release you tomorrow. How do you feel about the nurse taking out the catheter?" That was the best news Apple had gotten since he came in here last night. With that said, Dr. Duke walked out of the room saying, "I've got to go check on some of my really sick patients. See you tomorrow before you go home."

It was four o'clock in the afternoon and Morris Barton expressed to Apple to take as much time off as he needed. "Thanks Boss, but I am going to write a story tonight. I hope you will print it soon."

Bernie sat down in the big recliner, and Mr. Barton left them alone. A nurse came into the room, and while Bernie pretended to work on notes retrieved from her briefcase, the nurse quickly removed the catheter. "That wasn't so bad, was it?" asked the nurse. "Watch for blood in your urine, otherwise you're good to go."

With that Apple adjusted his laptop and began to strike the keys. Then paused and asked Bernie if she knew what the most overrated things in life were? No, she replied, tell me.

Apple said, "Catamaran sailboats, convertibles, Harleys, seven foot basketball players, want more?"

"OK, more."

"Superbowl halftime shows that last one hour, French wines, and craft beers. More?"

"You got more? No, enough already."

"Alright, two more, video games, and Bill Clinton. I've got more, but I will wait for the right time."

"Thanks, I appreciate that," said Bernie.

"Do you know something that is underrated?" He continued without waiting for an answer, "Removing a catheter is highly underrated."

Then he turned to his laptop. Apple spent the next three hours composing his article for the next day's news. He outlined his views that BAR Chem was sending out briefcases of cash for the purpose of gaining favor from everyone perceived to be blocking the return of the company to its former plant site along the Gulf Freeway. Apple discussed the murder of John Bishop and his beating at the hand of the union thugs.

He purposely left out his suspicions of the movements of the "Chump Change" and the shadowy captain, Bettis Tom. He did not want to scare off operations of the boat. He could prove the bribery allegations, so far, but the yacht was speculation, and he had no concrete evidence. Apple knew his way to Jeffrey Chung Dearcorn was his connection to the "Chump Change." He felt strongly that Bettis Tom was operating with the full knowledge and support of the Chairman of BAR Chem. The two of them, and probably more, were splitting millions through the illegal drug traffic. He very much wanted to find out everything he could about everyone on the BAR Chem Board of Directors. Apple knew in his heart that the yacht was very much at the source of Beer Can Billy's murder.

Apple did divulge that M. Ellis Winston had tried to give money to the Editor in Chief of the paper to prevent future articles such as this one. The bribe was rebuffed in the firmest tones. Apple stated his belief that the union leadership was acting in concert with BAR Chem to their own benefit and not for the members. He called for the ouster of Randy Filbin and Mario Santiago. He just hoped that didn't bring new retribution. But if it did, he would be more prepared next time. After all, this was Texas. He could carry a gun if he chose to. He would think about that one.

He finished the article and asked Bernadette to read it before he sent it in to the paper. After all, she would have to approve it in the end, as well as Mr. Barton.

All things considered, he thought an excellent story, especially since it was written from his hospital bed. Apple was eager to get back on his feet. Then things would get exciting. He intended to go to the big man himself, Jeffrey Chung Dearcorn, and just for the fun of it, Roy Jacobs. But, he did not intend to interview Bettis Tom, or Filbin, or Santiago without Sheriff Ben or perhaps Deputy Maggie by his side. He never wanted to end up in the hospital again. Those guys have proven they are ruthless. After all, someone murdered John Bishop and Beer Can Billy. Apple was sure he did not want to end up number three. He was looking forward to sitting across a courtroom from Little Joe and Fred Frederickson as soon as possible.

He was contented with his work, said good bye to Bernadette and went into a deep sleep.

At one o'clock, Apple was softly mumbling, "If you want to kill me, kill me. Don't hit me with that stick again! No, don't do it." He awoke suddenly and tried to sit up. The pain in his back and hip hit, and he slowly slumped back down onto the bed.

It was then that he noticed the figure slowly approaching him, and he began to mumble again, "No, no!" Then the figure sat easily on the side of his bed, and he noticed the familiar silver badge. Maggie softly said, "Take it easy, Apple, everything is OK. Nobody here but me. I'm watching out for you. No one gets through that door unless I allow them. Everything is fine. You want to talk about it?"

App slowly gathered himself and realized that he must have been dreaming, and was slightly embarrassed. "How long you been here? I remember you leaving early today."

"That was yesterday. I came back a few hours ago, just to check on you. You were uneasy so I decided to wait a while. Then I fell asleep, and here we are."

Apple was dismayed that she had returned to keep an eye out. Apple asked, "Are Little Joe and Fred still at the station?"

"Yes, and they will be in jail a while, at least for a few days. It will take that long to arraign them and conduct a bail hearing."

"Then why did you come back?"

"I wanted to make sure you are doing well. I might not be able to check on you for a day or so after you go home."

"Well, I am very glad to see you. Let's go back to sleep. I'm happy you're here. I feel safe."

"I know."

With that Apple quickly dozed off again. In a few minutes they were both breathing heavy with sleep.

Chapter 25
COLORADO BILLY STARTS PLANNING

Colorado Billy sat on his boat thinking. He was furious, but knew he had to clearly think about what to do. He knew he could not live the rest of his life looking over his shoulder for Bettis Tom and his crowd. He thought maybe, just maybe, I should do something to make them start looking over their shoulder for me.

He was disturbed about himself. Maybe I should have stayed on alert with Beer Can Billy he thought. Perhaps he died because I was not a good enough friend.

Colorado did not actually see what had happened, but he saw enough to be convinced everyone on the "Chump Change" that night was guilty of murder. A visual kept running through his thoughts about who he saw that night. Of course Bettis Tom was there. Four folks he knew were just deck hands. Colorado Billy didn't know where they fit in, but there was a spot for them. A queer thing, he thought, how small and short they were. He remembered Filbin and Santiago, the union bosses hanging around late into the night. Why, There were two others; he didn't know their names, but was sure they were tied to Santiago and Filbin in some way. He would later find out they were Little Joe and Fred. The last person was a fancy guy dressed in a business suit. He didn't know his name, but he had been around a lot. And of course there were always girls hanging around. Colorado was sure they had nothing to do with Beer Can's death, but they were there a lot. Might be one of them knew enough to help him.

What had set Colorado Billy's mind turning was the article in the Houston Announcer he had just read. It was the story about Apple's mugging, written by Bernadette Hannigan. He could read between the lines,. App had been severely hurt. Colorado knew that was connected to all this somehow, bur how? What should he do before more people were hurt?

Apple didn't know that Colorado had been only 50 miles away this whole time. He had not gone to the Caribbean as he had told Apple. He had started on the journey, but after about 100 miles, for some reason he did not understand, he had made a 180, and turned back towards Texas. Instead of Barbados or Road Town, he had ridden the southeast wind to the small town of Freeport, just down the coast from Galveston. There he had made his way to the new downtown marina where he prepared to hang out a while, until he figured his next move.

He had asked for a mooring slip towards the end of the pier. The marina was only slightly occupied with only one other boat on the entire pier. He could see who approached clearly. Let them come, he thought, I will be waiting. He kept his .45 automatic and his 12 gauge pump shotgun handy these days. But for all his vigilance, he was nervous and not sleeping well.

Two days after arriving, he had gone shopping for a car and had found one on a used car lot. An old Ford Focus, cheap and very common. The next thing he did was a little covert night shopping. He had driven to a nearby junk yard, slipped through the gate, and stolen a set of license plates. He wasn't sure why but thought they might come in handy.

These were not the kind of things Colorado had ever engaged in before. He was a successful businessman before he had retired and took up his life a sailor, but these were unusual circumstances that demanded unusual actions. Murder his friend, injure another, run him out of town. Maybe it was time he took some matters into his own hands. He determined to run and hide only so far.

Sheriff Ben was frustrated. After hours of questioning Little Joe and Fred, he had gotten very little. Both were street hardened and life hardened. The closing of the chemical plant had the effect of making them feel they had very little to hang on for. They were not one bit intimated by the Sheriff and his detectives asking questions about the mugging of Apple. Time and again they were questioned about who was behind the trashing of Apple's truck and the severe beating they gave App. But they held fast to their answer of "I don't know what you are talking about." They stuck to this answer even when they were told about the witnesses.

The Sheriff had done all the things right. He had separated them immediately, trying to get one of them to spill the beans, but no go. They were both holding to their story of knowing nothing.

Sheriff Ben was grateful he had a fall back plan. He had two eye witnesses. Big Henry had watched the two as they tore the pickup truck apart, and Apple could identify both as his assailants. They were guilty and Sheriff Ben knew it, but he would like to have them confess.

He knew they were aware of details about the shady deals coming out of the Filbin/Santiago office. They would not, in all probability, know in depth operations, but they would know enough for him to pick up the pair and question them, perhaps even bring some charges. Sheriff Ben had suspected they were guilty of several charges. At the very least, he felt strongly they were cheating their union brothers, the very ones they were supposed to be looking out for.

Little Joe and Fred, in all likelihood, would make bail tomorrow. The Sheriff did not suspect another attack on Apple because they were trying to intimidate, not shut him up forever., Nevertheless he was a little concerned about it.

He was mulling over a couple of unorthodox ideas about how to ensure Apple's safety, but he suspected Apple would never go for it. He intended to offer Apple a nice place to sleep at the jail, just for a few days. They had a clean but simple room for the officers held over in the evening, on call, to sleep. He could offer this to Apple. He doubted anyone would be so foolish as to attack him at the jail. He had two more ideas. App could come spend a couple of days at his house. He would not be there much of the time, but his wife, Ronnie was more than capable of watching over him. Apple would probably reject that too. But the Sheriff had one more idea up his sleeve. He was certain Maggie would agree to take him for a few days. He felt sure Apple would agree to that. Who wouldn't? The only problem was that Maggie would be gone during the daytime, much of the time. She could be there at night, but she was needed at the Sheriff's office. Perhaps he could spare her a few days. He would run it by Apple and Maggie.

Chapter 26
A NEW DR. DUKE

It was ten o'clock in the morning on his third day of his stay at Hermann Memorial. He was very sore but sitting up and eating on his own. He was delighted that he could make his way to the bathroom without help. Those first two days were the worst. He had to have help going to the bathroom, eating, and sponge baths. App would have been humiliated if he had not felt so bad. But, today was better. His left jaw was extremely sore, but he had still managed to eat a little oatmeal and drink a cup of coffee.

Bernie was there, and they were chatting easily about a few things, but mostly about work at the office. Bernie was most interested in what he was going to do now. She knew him well enough to know that very soon he would be back to his old self, and then the gloves would come off with BAR Chem. Apple had expressed his one goal - to find out who had murdered Beer Can Billy. Now he was more determined than ever. Now, since his attack, things were personal.

Bernie couldn't wait. She knew Apple was one of the best in the business, that he would know the facts before making blind accusations, but as soon as he was on his feet, the action would begin. He had an ability to really hold people's feet to the fire when he got going. BAR Chem and the ACW didn't know it, but their feet were inching closer to the fire.

Apple had investigated a lot of things over his time at the paper, but not murder cases. Bernie almost felt sorry for whoever would get in his sights. He looked a little young and naive, but that was all outward appearance. She knew the resolve and keep pushing attitude he had on the inside. Bernie thought this might be an exciting ride.

More than that, Mr. Barton was anxious to get this show on the road. He was still angry that M. Ellis Winston had tried to pay him off to get him to pull back the paper's reporting on the company's affairs. Mr. Barton could sense that BAR Chem had something in the works and did not need the Houston Announcer doing stories on their actions. BAR Chem needed their support, but that didn't seem likely.

Mr. Barton was unaware of Apple's suspicions that the company was looking at a return to the Gulf Coast. Everyone would actually welcome that, under the right circumstances, but not extortion and bribery to get a favorable outcome. Mr. Barton did not know why the ACW union had gotten so upset with App that they felt it necessary to beat him so severely. He was unaware of Apple's suspicion that Filbin and Santiago were on the take from the company, but he knew Apple would get to the bottom of it. Rest assured.

A rapid knock on the door, and Dr. Duke strode in. "How you feeling today? Better, huh?"

Apple told the doctor he was feeling much better, just very sore.

Every time Bernie saw the young doctor, she was amazed at how much he favored his famous uncle. The red mustache and the sandy, unruly hair were all present. He even had that same voice.

Bernie wondered if he had the same presence of self. She was remembering some years ago when the University of Texas Health Science Center at Houston made a name change. Not a big change, but almost like the old saying, "Do something, even if it's wrong."

The change was in the simple statement, The University of Texas, Houston Health Science Center. Moving the word Houston was not something the elder Dr. Duke approved of, so on his daily syndicated television segment, he said, as always, The University of Texas Health Science Center, at Houston. This infuriated the new president, but even though the signage changed, Dr. Duke did not. Bernie thought an amusing antidote. She wondered, "Does this new Dr. Duke have the same stuff?"

Houston needed a new Dr. Duke.

"I'm going to release you. Just take it very easy for a while, and come back in a week to have the stitches removed. It's been a pleasure treating you, but I recommend no more street brawling for a while. Got any questions?"

Apple did have a couple questions, "Will these nasty scars ever fade?"

"Well bubba, don't get impatient. It will take about a year, and they will diminish a bit, but they will never totally go away. Shoot, they give you a sort of intrigue. Anyway, the ladies will love 'em. I took a lot of time and sewed them real tight and close together so they will heal as good as anyone could expect. Taking care of the back of your head for right now is real important. Don't do anything risky for a while, and the hair will grow back soon. Wear a ball cap for a while, and no one will notice."

Apple had only one more. "How are my back and kidneys doing?"

"Just take care to take it easy," said Dr. Duke, "No

weight lifting. And if blood should appear in your urine, come in to see me right away, night or day. Otherwise, you're good to go."

"Doc, I am grateful to you. How about dinner sometime?"

"I might just take you up on that someday."

Bernie asked, "Any special diet or anything like that?" The answer was no, regular food and drink. Taking it easy was the only special need.

And with that said, the Doc exited.

Bernie said, "Get dressed, in the field reporter, and let's get out of here. We got stuff to do."

Some stuff Bernie was thinking about was assigning someone to do a story on the new, young, Dr. Duke. That would be a hell of a human interest story. She would bet not much of Houston knew of this new doc in the trauma unit. They would soon, and the Houston Announcer would be the first to bring it to them.

Apple pulled on an old faded pair of Levis with more difficulty than he had thought. He hadn't considered how it would feel to cover the still sore area on his right hip. It hurt a bit and he complained to Bernie. Not much outward sympathy there. Next he slipped on a favorite, very soft Astros jersey with Ryan on the back, his good luck shirt. No problem there.

"Alright associate editor, let's get outta here. Not that I won't miss the old hospital food."

Bernie said, "After you, my friend." With that App slumped himself carefully into a waiting wheel chair, manned by a very friendly staff member. He was sure he could make it by himself. He had been exercising a bit to keep his legs limbered, but was informed hospital rules stated every exiting patient was wheeled to their car.

They crossed through the big glass doors and onto the sidewalk. Apple was momentarily blinded by the bright sunshine, having been inside for three full days. He shaded his eyes for a full minute as he was wheeled down a lane in the parking lot. He wondered why. Most patients were picked up at the door.

Then he spotted a familiar face. And then another. Very strange he thought, the parking lot is full of people I know. There was Mr. Barton, and Maggie from the Sheriff's department, and Sheriff Ben, himself. Several co-workers from the Houston Announcer were there also. They were all smiling.

As Apple and Bernie moved closer, he got a peek past the small crowd and saw a bright red bow on the hood of a pickup truck. The pickup looked very much like his old truck, but that could not be since the last time he saw his, it had four flat tires and a broken windshield. Then Bernie stepped forward and said, "Your fans await, boy reporter."

By now, people passing by were slowing to see what the crowd was about. Mr. Barton extended his hand, opened the passenger door and said, "We wanted to show how happy we are at your recovery. We decided to chip in and get your old truck fixed up a bit." Apple thought the old hardback might cry for a moment.

Apple couldn't believe it, new upholstery, new tires, new paint, new dashboard, practically a new vehicle. He was very touched.

He looked over at Sheriff Ben, "And I wanted to drive the patrol car a while longer. After all I didn't get to do it much before."

Sheriff Ben said, "No can do. You might be bad luck to the department," smiling as he talked.

"She looks better than new."

Maggie came forward and kissed him on the cheek, "When am I getting my dinner?"

After thanks and gratitude all the way round, Apple inched into the passenger side, and with Bernie behind the wheel, they drove away toward Apple's apartment.

Apple, still touched, asked, "How did you get this thing patched up like this? It was totally wrecked when I left it at Big Henry's on the Galveston Causeway."

"Turns out Sheriff Ben knows every garage and mechanic in Galveston county. Most of the work was donated by friends you don't even know. The paint work is so fresh, they recommended we let it dry for one more day before we drove it, but as you can see, we didn't take their advice."

"It looks so good. I am touched."

"Actually, it was Maggie's idea, and Sheriff Ben arranged for all the work. The guys at the office pitched in and paid for parts that were not donated. Pretty good job, huh?"

The phone was ringing when Bernie and Apple opened the door to his apartment. He ignored the message light blinking on his house phone. "Bernie, will you pick up the phone?" Apple had quickly made his way to his favorite recliner and had slumped back into a comfortable position. "I don't want to talk to anyone. Well, maybe the President, Mr. Barton, or maybe Jeffrey Chung Dearcorn, heck, I'll even talk to Bettis Tom."

"How about Sheriff Ben, because that's who is calling."

Apple took the phone. "I am sorry to be calling so soon, but I have a couple of proposals for you," said Sheriff Ben, "You up to hearing them?"

"Fire away, Sheriff." Apple quickly grinned to himself, thinking maybe he shouldn't suggest to a fellow wearing a gun to fire away.

Apple said, "Right now I am open to proposals. I know! You want to give me back my patrol car."

"No," said the Sheriff, "I don't think you're gonna drive one of my cars anytime soon. You can't keep away from the lights and siren. Listen, here are my thoughts. By the way, the Mayor asked me yesterday if you were really driving one of our patrol cars."

"Really? What did you tell him?"

"I told him no, that the car was parked when you were attacked. But I did remind him that the car might have well saved your life."

"Thanks for the loaner, I'm grateful. Also for the restoration job on my pickup."

"Speak no more of it. It was fun rounding up all the help, and the truck looks great. No?"

Apple was beginning to wonder what the Sheriff had called about when Sheriff Ben said, "I just want to let you know that Little Joe and Fred are out on bail. I don't think you are in any danger. I believe they just wanted to give you a little heads up about poking into their affairs."

Apple said, "They could have just sent me a letter."

"Here's the deal. Since you might need a little help getting about, come to the office, I have a room you could stay in until you are back in the swing of things."

"You want me to come to the jail and stay? Are you sure Little Joe is finished with me?"

"Yes on both accounts."

"I would have to decline on that offer, but thanks."

"I knew you would not be very eager to come here, so here is my counter. How about coming to my house for a few days?"

"I'm sure Ms. Rodriguez would love that idea," responded Apple.

"I've talked to her and she is rather excited about it."

"Sorry, Sheriff, but I think recuperating at my own home is best. But how about when I am up and around, inviting me to dinner at your house? Then Ms. Rodriguez will be glad she didn't have me underfoot. What else you got on your mind?"

"Just one other idea. How about going to Maggie's for a few days, until you are able to go to the grocery and things like that."

"Now there is an idea that is very tempting. How does Maggie feel about that?"

"She was pleased. The only problem is she is gone for most of the day, and you would be there alone."

"No, but that is a great offer. I'll phone her myself and tell her, but I must still decline. Are you sure Little Joe and Fred are no problem?"

"No problem. Let me know how you're getting along? Too bad you're not up to it yet. Commander Johnson and I are meeting at his office tomorrow morning for coffee and to discuss what to do about the "Chump Change". We still think we should pay a visit to her."

Apple mused to himself about the turnaround in his and the Sheriff's relationship. Not long ago, Sheriff Ben was ordering him to butt out. Now he was being invited for coffee to discuss a murder investigation.

Chapter 27
COLORADO BILLY AND LITTLE JOE MEET

Colorado Billy was restless, but he waited until about four o'clock in the afternoon, then pointed his new, old Ford Focus toward San Leon. He wasn't sure why, but he stowed his .45 in the trunk along with a three foot piece of iron rod, the kind used in reinforcing concrete.

Colorado drove up Highway 288 through Angleton, turned east and headed down state Highway 6 towards the Gulf Freeway. He intended to intersect the freeway near the foot of the Galveston Causeway. He knew where Big Henry's Bait and Beer was located. It was a good boat launch that was popular with local fishermen.

Big Henry's sat on a little jut of land protruding into the marshy, salt grass landscape that was familiar up and down the Texas Gulf coastline. Colorado Billy had actually been here, he remembered, two times in the past. He had been here with a friend fishing. They had launched their small aluminum fishing boat at Big Henry's.

Colorado Billy and Beer Can Billy had enjoyed a cold beer at Big Henry's on their way to meet friends on Seawall Boulevard for dinner. They were early and decided to kill a little time at Big Henry's. He smiled as he thought of Beer Can Billy having a little fun at Big Henry's expense when he asked him why they called him Big Henry. Big Henry had answered with, "Just part of my name, I guess."

He remembered how Beer Can had looked at him with this big, stupid grin and said, "He didn't even get it, just part of my name, he answered."

Colorado Billy thought of reminding Beer Can not to push the big guy too far. He was a giant of a man.

Now as he sat alone at the long bar drinking a cold long neck, thinking of Beer Can's murder and the beating that his new friend, Apple, had received from someone. Perhaps the murderer had sat at this same bar. Colorado felt the back of his neck turning red from anger.

Big Henry approached and asked, "How about another one, my friend?"

"Sure, why not?"

Big Henry brought the beer over to Colorado, and Colorado asked him, rather casually, "Say, do you know my friend called Little Joe? I heard he had a scrape with Sheriff Ben Rodriguez. Heard about that?"

"Sure, I know Little Joe." Then in Big Henry's simple way said, "Don't like him much. You say he's a friend of yours?"

"Well, not very, but I just wanted to ask him how the jail over at Kemah treated him. You seen him around today?"

"Not today. Most of the boys are over at Jerry's on San Leon today. Jerry has happy hour all day today. This is Thursday, right?"

Colorado sat drinking his second beer and thinking. He knew Jerry's was over at San Leon. No more than a 20 minute drive from here. He decided to drive on over there and see what this guy looked like. And think some more about what he should do.

Bernie sat at her laptop. Perched on her desk was a note pad with a few scribbled notes about the short piece Mr. Barton had directed her to submit for the late edition. The article was to describe Apple's release from the hospital and a short description of his stay at Hermann Hospital.

She wanted to mention the young Dr. Duke and his excellent treatment of Apple Smith. But, she was to focus on the two characters that were arrested and released on bail for the assault of App. She wanted to be factual, but not specific, about their connection to the "Chump Change", the union, and through those to BAR Chem.

Bernie supposed her article was a sort of teaser for Apple's soon to appear series about his beating, his ongoing investigation of BAR Chem's move, and their desire to return. He would be connecting more and more of his investigation on Beer Can's murder and how the dots were pointing to the mystery movements of the "Chump Change."

Mr. Barton had told her to be hard hitting, up to a point. He wanted to "turn the heat up on all those characters." He wanted the article short, and to set the scene for Apple's upcoming series of articles.

The story she finished for print did just that. She was well aware of Bettis Tom, M. Ellis Winston, and the boss himself, Jeffery Chung Dearcorn. She was satisfied at what she had done. The stage was set for Apple's return in the next few days.

Colorado Billy sat at the end of the bar at Jerry's. From this vantage point he could see everyone that came through the front entrance way. He sat high enough to scan the entire place. Colorado could see most of the folks on the veranda enjoying the view across Galveston Bay.

His eye was drawn across the room to the tables near the opposite end of the bar. A group of five or six men were sitting and standing around, easily joking and enjoying a cold beer after a day's work. They looked like men he thought would be the kind that Little Joe might be a part of. Not too rough, but not polished. If he or Fred were not a part of this group, they might know of them since this was one of their regular watering holes.

Colorado wasn't sure he would recognize Fred as easily as he would Little Joe. Little Joe stood out in a crowd because of his diminutive size. For all he knew, Fred might be one of the guys already here.

As he sat nursing a beer, he wondered how long he should pursue this vigil and what he would do if either Little Joe or Fred showed up tonight.

He did not have to think about it long because there he was. It had to be Little Joe. Colorado Billy recognized him as one of the characters he had seen hanging around the "Chump Change," the sharp facial features. His eyes were set very close together and far back into his face. He had a light complexion, and of course his short height made him stand out.

Another man that Colorado thought had to be Fred Frederickson entered a bit behind Little Joe. Both strolled over to the edge of the group already gathered at the far end of the bar, picking a table nearby. One or two of the men nodded, and one walked over and shook hands with the pair.

They quickly had beers in their hands and began conversing together. Colorado moved down to the middle of the bar. He was so close he could hear mumbling, but not intelligible voices.

Colorado had been on his hunt for about four hours and was growing tired. Perhaps he should call this whole thing off. Maybe it was foolhardy to have a gun and a metal rod in his car. What was he going to do with them?

Then he heard a voice call out from the group, "Hey Little Joe, how did Rodriguez treat you at the jail?" All the guys got a chuckle out of this. Colorado Billy did not know if they were razzing Little Joe and Fred in good sport, or was there something deeper going on.

Little Joe got up from his seat, and with a grin, walked over to the table. Colorado could now hear clearly, "Someday that Sheriff is going to cross the line. Maybe he will get beat next election."

"Yeah, well I heard Big Henry had something to say about it."

"Everybody knows Big Henry hasn't the sense of a mule, he didn't see anything. That Sheriff had no business treating us like suspects in anything."

Colorado had enough beer for one day. He decided to go to his car in the parking lot, position it at the entrance, and try to identify the cars Little Joe and Fred were driving. His idea was to wait until they left for the evening, if he could stay awake that long.

Colorado was ready to call it a day and give up his chase when Little Joe emerged from the doorway and strode into the parking lot. He was alone. Colorado had hoped that they were together and he could, so to speak, kill two birds with one stone. But, he was grateful that one of them was making a move.

Little Joe walked toward an old beat up Chevy pickup, opened the door and got in. Colorado's plan was to follow him home, just see what the lay of the land was, then go home and think of what his next move would be.

Little Joe moved onto the roadway at a slow pace and headed towards the end of the peninsula, Eagle Point. "Damn!" said Colorado. There sat a County Sheriff's car on the side of the road, obviously watching for speeding traffic, or fellows who'd had one too many, on their way home from the ice house. That would be just his luck, Little Joe would be pulled over and taken to jail once again. What if the patrolman pulled them both over for driving too slow, and they spent the night in the same jail cell?

He was in luck, Little Joe passed by without incident, still driving 32 miles an hour. After about five minutes, he pulled into the front of a run down, small, paint-weathered, wood framed house, perched on cinder building blocks. The place appeared to be abandoned. Overgrown oleanders blocked the sides of the house. Only the porch and doorway were accessible.

Colorado Billy was following Little Joe about 500 feet behind. He doused his headlights, and creeping along very slowly, moved onto the grassy shoulder of the road, coming to a stop.

Without thinking, Colorado quickly opened the door and moved to the rear of his car, eased the trunk lid opened and grabbed the iron rod. He was watching Little Joe fumbling in his pocket for the front door key. If the door was not locked, he would have been inside, but the door was shut firmly, and he needed the key.

As Little Joe was standing in the dark on his front porch, he suddenly was startled. He felt the end of something extremely hard pushing on his back, under his shoulder blades. Little Joe said, "If you're trying to rob someone, you're out of luck. I've only got about ten dollars in my wallet."

The voice he heard sounded very common, almost as if he had heard it before, "I'm not after money, Little Joe, I've come for revenge."

The first thing Little Joe thought about was Apple

Smith, the reporter, but he somehow knew it wasn't him, that wouldn't be his style, besides he was still more than likely in the hospital. He had heard that the reporter had become pretty good friends with several at the Sheriff's office. Could it be one of the deputies?

Colorado's voice told Little Joe, "Stand still, and don't turn around. If you move I will bust your head open."

Little Joe wasn't much concerned with the rod in his back. He was thinking, is this guy holding a gun in his other hand?"

"Alright buddy, I'm standing still, what do you want? I'm sure we can work this out."

Colorado said, "I want you to tell me where the baseball bat is you beat the reporter with, and I want to know why you murdered Beer Can Billy down on the pier."

"What are you talking about? I don't know any Beer Can, although I like his name. Are you sure you got the right guy?"

Colorado had been extremely nervous driving down the road following Little Joe and was shaking when he was getting the rod out of the trunk of the Ford, but now he had regained the calm demeanor that was his hallmark. He was blinded with anger, more than nervous. He was remembering his buddy, Beer Can.

Colorado quickly moved the iron rod back about four inches and hit Little Joe sharply on the right ear. Blood started running down the back of his neck. "I got the right guy, now where is the ball bat?"

Little Joe said, "I don't know what you are talking about."

Colorado jabbed the rod into the middle of his back so hard it moved Little Joe forward where he hit the front door. "I want to hear from you why you murdered Beer Can," at the same time he hit Little Joe across the back of the head, blood instantly poured from the two inch cut.

Quick as a cat, Little Joe moved to his left side, turned and faced Colorado Billy. In his right hand he was now holding a baseball bat that he had picked up as he turned around. He drew back the bat, and at the same instant Colorado swung with all his might at the bat. He caught the bat in the middle, and broke it in half. A wooden baseball bat might be made of hickory, but that will not stop a three quarter inch reinforcing rod.

Little Joe never had a chance. Colorado had the element of surprise on his side, and he had been an Army Ranger as a young man. He knew how to take a man down.

The next move caught Little Joe under the left rib cage, and he crumpled to the floor of the porch. As he was struggling to keep consciousness, Colorado kicked him squarely in the face. Colorado was wearing sneakers so the kick did not have the same effect as Apple's kick in the face with leather shoes, but nevertheless, Little Joe fell on his face quivering. Colorado Billy administered a few more kicks to the rib cage, turned Little Joe over and kicked him in the face several times. He wanted Little Joe to bear scars so that his friends could see how he had been beaten. Maybe before roughing up someone else, like Apple, they would know there were consequences.

Little Joe lay on the floor, very still, his face was a mess, but he would live through it.

Colorado picked up the two pieces of baseball bat and quickly made his way to his parked car.

Chapter 28
THINGS EVEN OUT

Apple awoke around six o'clock, feeling sore, but otherwise pretty good. After swinging his feet around to the side of the bed, he stood up. The bump on the back of his head hurt. He walked to the bathroom, flipped on the lights, and stood looking in the mirror at this beaten face. Not too bad for someone with nearly 40 stitches. He needed a shave, tricky on the left side. He would have to stay away from his wound.

After a rather slow shave, he was feeling even better. App was wondering what he would do today when it suddenly hit him, why not drive over to the Coast Guard station where the Sheriff was having coffee with Commander Johnson? He felt he was up to that. They would be discussing what to do about the "Chump Change."

He didn't want to miss any of that. Then he would come back to his apartment, organize his thoughts about his next article for the paper. He needed to get busy. This story was now turned upside down. His series needed to be hard-hitting, factual, and now sooner, rather than later. No time like the present to get started.

He walked into the kitchen where a note was laying on the counter. It read, "Sorry my friend, had to get to work, Bernie." Apple realized that Bernie had spent the night in the spare bedroom. He was immediately touched by her concern. He would definitely have to do something for her, and soon.

Apple ate a banana for breakfast, and a little coffee, then returned to the bedroom. He selected a very old pair of khaki pants, and a rather worn, soft, button up dress shirt. He needed the comfort of easy wearing clothing until the bruises on his hip and back faded a bit more. After slipping on a pair of old leather loafers, without socks, he opened the front door and walked outside for the first time in several days. He was thinking, what a great day to be alive. He eased into the driver's side of his pickup, paused a minute, opened the door, swung his feet outside, then slowly walked around his repaired Ford. He hadn't appreciated what a fine job someone had done on fixing up his wheels. He did now. Amazingly the old truck looked better than it had before it was vandalized by Little Joe and Fred. He wondered if he would have to testify at their trial. He thought, "It'll be my pleasure."

He rolled out on the Gulf Freeway and pointed south for the 40 minute drive to Galveston and the Coast Guard station. He hoped Sheriff Ben and Commander Johnson were still on for coffee. He was sure he would arrive just after they had their first sip.

Apple was thinking about how good his old truck was running and how great the new upholstery felt to the touch when he drove by Dot's Diner at 65 miles an hour. He began to rethink that night. How did Arnost fit into this whole affair? Maybe not at all, other than having a job with Bettis Tom on the yacht. It could be more important to find out what M. Ellis Winston was doing having coffee with the Mayor of Houston. They could just be old friends, or maybe that acquaintance was very important. Apple knew he needed to start finding some answers.

As he passed Big Henry's he smiled as he thought about how sensitive Filbin and Santiago were about some simple questions asked to clarify how the union's money was spent. He knew in his heart they were cheating the members. Apple knew when this was exposed, union members would be grateful. His charges were not against the ACW, they were against their local leadership. Truly, Randy Filbin and Mario Santiago are the scabs.

App had been driving for about 30 minutes, and he was still admiring his new truck. If he maintained his posture and stayed off his right hip, he felt no pain. Movement to his right still caused pain, so he favored his left as much as possible. He pulled down the sun visor and took a good look at his face in the mirror attached there. The swelling and the discoloration had reduced greatly. The stitches were very prominent. Anyone looking at his face would notice the trauma that had recently occurred there. But, all in all, he was looking and feeling well.

He passed through the gate at the Coast Guard station on the little jut of land on the east end of Galveston Island, and noticed the Sheriff's police cruiser parked directly in front, in a no parking zone. Rank had its privileges. Apple thought about the trip to Dot's with the Sheriff doing almost 90 on the Gulf Freeway, and smiled. He thought about how many times he had seen a police car with no emergency lights zipping down a street at breakneck speed and wondered where he was going so fast.

As he slowly made his way across the foyer towards the Commander's office, several coasties noticed, and from the other side of the room a familiar booming voice said, "Mr. Smith." Apple knew immediately it was Chief Petty Officer Decks. There stood Chief Decks, big and burly, leading a small dog that looked like the small image of the

Chief. The dog had a big head, straight, small black eyes that said, "I'm little but think twice."

"Hey there, Chief. What gives with the doggy?" Decks grinned, and said, "Trifle with this hombre at your own risk. Stormin' Normin' just lets me tag along." He explained that this little guy was the number one drug sniffing dog on the entire coast. He was in fact a miniature Bull Terrier. Tough looking little guy, but small. Not to be confused with his much larger cousin.

As he walked nearer, he was getting a better look on the damage to App's face and whistled through his teeth, "I heard about your brush with bandits. How ya doing?"

Apple assured the Chief that he was feeling pretty good. Chief Decks opened the door to Commander Johnson's office and said, "Commander, look what the dogs drug in!"

There sat Sheriff Ben. When he turned to see what the Chief was talking about, his jaw dropped to his chest. "Well, I'll be, you're looking well, Apple. How you feel? The last time I saw you, you weren't doing so good. Great to see you up and about."

After handshakes all around, and Commander Johnson poured him a cup of hot coffee, they all sat down. "Hang around, Chief, I want you to hear this." The Commander was friendly to all his crew, especially this experienced Chief Petty Officer. He practiced treating his men with respect, and they in turn did a good job. Makes everyone happy.

The four of them discussed what to do about the "Chump Change." After talking about his ideas of smuggling and secret passageways and storage areas, Apple was mostly silent and listened. Besides his face was stinging a bit, and his hip was hurting. He was beginning to think that perhaps he had rushed into this trip too soon.

About 30 minutes into their conversation, the Sheriff's cell began to ring, and he said, "I hate to answer this. Every time I am with Mr. Smith, it is bad news," spoken in jest. "Sheriff Ben here."

The Sheriff listened briefly and said, "What the hell are you telling me? You sure you got the address right? Is an ambulance on the way?"

Apple and Commander Johnson were in the dark. They figured the call was a routine Sheriff's Department emergency call until Sheriff Ben said, "Apple, you interested in coming along? This might be a call that will be very unexpected, but never the less involve you. Johnny, you too might be surprised. You're welcome to ride along."

"What is it Ben? I am looking at a full calendar this afternoon, you're gonna have to be more specific. Besides I have seen enough of your calls to satisfy me for a while. Can I take a pass on this?"

"Sure Johnny, it might not be anything of interest to the Coast Guard at all. Just a hunch, that's all. But you Apple, you've gotta go, or you will not be a happy man tomorrow if you miss this."

Apple said, "Count me in. How could I refuse after that come on?"

With that they jumped into the Sheriff's cruiser. This time Sheriff Ben turned on the lights and the siren. Apple said, "Alright Sheriff, what gives?"

Sheriff Ben explained that it might all just be a wild goose chase, but if not Apple would be very interested. Ben was sure it would make a good story for the newspaper.

The cars on the freeway were parting and moving over as the lights on the cruiser did their work. They were headed north towards San Leon. At this rate they would be there in about 15 minutes.

Apple was very curious, but thought it would be a routine drug bust or a serious auto accident. He doubted that it would be as interesting as the Sheriff made out.

They darted down a couple of small asphalt roads at 50 miles an hour. Apple noted the paradox of the small frame houses on one side of the road, and on the waterfront, million dollar properties. At the far end of one of the roads, Apple could see emergency lights flashing.

As they pulled to a stop in the middle of the road, Sheriff Ben spoke, "If this is who they tell me it is, you're gonna be shocked, so be ready. Pay good attention to the identity."

The Sheriff walked at a much faster pace to the front porch of the house than Apple could manage. Apple saw the Sheriff arrive at the front door of the house, stop, stand gazing briefly, then go down on one knee as he talked to one of the emergency ambulance crew.

Apple could see a man lying on the wooden porch. Blood was dried under his head as if he had been in that position for a while.

Sheriff Ben said to Apple, "Recognize that man?"

Apple, in his job had seen many knifings, shooting, and horrific auto accidents, so he was not squeamish when it came to blood. "No, not really."

"Walk around to this side and take a good look. Now who is it?"

Apple said, "Well, I'll be, I think it is Little Joe. Is he still alive?"

"Yes, but he is in bad shape. Seems to have been lying here for several hours. The lab people can take samples and put a good time frame on it. Someone has beaten him right to the edge. His wallet is unbothered, so robbery doesn't seem to be a motive."

Apple couldn't believe his eyes. Here on the front porch of his house is the man who, several days ago had no mercy on him with his ball bat. Now someone had returned the favor.

Apple backed away off the porch into the yard and stood there almost dumfounded with surprise. Then it came to him, "Will they think I had anything to do with this?" He knew that Bernie had stayed at his house last night, and she would vouch for his whereabouts. Anyway, no one in their right mind would look at him and think he had the strength to do this.

"What do you think happened?" he asked the Sheriff when he walked over and stood beside him.

"It's hard to figure. Little Joe is always into something. I have arrested him several times for this type of violence. Maybe someone thought it was time to get even. You can fill in the script. Joe deals crystal from time to time, and that is a rough crowd. Perhaps he did not pay his supplier on time. Could be almost anything. I'll know more later today. After he gets medical attention, I will be asking him some questions."

Apple said, "Well I would like to get even, but this is not my style. I feel almost sorry for him."

The Sheriff grinned, "This is as good a time as any. Where were you last night?"

"Home. I have a witness. You're kidding, right?"

"Had to ask. I mean you just got out of the hospital yesterday where this guy put you. Who would have more of a reason to beat the tar out of Little Joe than you? Rest easy, I know you didn't do this. You didn't, did you?" Sheriff Ben was joking with Apple about this.

"Then you're sure he is not going to die?"

"The medics say no. He will make it."

"I am glad," said Apple.

Colorado Billy sat alone in the cockpit of his boat, docked at the Freeport City Marina. He was drinking a cold Budweiser, thinking of the events of last night. He was sure he had not killed Little Joe, but knew he had dealt him a severe beating. Instead of feeling remorse about it, he felt rather satisfied. He was glad that he had stopped running and now felt more in control of his own destiny.

Of course he could not come forward and admit what he had done. Colorado had made sure to put the real license plates back on the little Ford. Colorado also had a recent haircut. His long shoulder length hair was now up over his ears. The hipster hair was now gone. He, in fact now looked much like a middle aged businessman.

Earlier this morning, Colorado had driven to the Freeport channel jetty, carrying the steel rod that he had given the severe beating to Little Joe with. He had walked to the end of the jetty and tossed the rod as far into the channel as he could. He was certain no one had seen him, nor would anyone ever find it. Even if they did, there was no way to connect it to him. He was certain that no one had noticed him, but he was going to take every precaution to keep it that way.

His next step was to figure how he would get the broken ball bat to the Sheriff without casting doubt on himself. The stains on the bat had to be blood from Apple's beating, or with luck, even Beer Can's. He would have to think about that a while. He couldn't just walk into the station and give them the bat. And he couldn't just place it at their door because they would surely have surveillance cameras placed about the police station.

Colorado was sure the bat had been used against

Apple, and may have been the weapon that had struck the fatal blow to Beer Can Billy.

Now that he had taken action, it would be easier next time. Fred Frederickson didn't know it, but as Gus put it, "The wrath of the Lord is about to descend upon him." Colorado Billy knew where to locate Fred. He only needed to hang out at Jerry's Ice House and he will eventually show up.

Suddenly, an idea came to him. Now Colorado Billy knew how to get the bat into the hands of the Sheriff. He felt good. Today he would relax. Tomorrow he would begin to figure out exactly how to handle Fred. Colorado Billy smiled.

WILLIAM WARREN

Chapter 29
MAGGIE IS ON THE CASE

Apple rode over to the Sheriff's Department with Sheriff Ben since his pickup had been left at the Coast Guard Station. Maybe he could get Maggie to drive him over to retrieve it, then maybe lunch. He felt good about this idea. Maggie was now more intriguing than before since he had found out she was also a police officer. He smiled. Funny how his mind worked.

Apple asked Sheriff Ben what he thought about the strange turn of events they had just witnessed.

"You know Mr. Smith," Sheriff Ben always returned to Apple's formal name when the talk turned serious, "Ever since I met you, things going on make no sense. And I am no closer to a solution than I was in the beginning."

Apple said, "Do you think this incident with Little Joe is somehow related to John Bishop or Beer Can Billy?"

"It's hard to say, the only thing connecting them together seems to be the "Chump Change", and that is very loose."

Apple agreed, "Somehow, the yacht has to turn up. Then you can search it for some clues."

"What kind of clues? We're looking for murders here. Smuggling is serious, but I don't see how that translates to murder."

Apple quickly, and with some emphasis, replied, "If

say, perhaps cocaine, meth, or any number of other illegal substances are discovered, then maybe that will lead to a motive for murder."

"What else?"

"There could be any number of things going on. Maybe they are just laundering money, very large sums of money. The Caymans are very close to the route the "Chump Change" travels often. They could be connected to the Mexican drug cartels in some way. Remember, if my hunch is right, we are dealing with some very powerful people."

Sheriff Ben said, "Maybe, and if you are correct, they are operating here within a few miles of my office. And, have been doing it right before my eyes, and I haven't a clue. Think I can get reelected?"

"Well, I don't know, Maggie might be some tough competition."

"Yeah, I know, but lucky for me she says she is a few years away."

Apple asked the Sheriff, "How about this Little Joe thing? What do you think is happening there?"

"Oh by the way, I have assigned your pal Maggie to investigate Little Joe's beating. She is very good, and believe it, every dot will be accounted. She is thorough. She might even have some questions for you, so don't be offended when she comes ringing you up."

"It'll be my pleasure."

"My other investigators are working on Beer Can's as well as John Bishop's murder and are tied up, but we will be coordinating all three incidents together because they seem to be related in some way."

The pair arrived at the Sheriff's Office, and waiting just inside the door was Maggie. Today she was wearing her khaki slacks with a blue blazer. Under the blazer was her service weapon, and attached to the belt was her Sheriff's Department badge.

"Hey guys, heard your coffee time was interrupted. How about a cup now for the road?"

Sheriff Ben replied, "I could use one after this morning. How about you Apple?"

It seemed to Apple that he had been drinking more coffee since his acquaintance with Sheriff Ben.

"Y'all come into my office. Let's discuss this deal with Little Joe."

The three of them settled into his office with their cups of coffee, and Sheriff Ben began with, "Maggie I want you to head up this investigation. It might be very important, and it might just be a mugging or a neighborhood dispute. Apple here thinks it is tied in with John Bishop and William Harrison's murders."

That was the first time since the day Beer Can had been discovered floating in the harbor that Apple had heard him called by his formal name.

Maggie interjected as she turned to Apple, "Since you are so closely tied to Little Joe, do you have any idea who could have done this? I know you were at the union meeting and that Big Henry witnessed Joe and Fred trashing your pickup. Do you recall anyone acting in a strange way towards either one at the meeting?"

The Sheriff said, "See, Apple. I told you she would have some questions for you."

Maggie continued, "I have to ask, even if it sounds preposterous. Were you at your home all of last night?"

Apple turned to face Maggie, reached up with his hand and began to gently rub the stitches in his left cheek. "I was home all night. Bernadette spent the night in the spare bedroom. I've still got the note she left this morning before I awoke."

If Maggie was disturbed by this info, she did not show it. "Good, now we can get on to the important business, which is who beat the hell out of Little Joe? And why?"

Sheriff Ben spoke, "Apple, I can't help but believe your trouble with Little Joe and the events of this morning are connected, and we know that Little Joe and Fred have been seen hanging around the "Chump Change", which, in some loose way ties to our murders, especially Beer Can."

Apple was a little surprised at this quick summation of events. Up until now, he wasn't sure that the Sheriff and his department were up to the task of investigating the murders on Galveston Bay.

The Sheriff continued, "That is why I stated earlier this Little Joe affair could be very important."

Maggie asked Apple, "Do you remember the friend of Beer Can Billy's? I understand that you have met him a couple of times over at the Galveston Yacht Basin. I think he goes by the name of Colorado Billy."

Apple returned, "Yeah, good guy. He told me the murder of Beer Can Billy hit a little close to home."

"Was he frightened? Or how did he react?"

"I think he was scared, but mostly because he didn't feel he could let his guard down. He told me he didn't see anything, but I didn't believe him all the way."

Maggie said, "Do you think you could introduce me to him?"

"Impossible. He left for the deep Caribbean the day after Beer Can was murdered. Wouldn't tell me where he was headed, but my guess is Road Town, Tortola, or Barbados. He had mentioned those two places before, so my guess is he would have struck out for somewhere very familiar to him. Why are you asking about him? I am sure he left for safer waters."

"Well, the way I figure it, he's someone who knows Little Joe did this, and he would have had reason to avenge his friend. Also, when he read the piece about your attack, he might have said enough is enough, and took matters into his own hands."

"That's a good theory. The good avenger, except he is out of the country."

Maggie paused before she said, "Maybe, I wonder."

Sheriff Ben said, "Alright you two, get outta here. We've got work to do. Maggie, how about giving our newspaper friend, alias crime detective, a ride back to his pickup? The two of you can hash this out on the way. Maybe figure out the next step with Little Joe and Colorado Billy.

When they got into Maggie's police cruiser, Apple asked her, "So what's your next move?"

"I intend to interview all of Little Joe and Fred Frederickson's friends and acquaintances. You know all of those fellows that hang around the local beer joints, maybe even Filbin and Santiago."

Apple told her it would really be interesting if the "Chump Change" would return to Galveston. He related his theory about smuggling and secret storage areas onboard the boat.

He asked her, "If the "Chump Change" returned, would you be bold enough to ask Bettis Tom some questions?"

"I'd love to."

"How would Sheriff Ben feel about that?"

"He'd be fine, as long as it was relevant. He would

caution me about hitting too soon with no ideas. You know alert them, or put them to caution."

"Yeah, that makes sense. But maybe it would throw them off their game." Apple was thinking that he himself could ask questions without anyone's permission. That is, if he was willing to take another beating, or worse. Something to think about.

They arrived at the Coast Guard Station. Apple got out at his vehicle and asked Maggie, "How about dinner tonight?"

"That would be nice, if you can keep from getting beat up again."

"How about my apartment? You know, so I don't frighten the patrons away with these awful scars?"

"What a trick. Okay, but I'm gonna bring my gun."

Colorado Billy got into his Ford and pointed it up Highway 288 towards Houston. One hour later and he was in the busy parking lot of UPS on Louisiana Street, downtown Houston. He was wearing a common pull over shirt with large, black frame glasses and an Astros ball cap.

He had wrapped only one of the pieces of baseball bat in plain newspaper and packed it in a shipping box prior to entering the store. He intended to keep the other half of the bat for safety. UPS never loses packages, but he was being sure. He might have to produce the bat later. It was so important. If Little Joe's finger prints were on the bat along with Beer Can's blood, that would be extremely important. He was sure Apple Smith's blood was on the bat.

He shipped the package to the Sheriff's Department, Galveston County, Texas. Two days, and Sheriff Rodriguez would have evidence in his hands. What he did with it then was his responsibility. Colorado Billy felt good about his day's work. He frowned as he contemplated his soon to be encounter with Fred.

WILLIAM WARREN

Chapter 30
BACK TO WORK

Apple awoke early the next day, feeling more sore than the day before when he had shared coffee with the Commander and Sheriff Ben. The excitement and the exertion had made him very tired. Or maybe it was the pain medication Dr. Duke had prescribed. The first thing he had done was spend some time gazing into the mirror, examining the slight bruising remaining from the beating. He was looking closely at the stitches, which would be coming out in a few days. He wondered what the effect on his face would be in six months or a year. He remembered an old friend who had run headlong into a car on his bicycle. Twenty years later and the scars were still prominent on his face. But, Apple smiled, and hoped it would give him the same handsome, rugged appearance it gave his friend.

Bernie had not spent the night. That must be a sign he was recovering nicely. He was happy to be alone, but a little disappointed.

As he was lost in thoughts about his face, the phone began ringing, jostling him back to the moment. He picked up the phone with, "Apple Smith here."

Bernie said, "Nice you are still at home. I came by yesterday, just before noon and you were gone. Where were you when you should have been at home recuperating?"

Apple recounted the events of yesterday, and Bernie

was very interested, from a newspaper point of view. "Since you felt good enough to drive to Galveston, when are you going to start working for your pay again?"

"Soon boss, soon."

"Well, how about today? That is good stuff about Little Joe. Put some ink to paper and get me a story."

Apple said, "My very thought."

Bernie noted, "Things keep happening to you. How do you account for being on the spot when the Sheriff got the call about John Bishop, and Beer Can Billy? And now you just happen to be having coffee with your partners in crime, Commander Johnson and Sheriff Rodriguez when Little Joe gets beat half to death. So you are the first on the scene again. Are you sure you're not the the Good Avenger?"

"Just my reporter's instinct, I guess."

Bernie said, "I'll bet that person Maggie is somewhere involved too."

Apple laughed, "How did you know? Sheriff Ben assigned her to investigate Little Joe's problem."

"I'll just bet you like that. Seriously Apple, this is good stuff and it just fell into your lap. You can write about most of this from first-hand experience, not from a third party. It don't get no better."

"I'm on it ma'am," and with that they said their good byes. Apple knew he needed to sit down and write a hard-hitting story.

His angle was to begin with John Bishop's murder and continue to Beer Can Billy's. He would emphasize how the "Chump Change" was nearby in each case. Apple was hesitant to spell out Bettis Tom Stovall as the primary captain of the yacht, but he threw caution to the wind and got his name in print. Then he explained how he came to be involved by doing a story on BAR Chemical Company.

Of course the Association of Chemical Manufacturers Workers was involved because they were left without jobs. Apple went into detail about his attendance at the Union meeting. He emphasized that the meeting was open to the public, and he was personally invited by the leadership, that being Randy Filbin and Mario Santiago. The meeting was amiable until he began to ask questions about how the union's money was spent by the aforementioned leadership.

Apple detailed how his truck was vandalized after the meeting. He specifically mentioned Big Henry having eye witnessed the event. He blamed Filbin and Santiago along with Little Joe and Fred. It was written so as to ask for rebuttal from Filbin or Santiago. Apple hoped that maybe they would challenge his accusation in court. He thought, "I would love that." But he knew that would not be forthcoming. He also wished BAR Chem would challenge the story somehow. Getting one of those executives on a witness stand under oath would be exciting. He was sure that would not happen.

Apple continued his story by chronicling his beating at the hands of Little Joe and Fred Frederickson. He pointed out that he recognized both of them from the union meeting. He worried that his detailed description was too graphic, but he felt that was part of the story and went ahead with it. He hoped Bernadette or Mr. Barton would not censor that part out of the story. He did recall Mr. Barton telling him in the hospital to hit them hard when he was able. He hoped Morris's fervor was still that strong.

App finished by writing about the beating incident of Little Joe. He told all of those details from his firsthand witness to the events he had described. He made sure to give plenty of applause to the outstanding job done by everyone at Sheriff Ben's department. He mentioned Detective Maggie Stosselberg as the lead investigating Little Joe's beating.

He smiled as he used Bernie's description of Little Joe's attacker as the "Good Avenger." He worried that it was beginning to sound a little like Hollywood instead of the hard news that the story really was.

Apple tossed and turned all night. He had spent most of the night thinking about his position and what he should do. He was thinking about the attack on him by Little Joe and Fred, and the subsequent attack on Little Joe. Maybe he should use a little caution about how to proceed. He realized that just one smack by that baseball bat in the wrong place and his life might have ended.

App was certain he was on the right track with Filbin and Santiago, otherwise why such an overreaction? They must surely be taking money from Bar Chem through Bettis Tom. Apple was hitting a little close to home with his questions at the meeting, so Little Joe and Fred were turned loose on him. Little Joe and Fred thought they were just teaching the smart ass a lesson. They would have no idea of the bigger picture.

Chapter 31
DEARCORN IS NERVOUS

Apple picked up his phone, searched the contacts and dialed the number of BAR Chem. When the lady with the pretty voice answered, he said, "Apple Smith with the Houston Announcer calling for Jeffrey Chung Dearcorn." "Hold please." Apple held the phone for a full 20 seconds before he spoke, "Hello Mr. Dearcorn," when he was interrupted by a voice. "This is Mr. Dearcorn's secretary, what can I do for you?"

After a little give and take, Apple was informed that Mr. Dearcorn was in, but his schedule was full for the day. Apple made an appointment for the next day at 11 a.m.

He knew it was brash to call Dearcorn, but perhaps Jeffrey Chung Dearcorn had been reading the paper recently. Maybe he would be curious about what was going on.

Dearcorn keyed his intercom and said, "Get me Ellis Winston and Bettis Tom Stovall in here now!"

It took ten minutes to round up Ellis, and another hour to get Bettis Tom in Dearcorn's office.

As soon as Ellis and Bettis Tom were seated, Ellis could tell that this was no "good ole boy" meeting. Jeffrey Chung Dearcorn was all business, stern, not even an offer for coffee.

He began with, "Ellis, as you know we are in

261

lengthy and serious discussions with Texas about returning some of our operations to Galveston County. And BT, you should know too, and if you don't you should."

Ellis volunteered, "We both are aware. Remember I am the one leading the discussions with the Gulf Coast EPA and all the others in the county for permits and other regulations."

Bettis Tom asked, "What's this got to do with me?"

"We're gonna get to that, hold your horses. Then you both know this Mexico move is not working out very well. Hold on a minute." Dearcorn rang his secretary, "Find out if Roy Jacobs and Everett are in the building, and send them in."

At the mention of Roy Jacobs, Bettis Tom laughed out loud, "If Roy isn't here, check on the "Chump Change." He sees to be making his home there now. I tell you Jeff, his lifestyle and girls and his friends on board all the time are going to get us in trouble."

Ellis asked, "What kind of trouble? What's he doing besides loafing and having a good time?"

"Dearcorn knows what I am talking about."

"Don't tell me. Isn't loafing and having a good time what that yacht is all about?"

In a short time, both Roy Jacobs and Everett McIvoy entered Dearcorn's office. Roy Jacobs was so rich in his own right that he hardly moved too quickly, even for Jeffrery, but McIvoy dropped what he was doing and got there on the double.

"What's this all about?" demanded Roy.

Jeffrey Chung Dearcorn began with explaining that this was an impromptu, but very much off the record, board meeting. No written notes; he even had everyone deposit their cell phones on his desk.

Now the boys assembled knew something big was in the air. He seldom, but not unprecedented, had all the members lay out their phones. Not everything that passed among the board was for outside ears. Not even ears down the hall.

"Everybody shut up, sit down, and listen up!" demanded Dearcorn.

That got everyone's attention. Dearcorn picked up a folded newspaper from the corner of his desk and pointed to the bottom right of the front page. "See this. It is a story about us, an accounting of everything that has happened in recent weeks: the John Bishop affair, the murder of some fellow at the yacht basin, and recently the mugging of some newspaper reporter."

Ellis asked, "So what is the big deal? We have had stories from one source or another since the explosion at the plant."

Roy Jacobs said, "What is the attack on some newspaper guy got to do with us? Specifically me?"

Dearcorn answered, "Are you out of touch with the world, Roy? This is the same reporter that has been asking a lot of questions about our operations. Especially the involvement of the "Chump Change.""

BT wanted to know how this involved the yacht. Dearcorn answered with, "The "Chump Change" has been nearby each time one of these events has happened. The reporter has been asking why. And now he is put into the hospital. Ellis, who are these two guys accused of beating up this reporter fellow, Apple Smith?"

Ellis deferred to Bettis Tom, "They are a couple of guys that are connected to the Union. It seems their union bosses, you are familiar with Filbin and Santiago, use them from time to time to do a little dirty business."

Dearcorn followed up, "Aren't we paying Filbin and Santiago to go along with our plans and to tone down the protests that have plagued us for a number of years?"

BT was now on the spot, and he knew it, "Yes. And they have managed to tone down the noise a bit."

"Then does it follow that in a sense these two thugs are working for us since Filbin and Santiago are on our payroll? And are we in anyway responsible for their actions?"

At this point Ellis spoke up. "We are not responsible for what those two punks do in the dead of the night."

"Don't you get it? Even if legally we are not at fault, think what the publicity would be if it were reported that we have been buying off union leaders. For heaven's sake, beating up a newspaper reporter. That's just about as bad as attacking a police officer. Dumb! Dumb!"

Jeffrey Chung Dearcorn was so upset, he was sputtering. The entire group was holding its collective breath waiting for the next assault.

Bettis Tom spoke. "Alright, Jeff, what do you want done?"

Dearcorn asked, "Who the hell beat this Little Joe character up at his own house? And why? What's going on here?"

"I will have a talk with Randy Filbin, tell him to knock this foolishness off. He'll do what I say, or maybe he will be in Hermann Hospital next."

Ellis said, "Roy, how about staying away from the "Chump Change" for a while? How about doing some work around here for a change?"

Roy Jacobs laughed this off. Jeff Dearcorn then ordered him to stay away from the boat and hang around the office a little more. Present himself as an executive instead of a playboy.

Ellis asked for an update on the state of the company, strictly off the record. Dearcorn gave a loose description of the company's troubles in Mexico and followed with a report on how the Congressional Committee on corporate tax reform was progressing. Dearcorn felt good about the chances of having the laws changed. He was confident that if the country's tax laws were changed, BAR Chem would indeed move back to the U.S. He outlined which Congressmen were lined up with the company's viewpoint, and how effective their lobbying efforts were. He was sure they could overcome the EPA and local officials that were not exactly on board about BAR Chem reoccupying their previous plant sites.

Jeffrey Dearcorn went back to the original reason for the hastily called meeting what is going on with their involvement in the two murders and the beating of the reporter.

He dismissed everyone when he said, "OK, back to whatever you were doing. And I mean it Roy, stay away from the "Chump Change" for a while. Have your parties somewhere else." Jacobs shrugged as he walked out of the office.

"Bettis Tom, stay behind for a few minutes," spoke Jeffrey Chung Dearcorn. The others moved out of the office to resume their duties at the helm of the BAR Chem controls.

Dearcorn told Bettis Tom that he wanted to put more pressure on the Houston Announcer to roll back some of the negative press they were currently writing about. "You know, I sent Ellis to talk to and try to persuade Morris Barton to pull back, but he turned his back on us. I want you to go yourself to see Barton, and this time turn up the pressure. We don't need the stuff he is printing about us."

Bettis Tom asked, "Just how much persuasion do you want me to use?"

"Apply pressure, but don't hurt anyone. We don't need any more of the rough stuff on the editor of the Houston Announcer. Play it cool. Just give him a look at the gun in your belt, sneer a little, but do not get physical. You got that?"

"Money, you want me to use money?"

"No. No money. I doubt if money can move this guy. Ellis offered him plenty. That may be what got him thrown out of Barton's office. No, just turn up the pressure. And, I want some results. But leave Barton and the Smith fellow alone. By the way, just for your knowledge, Mr. Smith is calling on me tomorrow."

"I get it, boss. No money and no rough stuff. I'll talk to Barton."

"Oh, how about coming back to my room." Dearcorn always referred to his inner sanctum as his room. "You got any of the stuff?"

Bettis Tom reached into the front pocket of his jacket and retrieved a small glass vial. He spread the stuff out on the marble topped coffee table, walked over to Dearcorn's small desk, picked up a pair of scissors and cut a drinking straw in half. He handed one half to Dearcorn. He leaned forward, inhaled deeply, with the straw in his nostril, then stood up very straight. BT passed as he usually did. He needed his head clear.

When they had finished, BT walked out of the room without a word being said. But, Bettis Tom was thinking to himself, "I know Morris Barton. Not easy to pressure this guy."

Chapter 32
BT VISITS MR. BARTON
MAGGIE CALLS ON LITTLE JOE

Maggie sat at her desk, thinking, jotting down notes to herself. She had something on her mind. What did Randy Filbin and Mario Santiago know about the beating of Apple Smith and Little Joe? She intended on a meeting with the two of them soon, like today. She thought, would it be appropriate to bring along Apple? He was not exactly an uninterested party. He could take notes about what is said, so no questions, no accusations. They could be made later.

She put those thoughts aside for the time being. A more pressing thought kept coming to her mind. Did this Colorado Billy fellow really travel all the way to the Caribbean to get away from whatever menace he felt? Maybe he knew something more about what was going on. She recalled Apple saying he thought Colorado knew more about the murder of Beer Can Billy than he had stated. And, he left before anyone could actually interrogate him. Perhaps he turned into Florida, or Louisiana, or maybe he didn't go far at all. Maybe down to Port Aransas. Maybe he was somewhere near. Maggie just knew she would really like to talk to him.

Maggie had to bring herself back to the job at task.

She was charged with investigating the beating of Little Joe, not the murder of Beer Can.

Who would have an interest in tearing into Little Joe in such a revengeful way? Well, there was Apple, but that would have been physically impossible, considering the shape he was in the night of the attack.

Of course it could have been any number of low characters Little Joe associated with. That was a real possibility. Little Joe antagonized most everyone he came in contact with. Did he owe money to anyone? But the strange thought kept returning. What if Colorado Billy did not go to the Caribbean, what if he never left Texas? He certainly had a reason to attack Little Joe. If he had witnessed the murder of Beer Can, then that would be a revenge factor. What if he was the one?

"Maggie! Can you get in here a minute?" asked Sheriff Ben.

Maggie entered the Sheriff's office and was surprised to see him holding the big end of a baseball bat in his hand. "Look what just came in the mail. What do you make of this?" He was holding a folded piece of paper in his hand.

"What's in the note?"

It just says, "Check the bat for William Harry Wilson's, aka Beer Can Billy, and Mr. Apple Smith's blood. Also advise to check for Little Joe's finger prints." It was signed a friend of the court.

Maggie asked the Sheriff if he thought it was the bat that had been used against either one of the victims.

Sheriff Ben said, "We just might have the break we need. One or both of them might have been beaten with this bat."

"What gives with half a bat. Why half?"

The Sheriff replied, "It looks like it was broken by an object with one blow. Makes no sense."

Maggie asked, "Do you think Little Joe could have used this in the murder of Beer Can Billy? The "friend of the court" seems to think this might have been the weapon in both of the assaults."

"When you talk to Filbin or Santiago, ask them if Little Joe has ever been involved with anyone else where he brandished a baseball bat. Do they know if he owned such a bat? Just check with them and get a feel. They will probably say no. But, maybe they would like a chance to distance themselves from Little Joe. Maybe they would throw him under the bus."

Maggie left the office on her mission, and Sheriff Ben turned the bat over to the lab for blood analysis and fingerprints. All in all he was feeling pretty good. Things were beginning to look up.

She was headed toward the union's office. And, unlike Apple, they would damn well treat her with respect when she asked a question. She had decided that it would not be good protocol to take Apple along. Instead she would just call him and ask if he had any questions to pass along.

Apple was thinking about dinner he and Maggie had shared just a night ago, and wondering if it was too soon to ask her out again.

And, it seemed to him that his face was puffier from the stitches today than yesterday. Maybe he would wait a couple more days, and after tomorrow he would be better. He was scheduled to have the stitches removed. He was looking forward to that.

Apple's phone rang. It was Maggie. They talked ten minutes. Apple suggested she ask if they had ever been on board the "Chump Change", did they know Bettis Tom personally? On the subject of Little Joe, ask if they knew of Joe's plan to attack Apple or if they knew of his and Fred's reputation for doing their dirty work. Apple said he would insinuate that they were being paid by BAR Chem for keeping the union protests of the recent past under control. He would also ask if they ever participated in drugs, using or selling. He suggested that Maggie watch their faces for reaction at that last question. He told Maggie he was still convinced the yacht was smuggling drugs to the USA.

When Maggie asked if he had anything for Little Joe, he responded with, "Tell the little devil that I don't mind him attacking me from behind, but I am going to repay him for trashing my pickup."

Maggie asked, "There is one thought that keeps coming back to my mind. What if Colorado Billy did not go to the Caribbean? Do you think he had it in him to attack Little Joe?"

Apple dismissed that thought. He was pretty sure that Colorado was somewhere very far south, drinking a Red Stripe beer.

Maggie said, "All right, I get the message, but one more question. If he didn't go to the Caribbean, and stayed in Texas, where would he be?"

Apple said, "There are several places that could accommodate a full keel sail boat of his size. He mentioned that he would just start with the closest place, that being Freeport. If not Freeport, then check out Bay City and Port Aransas." Port Arthur was on the list of suspect places, but Apple suggested that if she was going to check out those possibilities, then Freeport would be his first choice. Simply because if he turned back then he would have a reason to stay close,Freeport being the closest. "If he is not there, start at Pensacola and work south, ending in Key West. Pretty big territory, but a possibility."

Maggie said, "Well, I'm not going to check every place with water looking for him, just a thought. But since Freeport is so close, maybe I'll check there and give it up, although I would like to go to Key West. One last thought: if he did do this to Little Joe, he would be close by."

"Who should I say is calling, sir?"

"Just tell him Bettis Tom Stovall is here and would like a few minutes of his time." Then he wiggled his fingers, indicating that she should run along and tell Morris Barton that he was waiting.

"There is a very strange man waiting to see you Mr. Barton. His name is Bettis Tom Stovall. He's wearing blue jeans and a yellow palm tree shirt." Most of the people who came to see Morris Barton wore pinstriped blue suits, except for the Houston lawyers. They wore the obligatory cream-colored linen suits.

Barton paused a second, then said, "Go tell Mr. Stovall that I will be free in 15 minutes. Then buzz me."

Barton thought a minute, asking himself what does that guy want? He called for Bernadette, and when she entered his office he said, "Guess who has come a calling? Bettis Tom Stovall himself."

"He just walked in and asked for a meeting? You going to talk to him?"

"Yes, only I want you to go to the front first and feel him out. Let's keep this guy on hold a minute, just to see what his temperament is. Ask him what his business is, and say that he can talk to you, that you act on the full authority of the paper. But don't let him turn and walk away. I want to hear him, just for the experience. I haven't talked to a real gangster in a long time."

After a short wait, Bettis Tom strode into the office with Bernie following closely. She caught Morris's eye and just shrugged her shoulders as if to say he just barged past.

Morris Barton said, "Hello, Mr. Stovall, I don't believe we have met."

"No."

"Well, what can I do for you? It must be important based on your haste."

BT replied, "Mr. Barton, as you know, the Houston Announcer has a very powerful voice. We at BAR Chemicals consider that your recent reporting of our company has been harmful."

"Just how have we harmed your company? We haven't spoken a word that is not true. We reported on John Bishop's death in a truthful fashion. Was he not, in fact, an employee of BAR Chem, and was found floating in the bay after being dispatched with a bullet hole in the back of his head? Now that is good hard news, Mr. Stovall."

"Please call me Bettis Tom. He was employed by the company, and we have no idea how he came to be in the bay with our briefcase of money. We would also like to have that mystery solved. But, we feel it will do no good for your newspaper to continue to cast aspersions our way."

Bettis Tom's approach was to be polite and businesslike in dealing with Mr. Barton, try to reason with him.

Morris Barton asked, "We would also like for the murder to be solved because there are other issues here. For instance, what was he doing with so much money? That seems to be an issue for BAR Chem to answer."

"Truthfully, Mr. Barton, we have no idea what he was up to. There seems to be some indication that the money was his own private funds, and what he was doing with it is anybody's guess."

Mr. Barton doubted every word of what Bettis Tom was selling, but was intrigued by what he had to say, and his manner in delivering it. He wondered if he should print any of this in the paper.

Barton continued, "Mr. Stovall, excuse me, Bettis Tom, now let me ask you straight up, did the company yacht, or anyone connected with it, have anything to do with our reporter, Apple Smith being nearly beaten to death last week?"

"Your paper reported that it was all to do with two thugs that were not exactly happy with the questions your guy asked about the ACW in an open meeting, and the way they spend money. Now as you said, you've reported in a truthful manner, is your article truthful? I don't know those two fellows."

"I will take you at your word, but if facts ever prove otherwise, let me assure that the full weight of this organization will come down hard on the guilty parties."

Bettis Tom, not used to turning the other cheek, now snarled, "Are you threatening me, Barton?"

"Not a threat, a promise. Now, get the hell out of my office."

As BT turned to exit, his gun was prominently exposed in the back of his belt. Obviously meant to be exposed. Morris Barton was incensed, "Hey!" he shouted, "Don't ever come into this building armed! Don't even walk down our sidewalk. I'm filing charges against you for this assault." Barton, known for his calm demeanor, surprised everyone outside his office when he shouted, "Everybody look good at this guy so you can identify him later. See the gun in his belt. I hope you've got a license for that thing, Buster." People were stunned, but everyone got a good look.

Maggie, on her way to the ACW, turned on to the first exit off the Gulf Freeway near Greyhound Park. Off the road, safe from traffic, she sat in her Galveston Sheriff's patrol car thinking. She was feeling a little uneasy about her decision to see Filbin and Santiago before Little Joe. She was thinking that maybe some evidence about Little Joe's involvement in Apple's assault could be learned ahead of interviewing Little Joe. It was always good to go into an interview loaded with information about the suspect, but perhaps she needed to be loaded with knowledge about Filbin

She came to a quick decision, reentered the feeder road, made a U-turn and headed north toward the hospital to question Little Joe. She was hoping that he was in good enough shape to answer a few questions. Maggie knew this was an important mission. She had a funny feeling that she might be able to crack not only who beat Little Joe senseless, but also how Apple's assault was connected to Beer Can Billy's murder, and how Beer Can might be connected to John Bishop, and how Bishop was connected to Bettis Tom. And, maybe BT would involve the biggest culprit of all, BAR Chem.

Maggie motored over to St. John's Hospital. It was easy to find, if you could find NASA. The hospital is within sight of the space facility.

Technically she was out of her jurisdiction because the hospital was located in Harris County, just on the line with Galveston County. However, the two counties had a very good working relationship, so questioning a suspect was no problem. Especially since the crime had clearly occurred in Sheriff Ben's territory. Harris County had given Ben plenty of space to work his cases, that being John Bishop, Beer Can Billy, and now the assault of Little Joe. They were cooperative with Sheriff Ben in investigating Apple's assault, even though it had occurred within the shadows of Houston's downtown, even within walking distance to the Astros' ball field. Maggie was grateful for this little bit of bureaucracy lifted for investigations. Maybe the Galveston Sheriff's people could repay Harris County someday.

Maggie entered the curved drive and parked in a no parking zone. She was glad to be driving a police cruiser instead of her new Cadillac. Cop cars get up front parking. She entered a side door and immediately went to the critical care unit, only to be informed that Little Joe had been moved to the Intensive Care Ward. She was concerned because earlier today when she had checked on him, he was doing well. So, why move him?

As she moved to the main nurse's station, she was thinking that this place has more security and more rules than the police department. The nurse at the desk was concerned about Maggie being there for questioning, but allowed it. She followed Maggie into the small room. Blinking lights and graphs running on digital screens seemed to be in every space.

Maggie told the nurse that she would be brief, but "This could be a murder investigation, and the questions have to be asked."

Little Joe's eyes were open and he was cognizant. He immediately recognized the badge that Maggie was wearing prominently on the outside of her jacket. She flashed an official ID card in his direction.

Little Joe was heavily sedated, but, asked, "Who are you?"

Maggie answered, "I am the one assigned to find out who did this to you. Did you see the persons?"

Little Joe held up one finger, indicating that a lone attacker was involved.

"What did he look like?" asked Maggie.

Little Joe was silent. He had lived on the edge so long, his distrust of anyone wearing a badge was evident.

"What did he use in the attack?"

Little Joe was alert to this question, his eyes fluttered, and his lips twitched as if he was remembering a bad dream. He certainly understood the question. He struggled to muttered, "Re-bar."

"The kind used in concrete?"

Little Joe nodded yes.

"Have you ever seen the fellow before? Was his hair short or long? How old was he?" Maggie fired quickly before Little Joe nodded off.

Little Joe remained silent. Maggie could not tell if he was listening, maybe she should return later, when he might be more responsive.

"Little Joe, did someone pay you to assault the reporter? You know very serious charges are going to be filed against you for that. The reporter has positively identified you and Fred. You will be going to jail for a long time, but if you cooperate with me, maybe I could help you."

Little Joe stirred. "I have seen my attacker somewhere before. Does he own a boat?"

Maggie's heart raced, but she outwardly showed no sign of excitement. Was he about to identify his attacker? "Joe, you are aware that Randy Filbin said you vandalized the pickup, and that you were upset the reporter had asked those questions at the meeting." She had not even talked to Filbin as of today, but she was sure that he would dump Little Joe and Fred if pressured.

"You know, he is going to turn against you?"

Joe tried to move his head to more directly face Maggie. His eyes narrowed. "He would not do that to me."

"Oh yes, he would. In fact, he already has. Why don't you just tell me that Randy Filbin or Santiago told you to attack the reporter? And help yourself." Maggie noticed an ACW business card facing up with Filbin's name prominently across the bottom. She was sure that Little Joe wanted to speak to Filbin or Santiago.

Little Joe relaxed back into his pillow. "Me and Fred and Filbin and Santiago decided that the reporter needed to be taught a lesson, so that is why Fred and me did what we did."

"One more question, Joe. What do you know about the death of William Wilson? Maybe you know him better by his marina name, Beer Can Billy."

"I don't know any Beer Can Billy, but there was a fellow over at the yacht basin got beat pretty bad, and died, but it was purely accidental that he died."

Maggie stood up, stuck her head outside the door, and said to a passing nurse, "Please come in here immediately." She turned back to Little Joe and said, "Repeat what you just said." Whereas Little Joe told her again in the presence of the nurse that Filbin and Santiago were in on the beating of Apple.

The ballgame had just changed.

Maggie said, "You did right, Little Joe. I'm going to catch the person that did this to you. Now rest easy." Maggie was trying to encourage him, when in fact she despised this little man. She was not sure if her intense negative feeling for Little Joe was because he assaulted some innocent person, or because he did it to Apple. But, it was a fact she desperately needed his testimony.

Maggie left the room and immediately called Sheriff Ben. "Ben, you need to get over here to the hospital. I've just got a confession from Little Joe, fingering Filbin and Santiago for their part in Apple's beating."

Sheriff Ben told Maggie to hold tight. He would ask the judge for an arrest warrant for Randy Filbin and Mario Santiago, and be there as quick as possible. He wanted to hear Little Joe himself. Then he and Maggie would pay a nice visit to Filbin's office. The Sheriff was excited to be making some progress in the ongoing investigations. He was proud of Maggie for coaxing Little Joe into details outlining his accomplices in the assault of Apple. He didn't know about Little Joe also pointing a finger in the direction of Colorado Billy. Nor was he aware that Little Joe did know something about Beer Can Billy's murder.

Maggie was sitting outside Little Joe's room waiting for Sheriff Ben. One hour passed, then two. Finally growing anxious, she phoned the Sheriff, no answer. After one more hour, with no answer, she walked to her car, just to ease the tension. She was eager to get over to the ACW and arrest those two low lives. As she was walking toward her patrol car, the police radio in her pocket started buzzing. "Sheriff, where you been?"

"Sorry, Maggie, I've got the warrant, but there is a nasty wreck on the freeway. I should be there within 30 minutes. Be patient, Little Joe is not going anywhere," he chuckled, "We know where he will be for a while."

Forty-five minutes later, Sheriff Ben arrived, just as there was a rush of activity moving into Little Joe's room. Maggie immediately stuck her head into the room and asked "What's happening?"

Little Joe had two nurses intently bent over him, one with a stethoscope listening to his heart, the other holding a large needle, poised for action, when in rushed a young doctor. His white lab coat opened at the front. Maggie, ever the police officer, noticed his Levis and scuffed sneakers, looking like anything but a doctor, but he seemed to know what to do. After several minutes of intense action, the doctor stepped back. Little Joe seemed to be stabilized, with an oxygen tube forced up his nose.

Sheriff Ben stepped toward the doctor, and they moved outside the room. Sheriff Ben introduced himself and asked, "Is he going to be OK? He is an important witness in a criminal case."

"I know you, Sheriff, you're pretty famous around here. I saw your TV interview recently about the Houston Announcer reporter beating."

"You've just been listening to the heart of the man who is the alleged beater. So how is he?"

The young doctor said, "We're moving him back into intensive care. He has a collapsed lung, and severe bruising of both kidneys."

"When can I talk to him? It's very important."

Maggie informed the Sheriff that she had a nurse listen in to his answer to her questions.

"Maggie, you think of everything. Job well done."

"It was surprising to me. He thinks also that Colorado Billy did this to him, but cannot positively say so. But maybe more important, he hinted that he was there when Beer Can Billy was murdered. He says it was an accident. He fell into the water, and they could not pull him out."

"Did he mention Bettis Tom Stovall?"

"No, but he will if we can question him further."

"You have a reliable witness to this conversation?"
"Yes sir."

Chapter 33
APPLE SQUEEZES DEARCORN

Apple knew Maggie was at either Filbin's or the hospital talking to Little Joe. At the thought of Little Joe, he absentmindedly reached for the now healing scar on his left cheek. It still stung a bit. A good reminder to him how serious this story about BAR Chem had become.

App was near the offices of the company where he was eagerly anticipating his interview with Jeffrey Chung Dearcorn. He was contemplating asking him if he knew what Bettis Tom was doing with the company's yacht.

He entered the foyer of the BAR Chem office building and was struck at how simple the structure was. He considered what an important world entity the company was. It was not lost on him that this group was actually doing some good across the world. He wondered how it had come, in his opinion, to be controlled by men such as Dearcorn. What was the idea behind giving Bettis Tom such an important role in the company? In his research for today, he had learned that BT was listed in the company annals as a lobbyist. Apple thought that someday some novelist is going to write a pretty interesting book about the comings and goings of Bettis Tom Stovall. Perhaps he would be that person.

He climbed the stairs to the second floor where he was stopped by a security guard who escorted him to the desk of a very pretty older lady. She served as Dearcorn's personal assistant. Apple remained true to his instincts when he approached her with an outstretched hand and a big smile.

She wasn't in the mood. "You must be the reporter. Do you always wear blue jeans when you interview important men like Mr. Dearcorn?"

"Almost always."

"You should reconsider."

She showed Apple down the hallway to an office, opened the door, and an executive with a three-piece, gray, pin stripped suit stood from behind an oversized desk, the kind that appears to have been cobbled together from an old barn door. Smooth and varnished to a high polish. Apple thought he is wearing a suit just like John Bishop was wearing when he was pulled from the net of a shrimp boat.

The gentleman moved across the large room, extended his hand and said, "Mr. Smith, my name is Roy Jacobs. I will be pinch hitting for Mr. Dearcorn. He sends his regrets, but will be unable to attend today."

Apple was taken off guard a bit. He decided that the businesslike manner he intended to use was out the window. "Roy Jacobs, I understand you enjoy the "Chump Change" very much. You might say it is your second home."

Roy responded with, "You might say that. How do you know that?"

"I know a lot of the "Chump Change" crowd, including Arnost, the deck boy, and Bettis Tom, himself."

"Yeah, well who else do you know?"

"I know you took a recent cruise to the Caribbean, but for some reason decided at the last minute to divert to

Veracruz instead of Galveston."

Now Roy was a bit off stride. "Mr. Smith, what are you here for? Surely not my interest in the yacht. Please state your business, I've got other things to attend."

Apple asked, "The word is around that BAR Chem may be returning to Texas. Is that true?"

"It's in the works, but only if we can return to our old plant site. That is the best location for our business on the Gulf Coast. You know the EPA and other local interests have been balking at permitting our return. And, we currently own it."

Apple returned, "I hope you can. Mr. Jacobs, what are the Company's ties to Bettis Tom Stovall? He doesn't seem to fit the mold of a big chemical plant executive?"

"Plain and simple, he is what you would call a lobbyist. He pushes the good of the company, not just here, but around the world."

"I'll bet he is very effective. Would you care to comment on the fact, off the record, if you wish, that M. Ellis Winston has recently visited our office with an offer of money to our editor, Mr. Barton, to ease up on the reporting of your company's recent exploits?"

"I have no knowledge of Mr. Winston's comings and goings, though I doubt Ellis would try to bribe your paper. Do you know who M. Ellis Winston is? If you don't, he is a very powerful attorney that works in our interest.'

"I met him recently, having lunch with Bettis Tom." Apple reached up and touched his cheek where the recently removed stitches still were prominently visible.

Roy asked, "What the hell happened to you? I can't help but notice the scars."

"That brings me to my next question. Have you ever heard of another employee of yours, Little Joe Edmunds, and Fred Frederickson? These scars are their handiwork."

"I never heard of them. Employees?"

"It's a little around the corner, but may I ask what are your relationships with the two union bosses, Filbin and Santiago?

"I know who they are. The top execs of the ACW. Why do you say they are our employees?"

"I think your company pays those two to keep the ACW in check, and they paid Little Joe and Fred to assault me."

"Mr. Smith, you walked in the door insulting me, and I heard you out. Now we are finished. Please leave!"

Apple knew this interview was over, and he felt he had blew it. He gained nothing from the interview. On his way out the door, he told Roy Jacobs, "I think you are part of a smuggling ring, using the "Chump Change" to bring drugs into the country. I think someone on the "Chump Change" murdered John Bishop, and had a role in the murder of William Harry Wilson. I think BAR Chem is paying off anyone in Galveston and Harris County to help the company return. I think BAR Chem is partly responsible for my assault, and I intend to prove it. Have a good day, Mr. Jacobs."

Roy stood slack jawed for a second, then bolted down the hallway to Jeffrey Chung Dearcorn's office.

Apple was stopped at the front door by a harried young woman. "Sir, are you Mr. Smith?" Where upon she informed him that Mr. Dearcorn would like to see him. Apple's pride told him to inform the young lady that he was out of time, but gave into his good reporter's sense. He knew that sometimes you had to rattle the cage a bit to get results. It seems this was one of those times.

He was escorted into Jeffrey Chung Dearcorn's

office. Seated behind the desk was Dearcorn, Jacobs sat to one side of the desk, watching as Apple entered the room.

Dearcorn said, "I'll get right to the point, Mr. Smith, You've made some serious accusations. Would you be so kind as to tell me what proof you have for your belief that our company yacht is somehow connected to murder and smuggling?"

Apple explained his position, then asked, "If you want to return to Texas, why not just apply in the proper methods for permits to rebuild? Our paper would support your efforts in that direction."

"Let me assure you that BAR Chem does not engage in illegalities of any kind. We just do not operate that way."

Apple asked, "How about bribery? M. Ellis Winston offered Mr. Morris Barton money to stop our articles on your company. Why not just have a sit down interview and explain your point? Trying to trade cash for favorable reporting, come on."

"Mr. Smith, the next time we consent to an interview will be across the room with attorneys present. I have nothing more to say to you. Please leave."

With that, the same young woman who had escorted him to Dearcorn's office appeared to lead him to the front door. Apple said, "Don't bother, I am familiar with the building. I can find my way to the parking lot."

Apple would later learn of Bettis Tom's meeting with Mr. Barton and the intimidation tactics he had employed to once again stop the Houston Announcer from reporting on BAR Chem. Too bad he didn't know this during his meeting with Roy Jacobs and Jeffrey Dearcorn.

Apple entered the large parking lot, walked to his shiny, newly refurbished pickup, and drove onto the freeway. He was thinking, not of Jacobs and Dearcorn, but of Maggie and how her interviews were going, if she was learning anything of substance.

He was still very upset over the murder of Beer Can, and he thought that Little Joe had gotten what he deserved. Now if there was anything to be done about Filbin and Santiago, he knew those two were behind his beating. He hoped that he could be on the scene when Maggie or Sheriff Ben slapped handcuffs on those two.

Perhaps the route he should examine would be writing about how corrupt they were. Maybe their own union brothers would turn on them. The ACW really needed new leadership. He wondered if the members knew how close they might be to getting their old jobs back. If BAR Chem returned, many jobs would open, good jobs.

The young doctor had a conference with Sheriff Ben and Maggie and informed them that it would be four, maybe six hours before Little Joe would be strong enough and alert to answer any more questions. Little Joe's heart had suddenly slowed to a dangerously low rate. "Along with his lungs and kidneys, his heart was compromised by the savage beating he has received."

Sheriff Ben and Maggie decided, however monotonous, and a killer of time, she should stay nearby so that she could be close when he was again able to talk. The Sheriff was eager to question him closely about the "Chump Change", Bettis Tom, and the ACW. Sheriff Ben and Maggie knew they were very close to valuable answers about the recent murders.

Maggie was concerned about arresting Randy Filbin and Santiago, Sheriff Ben told her , "Sit tight. They can wait."

Maggie sat just outside Little Joe's intensive care cubicle waiting. She was deep in thought about the possibility of now arresting Randy Filbin and Mario Santiago for their complicity in the assault of Apple, when two nurses hurried into Joe's room. She immediately heard an urgent voice call a Code Red. She had been in enough hospital emergency rooms to know that cardiac arrest was what they were excited about. Maggie also had enough experience to know to stand aside and let the code team do their work. But she had a notion that something was not going in Little Joe's favor, nor hers. She was a bit puzzled because she had spoken to Little Joe a few hours earlier, and although he was not in the best shape, he didn't appear to be in any danger.

After a few minutes, a nurse emerged, and told "Maggie, he is going to make it, but the doctor has given orders that no one should speak to him until morning." Maggie called the Sheriff and advised him of what was going on, and they decided that she should go home, get a good night's rest, and they would both meet at the hospital early the next day. Maggie was very weary and thought, "Good idea."

Randy Filbin eased back in his swivel, hard-backed office chair, sipping yet another cup of coffee, thinking. He reached into his top desk drawer and found his bottle of Johnnie Walker, loosened the cap and poured a heavy slug into the coffee he was drinking. He loved that Scotch whiskey.

He could think quickly on his feet, but he was most effective thinking things through, always to his own advantage. He picked up a pen and a legal pad and began to sketch down a few thoughts. Evening shadows were quickly turning everything shady outside, but he ignored the lateness of the day. He had to figure a few things out.

Santiago walked by his office, stuck his head in the

door and said, "What's going on?"

"Come in here. We've got a problem. Did you know that Sheriff Rodriguez has that lady police officer hanging around Little Joe's room all day?"

"Yeah, so what?"

Filbin explained to his slow witted co-conspirator that Little Joe, under pressure, might talk to the detective about the meeting they had after the ACW meeting with himself and Fred. Filbin was worried, and so should Santiago be. They could be facing some serious jail time if they were convicted, as Joe and Fred were sure to be, if they were exposed as the leaders of the little party with Apple Smith. Could they count on the two keeping their secrets to themselves?

Mario asked Filbin, "Do you think he knows about the drugs coming off the "Chump Change?"

"Are you crazy? Of course he knows?

"Do you think he would use us as the source of breaking the fellow's thumbs?"

Filbin said, "I don't think he will talk, because he is the one that hit him in the head. Surely he wouldn't blame that on us."

Santiago wasn't so sure. "Maybe we should go to the Sheriff and say it was Little Joe."

"Yeah," said Filbin, "Then it would be our word against him. You know, two against one."

"There is only one problem. What if the Sheriff doesn't believe us? And they will surely ask what we were doing there. And many other questions. I think we are in big trouble, Randy. What are we going to do?"

"Maybe go have a talk with Little Joe. Make sure he is still on our side. I think we should maybe go to the petty cash drawer and make a withdrawal."

"Perhaps, and we know Bettis Tom has the key to the drawer."

WILLIAM WARREN

Chapter 34
HELLO, AND GOODBYE, LITTLE JOE

At six o'clock, Randy Filbin placed a call to St. John's Hospital and asked for Joe Edmund's room number.

He was informed that Little Joe was in intensive care, and that only family members were allowed in to see him.

Filbin was glad to hear that. He had never heard Little Joe speak of relatives, so there would not be anyone at the hospital.

It was still early in the evening when Mario Santiago and Filbin drove around the hospital. They parked their car about two blocks from the hospital parking lot and walked the distance. Filbin was wary of security cameras, so he and Santiago dressed so as not to be identified from film. Filbin wore a very old blue dress suit jacket, with a dark baseball cap pulled down low over his eyes, and kept his face pointed to his feet. Santiago dressed in a similar fashion. They wanted to look like a cross between two businessmen finished with the day's work, and perhaps two older guys out to visit a friend at the hospital.

At this early time, all the doors were unlocked and open. They walked down a secluded sidewalk to a side door and entered the building. ICU was easy enough to find. The problem was the nurses' station in the center. Timing would have to be on the spot.

They observed through the tiny window in the door that two nurses were on duty. They split and moved toward the end of the hall approaching ICU and found separate seating where they could observe anyone coming or going out the doors.

Filbin and Mario Santiago sat for one hour, just like any other visitors. They were getting very nervous, hoping they would be able to make a move soon. They were beginning to lose hope that one of the nurses would exit the doors, but one eventually did. She moved down the hall a short ways and entered another door off the alcove near the entrance to the ICU.

Filbin quickly stood up and nodded at Santiago, who moved rapidly toward the swinging doors. Once inside the unit, he approached the single nurse sitting behind a desk just inside a short counter. "Pardon me nurse, could you please help me?" as he again moved toward the swinging doors. The nurse followed him. She was not supposed to leave the unit, but she was only a few feet outside. Santiago moved down the hall with the nurse following. As the nurse followed him, Filbin, waiting outside the door, still looking every bit the visitor, stealthy entered the intensive care area.

There were only six rooms, each with a large window, Filbin quickly spotted Little Joe, and entered the room. Little Joe was sleeping in a painless sleep, when Filbin put a pillow over his face and held it tight. Randy Filbin sarcastically said quietly to himself, "Hello and goodbye, Little Joe." Little Joe struggled in vain, reaching out to push away the stronger man, but could not. Soon he stopped his frantic struggle and was still. Filbin mercilessly held the pillow very tight for a few minutes longer.

Randy Filbin had never committed violence of

this nature before, but he was a hard man and felt some satisfaction at the job. But the work was not finished. He and Mario had to get out of the area, and quickly, undetected.

Filbin knew he had done a perfect job, but had not noticed that Little Joe, ever the fighter, had ripped the pocket off the suit jacket he was wearing. In the excitement, Filbin never noticed the missing pocket.

He exited the swinging doors just ahead of the nurse who had walked down the hall. She noticed nothing strange. Santiago still held the other nurse in conversation. Filbin thought, "That Mario had a way with words. He could talk a bingo caller into his numbers."

He walked briskly down the hall, past Santiago and out the doors of the hospital, towards his parked car. Santiago followed, 50 feet behind.

As they were getting into their car, the ICU nurses issued an urgent call for help. At the same moment they were frantically working on Little Joe, Randy Filbin and Mario Santiago were driving away. Little Joe would do no talking to the police. They even foolishly thought that maybe it would just be deemed a natural death in the ICU. Filbin was sure that he had removed the pillow from Little Joe's face, or did he?

At any rate, Little Joe was dealt with and they had gotten away undetected, so who cares if a bum like Little Joe was murdered? He had committed many crimes that he had been unpunished for, so Filbin smiled and thought, "Justice is done."

WILLIAM WARREN

Chapter 35
LITTLE JOE, YOU DONE GOOD

Apple's deep connections as an investigative reporter for the Houston Announcer were about to pay off. He was a very good friend of the top administrator of St. John's hospital where Little Joe had just been murdered.

It was nine o'clock and Apple and Maggie were having dinner at Prego's in the Rice University Village. Strange coincidences were piling up over the last couple of weeks, since Apple had set out on his story about BAR Chem's movement to Mexico. For instance, he was with Sheriff Ben when John Bishop's body was pulled from Galveston Bay. He had just made the friendship with Beer Can Billy and Colorado Billy a few days before Beer Can was murdered at the Galveston Yacht Basin, and happened to be with Sheriff Ben once again as the body was pulled from the water. He, along with Colorado Billy identified Beer Can Billy's lifeless body.

App was very grieved because he liked the man, and felt some responsibility for the murder, having asked the two men to report to him if anything suspicious happened around the BAR Chem yacht, "Chump Change."

His luck or coincidence was holding. His cell phone began ringing, and he very much wanted to ignore it. He felt it in bad taste to answer a phone while dining with a friend. His friend was Maggie, Deputy Inspector for the

Galveston County Sheriff's Department.

They were having the dinner they were supposed to have the night Apple was beaten in front of his downtown condo. Maggie was currently the lead detective on the beating of Little Joe Edmunds.

He was half way into his vittelo prego, and his second glass of merlot. Apple was very much enjoying his evening with delightful conversation and the strikingly beautiful Maggie. App still couldn't believe this tall brunet was a police officer. She was dressed in a flower patterned, soft cotton dress. Who would guess this very gorgeous lady had a badge and a gun in her purse. He thought, "She can arrest me anytime, after I finish this veal."

The damn cell phone kept ringing. The person on the other end was Hector, his Doc boyhood friend at St. John's. "What's up Hect? Can I call you back in the morning? I'm in the middle of a dinner date with a very lovely companion."

"Shut up Apple, listen! You better get over here. Your pal Joe Edmunds has just probably been murdered in his hospital bed. I think if you get here soon, you will arrive as soon as the police."

"What do you mean probably?"

"Well, he's dead, and was found with a pillow over his face. Couldn't have been suicide. Just one more important thing. Don't you dare tell anyone, or your paper that I told you about this. I could be in a lot of trouble over privacy issues. The hospital would not like it one bit."

"Right, thanks a million. I owe you."

"You're damn right you owe me, and I intend to collect. Get over here."

Apple was a bit amused that he had got a call before Maggie, but as he hung up, Maggie's phone began ringing. Apple could guess what it was about. Maggie was a little disturbed about their great evening being broken, right in the middle. She wondered if this interesting, very handsome, curly haired guy might begin to think hanging out with a police officer turned out to be a little more effort than was worth it".

Apple said, "Remember when we were at Jerry's, I told you how I could guess what people drove, and what they did for a living? I'll bet you didn't know that I could guess about phone calls too."

Maggie, although serious, grinned, "Yeah, I have a feeling that I am about to find out."

"Right. Your call was about Little Joe, right?"

"I don't want to know anything, except, Sheriff Ben didn't call you first, did he? If he did I will have a piece of his butt."

"Relax, Inspector, it was not the Sheriff, but pretty impressive, right?" Maggie grinned, but said, "I've got to go, can you find a ride back to your apartment? And you still owe me a dinner. Tonight doesn't count."

Apple asked, "Why don't you just give me a ride to the hospital? You know that's where I am heading."

"Can't do. It just would not look good for me to show up with a reporter, and stay out of my way when you do get there. I will try to take my time checking things out till you get there, but hurry."

"You're the best police pal I've got. Thanks," he said smiling.

Maggie hit the door running, and jumped into her new Cadillac, sat a police light on the dash board, and much to Apple's surprise turned on a blasting siren. Apple thought, this woman is full of surprises. He was glad he knew her. A policewoman in a Cadillac, speeding down

University Boulevard. What a sight.

Maggie arrived at the hospital, and to her surprise, she had gotten to the scene ahead of Sheriff Ben. She entered Little Joe's room where hospital staff had begun to prep the room for the removal of Little Joe. Maggie was disturbed because it was evident some items had been moved from their original positions. "Please, everyone leave the room, except for the doctor! OK with you, Doc?" There were three nurses in the room and they began filing out. "Who found the body?" A nurse said. "I did."

"Will you please stay?"

"Doc, how did he die?"

"Obvious asphyxiation."

"How can you tell?"

"Well, detective, we found a pillow over his head."

"Place the pillow back on his face, exactly as you found it."

Maggie began taking photos with her cell phone, and asking questions. "Anything else strange?"

The nurse spoke up, "Yes, in his hand we found this." She picked up a piece of blue cloth and handed it to Maggie. A wadded up card was also found in with the cloth. Maggie unfolded the card and looked at it, and was amazed when she read the name, Randall Filbin, Executive Director, Association of Chemical Manufacturers Worker's Union, Seabrook, Texas.

She had a hard grin as she said, "Little Joe, you done good, very good."

She dialed a number on her phone, and said, "Sheriff, where the heck are you?"

"Walking in the door of the hospital right now, with, guess who? Your pal from the Houston Announcer." The Sheriff and Apple had driven up in the parking lot at the same time. Apple practiced good judgement and did not park beside the Sheriff's cruiser right in the front of the hospital. Instead he found a marked spot very near. He quickly fell into pace by the Sheriff's side, and said "We keep meeting in the strangest places, don't we Sheriff?"

"I don't know how you keep on turning up at these scenes. You must have my office under surveillance."

Maggie quickly handed the card to Sheriff Ben, and said Benson and McBride, two uniforms, are on their way to pick up Filbin. The Sheriff said, good, probable cause, no warrant needed.

No one said a word to Apple as he freely moved around the room, scribbling a few notes on a pad. The Sheriff had become so accustomed in the last few weeks at seeing him there, it seemed that he just belonged.

WILLIAM WARREN

Chapter 36
APPLE AND MR. BARTON GO INTO BUSINESS

Apple left the crime scene and speeded up the Gulf Freeway to his downtown Houston Announcer office. He regretted that he could not be in the background as handcuffs were placed on Randy Filbin and more than likely Mario Santiago, charged with the murder of Little Joe Edmunds.

Events were happening faster than he seemed able to keep up. He had barely finished his story on his own assault at the hands of Little Joe when Little Joe was savagely beaten himself. And now Little Joe had been finished off in his own hospital bed.

Even though Apple was aware that Little Joe had a crumpled business card in his hand with Randy Filbin's name on it, he had allowed his mind to wander with thoughts of Colorado Billy. Surely, even though Maggie suspected he did, had nothing to do with the murder of Little Joe. Perhaps Colorado Billy had not gone to the Caribbean after all.

Thirty minutes later and Apple opened the door to his office. Most of the lights were off at this time of night. Only a few folks sat humped over their desks, gazing into their computer screens. He went directly to his desk and spent the next two hours pounding out the events since he had suffered his attack. He subconsciously reached for his left cheek and rubbed the rough, red scar on his face, with thoughts of who, and why, anyone would take such a chance to murder Little Joe in his hospital bed. Why not wait until he got out of the hospital to do such an act? If Colorado Billy had wanted to kill him, he surely would have done it that night on Little Joe's porch. No, there was someone else and another motive.

Apple's thoughts kept returning to the business card in Joe's hand. He must have struggled with his murderer and pulled the pocket from the coat of his assailant. Since the card was in the pocket, and had Filbin's name on it, then surely the guilt lay with him. He wondered if Maggie had arrested him yet.

He finished his story, and emailed a copy to Bernadette, and placed a paper copy in the middle of her desk, for action first thing tomorrow. He turned out his office light, and went straight for his condo near the ball park.

Apple turned in around two a.m., and was sleeping soundly when his phone rang. He ignored it. The message light was blinking; he rolled over and looked at the phone. Bernie had just called him at seven. The phone rang again, and Apple roused from his sleep and answered, "What's going on? You know it is seven? I went to bed at two."

This time Bernie ignored his questions. "You better get down here. Something strange is going on."

"Yeah, well it better be real strange to get out of bed for."

"Morris is not in his office, and Damon the Dip is in there going through his desk."

Damon Dipington was Vice President in charge of operations, or put another way, administrative manager. He managed the accounting department, and paid the monthly bills. Bernie described him as making sure the toilet tissue was ordered. Damon the Dip knew nothing about running a newspaper. He could not write a piece for the paper if Superman jumped from the top of the Announcer building.

Bernadette said, "Mr. Barton barely permitted him to enter his office. You better get down here soon."

Twenty minutes later, Apple strode into the offices of the newspaper. Sure enough there sat Damon the Dip behind Mr. Barton's desk, rifling through papers gouged from the drawers.

Apple, without stopping at Bernie's door, went directly into Barton's office, "What are you doing? Where is Mr. Barton?"

Through the large office window, the entire office was watching this encounter with their star reporter. Damon said, "Sit down Apple."

At that time Bernie came into the office. She had no conversations with Damon, but had an idea what this was all about. She had heard office chatter and had a bad feeling.

"Sit down Bernadette," and Damon motioned to a chair. "What are you doing with Mr. Barton's files? Where is he?"

Damon began, "Mr. Barton has been relieved of his duties here at the newspaper by the board. And, they have appointed me to finish out his contract, as Interim Editor in Chief. Now, I know both of you have been very close to Morris, and I want to assure you that both of you are held in high esteem by the board. Nothing will change."

Apple asked, "If nothing will change, then why has he stepped down?"

"There will be a few changes, nothing significant."

"How significant?" asked Apple. "Give me a for

303

instance."

"For instance, all the copy you turn in to Bernadette will go to me for final approval before going to print. The board is not exactly pleased about your repeated stories on BAR Chem. They would like for you to go in another direction on those pieces."

"What direction?"

"Treat them as a friend, not as a foe. It would be a good thing for them to return to Texas with a plant, and you are making that more difficult."

"Do you have any idea what you are suggesting? There are two, maybe three murders directly connected to them. And, the beating that I endured, I believe, is because of my involvement. How does the board answer that?"

Bernie sat still, trying to assimilate this conversation.

Apple said, "I cannot accept those terms. BAR Chem is involved, especially in the murder of their own attorney, John Bishop. And I will not quit writing about that."

"Then you give me no alternate course. You will no longer be permitted to report on the BAR Chem angle. You will be reassigned to something else."

"No I will not. I will resign before I stop my reporting on that story. By the way, has M. Ellis Winston or Bettis Tom Stovall been to visit you? Has your bank account had a jump recently?" asked Apple.

Bernadette said, "Apple, can I speak to you a moment in the hallway?"

"No Bernie, I cannot turn back."

Damon the Dip abruptly said, "Then consider yourself no longer employed at this newspaper. Gather your things and vacate your office."

"It'll be my pleasure. And oh, did you know the

entire office refers to you as Damon the Dip?"

Angered, Damon stood up from Mr. Barton's desk, and turned his back to Apple, and faced out onto the avenue below, and mumbled, "It's a name I cherish."

Apple was in the elevator when his cell rang. Bernie said to meet her at Dane's Pub on Westheimer. Mr. Barton would be waiting there for them. A short drive, and as Apple was parking on the street, he spotted Mr. Barton sitting alone at a table in the sunlight. Bernie would arrive soon.

Mr. Barton said to the pair, "Well boys, and girls, I guess you know what has happened by now."

Apple said, "We have a pretty good idea, but do you know what has just happened to me?"

Mr. Barton stood, stuck out his hand, smiled broadly, and said, "Don't tell me. We are both unemployed?"

"Yep, boss, we are both on the street."

"And, you Bernie?"

"Not me. I like regular paychecks. Believe me, this will pass. Damon the Dip cannot hold things together very long, and then they will be asking you two back, but they might not ask me back, so I'll stay put until this all passes."

They all agreed that the best thing was for Bernie to keep plugging along and outlast Damon. And, with her on the inside, they would know what is happening at the newspaper they all loved.

Mr. Barton said he did not mind very much, that he intended to retire soon anyway. He just hated the paper had succumbed to BAR Chem's political clout. He was fuming that M. Ellis Winston and Bettis Tom had won, in the short term. He laughed, and said, "Maybe I should have taken the money, then went along with the same stories."

Bernie asked, "Now what are you going to do,

Apple?"

"Me? I am going to see this BAR Chem thing out."

"That's my boy," said Morris.

""You got any money?" asked Bernie. "Not much, but enough. Besides, I can freelance. I get offers all the time. Maybe now I can call on some of those."

Bernie excused herself with, "Gotta go boys, I still have a job. Apple, keep in touch. There may be some ways I can help out. The Announcer still has some influence, here and there." With that, she drove the eight blocks back to the offices of the paper.

Apple began, "Well, now then, boss, I have an idea."

Mr. Barton interrupted, "I have an idea also. Since I am the boss, let me go first. It might be important."

"Go for it," said Apple.

Mr. Barton laid out his plan for himself and Apple. He proposed that they would go together and finish the job on BAR Chem. Apple would now be the boss, and Mr. Barton would be his assistant. He told Apple to remember that he was a rich man, and could support their operation for as long as necessary.

Morris Barton had one idea, though, he insisted on, that being to take down the Board of Directors at BAR Chem, Including M. Ellis Winston, Jeffrey Chung Dearcorn, and that gangster Bettis Tom. When he finished, he said, "So, what do you think, reporter? Think we can bring those crooks down? You said you had an idea, what was it?"

Apple said, "You pretty much laid out the plan., I agree to your terms," he said with a smile. "And since we are not on the clock, why don't we just sit here in the sunshine and go over our plans, and have a few beers?"

Apple brought Morris Barton up on the latest details of the investigation, including the death of Little Joe. He told him of his close friendship with Maggie, and that they could not get in the way of Sheriff Ben and his official investigation.

Morris whistled under his breath and said, "I had no idea. I thought we were mostly looking into the business side of the company, but this is a hell of a lot more exciting."

Apple gave Mr. Barton his first assignment, which was to find out who the big investors were in BAR Chem, who owned all that stock, and to think about how they could use the info to their own good. Mr. Barton gladly accepted the assignment, and they sat happily drinking beer. No one would guess they both had just been fired.

WILLIAM WARREN

Chapter 37
HOUSTON TO NY TO SAN FRANCISCO

Apple slept in the next day, all the way to eight o'clock. He was in the bath, shaving, when his phone rang. He answered with, "Apple Smith here, what can I do for you?"

"Mr. Smith, this is Excelsior Publishing calling, can you hold for Mr. Papanicoli?"

Apple was immediately excited, but he kept his voice calm and low. Excelsior Publishing was one of the largest publishing houses in the country. It was like Hemingway calling. Definitely, he could hold. He wasn't exactly sure who Mr. Papanicoli was, but he could find out. This was Excelsior. He wondered how it would go over when they found out he had been fired from the Houston Announcer?

A pleasant bass voice came on the other end. "Mr. Smith, this is George Papanicoli from Excelsior Publishing. We have just learned of your disagreement with the Announcer, and we have a proposition for you. Are you interested?"

Apple explained his situation and Mr. Barton's with the newspaper. He put it on the line, and directly accused BAR Chem of bribery and extortion. "By the way, how did you find out about my mishap so soon? It only occurred yesterday."

George Papanicoli explained that he was an old school friend of Bernadette Hannigan's. She had made a call to him about the possibility of Excelsior working with Apple.

"The truth is, Mr. Smith, we would like to talk to you face to face about the possibility of a book about your investigation. Let me ask you directly about the possibility that BAR Chem could be involved in the." He stopped there and asked Apple about the possibility of him flying to New York to bring them up to speed. Apple knew he did not want to say the word murder on the telephone.

"How about tomorrow? I will fly out today."

"Great! We will have someone meet you at the airport. Just call my secretary when you know the flight arrangements."

And just like that, Apple became a partner of Excelsior Publishing. He immediately called Morris Barton. Mr. Barton told Apple, "Now boy, that's a good thing, but don't forget your newspaper roots. You are still, body and soul, a reporter."

Apple reminded him that now Morris would not have to pay the bills until this whole thing was finished. Mr. Barton didn't seem to care about the money, but told Apple that he had a plan, and a very good one. He wouldn't tell Apple details, but just said he was going to call on an old friend.

Apple sat back in his coach seat, as Mr. Barton sat down at his home, and sketched out his plan. Maggie and Sheriff Ben were still in the process of questioning Randy Filbin. Commander Johnson was still waiting for the "Chump Change" to depart Veracruz, and the "Good Avenger", aka Colorado Billy was plotting his next step.

Colorado was mulling over what he thought were

his options. His original plan was to find Fred Frederickson and give him some of the same medicine that Little Joe had received.

Colorado was very confused concerning Little Joe. He had read a short article in the Galveston Daily News about the death of Little Joe. The story gave a strong idea that Joe had been murdered. The police even had a suspect in custody, someone Colorado Billy had never heard of. What would a union executive have to do with this entire business? Colorado figured he could trust the news since the paper was the oldest newspaper in Texas. He knew he did not have a hand in Little Joe's demise. All he had done was beat him to an inch of death, but he did not murder him. So what was going on? Who had murdered Little Joe and why?

It was then that Colorado Billy made up his mind to go after Bettis Tom and not Fred. Fred may have been the feet in Little Joe's death, but Bettis Tom was the mover behind the scene. Colorado was also certain that Bettis Tom was behind his friend Beer Can's death. Colorado would spend the day thinking about how to find Bettis Tom.

Morris Barton spent the day researching the financial records of BAR Chem. Much of it was online and public since BAR Chem was a publicly traded company.

Near the end of the day, he felt he had enough background to have a conversation with Jeremiah Eckstein, one of his oldest friends. Barton and Eckstein had first met in boot camp during the Viet Nam war. They had been shipped out to the same unit and spent the next two hard years together. Sleeping in the mud and fighting off mosquitos - that experience created friends for life.

Jeremiah Eckstein was a very wealthy man. He was born into wealth. Morris Barton knew he was rich, but he had no idea how rich. He was about to find out.

He called San Francisco and finally was able to get a line to Eckstein's office where he was put on hold a very long time. "Who is calling, sir? And, what is your business with Mr. Eckstein?"

"My name is Morris Barton, calling from Houston, and the business is personal. Just tell Jeremiah that I am waiting, and I guarantee you, he will speak to me, and if you don't, I guarantee you will not be in his good graces." Morris thought a veiled threat, and a real supposition that a man of Jeremiah's importance would speak to an old military buddy so quickly.

After a healthy wait, Jeremiah Eckstein came on the phone, "Hello Morris, good to hear from you. What brings you my way?"

"Jeremiah, I need a favor that only you can provide." The two old friends engaged in a long conversation about their past days in Viet Nam, and brought each other up on what had been happening recently. The last time they had seen each other was about five years ago, when Morris had been in San Francisco attending a conference of newspaper men from across the country.

Morris explained to Jeremiah about the recent findings and happenings in Texas concerning BAR Chem. He discussed the peculiar circumstances of John Bishop and the other deaths that BAR Chem seemed to be involved in, even though the details were rather sketchy. Jeremiah was especially interested in the events involving the company yacht.

Mr. Barton pleaded his case rather strongly and asked for a meeting with Jeremiah as soon as possible. Jeremiah said he could meet with Morris and Apple three days hence, if they could come to San Francisco. Morris happily agreed.

Mr. Barton hung up the phone and felt a feeling of satisfaction because he had accomplished what he had set out to do. He had discovered that Jeremiah owned roughly 31 percent of the outstanding shares of BAR Chem. Mr. Barton explained how those shares could be impacted when he and Apple went public with their findings about the BAR Chem Company operations. He made it sound as if he was doing Jeremiah Eckstein a favor by giving him a heads up. But, he really wanted a big favor from Eckstein.

Apple landed in New York at JFK and his phone beeped indicating a text from Mr. Barton. The text simply said, "Don't vacation in New York. We have to be in San Francisco in three days." Apple couldn't resist. He texted back immediately, "Why?" Then his phone started ringing. "Apple, that you?"

"Yeah boss, what's up with San Francisco?"

"I think I just scored a breakthrough." Then he went on and explained who Jeremiah Eckstein was and that he was the single largest shareholder of BAR Chem.

Apple had to think back over his ten years at the paper to remember when Morris Barton had sounded so excited. Morris said, "You know what this means?" then went on to explain, "We have the ear of the most important man connected with BAR Chem. He is actually more important than M. Ellis Winston and Jeffrey Chung Dearcorn." Now Apple was excited too.

"By the way, did you sign your book deal yet?"

"First thing in the morning, then I will hop back on the first flight for Houston. Talk to you when I arrive. See you, boss."

Apple stepped out of his taxi and noticed the difference from the limo Excelsior had greeted him with last night. But, he was very close to the offices on Broadway and was just happy to be here. He had thought about writing books in the past, but had just never had the time. Now he would be paid for writing, and he would have time when the BAR Chem murders were put to rest.

Chapter 38
EXCELSIOR PUBLISHING GETS INTERESTED

Back in Galveston, Maggie and Sheriff Ben were in the interrogation room with Randy Filbin and a Houston defense lawyer named Joel Frazier. Either Maggie or Sheriff Ben had been talking to Filbin since five this morning. Maggie was now doing the talking. "Just so you understand Mr. Filbin, you are being charged with first degree murder. We know you did it. The business card you carelessly left behind is enough to convince a jury anywhere."

Mr. Frazier said, "All circumstantial. Little Joe has known Randy a long time. That card could have come from Joe's own clothing."

"Admit it, Randy. We have you on security cameras walking in the door at the hospital. Just confirm that Mario Santiago is the other fellow with you."

"Santiago, nor I were anywhere near that hospital. You've got the wrong fellow."

Someone tapped on the door, and Sheriff Ben was called from the room. In a few minutes, he opened the door slightly and said, "Maggie can you come out here a moment?"

"Don't go away, Mr. Filbin. I've got a few more questions for you," grinned Maggie. Filbin was not going anywhere.

Outside the interrogation room, Sheriff Ben looked at Maggie and said, "We seem to have one of our murders solved. Remember the piece of baseball bat that ended up at the office? Well, forensics have just confirmed what we suspected, Apple's blood was definitely on the bat, so that is absolutely the weapon used in his assault."

Maggie brightened up, and asked, "And where does that get us?"

"That gets us to the murderer. Little Joe's finger prints were all over the bat, and ready for the big one? Beer Can Billy's blood and DNA were unquestionably on the bat."

"That means Little Joe murdered Beer Can Billy, and was so fond of his weapon that he used it on Apple."

"A bit more info. That is not the only DNA on the bat. Apparently Little Joe has used it before, but we have no idea on who."

Maggie suggested someone in the office check past complaints that maybe could fit the bill. "Sheriff, that is good news. Now is there any way we can use that info against Filbin?"

"If Filbin paid him, that would be proof enough for any judge or jury."

Maggie went back into the interrogation room and straightforward told Randy Filbin that he should come clean. "We now have the irrefutable evidence that Little Joe murdered Beer Can Billy and that you either watched, encouraged, or paid him."

"I don't know Beer Can Billy."

"You might know him better as William Harry Wilson, or better, the guy on the dock who saw Bettis Tom hand you money or drugs. I am also pretty sure that you were there on that night, and I also know that Mario

Santiago was there, and as soon as I pick him up, he will rat you out. So, I am going to walk out of here for a while. You and Mr. Frazier talk about it." With that Maggie walked out of the room and immediately moved to the small one-way glass to watch the interaction between Filbin and his attorney.

As she watched, Sheriff Ben moved down the hallway and stood by her side as they watched. Maggie said, "I think his attorney is trying to convince him that his only way is to cooperate. I believe the line I fed him about Santiago selling him out got him thinking."

Sheriff Ben responded, "I've got a plan. Here is what we do. I have a couple of guys on their way to pick up Santiago. The judge issued a warrant about 30 minutes ago. He and the DA have been looking at the surveillance video all morning trying to decide if the video looked like Santiago or not. We both know that it is not much proof, but enough to issue a warrant."

Maggie said, "I sure would like to ask him some questions."

"You're gonna get to, soon. We will let Filbin sit a while. When we get Santiago, leave the door open to Filbin's room, then we will parade Santiago past. We'll just let Filbin know that Santiago is in the room next to his. One of them will begin spilling information."

"I think it will be Filbin. He is about to talk now. The old boy is squirming so much you can almost see the wheels turning in his head. He is close to spilling the beans on everyone. Filbin knows he is in serious trouble."

In New York, Apple was waiting for Mr. Papanicoli in a reception room that was indicative of a successful New York publishing house. Photos of well-known authors adorned the walls, along with posters and awards collected over the years. An autographed picture of Papa Hemingway standing at his typewriter in Sloppy Joe's Saloon was prominently displayed. Apple was impressed, and thought to himself, "What am I doing here?"

Shortly, George Papanicoli himself entered from a side room and escorted App to a small conference room where several others were gathered. The discussion began about Apple's possibility of writing a book about BAR Chem centered around the murders of John Bishop, Beer Can Billy, and Little Joe. They were particularly interested in the assault of Apple and were intrigued with the beating of Little Joe on the porch of his own home.

They were not aware of the details of any of this, but upon learning some of the inside information such as the suitcase full of money, and the yacht that Apple was convinced is smuggling drugs in large quantities into Galveston. They were cautious, but extremely interested in how Jeffrey Chung Dearcorn, as Chairman of the Board, was involved. One of the editors sitting around the conference table had actually met Bettis Tom Stovall in Afghanistan where she was reporting on the special ops of the Army Rangers. Bettis Tom was working for a private security company, Black Nights Security. She had thought at the time that Bettis Tom was probably more dangerous than the enemy that was prowling the mountains. She was glad he was on our side.

George Papanicoli and Excelsior Publishing were eager to sign Apple to a book deal. They had one condition, that anything written in the book was based on facts that could be proven, and that the book would not be written until the investigation was culminated.

Apple asked and was given permission to write as many stories on the progress of the events as he pleased.

He was confident that he could gain employment with any number of national magazines or newspapers, and desired to do so. Excelsior believed, and rightly so, that publicity along the way to the book was a good thing.

Just like that, Apple signed a very satisfactory contract, and with a sizable upfront bonus to begin. Excelsior was confident the finished book would be a best seller, and that was what they were all about.

WILLIAM WARREN

:

Chapter 39
COLORADO BILLY DEVELOPS A PLAN

Colorado Billy was frustrated. He had sat for three hours at Jerry's Icehouse watching for Bettis Tom to arrive. When he asked around, he was met with mostly blank stares. It seemed no one was eager to talk about BT. He did learn that his quarry was not as regular as Little Joe and Fred. Colorado had not expected to find Bettis Tom as easily as Little Joe.

He went to his boat for the night and decided to try a new tactic. BT was not listed in the phone book, few were anymore. Colorado could not find him even mentioned on his computer. It seemed that Bettis Tom was not a Facebook patron. He had called the offices of BAR Chem and got a, "Don't know of an employee named that."

Colorado had started out by going to the marina where the "Chump Change" docked, but no one had seen her for some time. He had no idea that the yacht was in Veracruz. He was frustrated but determined to find Bettis Tom when a thought came to him. He would try a new angle tomorrow.

Colorado Billy had taken his usual precautions. He had changed the license plates on his beat up car and stuck an old baseball cap on, then had abandoned his sloppy look for a more sophisticated, businessman look. He put on a pair of clean khaki pants with a blue jacket, and tie, then pronounced himself fit for his task.

He drove over to Seabrook to start his search. As he drove into the parking area at the city hall, he tried to stay out of reach of the surveillance cameras he knew were lurking.

Colorado Billy, a real businessman before his retirement to the vagabond life, knew how to look and act the part. He had played it before.

Once inside, he sighted the door marked city taxes and utilities. Colorado got in line behind a young woman holding a squirming child by the hand. He was a little impatient to get his game moving. "At last," he thought as he moved to the window where a bored-appearing middle-aged clerk, asked how she could help. Colorado Billy explained how he thought his water bill was overdue, and he was fearful of getting his water turned off.

"What's the name, sir?"

Colorado Billy answered with, "Bettis Tom Stovall."

The clerk looked his name up on the computer, and said, "No sir, you're up to date."

Colorado said, "Are you sure, because I received a past due letter in the mail, and I am real concerned."

With that she turned the computer screen so Colorado Billy could clearly see that he was indeed paid current. He also saw the name Bettis T. Stovall. Billy was always quick witted, and took just a second to memorize the address, a little side street just off Deke Slayton Way.

Colorado Billy walked out of the building, moved around the side of the building to his car, and once inside, immediately jotted down the address. He felt pretty good about the caper he had just successfully pulled off. "Much easier than I thought." He had made a lucky guess about

Seabrook. He did not really know if Bettis Tom lived there. He could have lived in any number of small communities that lined the shore of Galveston Bay.

Colorado knew he was close, so he decided to take a quick look see at the address. He was surprised to find a million dollar condo right on the edge of Clear Lake. He wondered, "How does a boat captain pay for a place like this?" That was when he really began to consider who he was dealing with. All the more reason to avenge the murder of his friend, Beer Can. Why murder such an innocent bystander as Beer Can? Colorado Billy resolved again, they would all pay a price for that. He knew he was just an aging ex-businessman from Colorado, but they had instilled a blind, burning rage inside him. Yes, dammit, they would all pay.

One problem. There was a coded security gate. He parked down the street and watched for about one hour. There was no security guard at the entrance. Cars drove to the gate, punched in their code and the gate swung open, pretty standard stuff. He did notice that several cars simply piggybacked through the gate, on the car in front of them. He thought, if he knew BT's car he could just follow him on through the gate. He had no clue what Bettis Tom drove, and knew that would be a little more difficult than finding out the address at the water department. So he waited and observed. He had patience and time.

He was reluctant to pass on through the gate onto the grounds. He had BT's house number and could find that easy enough. But hanging around in his shabby car would attract unnecessary attention.

After a bit, he decided to drive behind the next car, locate Bettis Tom's house, and examine the lay of the land so to speak. After 15 minutes a big, black auto drove thru the gate, and Colorado gave him a little space, then passed into the entrance, just as if he belonged. He found the entrance to a duplex condo, with the front door on the ground level. The door opened onto a small flagstone landing with no place to conceal himself while waiting for BT. One thing that concerned him was the likelihood that BT would just drive into his garage and close the door before he had a chance to confront him.

He had an idea. He would come back at night. Then Bettis Tom Stovall, soldier of fortune, murderer, would pay.

Colorado Billy drove his old Ford back to Freeport and the comfort of his boat, took off his jacket, made a sandwich, and retired early, his mind and conscience completely clear. He felt in his heart that he was doing the right thing, even the honorable thing. After all, Teddy Roosevelt said, "Speak softly, and carry a big stick." Colorado Billy had a big stick, and he fully intended to carry it. He thought, "Soon, Bettis Tom, soon."

Mario Santiago and his attorney were sitting in a room next to where Randy Filbin was being questioned. Two thoughts were going through each of their minds. Number one, will the other keep quiet, and number two, what will happen to me?

Mario was extremely nervous. He knew that he had not murdered anyone, he had only been the distraction. Surely that would mean something to a judge. His answer to the questions from the Sheriff and his deputy detective were, "I don't know what you are talking about," and "I take the fifth on that."

Santiago felt the only crime he had committed was taking money from Bettis Tom to help keep the ACW from marching in front of the BAR Chem office building. He had always felt badly about betraying his union brothers by taking the money.

His other crime was one of omission. He had seen money and cocaine passed hand to hand from the "Chump Change" to others on the pier. He knew they were smuggling, but kept his mouth shut because the money he was receiving was good.

If the situation demanded it, sooner or later he would give Randy Filbin over on the charge of murdering Little Joe, but the other activities on the yacht he would keep to himself. He was terrified of Bettis Tom. He had heard rumors of Bettis Tom, and the latest that he had murdered someone in the recent weeks and left his body in Galveston Bay. Santiago was fearful that he would end up on the bottom of the bay himself if he even mentioned Bettis Tom Stovall's name to the police.

He determined to tell Sheriff Ben that Filbin and he had been together the night they gave cash to Little Joe and Fred to vandalize Apple's pickup truck, to punish him, but he thought his strategy would be to let go piece by piece information concerning the death of Little Joe and his part in that. He would keep his knowledge of Bettis Tom and the yacht to himself and only use that for a bargaining tool, if need be, later.

Bernie Hannigan received a phone call early in the day from a person who identified himself as spokesman for the local at the ACW. He said that he wanted to inform her and the newspaper that they would be having a special called meeting tonight with the purpose of electing new officers for the union. This was in response to Randy Filbin and Mario Santiago likely facing murder and conspiracy charges, along with extortion. And drug dealing was likely to be added. They weren't so upset with that as they were learning they had taken money from BAR Chem to hold back the union protests. Extortion or conspiracy were bad enough, but to work behind their backs for the company was unbearable. They would be replaced.

The union understood that some publicity about the new leadership would be a good thing for them. Under the circumstances with Little Joe, Fred, Filbin, and Santiago so involved in criminal activities, openness would be prudent, so they called Bernadette.

Bernie decided that she would do the reporting on this event. She did not do field work anymore, but was trained in, and served in that capacity for several years. Bernie felt that this was an important event in the stories that Apple had already written. Since she knew more about the events than anyone, other than Apple or maybe Mr. Barton, she thought she should do the job herself. She was fearful that something would be missed by a reporter not up to date on the events.

After the phone call from the union spokesman, the first thing she did was call Apple. He answered right away. "Hey Bern, what's up?"

Bernie asked him, "Where are you and what are you up to?"

"I am sitting at JFK in New York."

"What are you doing there?"

"I just signed a book deal with Excelsior. I'm going to write a book based on the BAR Chem story." Then he added, "Think that will clear muster with Damon the Dip?"

Bernie said, "I can't wait to tell him."

"Be careful. Someone is behind Damon and my dismissal and Mr. Barton. They might not like the joke."

Bernie said, "I don't care. Here is what I called about. The ACW is holding a meeting tonight to elect new leadership. I thought it would be poetic justice if you showed up to observe. Also it might be some fodder for your book. I doubt the membership would mind."

"I am about to board the plane for Houston any minute. I might just make it. What's going on with the union?"

Apple did not know the latest with Filbin and Santiago. Bernie brought him as up to date as she knew. Maggie and Sheriff Ben were not as eager to inform her as they had been when Apple was on the case.

"I expect to land around five. I think I can just about make it. You're really going to report on the meeting yourself?"

"Yeah, I want this right."

"Does Damon the Dip know your plans?"

"No, I hardly ever talk to the Dip."

"I won't have much time. Morris and I are leaving first thing in the morning for San Francisco." Apple now was the one bringing Bernie up to date on his and Mr. Barton's activities. He had to explain who Jeremiah Eckstein was. Bernie said, "That Barton. I am aware of Eckstein, but I never knew he was a close friend of Mr. Barton's. Alright, in the field reporter, I'll see you at the meeting. Don't get lost."

Apple hung up and punched in Maggie's number. He didn't have any idea how busy she was with Filbin and his partner Santiago. Her phone rang and she stepped out of the room and took the call. "Hey Apple, where you been?" He explained about his trip to New York, and Maggie told him the latest on the two suspects. Apple knew that Little Joe had been smothered in his own hospital bed, but did not know that Randy Filbin and now Mario Santiago had been arrested in connection with the murder.

A shocked Apple said, "Boy, do I need to get home soon. This is moving fast." He then explained to Maggie his plan to attend the union meeting tonight at Big Henry's and sit quietly in the back and take notes, but not to ask any questions. "I am too proud of my new pickup truck to go through that again, not to mention the two fresh pink scars on my face."

Apple told Maggie that he would return day after tomorrow from San Francisco, and then he would explain how the San Fran trip played into all this. Apple wanted to know if she was up for a little gumbo when he returned. He knew she loved the gumbo at a little restaurant down the street from the 1894 Grand in Galveston, and he found himself wanting to see her as soon as possible.

Maggie said, "I can't promise anything right now, with this work load, but call as soon as you get back. We'll work something out." With that they said goodbye and see you soon. Then Apple boarded his flight for George Bush Intercontinental and Houston.

Chapter 40
A HEAVY HITTER COMES ONBOARD

Apple landed and went directly to his truck parked at one of the garages near his gate. He checked his watch and thought that he might just make it all the way to Big Henry's in time to observe the entire meeting. The trip to Galveston was about 70 miles, but the good news was he could take the freeway all the way. If the traffic was cooperative, he would be on time.

Apple made the trip with about five minutes to spare. The spot where his truck was vandalized was empty, but Apple thought otherwise about parking there tonight. Why tempt fate? People were still filing inside. He hoped Bernie was inside.

Once inside, he spotted Bernie sitting over to one side, near an exit door. He made his way around the back of the meeting room, tapped Bernie on the arm, and said, "Saving this seat for someone?"

"Yeah, I am, but he is not here, so you may as well sit." Same ole Bern, always handy with a comeback. Apple smiled.

Just as he sat down, the meeting was called to order by one of the union brothers. Apple scribbled a note, "Who's that?" Bernie leaned over and whispered in his ear, "That's Wilber Moses Wright. He is the president of the entire ACW. He lives in Detroit, came down to preside over this election of new leadership. An upright fellow, by

329

all accounts. Now shut up and listen."

The meeting began, and Apple noticed that this meeting was totally different from the one he attended the night he was attacked. He looked over his shoulder for Little Joe, just in case. This group was all decorum and businesslike, not like the almost impromptu atmosphere of the previous meeting.

In due course, Wilber Moses Wright called out three names that were nominated for president, vice, and secretary. No secret ballot here. If you were for, you stood up, then opposed stood. Unanimous for. Mr. Wright then immediately handed the podium and the gavel over to the new president to a standing ovation from the assembled members, about one hundred total.

Apple was bored. He wanted to ask a few questions, but thought the better of it. He turned toward Bernie and mouthed the words, "I am going to ask a few questions."

Bernie shook her head no.

Apple stood up and said, "Mr. President, my name is Apple Smith. I was, until a few days ago a reporter for the Houston Announcer. They fired me because I would not moderate my stories about the mess BAR Chem has made of the Gulf Coast. Mr. Filbin and Mr. Santiago were part of the corruption that I believe BAR Chem is engaged in. If you were closer you could see the evidence on my face for crossing them.

"As you probably know two of your union members were responsible for putting me in the hospital, all because Filbin didn't care for my questions about his receiving money from the company." There was a low murmur from the members when Apple asked the question, "Will your new leadership be a vast difference from the way Filbin went about the union's business? And have you heard rumors that BAR Chem may return in some way to our area?"

"Mr. Smith, we are glad that you are here tonight. We hope that you will have a more favorable view of us from now on. On behalf of the ACW I would like to apologize for the way you were treated before.

Anytime you want to look at our books, you are welcome, and I don't have to do this, but to my brothers, I intend to issue a personal financial statement regularly as long as I am President. We are also happy tonight to welcome Ms. Bernadette Hannigan, Associate Editor of the Houston Announcer. We can use all the good publicity we can get. And I am aware of the notion that BAR Chem will return. We are hopeful that we can get back to work. And Mr. Smith, I guarantee that your truck will be fine in our parking lot."

In the parking lot a fellow approached Apple and handed him a folded piece of paper with a telephone number written on it. The man said for Apple to call him some time. He had some information that Apple might be interested in.

Bernie said, "I am the reporter here. Why didn't he approach me?"

Apple answered with a grin, "I have a history here. Get beat up with a few scars and they will give you notes."

With the promise to get together as soon as Apple returned from San Francisco, they said good night and departed.

The next morning, Bernie wrote a concise report of the previous night's meeting of the ACW. She said nothing about Filbin or Santiago being in jail pending murder charges. She included a nice interview with the head of the union who had flown in from Detroit. In keeping with the

Houston Announcer's new policy, she made no mention at all of BAR Chem.

Morris Barton and Apple boarded a plane, and four hours later landed at the international airport in San Francisco. They did not check into a hotel because they were planning on returning to Houston as soon as their meeting with Jeremiah Eckstein was over.

They arrived via taxi, pulled up to the curb at 420 Montgomery Street. Apple immediately noticed that the building housed the world headquarters of Wells Fargo. Apple said, "Wow! Tell me again who this guy is we are going to see?"

Mr. Barton, not so impressed because he had been here before to visit his old friend, and as editor for many years of the largest newspaper west of the Mississippi, had many occasions to visit places like this, said, "Just an old Army buddy. Pull your tongue back in and try to relax. Enjoy the moment. We are, as they say, about to pull some strings, some very big strings."

"Boss," Apple said, "I have always underestimated you."

They entered the offices of Eckstein Investments, LLC and were immediately greeted by a middle aged matron who looked up from her desk and said, "May I help you?"

"I am Morris Barton, here to see Jeremiah."

"Yes, I remember talking to you. You ordered me to get Mr. Eckstein on the phone quickly. And, to my surprise, he came right away. Pleasure to meet you, sir. Let me show you in. I believe he is waiting for you."

Apple continued to be amazed, and not too many things amazed him, especially businessmen. But this businessman was different. Apple was looking forward to this meeting but held out little hope for achieving anything. BAR Chem was too big and too important.

Colorado Billy, on a strange whim, took his phone out of his pocket and dialed the offices of BAR Chem. A person answered the phone, "BAR Chemicals, how may I direct your call?"

"Please give me the office of Mr. Roy Jacobs."

"And who, may I tell him, is calling?"

"My name is Jackson Beauregard Boudreaux calling. I am an attorney representing the Royal Deals Gambling Casino in Lake Charles."

Directly Roy Jacobs answered the phone. He had gambled some in the Royal Deals Casino, but knew no reason they should be calling him. His gambling was strictly low boy now. He held back ever since he had that one bad night in Las Vegas two years ago.

"Roy Jacobs here. How can I help you Mr. Boudreaux?"

The voice on the other end said, "Listen to me very carefully. I witnessed you buying drugs from the "Chump Change" and I have it all on video."

"So how can I help you?"

"I want $20,000 and you can have the video."

Roy was stunned. But he had bought cocaine from Bettis Tom on the yacht many times. He usually did not leave the boat, and would stay two or three days. Bettis Tom himself never delivered, but had a deck hand named Arnold or something, maybe Arnost, handed over the stuff. Jacobs said to himself the dirty little bastard is blackmailing me. "Does Bettis Tom know you are calling me? Do you know what he will do if I tell him?"

"Shut up and listen." He gave Roy Jacobs the address of an old broken down house in San Leon with oleander bushes growing wildly alongside and in front of the porch. "Meet me there tonight at 10 p.m. with the money. Don't try anything smart. The two of us will be watching until we are sure you are alone. Mess this up and BAR Chem, your wife, and the Smith reporter guy from the Announcer gets the video."

"I can't get $20,000 at this time of the day."

"Hear me smart guy, that kind of money is chump change to you. Get it, and bring it to me, and I won't bother you again." He smiled as he understood his joke about the "Chump Change."

Roy Jacobs was visibly shaken as he hung his phone up. He said to himself that he needed to slow his life down a bit. This kind of excitement was too much. Getting that much money was no problem for him. He sometimes kept that much in his briefcase, just for fun. He recognized that he lived life on the edge. He also wondered if he should try to get in touch with Bettis Tom. He decided against that. What if Bettis Tom were behind this shakedown? Roy doubted that since BT was very rich and wouldn't worry about $20,000. He knew if Jeffrey Chung Dearcorn got wind of this, there would be repercussions. Roy decided to just keep his mouth shut, deliver the money, and hope that Boudreaux would keep his word about handing over the video.

Apple and Mr. Barton entered a large office where Jeremiah Eckstein was waiting just inside the door. He greeted Morris Barton warmly. Apple grinned as he watched the old war buddies take a step back, pop to attention, and salute each other, just like they were young men. Jeremiah said, "That is for General Westmoreland. How I hated that old dog."

"Yeah, the food was terrible," and they both laughed.

Mr. Barton introduced Apple and said, "This young guy is the best investigative reporter that I have ever known, and I have known a few. He will someday win a Pulitzer, wait and see."

After a few pleasant exchanges, Jeremiah said, "After your phone call, I have been waiting for this conversation. Please tell me all the details, and what do you expect me to do about it?"

Mr. Barton said, "Apple, you begin, since it is your story."

Apple started from the beginning about how he wanted to do a story on BAR Chem leaving Texas for Mexico. Eckstein broke in, "I was never in favor of that. But, I was not in the line of command to have much influence. Please continue."

Apple went through the whole litany of events, bringing Eckstein up to date. He even talked about the union affairs and his recent beating at the hands of Little Joe, and the recent death of Little Joe in the hospital.

He told of how the two union leaders were accused of murdering one of their own, Little Joe. Mr. Eckstein asked, "Is that where you got the fresh scars?" At that, Jeremiah Eckstein leaned in close and pulled back his own hair to reveal a dimming scar running from the front of his scalp to the top of his left ear. "Got that from a mugging about ten years ago as I stepped from my car. My wife and I were strolling Market Street, relaxing, eating, when we were attacked and robbed."

At this bit of news, Apple knew he had a kindred spirit. Apple left out the parts concerning Mr. Barton from his narrative, leaving that for him. Morris Barton related how first M. Ellis Winston tried to bribe him, and when that didn't work, Bettis Tom had shown up with a different tactic. Mr. Barton described it as strong armed extortion. He was calm, but had a hard tone in his voice as he described BT's visit to his office. What he was particularly upset about was not losing his job, but that the newspaper he had given his heart to for so many years caved in to the demands of BAR Chem. "And so, Jeremiah, that brings us to you."

Jeremiah asks, "Were the stories in your paper so devastating that the company felt like it needed to shut you off?"

Apple, up to this time, had sat back and allowed Mr. Barton to answer and speak, but this time he spoke up, "We only printed what is true. What started all this was the murder of one of the company's own employees, an attorney named John Bishop. I was interviewing the Sheriff when he got the call, and he allowed me to go along. A shrimp trawler had pulled his body out of Galveston Bay. That in itself was not so unusual, but he had on a charcoal gray business suit with a briefcase locked to his arm that was filled with cash. Now we only reported those true things. I personally witnessed them myself. I might add, he had a bullet hole in the back of his head.

"The BAR Chemicals company yacht was spotted in the vicinity the night before Mr. Bishop was murdered. We printed only those facts concerning Mr. Bishop."

"Why would BAR Chem murder one of their own employees?"

Mr. Barton said, "Simple. The money was to have been used to bribe local officials to smooth the way for BAR Chem to return to Texas, and the way I figure it, someone got greedy, decided to take the money for themselves, Mr. Bishop jumped into the water and was shot in the process. But the persons were unable to locate his body in the water

336

in the dark.

"You know the entire Houston Ship Channel area is the best location in the world for chemical companies. BAR Chem owns all of the land they used to occupy. They want to go no other place and begin again. Occupying their old property is very important, but permits, the EPA, including state and national officials, have to approve the reoccupying of that tract of land."

Jeremiah Eckstein added, "Buying another suitable tract would cost the company about one billion dollars. We are not prepared to do that. On the other hand, we are interested in doing things the right way."

Apple said, "I know there are at least two other murders connected with BAR Chem, and I believe I can produce numerous other officials that will attest to the bribery charges. Personally, I was attacked for asking questions at the union meeting, and the money paid to the two thugs came from BAR Chem."

Mr. Eckstein said, "I will tell you for certain that the company is losing money in a big way in Mexico, and we need to stop the bleeding. One way is to move at least part of the operation back to our old site in Texas."

Mr. Barton interjected, "Here is our proposal. Use your influence to replace the entire Board of Directors, including that soldier of fortune, Bettis Tom Stovall. If you don't, he and the board will pull you down. Everyone that knows anything will have the finger pointed at them when we finish our reporting on the company. There will be many newspaper and magazine stories about what is going on, not to mention the new book that Apple will write for Excelsior Publishing."

"You've convinced me, Morris, but that will be a big job. Dearcorn and the entire board own a large number of the stocks. Let me work on it, and I will see what I can put together. I just ask that in the meantime, lighten up on us a little bit. Don't stop reporting, just give us the benefit of the doubt. And perhaps help us return to the Gulf Coast."

Everything was agreed on in gentlemen to gentlemen handshakes. Nothing recorded, nothing written down, just three men looking into the eyes of the other and agreeing.

When Apple and Mr. Barton were in a taxi cab heading to SFO airport, Apple asked, "Do you think he will keep his word?"

"He will or die trying, which he might with that crazy Bettis Tom around."

They arrived at the airport where only Apple got out. Morris informed him that he was going to stay in San Francisco for a few days as the guest of Jeremiah Eckstein at his house.

"Wow, boss, you amaze me. We just threatened to take the man's billion dollar business down, and he invites you to visit with him for a few days. How do you do it?"

With that, Apple walked into the terminal for his flight to Houston. He was already looking forward to seeing Maggie tonight. He mused in his mind that she was the most interesting woman he had ever met, and, he grinned, not too bad to look at either.

Chapter 41
THE GOOD AVENGER MEETS ROY JACOBS

Colorado Billy sat around all day, nervous, drinking coffee, and finally a Jack Daniels and Coke. Nothing helped. He was jittery. But through all this introspection, he knew he was doing the right thing. Roy Jacobs was a despicable, uncouth man. Roy was willing to sit around and watch, never hands on, as people were hurt. He may or may not have the power to change anything, but he never tried. He did not care.

Colorado figured, after this night, Roy will care. Maybe he will even be convinced to change his ways. He might even turn out to be an ally. Roy just needs to see the error of his ways, an epiphany. After he feels the pain in a personal way, he could be a help.

It was finally time. He changed the license plates one more time in the dark. If he hurried he would just have time to make a stop at Lowe's to pick up a few items.

After arriving at the store, he went straight to the yard tools area. He bought an axe and a cheap handsaw. Later as he made his way to pay, on a last-second thought, he bought a roll of duct tape.

On his way to San Leon, he made one stop at a small local supermarket. He was careful to scan for security cameras. When he saw none, he pulled into the back of the parking lot. Once parked, he popped the trunk and took out the axe and the handsaw. He glanced around to make sure no one was nearby, and proceeded to cut the handle out of the axe, up near the blade. He grinned to himself as he thought, maybe I should leave the blade on. A couple of whacks with that will change his attitude. But, he recognized he did not want to kill him or leave him permanently harmed, only a little pain, and scare the hell out of him.

Colorado took the back roads, aiming to hit the Gulf Freeway through Santa Fe, Texas. Along the way he threw the head of the axe and the handsaw over the rail on the high bridge over Chocolate Bayou. No cars in sight, so he was sure he had not been seen by anyone.

Arriving at San Leon a little early, he decided to kill an hour or so at Jerry's Ice House. He felt he could use a drink before his appointed hour with Roy Jacobs.

He walked into the popular but very informal eatery, and walked straight to the bar on the far side of the room. This is the same seat he had occupied once before. Close enough to see the veranda with the half-moon shinning across Galveston Bay. Altogether a beautiful evening.

He had calmed down a bit from his planning and activities of the last several hours. "What'll it be buddy?" He ordered a Bud in a longneck bottle, and noticed that he was contented and calm. He felt good, knowing that he was acting responsibly, considering the way he and his friends had been treated. Not to worry, for he would soon even the score a little.

Roy Jacobs entered Jerry's and walked straight out the large open doors to the veranda. He sat at a small table near the rail of the patio. He appeared to be a man without a trouble in the world. But, on the inside he could hardly keep the trembling from being noticed. At this time he still was contemplating whether or not to keep the ten o'clock meeting. He was pondering if he should call the cops, tell Dearcorn, or even call Bettis Tom. Maybe the call to Bettis Tom was the answer. He would know how to handle this kind of situation. Whoever called him would be sorry when BT stuck that big gun in his ribcage.

After one beer Colorado Billy got up and started to the men's room, when he was struck by the sight of Roy Jacobs sitting alone having a drink. He was not absolutely sure it was Roy. He had only seen him coming and going from the "Chump Change" late at night, never in a good light. On the way back to his barstool, he purposely detoured for a closer look. He was pretty sure it was Roy.

He smiled because he knew Roy would be at the meeting place. Before he wasn't sure if the cops would be waiting for him, or perhaps some more thugs hired by Bettis Tom. Now he was sure Roy would be there alone. At any rate he could watch and wait. He was confident that Roy Jacobs did not know him from anyone else in the bar.

Apple called Maggie as soon as his plane touched down at Bush Intercontinental, and they agreed to meet at a local Tex-Mex restaurant just off Nasa Road 1 and the Gulf Freeway. He was happy to arrive a little before she did. He thought it bad form to have his lady dinner date meet him and arrive before him.

She arrived soon after him, and they were seated rather quickly. It was always a good plan to have dinner during the middle of the week rather than on the crowded weekends.

They were sipping on margaritas, enjoying the evening. Maggie was saying, "I believe Filbin or Santiago, or maybe both are near talking. Especially Filbin seems to be feeling the stress. After all, we have had him in custody for three days. That means after about 18 hours a day questioning, he is very tired and feeling alone. Even his attorney is not there all the time with him.

Maggie's phone rang and said, "Really? I'll be quick. I am only about 20 minutes from there. Has anyone called the DA? Yeah, right. Hey Sheriff, I'm having dinner with Apple, OK if I bring him along?"

Apple, very puzzled, said, "What is going on? OK if I come where? Maybe I don't want to come along."

"Believe me, you want to be on this stage. Pay the bill and let's go. Filbin wants to make a statement, and he said he will only talk to me."

"Well how about that? Only you, huh?"

"Yes, only me. You want to come or not?"

"Wouldn't miss it. I would love to see those two squirm. You really think they murdered Little Joe?"

"Positive."

Colorado Billy sat watching Roy Jacobs, making a plan in his head. Presently he got up from his bar stool, placed a five dollar bill on the bar, and strolled slowly out of Jerry's Ice House. Colorado drove slowly over the familiar road to Little Joe's house. He had chosen Joe's house because it was familiar to him, provided some cover from the street, and he knew no one would be home.

He parked his car two blocks down the street over on the grassy shoulder. His old Ford fit in perfectly with the surrounding neighborhood. He had no worries about it drawing attention parked as it was.

Colorado Billy walked around to the back of the car and found the axe handle stowed in the trunk. He put on a pair of latex gloves, pulled his cap down low over his eyes. He hoofed the two blocks on the opposite side of the open drainage ditch, near the shrubbery. He was in luck. Not a single car came down the street.

He was confident that he would arrive ahead of Roy, since he was still sipping a drink when Colorado left Jerry's. He cautiously approached the front of the house from the side, found a concealed place in the oleander bushes, and dropped to his knees to wait.

He had been sitting, waiting one hour. He knew it was near ten, it had to be. Presently a car turned into the driveway and immediately doused its lights.

Roy sat in the car looking out into the night, trying to notice anything that he might recognize. He thought that he was here before his blackmailer. Maybe he would just sit in his car and wait. After about 15 minutes, Roy grew restless. Maybe he was supposed to knock on the door? He would love to just drive off, but he knew the kinds of things that were on the video would bring him plenty of trouble with the company, and maybe even the police. No, he would just wait. Presently he felt the urge to urinate. He had two drinks and a beer while killing time at Jerry's. He stepped out of the car and cautiously walked to the edge of the oleander bushes.

Suddenly he was struck on the side of his head with something very hard. Roy went down to the ground. Another blow hit him savagely across his shoulder blades. Roy tried to turn over on his side to see his assailant, but was struck across his cheekbone with the hard object. Blood was now flowing freely from the back of his head and the cut on his cheekbone.

"Who are you?" choked out Roy.

"Just take it that I am not a friend of the family," whereas Colorado delivered another blow below the chin with his well-placed foot.

Then Colorado laughed out loud and said, "Just call me the Good Avenger." He remembered the quote from the

Houston Announcer when they had described him so, after his beating of Little Joe.

"Why are you doing this?" groaned Roy.

"I know you were there the night Little Joe murdered Beer Can Billy, and you sat by and watched without doing anything to stop it. Tell me the truth, and I will not hit you again."

"I don't know what you are talking about. I never heard of any Beer Can whatever."

Colorado hit him across the left collar bone with the axe handle, and broke the bone with ease.

"Tell me the truth. You saw everything, right? The night on the pier after gambling and doing drugs on the "Chump Change."

"OK, I did see, I was there, but I was powerless to do anything to help your friend."

"Here's what I am going to do," said Colorado Billy. "Give me your cell phone. I want you to go to the police and tell the Sheriff's Department what you just told me. I want you to tell them that Bettis Tom, as I know he was, told Little Joe to rough up Beer Can Billy. I also want you to resign from the board at BAR Chem. Just lie still, and when I am a safe distance down the road, I will call for an ambulance. If you don't do as I say, I will kill you next time, and soon. Do you understand me?"

Roy said nothing, Colorado Billy hit him across the kneecap, hard enough to fracture the bone. "Do we understand each other? Speak to me!"

Roy struggled to say, "Yes."

Colorado Billy said, "That's good enough for me."

When Maggie and Apple arrived at the police station, she directed Apple where to stand outside the interrogation room viewing through the one-way glass pane. Maggie had given him stern directions about not being seen and not saying a word, but he would be able to hear everything inside the room. He just nodded his head, took up his station and notepad. This was important stuff and he did not want to miss a word.

Maggie walked into Filbin's room, accompanied by the Galveston County District attorney, and said, "You wanted to see me?"

Filbin just shook his head in the affirmative. His attorney had not arrived. She turned the conversation over to the DA where he explained his rights in clear, concise statements.

Then he turned back the questioning to Maggie, who said, "So you are prepared to give me a statement? Did you kill Little Joe Edmundson? How, and why?"

Randy Filbin just shook his head up and down in the affirmative. Maggie said, "You're going to have to speak, not just nod."

Filbin answered, "Yes, I did."

Then Maggie exited the room. "I'll be right back." She walked to the room next to Filbin and knocked lightly, stuck her head in the room and nodded to Sheriff Ben who was locked in conversation with Mario Santiago. Sheriff Ben said to Santiago, "Your friend in the next room has just admitted to the killing of Little Joe, and has said you were his accomplice. Do you want to make a statement? It will go easier for you if you volunteer. You can tell your side. Otherwise, Filbin will tell his version and you will have no rebuttal. If you were smart you would tell your side of the story."

Mario Santiago's eyes were blazing, "I don't believe you. Randy would not do that to me."

"Hang on a minute," and Sheriff Ben left the room.

He knocked on the door and motioned Maggie outside. "Give me details, my guy doesn't believe me."

Maggie said, "Santiago distracted the nurses while Filbin held a pillow over Little Joe's face. He even described exactly what Santiago was wearing. Tell Santiago that only Filbin could know that. He has also admitted telling Little Joe and Fred to vandalize Apple's truck and to punish him. Add that we even know how much money they gave them to assault Apple. He has also told me Bettis Tom Stovall has been funneling drugs and money to Filbin and Santiago to keep the ACW union in line. Sheriff Ben, one other thing. Filbin thinks that the "Chump Change" has double bulkheads to hide drugs, spaced all around the yacht. He says in the master stateroom, there is a panel that comes off exposing a very small entry. Filbin says that a fellow named Arnost is in charge of stowing and maintaining all the secret cargo onboard. I think we got them, Sheriff."

"Good job, Maggie."

Maggie added, rather sadly, "They murdered Little Joe because they were fearful he would spill the beans on all of them. Now they are here." She turned to Apple and said, "Be careful how you report. It is highly unorthodox to allow a reporter in to witness this, but you earned it. Look at your scars."

Apple nodded, "Thanks."

Colorado Billy drove down the Gulf Freeway a piece, and directly turned into Big Henry's Beer and Bait. He quickly found a vacant parking space, not too busy this time of night. He walked around to the back of the car and called 911, gave them the address where they could find Roy Jacobs. "And hurry, he's been beaten very badly." Colorado then took the phone, tossed it down on the asphalt and hit it with a claw hammer from the trunk of the car.

The phone shattered into about six parts, which he threw one by one into the water.

He then took the handsaw and quickly cut the axe handle into four parts. Colorado then walked over to the edge of the tidal pool and tossed two of the pieces far out into the eddy. He was confident that the tide would take the pieces quickly into the bay and eventually into the ocean. He kept the two smaller pieces for later disposal. He was careful to keep out of view of the two security cameras located at the front of the parking lot.

He then casually walked into Big Henry's and ordered a Budweiser in a long neck. He was contented with his day's work. Another of the cold blooded killers had been dealt with. Colorado figured he would relax a few days, then pay Bettis Tom a visit. After all BT was the one deserving justice more than the others. Colorado vowed that he would get his justice soon.

WILLIAM WARREN

Chapter 42
APPLE IS ON THE SCENE

Sheriff Ben came quickly out of his interrogation room, paused in front of Apple and said, "I swear, every time I see you, somebody turns up beaten or dead."

Apple said to the Sheriff, "I'm good job security for you, Sheriff."

"Hang loose, if you haven't had enough for the night. I'll explain later."

He stuck his head into the room where Filbin and Maggie were finishing up signing papers that the District Attorney was shoving in his face, "Maggie, are you finished? Please come out here."

"Yes sir, Sheriff, what gives?"

"911 just got an anonymous call. There has been another, so called, beating at Little Joe's house. Got a feeling we need to get over there quick."

The Sheriff turned to Apple and said, "Almost seems like you work here. You can ride with me, or follow along, I know you are going regardless."

"Thanks Sheriff, I know the way. I'll just follow." He looked at Maggie and just shrugged his shoulders and said, "What?" She shrugged back.

All three arrived directly behind an ambulance, whose crew was kneeling over a very still person lying on the porch of Little Joe's house. It was very strange how close he was lying to the position where Little Joe had lain so recently.

Apple got out of his pickup with his note pad in hand. He did not want to forget any of the small details. He moved in as close as he could risk without getting in the way of the emergency crew or Sheriff Ben.

He overheard the Sheriff say to Maggie, "Some guy named Roy Jacobs. You ever hear of him?" Maggie did not know him. It suddenly hit Apple who this guy is. "He is a member of the Board of Directors at BAR Chem."

Sheriff Ben asked Apple, "How you know this?"

"I recently had an interview with him over at the BAR Chem offices. I was supposed to meet with Jeffery Chung Dearcorn, this guy substituted for him."

"What do you know about him?"

"I know that he is rich, and spends a lot of time loafing on the "Chump Change.""

Sheriff Ben spoke to Maggie, "This is strange. Why would he be on the front porch of Little Joe's? Got any ideas why? Hold on a minute."

The EMTs were talking to the Sheriff. "He will live, no life threatening issues, but he is beat severely. Appears to have a shattered collar bone and a crushed knee. He has sustained several sharp blows to the head and face. We have stopped the bleeding and given him a painkiller."

Sheriff Ben asked, "When will I be able to talk to him?" The Sheriff was looking through Roy's wallet. "Seems you are right, Apple, he is Roy Jacobs. And, he does work for BAR Chem, at least this ID card shows that he does. You continue to amaze me, how you keep turning up in places like this."

"Just a gift, Sheriff."

The ambulance raced away with their patient, lights blazing. Again this neighborhood had been awakened in the night to the sound of sirens and bright lights. The Sheriff had his men looking around the house for anything out of the ordinary. The only thing they discovered was where the assailant had crouched in the bushes waiting for Roy.

Maggie looked at the Sheriff and at Apple and said, "I think I have a pretty good idea who is responsible for this. I need to go by the office and look at the report from the night our friend Beer Can was murdered. I wonder if there is any record of Roy Jacobs being around that scene?"

Apple said, "I know what you are thinking."

"Oh, you do, do you?"

"Yes, our 'Good Avenger,' aka Colorado Billy, has struck again."

Sheriff Ben added, "You're thinking the same guy who assaulted Little Joe is responsible for this?"

"Well, yes. The similarities are too striking to ignore. If we find out who attacked Little Joe, we will have our guy. I just don't know how this fellow fits in with Little Joe and this whole business.

Sheriff Ben told Maggie, "Since you are already on the case, just add this, and keep at it."

Maggie replied, "I am going by the office to do some research, then turning in. First thing in the morning, I am going to begin searching for Colorado Billy."

Apple said, "I'll bet if we could find the "Chump Change" we would have some answers to this puzzle."

They departed the scene, and as soon as Apple was in his car he dialed up Bernadette at the Houston Announcer.

"Apple, why the hell are you calling at this hour? This better be good. You're not dead, are you?"

"Wake up, associate editor, I've got a scoop for you."

Apple then detailed the entire Roy Jacobs affair. They both agreed that the beating of Mr. Jacobs was indeed a newsworthy event. He was a very important cog in the BAR Chem operations, even if only in name. And, Little Joe's beating and this assault, and even Apple's assault were all connected. They knew Little Joe and Fred were responsible for Apple's beating, but who was responsible for Little Joe's and now Roy Jacobs? They were too closely tied for a simple coincidence.

Bernie, now fully awake and interested, asked Apple, "Can you write up a story, say 500 words, summing up what you witnessed?"

"What? You want me to write a story under an assumed name for the newspaper that just recently fired me for writing stories on this subject? Are you crazy? Plus I used to get paid for stuff like this."

"Come on Apple, You probably owe me more than this one."

"What do you think Damon the Dip will have to say about it?"

"We won't tell him that you wrote it, and besides I approve everything anyway, he will never even see it. All he does is play golf all day, he never reads any copy. Please do me this favor, and by the way, early tomorrow."

They agreed and Apple wrote a short summary of what he had witnessed. He smiled as he made reference to the "Good Avenger" at least twice in the article. He knew Bernie might edit out one of those references before the article made it to print. The story was more vague than he would have liked, but he was not sure how much BAR Chem could be mentioned and connected since Mr. Barton and himself had been dismissed over that very issue. He was humored thinking about the book he would write.

BAR Chem would be bashed and hammered as he would determine they deserved. He smiled as he thought that he just might take a shot at the Announcer, as well, for dismissing his story.

WILLIAM WARREN

Chapter 43
MAGGIE GETS CLOSE

Colorado Billy had just returned from a quick trip to Surfside Beach where he had walked into the sand dunes and buried the remains of the axe handle that he had used to beat Roy Jacobs. He returned to the marina and walked down the end of the pier where his boat was tied. Right away he noticed something different. The swinging hatch leading to the entrance of his boat and living quarters was standing wide open. Colorado knew he had not left it open. He cautiously entered the hatchway and mounted the four steps leading into the interior of his boat. Someone had been here. Not much was disturbed, just some papers he kept in his navigation table. He knew his car title and boat insurance were there, so whoever was here now knew his identity. Colorado Billy thought, not good.

He found a note which stated, "Good Avenger", aka Colorado Billy, stop your business and we'll call it even. Continue at your own peril.

The next morning, Colorado Billy unlocked the hiding place inside a cupboard, found his .45, and tucked it into the back of his belt, under his shirt. Then he walked to the marina office. He warmly greeted the office attendant as if he had no troubles in the world, and said, "Well, today is the day, I am heading south. The weather is good, and I am getting restless." He made arrangements to pick up his car at a later date.

He informed them that he was heading for Venezuela, about a two week trip if the wind favored him. They said their goodbyes, and Colorado paid his fees up to date.

His tanks were full of fresh water, his fuel topped off, and he had enough food to last him a month. He was ready. Colorado motored out of the marina into the Intracoastal Waterway, and motored right on by the jetty that led to the open Gulf of Mexico. He had no intention of going to Venezuela. He was still pissed about his friend Beer Can's murder and the beating of Apple Smith. His determination was stronger than ever to punish those responsible. So far it had been easy. Now it was perhaps going to be a little more difficult. But he figured that the closer he got to the bear's den, the tougher it would be.

After thinking about his break-in, he knew it could be only one person, or at least his hired hands, Bettis Tom himself had paid a visit to his boat. Well, they can come back, but I will be gone. He laughed loudly as he thought, "I'll keep them guessing. They have to be a little worried about where I am." He wished he had left a note for Bettis Tom at his home when he had visited. Maybe he would just do that to even the score. He thinks he is hunting me, well, let him be the hunted.

Four hours later and he had crossed Galveston Bay and was entering the Watergate Marina on Clear Lake. He had called ahead and made arrangements to dock his boat there. He was very familiar with the marina, having been there many times. A nice place with swimming pools, laundry facilities, internet, and restaurants close by.

Registering under a false name, he chuckled. William Bonney, Billy the Kid. "That I am," he said to himself.

Colorado Billy called a taxi, went to a rental car

agency on NASA Road 1, and rented a car, one way to Freeport where he retrieved his old Ford Focus. He would need his car soon.

Maggie was busy with her police contacts up and down the coast searching for a fellow named William Jack Burleson, most of the time referred to as Colorado Billy. He would be sailing a 46-foot Island Packet sailboat. She had systematically started at Beaumont, moved down the Texas coast from there. She rightly figured that Colorado was somewhere close, not as far as Florida. He had to be close because it would just be too much trouble to travel from far away, put his victims in the hospital, then travel back, so he had to be nearby. She figured Freeport, or perhaps Bay City. The Matagorda Harbor Marina answered promptly and stated that there was no one or boat matching that description. She moved on down to Aransas Pass. Same result, no one matching her questions there.

She tried Freeport again, both Bridge Harbor and the Municipal marina at Freeport. Bridge Harbor said not there, and only one Island Packet, but only twenty nine feet. The city marina at Freeport did not answer the phone.

Maggie figured that by the time she got someone from the Freeport Police to drive over and check it out, she could take a look see for herself.

She was becoming confident that her quarry was there. She somehow, instinctively knew he was the one that had beaten both Little Joe and Roy Jacobs. She now had proof that Randy Filbin and Mario Santiago had murdered Little Joe, and that Little Joe, with unknown accomplices had murdered Beer Can, but she needed Colorado Billy for the assault on Roy Jacobs. She felt that if she could question Colorado for the Jacobs affair, then those two cases could be sewed up. Maggie knew that she was making end roads into the whole BAR Chem entanglement, specifically the murder of John Bishop. What she was hoping for was some evidence to tie all this to Bettis Tom. She knew he was at the heart of this whole affair.

Maggie climbed into her unmarked police cruiser and pointed her car in the direction of Hwy 6 and Freeport. She smiled to herself as she thought, "I might just catch Colorado Billy by surprise." She thought of calling Apple, but in her haste, decided against it. She didn't want to spend time waiting for him to arrive.

Maggie was thinking as she was driving that maybe things would be better if she just allowed Colorado do his thing. Bettis Tom has to be on his hit list sooner or later.

Chapter 44
CHASING COLORADO BILLY

App was emptying his briefcase when a small folded piece of paper caught his attention. As he unfolded its creases, he remembered the fellow that had given it to him a few days ago, after the ACW meeting at Big Henry's. Bernie had remarked as to why the guy had given it to Apple instead of her. He had almost forgotten about the man saying, "Call me, I have information you may want."

He dialed the number written on the note, and a sleepy voice answered. Apple reminded him of the note. The fellow, whose name was Jim Argile, told App that he was a friend of Colorado Billy's, that he had met him after a fishing trip at Big Henry's Beer and Bait.

Apple was astounded when he was told that he had received a phone call recently from Colorado Billy. "How can that be since he is in the Caribbean, somewhere?"

Jim answered, "He's not in the Caribbean. He is somewhere nearby, and that is all I want to tell you on the phone."

Apple said, "How about one hour? Can you meet me at Big Henry's? I need to hear more. You know Colorado is a friend of mine. I would like to help him."

As Apple turned in the lot at Big Henry's, he noticed the boat ramp where two guys were launching a boat for a day's fishing. They reminded him of the first time he had met Randy Filbin and Mario Santiago. How times had changed. Now they were in jail charged with murdering Little Joe, and replaced by the ACW as the local leaders. Well, good riddance to them.

He went inside where there were only two other patrons at this time of day. He sat at a bar stool, and presently one of the fellows approached him. "Hey, are you the reporter?"

"That would be me. Are you Jim?"

After pleasantries, Apple got down to business. "How do you know it was Colorado Billy on the phone?"

"I recognized his voice, and he told me so. I have exchanged calls with him several times."

Apple explored, "Why are you telling me this now?"

Jim said, "I expect he is the "Good Avenger" that the Announcer is now calling him. Colorado told me he was the one that gave Little Joe his trip to the hospital. He had it coming, but I don't know this other guy."

"But why tell me?"

"I believe Colorado is getting in serious trouble, and maybe you can help, without involving the cops. Perhaps you could locate and talk to him. Maybe get him to really go to the Caribbean."

"If he is actually nearby, I would love to talk to him. You know, he might not be the "Good Avenger". Many people held grudges again Little Joe and are glad he is gone."

"Yeah, me for one. I had an altercation with Little Joe a few years back, when the company first left for Mexico. I would have whipped his ass if he had not pulled out that big Buck knife." At this Jim turned his arm over to expose a nine-inch scar inflicted by the knife.

"What was the fight about?"

"Little Joe was siding a little too far on the side of

BAR Chem and I called him out for it. He went to jail and was bailed out by his pal, some guy named Bettis Tom Stovall. Got off easy, claimed self defense. He got out of jail, and I got this scar."

Apple asked Jim, "Do you know that it is almost certain Little Joe was paid by Randy Filbin to do just such things? And, that the money came from Bettis Tom, he got it from BAR Chem. He is on their payroll now."

"We, meaning all the union brothers, have suspected that for a few years. We are all glad they are gone."

Apple asked, "Jim, do you have any idea where Colorado might be hiding out?"

"I have a pretty good idea, I think it is somewhere in Brazoria County."

"Why Brazoria County?" Apple knew Brazoria County as the county down the coast from Galveston and only 30 miles or so from where they were sitting.

"The call was from 979, which is the area code for Brazoria County. I believe he tossed his old phone into the ocean and bought a new one there."

Apple knew that he could only be in one or two places, that being Bridge Harbor near the high bridge at Surfside Beach or the City Marina at Freeport. He had an urge to finish this conversation and get headed to Freeport.

"You've been a big help. I will find Colorado and try to help him out of this sticky situation. I'm fearful if he keeps this up, he will be hurt himself, or land in jail."

Jim asked, "What do you know about this Bettis Tom character? I hear he is a very bad fellow to get mixed up with."

Apple said, "Just that he has been a soldier of fortune, but in recent years has been involved in shady deals on behalf of BAR Chem around the world. My

WILLIAM WARREN

research indicates that he was in up to his neck in Italy a few years ago, convincing their Minister of Foreign Trade to do exclusive business with BAR Chem, for construction steel. He is a scary fellow. Keep away from him if you can."

"I think Colorado holds him responsible for Beer Can's murder. He told me that he may just look up this Bettis Tom fellow."

Apple said, "I hope not, this BT is a different kind of cat."

Jim replied, "If I were Bettis Tom, I would be looking over my shoulder. It would be a bad thing to underestimate Colorado Billy. I think he can more than take care of himself."

Apple just shook his head, "I am beginning to think you are right."

Jim gave Apple Colorado's phone number, and they departed. Apple promised that he would keep Jim up to date on the happenings of the investigation. That was the least he could do for such valuable information.

Apple drove out of the parking lot and immediately hit the accelerator on his pickup. Because he was a cautious driver, he had forgotten how well his truck ran. He bumped up to 80 quickly and headed for Hwy 6 towards Freeport. He knew he would find Colorado Billy there. The Brazoria County area code pointed there clearly. Just like Maggie, he felt it in his bones that Colorado was at the City Marina in his big sailboat.

He smiled as he remembered the name of Colorado's boat, "Rocky Mountain High." Apple felt a tinge of sadness for all the events that had happened. Beer Can's death, and now Colorado in so much trouble. Those two had only been doing what they enjoyed in their retirement, enjoying their boats, and each other's company.

Apple mused about what type of individual would sail single-handed across the globe as both these exceptional gentlemen had. All they had wanted to do was live their lives on their own terms. Apple thought, so much evil in the world. He knew all Colorado was trying to do was even the score. Apple admired him very much. Not so much his methods, but thanking him for beating the hell out of Little Joe, after what Little Joe had done to him. He instinctively reached up and touched the big scars on his face. He smiled. He vowed to find Colorado Billy and help him in any way he could.

Apple noticed that he was gaining on the rather plain white Chevy Suburban running south on Hwy 288. Whoever was driving, was set on 78 miles an hour in a 65. He figured they must trust their police radar detector. So he thought he could just piggy back and avoid State Troopers all the way to Freeport. His Ford pickup with the big v8 was effortlessly moving down the road, and he was enjoying the trip. He felt somewhat of a sense of urgency in making this search for Colorado Billy, but still managed to listen to some Sinatra on his XM.

The white Suburban and the Ford Pickup followed and led each other past the football stadium and the high school, turned left and made their way down the center of old Freeport. What a sad looking place, thought Apple.

Indeed it was, a once thriving small town back in the fifties, just ran out of growing room. Businesses moved to better locations, or just gave up. The once thriving party boat industry had been killed by the limit on red snapper. Not many people were waiting in line to kill all day for two fish. So, the snapper business just ended abruptly.

The Port of Freeport thrived, but most of the money

earned there went elsewhere. The huge chemical complex did not contribute much to the locals, so the city was just dying. Ten years or so ago, the city fathers had an idea to build a new state of the art floating pier marina, to accommodate sport fishermen and pleasure craft. But, as people soon discovered, there were no local restaurants, or points of interest near the marina. Promises of hotels and restaurants never materialized. Boaters stayed away. Too bad, thought Apple, it is a good marina.

The white Suburban, much to Apple's surprise, turned left at the light and made for the marina, crossed the low levee bordering the old Brazos River, and turned into the marina parking lot.

Apple looked around and thought this is the perfect hide away for Colorado Billy. He had high hopes that he would find Colorado here. His intentions were not entirely honorable. If he did find him, he had determined to warn him that the Galveston County Sheriff considered him the prime suspect in the two recent assaults on Little Joe and Roy Jacobs. If he had not gone south, maybe now was the time.

Apple had admiration for Colorado, if he was the "Good Avenger." After all, he had evened the score for the beating Apple had endured. It all made common sense. Who would be interested in whipping Little Joe, or for that matter Roy Jacobs? Only Colorado Billy fit the bill. Beer Can had been his friend, and those who sail across the oceans single-handed aren't easily put off. "Yes," he thought, "It has to be Colorado Billy." Apple hoped to find him.

The white suburban found a parking spot near the marina office. Apple parked back down the end of the lot. He exited his car and walked toward the office. He stopped and glared into the high sky, sunny day, trying to make out the person moving toward the office. He was smiling big. He saw the back of those khaki pants open the door, and he knew who had been in the suburban all the way to Freeport.

"I'll be damned, it's Maggie!"

Maggie hadn't seen Apple, so rather than intrude on her space, not to mention her authority, he waited by the door outside. Presently she exited, and pretended to be surprised when she saw him waiting. "Hello there, Mister Reporter."

"Out of your territory, aren't you, Deputy Inspector?"

"No, the guy inside seems to like me rather well."

"Any luck? It seems we are both chasing the same shadow."

"Bad luck. Our man seems not to be here. But, at least our instincts were right. He was here, but the fellow said he had checked out only yesterday."

"My guess is he didn't leave a forwarding address."

"Yes, he did. Venezuela." Maggie did not believe it. "I am more than ever convinced that Colorado Billy is the "Good Avenger.": She laughed as she said this. "He has been here under my nose all the time. After the death of Beer Can Billy, he just pulled out of Kemah, and pulled in here."

"I believe he originally planned to head into the deep south, but something changed his mind. You know what, Maggie? I hope you don't find him, but my money is on you. I wasn't at all surprised to see you here. I only came because you set my mind to thinking about Freeport. I was surprised, a bit because I followed you all the way. I wish we could have ridden together."

"Yeah, well, you know it is my job. I have to catch

him before he hurts someone else, even if I don't care much for the people he has hurt so far."

"OK, so what now?"

"How about something to eat? I saw a seafood place back down the road about a mile."

"Great! I am always up for seafood. You can pay, put it on your expense account, since I don't have one anymore."

After food was ordered, Apple asked, "Really, now where do we go from here?"

"I'm not sure. But I think he is around here somewhere close, and everyone will be surprised when he is found."

"Well we better move fast, before he finds a new victim."

Maggie asked, "Who is next in line for some of his discipline?"

"I'm glad you asked. Here is my theory. Since we are assuming that he is the one who beat the hell out of Roy Jacobs ... by the way, have you questioned Jacobs? He skipped over Fred Frederickson, maybe because you have him in jail, and he didn't bother with Randy Filbin or Santiago when he had plenty of opportunity, he went higher up the ladder to Jacobs. I believe Colorado Billy saw Jacobs on board the "Chump Change" the night Beer Can Billy was murdered. Who else was there, and probably knows what happened? My guess is two other fat cats, either M. Ellis Winston or the man himself, Bettis Tom Stovall. Beer Can and Colorado both have told me that someone in a black Jag regularly visited the yacht. Winston played high stakes poker there several times a month, but would not order for Beer Can to be beat up, nor especially murdered. My idea is find Bettis Tom and watch him, and Colorado Billy will eventually turn up. Colorado is going to give Bettis Tom a run for his money."

"I am thinking the same thing. Should be interesting."

They didn't know it, but they had passed Colorado Billy in his old Ford Focus going in the opposite direction, north on 288. They had only missed him by one hour.

Apple asked, "Are you working tonight? How about a movie at my apartment?"

"Sorry pal, but I have a ton of paperwork to catch up on, not to mention all the characters that are winding up in our jail. I would still like to talk to Roy Jacobs. Sheriff Ben was questioning him in his hospital room today. And, a big thing, I think I need to figure out where Bettis Tom is hanging his hat these days. How about this weekend? That is if we have no beatings or murders for a few days."

They made a date, then got into their respective vehicles for the trip back to the city.

WILLIAM WARREN

Chapter 45
REMINISCING, AND OLD MOVIES

Apple was sitting alone in his apartment, eating a ham sandwich which was not holding his interest. He threw the thing in the waste disposal and poured himself a stiff Jack and Coke. Damn, he wished Maggie had been able to make it tonight. He had fallen into something with her. He hesitated to say love. He had many girlfriends, or at least willing lady friends. He was a handsome guy, and he knew it, but never thought of it in that way. He smiled as he thought about the two jagged scars on both cheeks. Only thanks to that gifted surgeon, young Dr. Duke, that they were presentable. Bernadette said, "They give you a certain rugged, charm. Don't worry about it."

He had taken her advice, and only occasionally noticed them. His only surrender was unconsciously reaching a finger to touch and run the outline down his cheek. He wasn't even particularly upset with Little Joe, now especially that he had met his end so hard.

Before App realized it, he was having his second whiskey and Coke. He was trying to figure things out, like why Beer Can Billy was murdered, and where was Colorado Billy, and what the hell did the "Chump Change" have to do with all of this?

The doorbell rang, and he got up, barefooted, padded to the door. He peered out the peep hole, and a big grin spread across his face. It was Maggie! He couldn't slip the chain quick enough.

"What are you doing in here, App? Took you long enough to open the door."

"Just sitting, thinking, having a drink. Come in copper. Put your badge and gun on the table, and join me for a drink."

Maggie smiled. "She's not here, is she?"

"Who's here?"

"That good looking editor friend of yours from the paper. You know who."

"She just left. She's coming back later, when the coast is clear."

Apple poured Maggie a chardonnay and said, "Here's looking at you kid."

Maggie asked, "What does that mean?"

"I don't know, but it comes from my favorite movie."

"I think it means, we're watching you, what will I do now? Apple, where do you think Colorado Billy is hiding? Is it possible that he really did go south? If I didn't know that he would hit again, I would just walk away and figure the score is even."

"We both know he is somewhere nearby. Hey, we were going to watch a movie tonight, and forget about all this stuff until tomorrow. I thought you had work to do tonight."

Maggie said, "I do, but it can wait until tomorrow, that is if nobody is murdered or ends up in a hospital."

Apple poured himself one more drink, and decided to himself that was enough. "We have been seeing each other about every other day, and I don't know anything about you, except that your father is a surgeon in New York, and your mother sells a lot of real estate in the Bay

Area."

"You also know that I can afford my own car, that I went to Rice University, and that I have a law degree."

"Yes, but that doesn't surprise me. Tell me something that will surprise."

"Alright, here's one of my favorite quotes from a movie. "Rules in a knife fight?" How about, "You can't swim?, Well, the fall will probably kill you.""

"You're obviously a fan of Butch Cassidy."

"Yeah, I love that movie, but what appeals to me is the absurdity of the comments. They are funny because they are so obvious."

"What appeals to you is a couple of guys named Newman and Redford. And the follow up to the knife fight, "If he wins, kill him." Apple had seen that movie himself.

"How about you, any favorites besides Casablanca?"

"Sure, how about, "They don't know it, but come night the wrath of the Lord is going to fall on them.""

"Too easy, Lonesome Dove. Do you think, that maybe come night the wrath is going to fall on someone else? Perhaps Bettis Tom Stovall?"

Apple said, "I don't know about Bettis Tom, but in the movie, Blue Duck had it coming."

Maggie answered, "Since you won't drop it, here's one from another movie I like very much. "It's not personal, it's business."
You don't know that one, right?"

"No, but maybe with Colorado it has become personal. With Bettis Tom it's just business. Who do you think will win?"

"I knew you wouldn't get that one, it's from You've Got Mail."

"Yeah, well I'm not up on my chick flicks. I do know

Tom Hanks said it, though. I think Colorado has 'Gone to the mattresses'."

"Everyone knows that one. Sonny's righteous anger got him killed, as in the Godfather. I just hope that don't happen to Colorado, at least before I get the chance to meet him in person."

"Rest easy, you're gonna catch him soon." But as Apple said those words, he was far from sure. "Dangerous game Colorado's playing."

Their scanning the cable guide was interrupted by App's phone ringing, "Hey Boss, how are things in San Francisco? Watching TV here."

"Listen, ex-reporter, get your pencil sharpened. Things are about to happen soon, and you're going to need a good accurate description."

That got Apple's attention. "What's about to happen?"

Mr. Barton explained that Jeremiah Eckstein had pulled together a coalition of major stockholders of BAR Chem. Enough to oust the current Board.

Apple asked, "When, Boss?"

Mr. Barton said, "No time, but probably within a couple of days. Another development, and it might require some direction from you. Jeremiah has contacted the Feds in Mexico, he has a lot of swing down there because of BAR Chem's presence in Matamoras, asking them to board and search the "Chump Change." I know that is something you have been waiting for since this whole affair began."

"What can I do?"

"To start with, what is the name of the fellow you said knew about everything with the smuggling, had a European name?"

Apple filled him in with Arnost's place in the

operation of the drug smuggling business. Apple asked what were the chances of the Mexican authorities allowing the Galveston Coast Guard to observe when they boarded and searched the "Chump Change." App thought it would be a huge advantage for Chief Decks and his drug sniffing pooch to be a member of the team. He knew it would be out of the ordinary, but maybe with Jeremiah Eckstein's influence it could just happen. He was sure Commander Johnson would be in favor of the Chief being there. They had been waiting a long time to inspect the "Chump Change."

Apple was excited, he was going to have a hard time returning to watching movies, even with Maggie. He didn't have much time to switch gears when Maggie's phone began that funny ring tone she liked so well. She was not in the mood for phone calls from Sheriff Ben, but knew it was important so she frowned, and quickly answered with, "Hey, Sheriff Ben, what's going on?"

"I know you are off the clock, but some information I want you to be up to snuff on, and I need your input. Roy Jacobs has confessed to being on board the "Chump Change" the night John Bishop was murdered."

Maggie, holding her breath, asked, "Did he see it?"

"He says not, but he confirms that John Bishop was on board just before he heard the gunshot that probably killed Bishop. He also says he does not know what the money in the briefcase was all about, but states that Bishop routinely carried lots of cash."

"So, Ben, where does that leave us?"

Answered Sheriff Ben, "For one thing, everybody on board is a suspect. The DA is working on an arrest order for Bettis Tom Stovall. We don't know who else was on board, but we will find out.

Maggie said, "Bettis Tom is the big fish."

Sheriff Ben continued, "Another development, I received a call from M. Ellis Winston, you know, the attorney for BAR Chem, advising me that Roy Jacobs would officially be removed from the Board at BAR Chem first thing tomorrow. They are abandoning ship now. My guess is they are panicking a bit over there."

"It appears Roy is the key to finding out a lot about all the mayhem that has happened."

"Maggie, there is something important I must tell you. I myself have participated in poker games on board the "Chump Change.""

"Sheriff, I already know that. Colorado Billy told Apple, before he disappeared."

"Well, just be aware, that might bite me in the backside before all this is over."

Maggie said, "You might have to answer a few questions, that's for sure, like why were you playing instead of busting the game up."

"There is one more thing. When this is all over, I am going to retire, and I want you to take over the Department. Will you do it?"

"That is my long time goal, but are you sure? Do not make any rash decisions. At the worst, you will just get a smack on your hands. Hell, everybody in Galveston County loves you. You would still win re-election in a landslide."

"I will retire, I am tired of all of this. And, you will make a great Sheriff."

Maggie briefed Apple on the full account, except for the part about his playing poker with the crowd on the "Chump Change."

Now after the two phone calls, neither was much interested

in watching a movie on TV, so they said their goodbyes. Maggie returned to Kemah, and Apple went to bed. He had a lot on his mind, like how to persuade Commander Johnson to allow Chief Decks and his dog to go to Veracruz for the boarding of the "Chump Change."

Maggie was consumed in finding Colorado Billy. She had no idea that he had relocated just a few miles from her apartment. She thought that if she could find Colorado he would quickly admit to the assaults on Little Joe and Roy Jacobs. She knew he was nearby. She figured if she could locate the big sailboat he lived on, then she could find him. First thing tomorrow, she would begin searching all the marinas in the area that could accommodate his boat. She had to find him before he assaulted Bettis Tom or someone else connected to BAR Chem, like M. Ellis Winston, or Dearcorn himself. She smiled as she thought of Colorado Billy taking a big stick to Bettis Tom.

Sheriff Ben and Maggie were meeting at 7 a.m., both drinking coffee and discussing the plan of the day. Sheriff Ben's efforts the night before to apprehend Bettis Tom for questioning concerning Roy Jacob's assertion that he was highly suspect for the murder of John Bishop, had not produced BT.

The Sheriff had stationed men at Bettis Tom's residence all night, but he had not shown up. He did not know the Sheriff was looking for him, he had just been fortunate. Bettis Tom had a small place on the east side of Galveston Bay, at Smith Point that he used frequently. Soldier of Fortune that he was, made him cautious, this was his "safe house."

Sheriff Ben said to Maggie, "Is it possible that Bettis Tom stays somewhere else, rather than his primary residence? I wonder if he has a sister, aunt, or someone like that around here."

Maggie said, "Maybe we could check tax records and find out about all the Stovalls, or maybe he just owns two residences."

"Let's have someone check that out."

They were sitting, trying to get a foothold on where to start when Ben's phone rang out. "Looks like Commander Johnson. Hey Johnny, long time no see."

"Sheriff Ben, get your hat on. The "Chump Change" is on the move. I just received a call from Veracruz that she has cleared the break water. I just know they are heading to Galveston."

"All right! How long will that take?"

"Just happen to know the answer. It is about 640 miles, so at ten knots, it would take a little over two and a half days. She could be here sooner, because that big yacht can do well over ten knots. First thing in the morning, we will station a couple of boats out at the end of the Galveston jettys. I do not intend to miss this time. You coming?"

"You know we will be there."

Maggie had given Sheriff Ben the latest on Apple's conversation with Mr. Barton the night before. He thought Jeremiah Eckstein's suggestion that the Mexican Police board the yacht had probably made it's way to the "Chump Change", and everyone knew they had outstayed their welcome.

Maggie wanted to know if it was good to invite Apple along. The Sheriff had said by all means, "Commander Johnson has a standing invitation to him since this waiting for the "Chump," this is his story as much as anyone's. He deserves a front row seat. How about calling him with the details? But, I want you to stay behind and mind the ship. With Filbin, and Santiago in jail, and Jacobs about to be released from the hospital, one of us familiar with those cases needs to be close."

"Fine, you know I don't care for that tossing from a boat anyway. I would rather you phone him, Sheriff. It will be much more official if the call came from you." The Sheriff called Apple with the news. Apple said he couldn't wait, he would be at the dock promptly at 6 a.m. tomorrow.

He called Morris Barton with the news of the "Chump Change" movements, then decided to spend the first few hours of the day writing. The Boss had laughingly told Apple that he would call the Eckstein dogs off the "Chump Change" since she was leaving Veracruz.

WILLIAM WARREN

Chapter 46
COLLECTING "CHUMP CHANGE"

Colorado Billy had been watching Bettis Tom's house for two days, and no sign of him. Now he was beginning to formulate a new plan. The trip he had made to Tahiti, alone, on his sailboat, had taught him patience. He could wait Bettis Tom out. Sooner or later he would return to his lair, and Colorado would be waiting. His plan was so simple, he did not know why he hadn't thought of it sooner.

BT's condo was on the end of a row of houses, with a balcony and windows facing out toward the north across the bay. Colorado would just bring his boat, "Rocky Mountain High," to a point just off Bettis Tom's side windows and balcony. He would anchor about 1,500 feet from the shore and keep watch. He would be able to see the entry to the house and whoever went in the front door. He would watch for lights in the house. Colorado would do most of his watching through a fine pair of Bushnell binoculars. He could distinguish faces with those binocs from this distance, and he could see figures perfectly clear, even without the binoculars.

Sitting in the dark for long periods of time, in his car, would no longer attract attention, and he would be very comfortable. He loved sitting on his boat anyhow. Good, he thought, this could even be fun.

When the time came to go ashore, he would just

jump into his dingy and motor ashore. The water was shallow, but he could easily beach his dingy on the sandy coast line. He thought when he was finished teaching BT a lesson or two, he would just jump on his dingy, motor out to his boat, and get a good night's sleep. Then he could give some attention to really going deep into the Caribbean. Good plan, he thought.

Apple awoke at 4 a.m., hastily wolfed down a boiled egg that he had prepared last night, and half a glass of orange juice, then was out of the house at 4:15 a.m. This was one day he did not want to miss. His senses were acutely aware of the importance of putting his theories to the test. He knew there was something more to the "Chump Change" than just another huge yacht.
The boat was hauling something of value when it returned so regularly from Venezuela, or elsewhere, to Galveston. He could think of diamonds, or computer chips, but more likely was illegal drugs. There were millions to be made transporting meth, coke, or even grass. And, there was only one way that could be so successful. Jeffrey Chung Dearcorn himself had to be in on it. Even Bettis Tom could not pull this off without permission from Dearcorn.

It all seemed so preposterous, someone as head of a huge corporation like BAR Chem could be involved in something as base as smuggling drugs. He thought of the scam that Enron had pulled a few years ago. Money makes people crazy. Apple still thought the split for each was hundreds of millions of dollars. Boy! He would like to look at Jeffery Chung Dearcorn's and Bettis Tom's off shore bank accounts. They were hiding the money somewhere.

He had better be right. This was a big gamble on the part of the Sheriff, the Coast Guard, and Jeremiah Eckstein. If he was wrong, this could end up in court for a very long time. The escape clause would be the yacht and Bettis Tom, both instrumental in the murder of John Bishop. Now with Roy Jacobs confessing about everything he knew, the search was on steady grounds. Commander Johnson and the Sheriff were not only looking for contraband, they were looking for Bettis Tom, so searching the yacht was a legitimate enterprise. He was so sure of himself that he was betting his all on his theories. Evidently some very important people behind him were too.

They all were on time to cast off. Apple was impressed. Besides two 25- foot chase boats, equipped with a .50 caliber gun on the bow, a 65- foot Coast Guard Cutter would be standing by as the command vessel. Commander Johnson was commanding the cutter, and the entire operation. Apple would ride on the cutter until the "Chump Change" was dead in the water, then he and Sheriff Ben would board one of the chase boats.

Commander Johnson wanted Apple with his head of ideas on the yacht, once it was secure. Also boarding would be Chief Decks, along with his drug sniffing dog, Stormin Normin. There would be ten Coast Guardsmen, all armed, plus the Sheriff and Apple.

Apple was standing near the rail on the starboard side taking it all in. Galveston was impressive with the ship channel entering the bay, and the city still lit from the night. Darkness had given way to a still, shadowy morning light.

Chief Decks approached and said, "Wondering if we are right? I am. My friend, you better be correct in your theories about hidden bulkheads and drugs, or we are all up the creek without a paddle, so to speak."

"I'm right. Chief, there might even be more money, in cash, than any of us have ever seen before. You might even find Escobar's cousin stashed away. Know what I mean?"

Just before 6 p.m., a large blip appeared on the cutter's radar. One of the boat's radarman calculated the speed at 30 knots, about the speed a cruise ship can travel at top speed. Commander Johnson said, "That has to be the "Chump Change." No tanker or cargo vessel travels that fast. And, her vector leads her straight from Veracruz. Boys, get ready. This is our guy."

After boarding plans were laid out to the initial boarding party, the Commander turned to Apple and said, "Mr. Smith, do you have any particular ideas about what and where we are to look for hidden contraband?"

Apple again explained his theory that there were hidden, false bulkheads throughout the yacht, and he was certain Arnost knew where all of them were.

The "Chump Change" appeared on the horizon, and Apple thought what a beautiful boat, "Too bad she is being used for such nefarious work."

Every eye was on the "Chump Change" when Commander Johnson said, "Look at that, Chief, I believe she is turning."

Chief Decks exclaimed, "She's running, Capt!"

"Call him on the radio, Chief!"

"Chump Change" this is the US Coast Guard. You are ordered to immediately come to a halt, repeat, come to an immediate halt and prepare to be boarded."

No answer from the yacht. Instead she added more throttle. After repeated radio instructions, the Commander said, "Chief, we can't keep up with her. Prepare to fire across her bow."

"Aye, aye, Capt."

The Chief scurried from the small bridge to the bow

where the gun mount was already manned, "Lock and load boys. On my order, fire a burst along her side. Do not hit her, got it?"

Commander Johnson nodded his head from the bridge, and the gunners opened up with a dozen rounds from the MK38, 25 mm cannon. That got the attention of the running yacht. They immediately raised a white flag from the staff, and shut down.

One of the chase boats pulled alongside the cutter and Chief Decks and Storming Normin, the drug dog, hastily jumped on board.

They quickly covered the half mile, and pulled alongside the yacht, where Chief Decks got on a bullhorn, and ordered, "Kill all the power and everyone on board come alongside the lifeline. Anyone not complying immediately will be considered hostile."

After five minutes, two diminutive fellows came out of a side door and walked to the lifeline. The Chief asked, "One of you named Arnost?"

One of the men said, "I am Arnost."

"Commander Johnson, of the United States Coast Guard sends his regards. Who else is on board?"

Directly another fellow came along to the lifeline. "Anyone else on board?"

The answer was no, only three of us.

"We are coming aboard. Stand still in your position."

Quickly, five coasties climbed over the side and immediately handcuffed all three of the deckhands.

Chief Decks came aboard, and immediately asked, "Anyone else on this yacht? Are there any booby traps? And, why did you run? Don't you know you can't run from the Coast Guard? Where is Bettis Tom Stovall?"

The boat was quickly given the safety once over

and determined no one else was hiding.

By now the cutter was alongside, and Commander Johnson took charge. "Chief, leave Arnost behind, and bring the other two over."

Apple was intrigued by all this military preciseness, everything planned, nothing left to chance.

"Mr. Smith if you care to board her, go ahead. Sheriff, how do you think we should proceed?"

"Let's do a quick preliminary search before you escort her into Galveston. I just want to get a good idea of the layout."

Apple clambered over the side, and thought, "This is way bigger than I thought."

Chief Decks was inside when he shouted, "Go get 'em, Stormin Normin," and with that he released the dog. Normin started jumping around and barking while seemingly only barking at a bulkhead.

Arnost was standing aside, not saying anything, or volunteering.

Apple said, "You're caught Arnost. Why not just tell the Chief where it is, and save all of us some time and trouble." With that, Arnost seemed to shrink into himself, and just nodded with his head toward a passageway. They followed. Arnost abruptly stopped, opened what seemed like a broom closet and pointed.

Chief Decks brought his dog by his side, reached into a pouch he had attached to his waist, and produced a tiny camera and a very small video screen. He fastened a strap under the dog's belly with the small camera on his shoulders, just behind his head. He sat the dog inside the closet, where Arnost had opened a small door, barely one foot by one foot wide, "Go get 'em Stormin." The dog immediately entered the tiny opening, carrying a small camera on his back.

Apple was astonished, "What the heck is that?"

"Your tax dollars at work, sir. We'll know what's back there soon enough, Ole Storming Normin will see to it. He loves his work, and seems to know what we are looking for." Chief Decks adjusted his tiny screen, and leaned forward with a big smile on his face. "Apple, take a look at this."

App thought it looked like one of those screens from the ocean floor, but was clear enough. In a space hardly five feet tall and three feet wide, and about ten feet long, was tightly packed, plastic wrapped substances in three inch by six inch packages, white in color. Apple said, as Bernadette had done many times, "Bingo!"

Chief Decks turned to Arnost, who seemed to have seen a ghost. "What are we looking at?"

Arnost said nothing. Chief Decks said, "No matter, we'll have an answer soon enough."

Sheriff Ben, who had been standing by, read Arnost his rights.

Chief Decks said to the Commander who was standing by on the cutter, "Sir, looks like we've got tons of the stuff!"

Apple was so relieved from the pressure of his accusations that he felt wobbly in the knees. He was aware of the significance of this find. Both Bettis Tom and Jeffrey Chung Dearcorn were the chief suspects in what might be the biggest drug smuggling operation in the country. I hope we can prove culpability. It just wouldn't be fair for guys like Arnost to take the fall for such an enterprise.

"So what do you think, Sheriff?" said Apple.

"Looks like this might go down in history. Maybe it will lead us to the promised land for some of the pending cases in the files."

Somehow Apple sensed the Sheriff was not as happy as he should have been.

After Commander Johnson consulted with Chief Decks, it was decided that the Chief would take charge of the "Chump Change," and follow the cutter into the port at Galveston. "Can you run that thing?" asked the Commander. Chief Decks just smiled and snapped off a sharp salute, "Aye aye, sir. Can do."

One of the chase boats, with blue and red lights flashing, took the lead with the cutter following. The "Chump Change" followed the cutter, and the second chase boat took up the rear, also with lights flashing. Commander Johnson took this very seriously and had all his gun positions manned but not loaded. Once the Commander entered the channel, he had the last boat close the ship channel entrance. The Commander wanted no one coming up behind them. Tankers and car haulers, and cargo ships were circling the harbor waiting for their turn and the all clear, before entering the Houston Ship Channel.

Chapter 47
THE NEW EDITOR

As they entered the ship channel headed for the Coast Guard Station at Galveston, Apple made a phone call to Bernadette. It was now 8 p.m. When Bernie answered, Apple told her, "Ms. Hannigan, stand by for a news scoop from your now defunct reporter."

Bernadette fired back, "No, you standby for a news flash."

"Look, I called you first, so I get to go first. This is so big you will not believe it."

Bernie said, "Well! You're going to have to go second. Now listen up. Can you guess who is the new Senior Editor at the Houston Announcer? You guessed it buddy boy. Yours truly, Bernie Hannigan has just been named new editor. Now what do you think?"

"No doubt about it, you should have gone first. Great news. I knew it was just a matter of time. What happened to Damon the Dip?"

"Promoted down to his old spot. I think I will consider firing him next week."

Apple asked, "Have you talked to Mr. Barton? How does he feel about you getting his old job?"

"I did, he was excited for me. I asked him what he thought, and he said that he loved being retired. He was still in San Francisco. Now what is your news? You can't top mine."

"No, but I called to tell you to 'Stop the presses!' We just boarded the "Chump Change" and she is loaded with heroin and cocaine. We are bringing the "Chump" into the Coast Guard Station as we speak."

Apple proceeded to give her a detailed description of everything that had happened. The news would hit the stands on the morning edition. Bernie felt she had a good start to being the new editor.

Bernie said, "By the way, want your old job back?"

"Hell yes! I want my job back, but first I need to finish this BAR Chem business, and get started on my book contract. Can you wait?"

"For a boy reporter, you ask a lot. Yes, take your time, but not too much. In the field reporters are knocking on my door. Maybe I can find a youthful one, with no scars."

It was now about nine at night, Apple thought, seven on the west coast, just right to call Mr. Barton, so he did. He gave Mr. Barton the news about the "Chump Change." Mr. Barton said, "Extremely good news, I'll tell Jeremiah as soon as we hang up. He has been very concerned with this boat business."

"I know, Boss. He has moved far out on a limb to support us with little more than accusations."

Morris Barton asked, "What happens now to the board, especially Jeffrey Chung Dearcorn?

"Well, for sure we will have to directly connect him to the drug smuggling, but Roy Jacobs has already said that he knows all about it."

"What about this Bettis Tom character? I still remember that bastard walking into my office demanding that I stop printing stories about the boat and the company."

"He is still on the loose, but I am sure that the Sheriff

will catch up to him soon enough. If the "Good Avenger" doesn't find him first."

Mr. Barton asked, "Do you still think it is your friend, that Colorado fellow?"

Apple replied, "I am not positive, but Maggie, the Galveston County Inspector, is convinced that it is him. One side of me hopes that it is him, and another hopes that it is not. By all accounts that Bettis Tom fellow is more clever and nastier than the others. He is very dangerous, and Colorado Billy could be walking into a lion's den."

The Boss asked, "When do you expect Dearcorn to be arrested? Jeremiah needs to move quickly with this Board of Directors dismissal. There will be many things he will have to be prepared to answer."

Apple replied, "Probably not tonight. I heard the Sheriff talking to his office, and they want to move very carefully with this. Can you imagine the things that had better be right? Arresting the entire Board of BAR Chemicals Company? But, the answer is more than likely tomorrow or the next day. The boat is loaded with narcotics, but they have not even tested any of it as of yet. My guess is there are tons of the stuff hidden away on board. We are just now pulling into the Coast Guard Station. Talk to you tomorrow, Boss."

WILLIAM WARREN

Chapter 48
BETTIS TOM'S SURPRISE

Colorado Billy sat still, sipping a cold long neck, looking toward the shore from the cockpit of his big boat. He had anchored late this afternoon, and didn't expect anything to happen soon. He was not aware of the "Chump Change" being escorted into port. And he was not aware of others watching the condo where Bettis Tom hung his hat.

Maggie sat in her unmarked, plain white, Chevy Suburban patrol cruiser, just down the block from the security gate that led to BT's condo complex. From her vantage point she could not see the water, so Colorado's "Rocky Mountain High" was hidden from her view. Frankly she had not anticipated anyone coming from the water. She had the security code of the gate, and could have parked much closer to the entrance of Bettis Tom's building, but did not want to attract attention. After all, she was not sure if she was watching for Bettis Tom or Colorado Billy.

Maggie had been thoroughly briefed by Sheriff Ben as soon as the contraband had been discovered on board, and the crew arrested. He had called Maggie and told her that Bettis Tom was not on the boat. They had agreed that she would watch his condo and arrest him upon sight.

Maggie wanted to go alone for the bust, but the Sheriff ordered her to take another officer with her. Sheriff Ben knew that BT was a dangerous man, and wanted to take no chances. No chances with Maggie's safety, nor with BT eluding arrest. He smiled at Maggie's brashness. She was totally fearless, to the point of recklessness, and Ben was taking no chances. He liked her and knew she would be the next Sheriff of Galveston County, probably sooner than she knew.

Colorado sat glancing at his watch. It was now a quarter till 10 p.m., and he was growing sleepy. His mind began to drift to Beer Can Billy, and what an unusual fellow he was. The guy had sailed the world, alone, and didn't think a word about it. He had several magazines write articles about his prowess at sailing a boat single-handed around the world. He loved the Southern Pacific, and had begun to plan his retirement there. He particularly was fond of out of the way places like Tahiti, and he mentioned Bora Bora often. Colorado smiled as Beer Can Billy described local beers brewed in Tahiti and Bora Bora. Beer Can had a lot to live for. Suddenly Colorado was becoming angry.

He recognized the anger from his last two victims. How out of control he had been, especially with Little Joe. Little Joe was the one who had struck the blow to the back of the head that had killed Beer Can Billy. And then he did not have the decency to pull him from the water, just left him there. Now he was really hot. His heart was pounding with a rage rising. And that is the reason he had attacked Roy Jacobs. He was sure Roy had been there the night Beer Can was murdered, and had chosen not to be involved. He had just let the man float in the water.

Colorado went below, and rifled through a tool box. He selected a long handled carpenter's claw hammer for his weapon. He intended to break some bones of Bettis Tom Stovall. He had been thinking about this for several days, what he should choose for his weapon, and had settled on the hammer. He intended to throw the hammer into the Houston Ship Channel when he was finished with this business. Colorado had decided that he would really sail south, far into the Caribbean, maybe alight somewhere in South America. He had determined that tonight would be his last night as the "Good Avenger." He would be done with this affair, and consider the score evened for Beer Can's murder. Whoever got in his way was in trouble, because he intended to finish his quest.

On his way up the ladder and onto deck, he paused before a cabinet over his cooking stove, seemed to think a bit, then removed the .45 automatic from its storage place. He thought this BT fellow is no ordinary punk, like Little Joe, and he knew that Roy Jacobs would not be armed, but he was aware of BT's reputation for always carrying a pistol, so he tucked the .45 away in a fanny pack, just to level the table.

Colorado had seen no lights or movement at the condo, but had grown weary and impatient waiting, so he determined to go ashore and check out things, up close. He started the little Mercury outboard on his dingy and puttered away from his anchored boat.

He covered the quarter mile to the sandy shore, and beached his little dingy. He had driven his boat up onto the beach so well that he was able to climb from the boat without so much as getting his feet wet.

It was not a perfect night for his revenge tour. The moon was half full, providing a reasonable light for him to make his clambering in the dark up the sandy beach, but also making his shadowy figure visible to anyone looking his way. He walked up the four-foot incline and immediately stepped onto a freshly mowed St. Augustine grassy common space. The grass was wet from the night air, and spongy to his feet. He smiled as he thought that maybe he should just pause a minute and relax in this perfect environment. But, he couldn't tarry.

Colorado had been watching for movement from his boat anchored just off shore, and had noticed several lawn tables equipped with chairs and summer umbrellas spaced in the grassy area above the beach. He passed one and decided to sit and watch a bit. He had not smoked in years, but as he sat and watched he was craving a cigarette. He smiled to himself, thinking that he would light up, if he had a smoke. The tranquil setting had started him thinking, "Was this necessary? If all this had not happened, he could be happy living in this beautiful spot, in one of these lovely condos. Hell, what if he and Bettis Tom had been neighbors?"

As he sat pondering what he was doing here, he noticed through a tiny slit in the front curtains a dim light glowing from what must be the den of the condo. His first thought was that someone was in the place watching television. Maybe Bettis Tom had come in during the daylight hours and he had just missed him.

Colorado moved from his comfortable chair under the umbrella and slowly walked over to the parking lot. He was thankful that no one seemed to be stirring, he was alone. He didn't know that Maggie was watching from across the street. What if she noticed someone walking in the darkened lot? Colorado Billy was trying to figure out which car belonged to Bettis Tom.

Then he decided it did not really matter. He slowly approached the crossover SUV nearest BT's front door entrance, but his instinct told him not this one. He looked about and picked out a ten-year-old Jeep Wagon, much more Bettis Tom's style. He took the hammer he had been carrying, and thought this is it, then abruptly changed his mind. He did not want to attract the attention of neighbors. He backed away into the darkness of the covered entryway, and thought about what he should do. It was obvious he could not wait forever, and he did not want to set off a car alarm. He reached for the zipper on the fanny pack where his .45 was heavily sagging, and unzipped the top. He wanted to be ready for anything, but sincerely hoped he would not need his gun.

"How simple," he thought. I will just ring the door bell, and hope Bettis Tom answers the door. Slowly, and with a trembling hand, Colorado Billy pushed the doorbell. He was thinking, "Too late now, Beer Can is murdered, and nobody has answered for that horrible crime, brought upon his innocent friend. Well! I know who to blame, and tonight he will meet justice. I just hope he is home."

Colorado pushed the bell a second time, and thought he could hear a rustling from inside the door. Then slowly the door opened just a crack, only opened as far as the chain latch would allow. From within, "Yeah, who is it it?"

Colorado answered, "Are you Mr. Stovall?"

"No, who wants to know?"

"Tell him Colorado Billy is calling." Then with all his force, Colorado plunged the end of the clawhammer into the gap of the still-chain-latched door, into the eye of the fellow behind the door. Then with his full weight lunged at the door, hit it hard, and the door flew open with pieces of wood still attached to the lock. The man lay crunched on the floor holding his eye and moaning.

Colorado looked across the room where Bettis Tom was sitting in a recliner chair. It had all happened so fast BT had no chance. As he was rising from the chair, Colorado hit him across the shoulder with the full force of the hammer. Billy could feel through the hammer handle the bone crunch under the force of the blow.

Bettis Tom fell forward to the floor, clutching his shoulder. "So you are the big, bad ass Bettis Tom Stovall. Can't say it is a pleasure to meet you."

Bettis Tom was slowly struggling to his feet when Billy delivered a second blow with the back side of the hammer to the side of BT's face. Blood poured from the wound. Colorado thought, "Easy Billy, you don't want to kill him, just make him pay.'"

Bettis Tom, through a strong will, asked "Who the hell are you? Why have you done this?"

"Perhaps you don't remember the fellow you murdered on the dock, a few weeks back. His name was Beer Can Billy, and I am Colorado Billy. I have come seeking justice. What have you got to say for yourself, Mr. Stovall?"

"I'm not who you think I am!"

"I know who you are. You're the gutless ass who murdered my friend."

"No, you've got the details all wrong, I tried to save him. Filbin and his crew are who is responsible."

This type of lying to save his own skin infuriated Colorado, and he savagely hit Bettis Tom across the shin with his hammer handle, causing BT to cry out in pain. "I think you just shattered my leg! You better back off, Mister."

"Alright Bettis Tom Stovall, then who are you?"

"I am Beverly Thomas Stevens, undercover FBI."

Colorado Billy stammered, "Yeah, and I am the "Good Avenger" sent here by J. Edgar Hoover. Mr. Stovall, you have beaten and maimed your last person, I am going to give you a crippling beating, I plan to break your thumbs, just like you did Beer Can's, then you won't attack any more innocent men."

As Colorado approached, Beverly Tom Stevens struggled to reach under the sofa for his hidden .357. He whirled from his sitting position and fired a double click at Colorado, hitting him in the right calf muscle, and missing with the second shot.

Colorado, pumping adrenaline, frantically reached into his fannny pack, and grabbed for his .45, then remembered that he had not chambered a round. Beverly Tom was trembling from his beating, having a difficult time pointing his weapon.

Colorado Billy told him, "Buddy, you shouldn't have done that. Now I am going to shoot you in the heart, and be damned with you," but he also was having trouble, fighting for control over his wounded leg. He fired his weapon, hitting Stevens in his upper leg, causing Beverly Tom to collapse in front of the sofa.

Colorado Billy, only slightly aware of the circumstances, but realizing that he was going to attract a crowd with the gunshots, backed out of the front door, with two men collapsed on the floor of the condo. Colorado was limping, dragging his leg behind him, toward the beached dingy, and the safety of his anchored boat.

Maggie had her hand on the door handle of the Chevy Suburban. She had noticed the extra light streaming from the slightly opened door, and decided to wait no more, and investigate, when she heard the report from three gunshots. Damn! she thought, and hit the gas petal of the big cruiser, lunging the truck toward the opening security gate. She crashed the front of the truck into the gate, and kept moving to the gun shots.

Maggie flipped the cruiser's police lights on as the vehicle jolted to a halt in front of the condo. She hit the siren, and the screeching noise erupted in the quiet of the night. She instantly turned it off. She hated the sound, and even in the middle of an emergency, she couldn't stand it. Maggie thought it always made circumstances worse.

Weapon drawn, she ran to the light, noticing blood smeared on the front of the walkway, leading to the beach. She thought she heard the quiet hum of a small outboard, but couldn't waste time in that direction. She entered the condo, and instantly saw one man lying near the front door, moaning and holding his head. One man was lying near a sofa, with a gun in his hand, apparently suffering from a gunshot wound, and appeared to be unconscious.

She approached, and said, "Bettis Tom! Loosen the gun, right now." And, she began to call for an ambulance, and backup, "Two men down, one shot, possibly both, need backup!"

The business at the Coast Guard station with the "Chump Change" finished for the day, App was having a chat with Sheriff Ben. Apple had determined to ask the Sheriff what he had been doing when he played poker on the big yacht. They were standing by the door to the Sheriff's vehicle when the radio began blasting with an urgent request for an ambulance on San Leon. Sheriff Ben said, "Gotta go App. Every time I am entertained by you, things happen. Might be some kind of sneak attack, call me later." He jumped in his cruiser, and with lights blazing, took off at a great speed.

Apple, by now, accustomed to the Sheriff speeding up and down the Gulf Freeway, between Houston and Galveston, hastily slid into his own Ford pickup, and throwing caution to the wind, speeded after the Sheriff. They roared across the Galveston Causeway, connecting the island to the mainland, and made their way directly to

San Leon.

Apple was thinking, "Not another beating at the house owned by the late Little Joe." But, they did not go to the street Little Joe lived on. They were speeding toward the costly waterfront properties, when Apple realized they were rapidly moving in the direction of Bettis Tom Stovall's house. Bernadette's research had revealed his location. Apple planned to see who was coming and going there, himself, as soon as he found the time. He hoped this was something big, or the Sheriff was going to be very unhappy with him following at 90 on the freeway. He had no idea what awaited.

Quickly, before the ambulance arrived, two Galveston County Deputies arrived at the scene. They sped into the door with sidearms at the ready, and saw Maggie kneeling beside a prone figure with her arms covered in blood. She was holding pressure on Bettis Tom's wounded leg, with the only thing handy, a blood soaked cushion from the sofa. Bettis Tom was moaning softly, close to unconsciousness. One of the officers began to examine the wound on the side of his head, while the other had rolled the other fellow over, and was examining the wounded eye, the one Colorado Billy had slammed the end of the hammer into. The eye appeared to be intact, but the guy was as still as a windless night, clutching his head. The officer applied ice from the refrigerator to the eye, and said, "Easy friend, the EMT will be here soon. Who are you?"

The officer was stunned when the guy whispered to him, "Special Agent, Harold Polanski, FBI."

Then the officer asked, "What are you doing here?"

The response was, "Conferring with my colleague, how is he? Hit bad? I heard gunshots!"

"He's hit, but he will survive? Who did this?"

"I don't know, just some maniac struck me with a hammer when I opened the door."

"Yeah, who is your friend?"

"That's Special Agent, Beverly Tom Stevens, undercover agent, FBI. You probably know him as Bettis Tom Stovall."

The surprised officer turned to Maggie and said, "Inspector, guess who you are tending? He's not Bettis Tom Stovall, name's Stevens, undercover FBI."

Maggie leaned closer to Beverly Tom, and asked, "Is that true, are you FBI?"

Beverly Tom motioned with his eyes to the desk, and quietly said, "Open top drawer." The other officer quickly stepped to the desk, and withdrew a leather protector, inside was an FBI badge, along with an ID card, reading Beverly Tom Stevens, Department of Investigation.

"Looks legit, Maggie."

Maggie just declared, "Well, I'll be damned. Beverly Tom, can you hear me? He shook his head, affirmative. Maggie said, "Looks like we've been investigating the same thing. Got any idea who did this?"

Beverly Tom said, "I know for sure," and he managed a slight grin, through the loss of blood, and pain, "It's the "Good Avenger," the boat guy that's been going around assaulting folks. I guess it was my time. I figure we did not take him serious enough."

Maggie said, "I'll catch him soon. Where did you hit him?"

"I missed his chest and hit him in the calf. Don't worry about him. I want you to arrest that damned Chairman of the Board, Jeffrey Chung Dearcorn, for running the biggest drug business any of us have ever seen."

Maggie simply replied, "It'll be my pleasure."

Unknown to Maggie, Sheriff Ben had arrived, and had heard most of the conversation, and two minutes after the Sheriff, Apple had appeared, and had missed the firsthand knowledge of the FBI disclosure.

One minute later an ambulance screeched to a halt in front of the condo's door. Upon entering, one of the EMTs simply said, "Wow!" and immediately called for a second ambulance.

Maggie was relieved of her duties, and immediately turned to Sheriff Ben, and said, "Did you hear that? Answers a lot of questions, right? Beverly Tom was on a stretcher, being moved to the front door when he spotted Sheriff Ben, and managed to say, "Hey Ben, quite a mess, huh?" Beverly Tom turned to Maggie and struggled to say, "Sheriff, I guess cat's out of the bag. Inspector, did you know Sheriff Ben has been playing poker for the FBI?"

Apple, hearing this, was beside himself with glee, and out of character, turned to the big Sheriff and bear hugged him. Then composed himself, and said, "Sorry about that, Sheriff."

Sheriff Ben, grinning, said, "You thought I was a bad guy, didn't you?"

"Never doubted you for a minute," said App. When in fact just the opposite was true. He figured the Sheriff was caught up to his eyeballs in the poker games, and maybe even in the drugs. He liked the Sheriff, and was greatly pleased to find out that in fact the Sheriff had been "undercover" himself. It must have been a great burden lifted from the shoulders of Sheriff Ben for Beverly Tom Stevens to reveal the true nature of his visits to the "Chump Change."

Apple said to the Sheriff and to Maggie, "All this

time we have been searching for Bettis Tom Stovall and he didn't even exist."

Chapter 49
THE GOOD AVENGER HAS A CONSCIOUS

Colorado Billy, suffering from the gunshot to his calf, made his way to his boat, the "Rocky Mountain High." The shot had missed the main part of his leg, and had only grazed him, ripping out a finger's size of skin and meat. Colorado took an old kapok life preserver from underneath a seat and pressed it tightly to his leg, effectively stopping the flow of blood. His leg still hurt like hell, but he knew his life was not in danger.

He wanted to feel some satisfaction of his escape from Bettis Tom, but was troubled. BT's words about his position at the FBI bothered him greatly. Surely he was just saying that to save his stinking life. People like him would say anything, and do anything. After all he had been the boss around Beer Can's murder. Even though it was plain that Little Joe and Fred Edmundson had done the actual deed.

Colorado was also bothered by his realization of what he had become. He had beaten Little Joe to within an inch of his life, then given Roy Jacobs the same treatment. He had full knowledge that Jacobs had little to do with the actual beating, but he was present, and that was enough. And, now he had left Bettis Tom with a gunshot wound, a busted shoulder, and a large lump on his head. What if the guy was really an FBI agent? He knew he might be in a lot of trouble. Not to mention the guy at the door he had poked rather fiercely in the eye with his hammer handle. If Bettis Tom was FBI, then there was a good chance so was the other fellow. And, again they were probably just big time gangsters, not FBI, the good guys.

Colorado managed to pull his anchor and get his boat moving, despite the terrible burning in his leg. He didn't know where he was going, just away. He knew he needed to see a doctor if an infection set in, so he decided to move to a safer location on the bay, and wait a few days and doctor the wound himself. His idea of a good death was not with a raging fever, all alone, on the ocean. Besides, the idea of shooting an FBI agent bothered him. He would just move across Galveston Bay to Trinity Bay, and anchor, then when he felt better, he could move back to his pier at the marina, and bring himself up to speed with events. He had an Apple Mac laptop with a satellite hookup, so he could check tomorrow and find out, maybe, if an FBI agent had been shot. Colorado Billy didn't think the police had a clue he was the "Good Avenger."

Maggie stepped outside and walked down to the beach. She could make out where a skiff had recently been dragged onto the beach. As was usually the case, on the bay at this time of night, visibility was not good because of the haze shadowing everything, but she peered into the night and thought she could just see the outline of a large sailboat moving away from shore into the vast bay. "Surely not," she thought.

But the words of Beverly Tom kept coming back to her. It was the "Good Avenger," aka Colorado Billy. Just as Maggie had suspected all along, Colorado was around here somewhere close.

BT had given Sheriff Ben the number of his contact man at the Houston office of the bureau. The Sheriff made the call, informing them of the situation. Even at this late hour, the FBI chief wanted to meet Ben at his office to decide how to proceed.

It was agreed to not wait for daylight. Jeffrey Chung Dearcorn, based on the "Chump Change" being loaded with smuggled drugs, and the information from their man, Beverly Tom, was arrested at his home in swanky River Oaks. Sheriff Ben wanted to do the deed himself, but it was not in his jurisdiction, and since the FBI had been involved, he and Maggie gave way. Dearcorn was arrested, charged, and immediately posted one million dollars bail. He spent part of one night, and part of the next day in jail. He was not even questioned. His attorney was at the jail waiting for him when he was brought in. As he was riding in the backseat of a Houston Police cruiser, his wife immediately called his long-time personal attorney, and the Governor of Texas, who placed a call, and rushed the bail hearing along.

On words from Beverly Tom, no one on the BAR Chem Board of Directors was involved, except Dearcorn. M. Ellis Winston had no knowledge, or participation, and was not charged.

The crew of the "Chump Change," especially Arnost, who was now facing murder charges in the shooting of John Bishop, had been arrested the day before, and was now sitting in jail.

The next two days were spent by Maggie and now the FBI searching for Colorado Billy. As he sat alone nursing his wounded leg, he knew he was going to need medical attention, and soon. The calf muscle was dark red from a nasty infection that he couldn't ward off, even with the hydrogen peroxide that he bathed the leg in continuously, and changed the bandage frequently.

Colorado made a decision. He would turn himself in. Not only because of the wound, but because he had shot an innocent FBI agent. His conscience was eating away at him. Funny, he thought, the assault on Little Joe didn't bother him at all, nor Roy Jacobs. Maybe Roy was innocent of participation in Beer Can's murder, but he needed it anyway.

Colorado picked up his phone, and called Apple. He felt he could trust Apple to help him. Colorado wanted only Apple to motor out to his boat, now anchored across the ship channel in Trinity Bay. His boat appeared to just be another sailboater enjoying some solitude.

Apple agreed to Colorado's request, but insisted on being allowed to bring Bernie along. Colorado's other request was for Apple to secure a top notch criminal trial attorney. Apple knew just the man. Colorado said he could afford to pay whatever it cost. Apple called M. Ellis Winston, now released from service with BAR Chem. Ellis, incensed to find out that Jeffrey Chung Dearcorn had been fighting his every move to secure permits from the various agencies for the return of BAR Chem to Texas, quickly agreed to represent Colorado Billy. Despite having the wool pulled over his head, M. Ellis Winston was one of the best trial lawyers in the country. He said, "This will be payback."

Apple and Bernie motored out to fetch Colorado on a friend's borrowed boat. When they arrived, and boarded the "Rocky Mountain High," Colorado was on the edge of delirium. The infection from the wound was raging full bloom. They motored back to shore and brought Colorado to the same hospital where Little Joe, Roy Jacobs, Beverly Tom, Harold Polanski, and now Colorado Billy were treated.

The doctor took one look at Colorado's leg and said, "You saved his life. He would have only made one more day."

The Coast Guard and the DEA finished their tearing apart of the "Chump Change," found 2,000 pounds of cocaine, the same amount of heroin, and 5,000 pounds of marijuana. Jeffrey Chung Dearcorn's dope business was supplying most of the eastern seaboard with heroin. The folks in Vermont and Connecticut were especially happy. The goods were estimated at 50 million dollars. Dearcorn would split that with the man he had thought was Bettis Tom Stovall. The irony was, Bettis Tom's share was financing their case against Dearcorn.

Apple finished his book, which six months later became an instant bestseller. Then he took up Bernie's offer of his old job back at the Houston Announcer.

Sheriff Ben finished out his current term of three months as Sheriff of Galveston County, then retired. He went out as he had come in, a hero to the folks he served.

Maggie was elected Sheriff in a landslide. So the Rice University and South Texas School of Law graduate began what she hoped would be a long career as Sheriff of Galveston County.

Beverly Tom Stevens was expected to walk with a limp for the rest of his life. The FBI assigned him head of the New York office investigating white collar crime.

Colorado Billy received one year in federal prison, a $50,000 fine, and ten years probation. M. Ellis Winston got him off light. He will suffer with a guilty conscience for the rest of his life.

At this time, Jeffrey Chung Dearcorn was still free on bail and allowed to move around the country as he desired.

Randy Filbin was charged with first degree murder. Mario Santiago was charged with second degree as an accessory. Both were charged with extortion and racketeering. They are both now in jail.

BAR Chem recently broke ground on their new chemical plant complex on a large section of salt grass prairie outside of Galveston near Texas City, Texas. The ACW was especially pleased.

Apple was recently seen holding a pretty, dark haired lady's hand. She was wearing a white shirt and khakis. He was wearing an old pair of Levi's, with a large hole in the knee, and driving a very shiny Ford Pickup. She was driving a new Cadillac CTS with an inconspicuous red light on the dash. They were laughing, and eating crawfish at Jerry's in San Leon, Texas.

The End

Lightning Source UK Ltd.
Milton Keynes UK
UKHW041556121218
333881UK00001B/88/P